Magician's Journey
by
Jay Seaborg

Book One in *The Land of Magic* Series

To Maria, who has made my own journey a thing of magic

Chapter One

God's eyes, will this line ever move? Herin Freeholder looked around in wonder at the crowded room. He was still getting used to the fact that his lifelong dream was close enough to touch. The hall was filled with dozens of young men in long lines. *I'll bet there's more people here than in all of Chesterfield,* he thought. Kress was the financial and political center of the Empire, and being here was necessary if he wanted to become a trained magician. *Well, I wanted a new life, and this is certainly different.*

Herin had lived all of his twenty years as the son of a farmer, but it was his ability to handle magic that had brought him here to the city. His broad shoulders and tanned skin marked him as one who had spent years performing physical labor, a marked contrast to the paler faces and slender builds of almost all of the other applicants in line. The prospective students were waiting for admission to the prestigious Institute of Metaphysics, the school run by the Council of Magicians. Herin felt a bit out of place, even just standing in line. The stylish cut of the clothes and the cultured accents of his future classmates clearly identified them as members of the upper class, several levels above where Herin dwelt.

Since childhood, he had been taught that only the elite lived in Kress. It was difficult to overcome years of conditioning overnight, but sooner or later he knew he had to push aside his old ways of thinking if he hoped to be successful. Herin had every intention of completing the course and becoming a full-fledged magician. It was his passport to a new life, one far removed from days spent behind a plow. Finally, the line moved forward enough for him to hand over his paperwork to one of the Council officials. Herin took the opportunity to study the man as he looked over the documents. *He seems pretty ordinary to me. Nothing special that I can see, just a tired-looking middle aged man.* The official paused in his reading to fix Herin with a curious stare.

What's wrong? Herin thought. *I know everything is in order. There is no way they will reject me now, not after I've come all this way.* He would not go back to his old life. Herin could just hear his father already, his "I-told-you-so's" full of venom and spite.

"Master Orbinsson gave you high marks on your initial examination," the man said, signing the bottom of the last sheet before handing back the documents. "If you don't mind me asking, how did you come to apply to the Institute? We don't get many students from the Provinces."

"Master Orbinsson traveled through the province and tested boys for magical aptitude. He advised me to come here for more training. He said I showed real promise." Herin remembered the long-heated arguments with his father about leaving the farm and venturing to Kress. Orbinsson had intervened on Herin's behalf, holding out the prospect of Herin someday being appointed to a high position, with the commensurate salary. Herin's father had reluctantly agreed to allow him to travel to the capital for training.

"Promise indeed," the man smiled. "I was in the class with Orbinsson here more than twenty years ago. He was a first-class magician. Based on what he put on your application I will recommend that you begin at Level Two rather than One. If even half of what he says here holds true, you are already more advanced than most of the students who are in their second year."

"Level Two?" Herin's breath caught in his throat and his heart began to pound harder. He had anticipated taking six or seven years to complete the four levels of training needed to achieve a degree from the Institute. To start at the second level was a surprise. "Thank you sir," he managed to gasp.

"Hold your thanks, son," the man said holding up a hand. "I am not doing you any favors. The second year students will resent you for starting even with them without having to go through a year of schooling. The first year students will hate you for getting to skip all of the work they will be doing. But if you can ignore all of that, focus on your studies and keep working hard, in a few years you could be graduating here and moving ahead with your career. Keep that in mind."

"I will sir," Herin promised whole-heartedly, his mind still trying to get a handle on the unexpected turn of events. "Where should I go now?"

The official pointed to a doorway leading off into the interior of the building. "Go to the end of that hallway and you'll find a desk. Hand everything over and they'll write out your schedule for you. Good luck." He reached out to shake Herin's hand, a gesture Herin had not seen the man make with any of the other candidates. "I look forward to hearing good things about you, Herin."

A group of upper level students lounged near the hallway, making sarcastic comments about the incoming class. They all wore tailored tunics, and the sunlight slanting down through the skylights glinted off the gold rings adorning their fingers.

Herin approached the group, head down as he glanced over the papers in his hand. One student moved in front of him, reaching out to rub the rough material of his homespun tunic between his thumb and forefinger while he slowly looked Herin over from head to toe.

"Brown hair, brown eyes, brown clothes, brown boots…no doubt brown shit on the bottom of the boots as well." The others laughed. "Don't you have any colors out there in the Provinces, farmboy?"

"I suppose not," Herin replied with a shrug, shifting his feet to pass by.

The student moved in front of him once more, blocking his progress. "I'm not done talking to you. When an upper classman addresses you, the correct procedure is to wait until he dismisses you before you move. Understand?" He flicked an imaginary piece of dust from Herin's tunic.

Herin could feel the heat rushing into his face, as he fought down the anger that threatened to boil over. "Is that so? Back where I come from out there in the Provinces, if a jackass won't move, we have to persuade it to move. Do I need to move you?"

"Threats now? I don't think you realize what is happening here, farmboy. You are in Kress now, and the rules of the game are different from whatever little pigsty you came from. Here we don't talk back to our betters, and here only certain people have power. You aren't one of those people."

Herin did not answer directly, merely shifted his pack to his left shoulder and began to flex the fingers of his right hand. "Watch it, Loki," laughed one of the others. "You're getting him all riled up. I think he means to hit you."

"That right, farmboy? Want to try your luck?" Loki prodded him with a finger, a smirking smile on his face.

"I just want to get my schedule and room assignment," Herin answered, his eyes locked on Loki's. "Are you going to move or do I need to move you myself?"

"Touch me and you'll be out of this place so fast you won't know what …"

Herin bounced Loki off the wall by the simple expedient of lowering his shoulder and shoving as hard as he could. Recovering, Loki aimed a vicious back-handed slap at him as he passed, but Herin had been anticipating something of the sort and easily caught Loki's wrist in his hand. Herin had been involved in more than one tavern brawl in Chesterfield, and he could see that for all his bluster, Loki was no fighter. "If you want to hurt someone, learn to fight like a man, not a little girl." He flipped Loki out of the way and began to make his way down the hallway.

"You bastard! You'll pay for this," Loki promised, rubbing his wrist.

"Just leave me be," Herin said quietly. "I came here to be trained as a magician and that's what I intend to do. Go your own way and let me go mine."

"Watch your back, outlander. My father is the most powerful man in Kress and no one insults our family without paying for it. Especially not some clodhopper with the smell of manure barely washed from his hands. You will pay, I promise you that."

"Gentlemen, is there a problem here?" The voice was calm and steady. They all turned to see a distinguished looking magician watching them closely, his eyes missing nothing. His hands were folded inside the large embroidered sleeves of a dark blue robe that denoted a master magician. Herin quickly composed his face and shook his head.

"No sir, no problem at all," he said, praying that the magician had not seen the incident from its beginnings. He didn't know the rules yet, but fighting before even leaving the enrollment area certainly couldn't be something that was tolerated.

"Good. Loki, you and your friends have no business being here. Get back to your dorms right now. Young man, walk with me."

Herin walked nervously beside the man, wondering if he was going to be in trouble before school even began. The magician looked down at him once or twice, but kept his silence until they had entered the long hall leading off the entranceway. "My name is Thorsson Valgaard."

Oh, shit! Thorsson Valgaard. The name made Herin's stomach drop. Master Valgaard was the Council Master, the most powerful magician in Kress, or anywhere else in the empire for that matter. This was not the manner in which Herin would have chosen to meet him. But what was done was done and he had no choice but to nod weakly and follow the magician.

They went through an arched doorway into a hall of white marble, lined on both sides with stained glass windows that created the illusion of walking through a rainbow. A pleasant aroma not unlike baking bread filled the air, and Herin reached out to gently rub his fingers along one wall. As he suspected, it had the slightly oily feel that told him a beautification spell was in place.

Beside him, the older man watched his actions and cocked his head in curiosity. "What are you doing, young man?"

Herin was a bit embarrassed to be caught and shrugged his broad shoulders. "Just checking something, sir. I've never experienced such an extensive beautification spell close up before. Are all of the buildings a part of it, or just this one?"

Valgaard's eyebrows shot up in surprise and he frowned down at Herin. "And what makes you think there is such a thing in place here?"

"I wasn't certain until I touched the wall. I'm not quite sure which one though. Maybe *The Eternal Flame…?*"

The magician frowned even more deeply and shook his head. "This isn't possible," he murmured as he stared at Herin. He stroked his beard thoughtfully and his eyes narrowed. "How could you possibly identify that spell?" he demanded. "It isn't something a novice should be able to detect."

"Master Orbinsson taught me dozens of spells," Herin replied, puzzled by the man's reaction. *The Eternal Flame* wasn't even one of the more difficult spells he had mastered. As he recalled, it had only taken him a few hours to learn it.

"Did he now? That's a spell we don't even try to teach until the third year and you already know of it? Strange. Do you know how to invoke it?"

"I can use it, sir." Herin answered, still wondering what the fuss was about. *Of course I can use it. Why wouldn't I be able to? Students here must know how to do spells like this one. Why wait until the third year? Damn, I hope it doesn't take years to be given the chance to learn every spell. What would be the point of coming here?* Orbinsson had thrown spells at him as quickly as he could show he could control them. In the beginning, he had sometimes learned two or three spells in a month's time.

"How did you know there was a spell laid on these stones?"

Herin hesitated. There was a simple explanation, but it was a secret he had hidden even from Master Orbinsson, afraid that if anyone knew the truth he would be regarded as something of a freak.

The reality was that Herin could smell magic. He didn't know where the ability came from or how he had acquired it, but it accounted for his ease in picking up spells. A correctly performed invocation gave off a pleasant smell, one done incorrectly gave off a foul odor.

"I just wondered if there was any magic being used and wanted to check," he said, wondering if the excuse sounded as thin to the magician as it did to his ears. "The walls tingled a little when I touched them so I knew there was some sort of spell in place. *The Eternal Flame* seemed the most logical."

The magician reached out to touch the wall himself. "So it does," he said in quiet surprise. "I suppose I never thought to touch them before. What is your name?"

"Herin Freeholder."

"Where are you from, Herin? It's obvious from your accent that it is not Kress."

"Chesterfield. It's a little town in the Great Grasslands."

The magician smiled a bit and his eyes took on a knowing look. "I see," he said with a soft chuckle. "That explains your encounter with Loki Tybold and his friends. He has a rather inflated sense of entitlement. Loki usually looks down on anyone not of his social class. His father is the head of The First Families and a very generous contributor to this Institution. Be careful, Herin. You have made a real enemy there. But you appear to be someone who knows how to protect himself."

"Who are the First Families?" Herin asked.

"Ten families who control virtually all trade in the city. They run everything from baking to banking, and nothing moves in or out of Kress without them having a finger in it somewhere. They are very rich, and very powerful. Come, let's get you registered and settled in, and we can talk while we walk. I want to hear more about your training."

The registration process took very little time, greased by Valgaard. The Council Master questioned Herin closely, asking about every facet of training he had received. Herin answered as honestly as he could, flustered to be in the presence of such a powerful magician, and wanting desperately to make a good impression. There was little time to take in the grounds of the school as they walked, but he was painfully aware of the glances the other students sent his way. Some looked envious, others merely curious, but Herin knew that the chance of remaining unknown while he acclimated to his new life was over. After today he would be that strange outsider who was singled out by the head of the Council for individual attention. It would not make his life any easier.

The dorm attendant consulted a ledger before shoving a key across the desk to Herin. Etched into its face was a room number, one located on the third floor of the building. Herin silently climbed the spiral staircase and easily located his room, surprised but relieved to find that he would not have to share it with anyone.

The room itself was tiny, barely big enough for the rude bed, desk, and small wooden chest where he stored his few belongings. Even Herin's meager collection of clothing filled the chest to capacity. Obviously, students were expected to lead a frugal existence. That would be no problem, accustomed as he was to living a hard life already. He flopped back on the bed and stared at the thick wooden beams running across the ceiling. It certainly had been a busy morning, but the important thing was that he was finally here. He was a student at the Institute. Everything would work out fine once classes began.

A month later Herin would remember that first day as a time when he was still naïve enough to believe that things would go according to some Divine Plan. In the first four weeks of class he had found himself living two different lives. In the classroom, he soon exceeded even his own expectations, and his instructors quickly realized that they had a skilled and exceptional student on their hands. Herin was moved into the advanced section in a half dozen different classes, sitting next to students who were in their third or fourth year of studies. Despite his innate ability and his unique gift, Herin found the work challenging. But it was satisfying all the same.

Outside of class was a different matter altogether. Roomed with other first year students, Herin found he had nothing in common with his fellow classmates. Those would-be magicians were all in rudimentary classes, learning things he had long since mastered. When they gathered in the dining hall to engage in the age-old student art of complaining about courses and teachers, Herin was left out since he had none of the classes or instructors they were complaining about. In addition, they tended to regard him as something of an oddity. Not only was he the only outlander in the hall, but he was taking classes that none of the others could even hope to gain entry to for at least two more years. It was not a situation designed to make things easy.

The story of his confrontation with Loki only added to his difficulties. Everyone in school knew the Tybolds. Loki Tybold was a third-year student, though Herin believed it was more because of his father's deep pockets than for any skills shown by his son. Herin only had one class with Loki, but he had seen that the aristocrat, for all his bluster, was an unskilled magician at best. He could barely control even the most basic spells, and more than once Herin had seen the teacher sigh and shake his head in exasperation as he watched Loki fumble his way through an exercise. "Freeholder, come over here again and try to teach this young fool how to do a basic spell," Master Groves seemed to say at least once a week. "Maybe we'll be lucky and he'll get it before the end of the millennium."

In truth, Herin found that performing magic, even in front of the instructors at the school, was just as easy as it had been back in his village. Master Orbinsson had been a good teacher, and Herin had a solid grounding in the principles guiding spellwork. Whatever fortunate combination of factors bestowed upon him the ability to smell magic had also made it easy for him to channel those energies in the first place. Herin was no philosopher so he didn't spend much time wondering about it, though he felt incredibly fortunate to have the ability.

The part of the training that was most difficult for him was the Council's insistence on a methodical approach to the art. Each student was required to keep a notebook containing formulas for spells, observations from labs, and essays on magical theory. It was these last exercises that proved the biggest roadblocks. The Master Magicians who ran each class would give nightly assignments that usually consisted of a question for the students to answer and expound upon. These excursions into the theoretical realm gave Herin the biggest headaches. He had never spent any time thinking through the reasons behind why magic worked, when it was appropriate to use, or the ramifications of each spell. This part of the course seemed to come much easier to the other third year students, which in fact was the case, since they had been exposed to this method since their first year of entering the school.

Notebooks were collected on a weekly basis so that the magicians teaching the classes could check each student's progress. Herin's grades in that area crept lower and lower until he was summoned to Valgaard's office a month into the semester. As he stood in front of Valgaard's secretary, a fussy little man named Dagmar, he wondered if he was failing to meet the school's standards for academic achievement.

After an uncomfortable half hour in the Council Master's office he had his answer. Valgaard had informed him in no uncertain terms that his written work was not acceptable. "Your writing would disgrace a five-year old," had been the older magician's succinct evaluation.

Valgaard had no intention of losing such a valuable pupil, knowing that magicians with Herin's potential were rare. Nonetheless, he fully expected every graduate of the school to meet the minimum standards he had established, and Herin was no exception, ability or no. To Herin's chagrin, Valgaard informed him that he would be enrolled in a tutoring program until such time as he showed enough improvement to cancel it. What little free time he had possessed would now be spent in the school's library with a Master Magician.

"By the end of the term I expect improvement," Valgaard had sternly warned him as he terminated the interview.

Herin left the office in a state of depression, promising himself that long before the end of the semester he would have his grades to an acceptable level. The alternative, going back to Chesterfield a failure, would be more than enough incentive to keep him at his task.

Chapter Two

"Look Loki, there's the boy genius," smirked one of the pack of aristocrats gathered for lunch in the main hall of the school.

"Genius?" Loki snorted. "You haven't heard? Our future Master Magician is being tutored every night after class. Seems he is having a bit of a problem keeping up with all the work. Flash only gets you so far I guess."

"Really? Then why are the instructors still calling on him all the time to demonstrate how to do things? I heard he met with Old Man Valgaard for more than thirty minutes a couple of weeks ago. Who gets that kind of time from the Head? I think you're wrong. I think he's connected."

Loki laughed and shook his head. "Oh, he met with Valgaard all right. To be called on the carpet. I heard from one of the people waiting in the reception room that when Freeholder came out of the office he had his tail between his legs. Besides, I've seen him being tutored. He goes to the fourth floor of the library where he won't be seen. I suppose it wouldn't look so good if the boy wonder was found to be a fraud."

"Then why keep him in third year classes?"

"Politics," Loki guessed. "Maybe they think it will make the rest of us work harder if we think a first-year student is showing us up. But now we know how he's doing it. They are obviously feeding him material ahead of time so that he can look good in class. For all I know, he isn't even capable of doing any magic on his own. The instructors must be manipulating things while everybody is focused on Freeholder so we think he's doing it. He's a stooge I say, planted here by the administration to keep the rest in line."

"Don't get carried away with conspiracies," added another. "I admit I find Freeholder completely unsophisticated, but he knows his way around a spell, you have to grant him that."

"I'll grant him nothing," Loki replied, staring across the room. "And I haven't forgotten the first day either. A reckoning will come, I promise you that."

"When?" asked a third. "That incident was nearly two months ago now."

"You have a lot to learn about revenge." Loki headed to a choice table and jerked his head to clear it of its current occupants. He didn't notice the looks of resentment on their faces, nor would he have cared had he done so. Loki floated through life secure in the knowledge that no one would be willing to confront the son of the richest man in the city.

Picking up the thread of conversation, Loki continued to hold court. "I've watched my father for years when he decides to crush someone. He's told me time and time again, 'Pick your time and place of battle and make it on your terms, not theirs.' It's a lesson that young barbarian is going to learn first-hand. If I had done something the next day, what would have happened? Valgaard would have been on me straight off. I've waited patiently until people have stopped thinking about it. Now we're really into the semester, and everyone is starting to worry about the mid-term examinations, so they have little time for anything else."

"You have a plan?"

"I always have a plan. Another thing I learned from my father."

Herin was unaware of the by-play as he sat eating alone. At the moment all of his thoughts were focused on his upcoming tutoring session. *I know I've made progress,* he thought. *They have to stop sometime. Don't they? I need a break, a night on the town to blow off steam. I haven't had a nice mug of ale since I got to this city.* Herin had been in Kress for two months and had yet to see the inside of a tavern. He was thoroughly tired of spending every weekend cooped up in the library, writing essay after essay while the other students were off carousing at some local alehouse. *That changes this weekend,* he promised himself.

Hours later Herin watched nervously as the magician assigned to tutor him scanned an essay he had written for his *Politics and Magic* class, a seminar on using magic as a political tool. Herin had wondered at the purpose of the class and frankly had been bored almost to the point of despair the first few days. He had come to the Institute to learn how to perform spells, and a dry class on how to manipulate politicians struck him as a complete waste of time. He remembered thinking: *Why not just use magic to make them do what you want? Who could stop you?*

The essay Master Mellon was perusing was one he was particularly proud of, and he thought it far and away the best thing he had produced so far. In it, he put forth his own theory of how the Council should operate.

The magician finished and took a few moments to fill his pipe with tobacco and light it. He rocked back and forth in his chair, eyes on the ceiling. After a moment or two of thought, he looked fixedly at Herin. "Where did you come up with this? Did you find it in a book somewhere?"

"No sir, it's all mine."

"This is quite advanced thinking for a first-year student," Mellon continued.

Herin waited to see where the conversation was headed before saying anything more. He said a silent prayer, hoping his work had improved to the point where he wouldn't have to do so much writing and research. The only thing he hated worse than writing was reading the ancient manuscripts that filled the library.

"I must say, it's an interesting angle."

"I haven't yet had a chance to do any field work," Herin reminded him. "But I am sure my theory will hold true. People either fear magicians or they respect them, but right now they only associate us with magic. If a situation doesn't call for magic, they won't call for a magician. We are almost a sideshow, only called for if there is some sort of emergency. But what about the day to day operation of the government? We are being closed out of that, and it is limiting our power."

"We have a seat in the Senate," Mellon reminded him.

"We do, a non-voting one. But does anyone even bother to attend any sessions? My understanding is that we rarely have a representative at any of the meetings."

"True enough," Mellon conceded. "What made you think of this in the first place?"

Herin could identify the exact moment when his epiphany had occurred. "I was thinking about Master Orbinsson tutoring me back in Chesterfield. He was supposed to be a very skilled magician. So why in the world was he out in the middle of nowhere working with a bunch of country boys?"

"If he hadn't been, you wouldn't be sitting here with me now," Mellon reminded him.

"I am well aware of that, Master," Herin replied. "But I don't want to spend my life running around the Outlands trying to find that one candidate in a thousand who might be able to handle the work here at school. That isn't a very good use of our resources, if you ask me. He was out there because the Council didn't have anything else for him to do. But what if we could re-establish ourselves as councilors as well as magicians? That would open up more positions in all of the Provincial governments, and would increase our prestige. I don't see how that would be a bad thing."

"Nor do I," Mellon agreed. "This is good work. Better than anything you've done so far. It seems to me that you have passed the crisis point. From here on out it's going to be on your shoulders to keep up. No more using the excuse that your schooling out there in the provinces didn't prepare you for the academic rigors here. Do you agree?"

"Yes, sir." At this moment Herin would have agreed to almost anything if it meant he would be done with the tutoring sessions.

"Meaning you've had quite enough of tutoring," Mellon smiled through his beard. "I understand your desire to be finished with these sessions. But understand something Herin. You were moved up in class because it was felt that you had a talent that not many students display. That won't mean that you get special treatment. In fact, in many ways it is going to be harder for you than for most other students here."

Herin spread his hands on the desk. "I've tried to do what was asked of me, Master."

"You have done that much. It isn't that you slough off on your work. I think it's because magic has always been so much easier for you that these other parts seem wasteful by comparison." Mellon picked up the paper and let it fall gently back down to the desktop. "Everything we do here has purpose. Every assignment, every lecture, every lab is meant to prepare you for the day when you leave here and become a full-fledged magician. On that day you will be representing the Council, and we must be sure you are ready for the task. Enough lecturing for one day. Off with you."

"I am finished for today?" Herin said eagerly.

"Finished for good unless you fall into sloppy habits in the future."

"That will not happen," Herin promised, getting to his feet before the magician changed his mind.

Mellon chuckled as he watched the youngster fly down the stairs. He picked up the paper to re-read one of the sections that had caught his eye. The wording was still a bit crude, a legacy of Herin's educational background, but the ideas were first-rate. He intended to bring it to the attention of Valgaard as soon as possible. It was a radical idea that could completely change the traditional role that magicians played within the Empire's power structure.

"That boy might go far," Mellon murmured as he settled himself.

Herin had already rushed out into the sunshine of the courtyard, as ecstatic as he could ever remember feeling. It puzzled him for just a second that the yard was empty, until he recalled that there was a full schedule of games today at the Coliseum. It was not quite midday yet, and the contests would go on until well after dark. He could still see most of the action if he hurried.

Quickly running back to his room, Herin changed into something more practical than his Institute tunic, opting for the clothes he had worn during the caravan journey from Chesterfield. The trousers and shirt had been laundered and he decided to wear boots rather than sandals since it would be chilly by the time he returned to his quarters that evening. He threw a dark cloak over one arm against the upcoming night frost and trotted to the front gate of the school. What little money he possessed rode in a small leather purse tucked inside his belt.

Herin paused for a moment outside the main gate to get his bearings. He had not left the school grounds since his arrival seven weeks before, but he had a general idea of which way to go and set off confidently in that direction. Herin's decision was vindicated a few minutes later when he rounded a corner and saw the massive upper tiers of the Coliseum jutting above the surrounding buildings like some strange mountain in the middle of Kress. It was such an arresting sight that he stopped for a moment to take it all in before jogging in the direction of the Stadium.

"Looking for some fun, handsome?" Herin felt a hand on his arm and turned in surprise. A young girl, her face made up in garish colors, moved closer and slid her hips seductively against his. Her hand reached around to brush his crotch, squeezing him gently and making him jerk backwards in shock. "I've a room just upstairs here and we can be alone. I'll show you things you've never dreamed of. When I'm done with you, you'll be ruined for anyone else ever again."

Herin could believe that. If he was foolish enough to go off with this girl there was a good chance of emerging from such a session afflicted with any of a dozen maladies. He was not a virgin, but his forays into sex so far had been with the girls in Chesterfield, not with the whores of Kress. There would be no joy in such an encounter, no matter what exotic technique she used; he could see that by the deadness in the girl's eyes. He realized with a start that she could not have been more than fifteen or sixteen, though she had the gaze of a woman a thousand years old, devoid of any real emotion and tired of life.

Herin detached himself and shook his head. "Some other time."

"You have the time now," the girl said, in what he imagined she thought of as a seductive voice. "No one walks these streets unless they are looking for some pleasure. And lucky you, you found me right off."

"No," he said more firmly, turning to go. She clutched at his arm in desperation and her voice took on a more frantic tone.

"Please," she begged. "If you don't come up to my room with me, I will be beaten. See that man over there?" Herin saw a dirty looking man lounging in the shadows of a building, watching them. "He is my owner. I have fallen behind in my quota, and if I don't start to catch up he will beat me. Please."

There had not been any situations in Chesterfield to prepare Herin for moral dilemmas such as this one. *She isn't my responsibility,* he told himself. *I can't save every whore in Kress who has a problem with their pimp.*

"I'm sorry," he said, walking several more steps up the street. "What happens between you and him isn't my concern."

"Bastard! You're like all the rest." Her face twisted with sudden hate. "You'll come to me when you need a warm hole to satisfy that itch between your legs, but I'm nothing other than that. Go then, and may you rot in hell!"

Her face held such an expression of hate that Herin made sure to keep his eyes on her as he moved away, knowing full well that a knife in the back might be his reward for dropping his guard. The man he had seen on the sidewalk detached himself from the shadows and sauntered into the street, blocking his way.

"Is there a problem?" he said in an oily voice.

"No problem," Herin said, trying to keep them both in sight at the same time. "I'm just going to the Games."

"Ah yes, the Games," the man chuckled. "Well we have our own Games right here, and you, my friend, are welcome to play."

"He is trying to get out of coming with me," the girl said. "And we've already set the price." Even in the tenseness of the situation, Herin could hear real fear in her voice.

"Is that so? It isn't polite to renege on a contract. Not only not polite, but not really healthy either. We take a dim view of such things on the Street of Dreams."

"What are you talking about? I don't know what you two are playing at here, but I am leaving."

Herin backed away a few more steps and the man quickly shuffled in front of him, blocking him again. A knife appeared in his hand with such swiftness that Herin could almost believe the man had conjured it there. The thug slowly turned his wrist back and forth so that the blade caught the sunlight and reflected it towards Herin's eyes. What had been an uncomfortable situation had turned deadly, and Herin realized that they could easily kill him and take whatever money he had.

He whispered a spell and felt the familiar surge of energy flowing through him that indicated it was working. The man's knife flew from his hand to clatter up against the brick wall of the building behind them.

"Darla you fool, you picked a magician!" the man snarled. "Get away from him before he does something worse."

Darla ran to the building and ducked inside.

"My apologies, Lord," the man croaked, and Herin could see that he was truly afraid. "A thousand pardons. I beg you not to take your revenge on us. It was an honest mistake and the girl will be punished."

"We are finished here," Herin told him, his body still tingling with the after effects of the magic he had channeled. He spun on his heels and almost ran the rest of the way up the street, pausing only when he had turned the corner and found himself in a wide, well-traveled road. There were still hours to go before that day's contests would be done, and he would have plenty of time to see what he came to see.

Herin expected the interior of the stadium to be chaotic. He was pleasantly surprised to find that crowd movement was orderly and efficient, the result of more than a century's experience by the officials of Kress. Like a leaf borne on a swift stream, Herin found himself taken up several levels by the crowd, and moved almost before he knew it back into the open air inside the Coliseum. It had all happened so quickly that he hadn't even had time to absorb his surroundings, an oversight he set about to correct at once, turning around in his seat to survey the vast amphitheater that had such a glorious reputation.

Herin had arrived at intermission, with the morning contests completed, and slaves working to ready the arena for the afternoon matches. A dozen or so were using rakes to scrape the surface so that it was level, in the process covering up the scattered splotches where blood had soaked the sand. Others were moving small wooden carts filled with new sand, dumping the contents here and there to be raked in as filler in the worst spots.

A vendor selling large, flat ovals of bread slathered with olive oil and sprinkled with salt emerged from one of the tunnels and began hawking his wares. Herin's stomach growled at the savory aroma, reminding him that he had not eaten since breakfast. He paid two coppers for a piece, closing his eyes in pleasure as he bit into the warm crust. Looking closer at the architecture of the gigantic building as he ate, he was awed by the workmanship apparent in every curve and archway. Herin knew very little about the Games, but he did know that this edifice had been built in the time when his great-great-grandfather would have been a boy. As with most twenty year olds, that time span seemed so far in the past as to be shrouded in legend.

Above the last row of seats were private boxes, cubicles set off from the rest of the stadium by recessed porches and walls four feet high. On the front of each wall was painted a crest and he could see that each box had its own set of slaves to serve the occupants.

"What are those?" he asked the man sitting next to him, as he pointed upwards.

The man barely spared a second to glance over his shoulder. "Not for the likes of you and me, mate, I'll tell you that. Boxes for the rich and powerful, First Families and the like."

First Families. It was a term Herin was now familiar with. He had heard Loki use it virtually every day. The Tybold family, he had found out, controlled among other things, the grain shipments into Kress. This put them in a position to manipulate the supply, and through that, the price, so that their fortune was vast and seemingly immune to any economic downturn. No matter what the economy was doing, people still had to eat.

"I see twenty boxes," he said to his newfound informant. "Are they all owned by one of the Families?"

"No, there are only ten Families. Different big shots own the rest of them," the man told him, scratching his head. "Never gave it too much thought. Won't be me up there one day, now will it? There are some others besides the Families that have money to burn on something like that."

"That's a big deal here, isn't it? Being connected, I mean."

The man looked at Herin and smiled. "Connections are a big deal everywhere, mate. Everywhere. Can't get anywhere in life without connections, even if you isn't rich. We're all connected, one way or t'other. Can't do without each other, now can we?"

Herin was struck by the truth of that, and he sat in silence for some time mulling it over. *Connections. Kress is a city where connections mean everything, and my only connection is with the Council. Without my ability to control magic, I would be nothing here.*

"Do you know who owns each box?" he persisted.

Since nothing much was going on in the arena just yet, the man was willing to oblige Herin. He cocked his head and pointed to a box directly across from them. "That one there belongs to the Mayor. Well, not to him personally, but to the government. That one is the Jensens, the Kalvarias, the Uhls…" He went on naming all the boxes until he came to the largest one, which Herin knew without asking, belonged to the Tybolds. "Jarl Tybold is the most powerful man in Kress. Got more power than the Mayor when you come right down to it. Made a pact with the Evil One some say, and it wouldn't surprise me if it was true. Course, Tybold would no doubt get the better of that deal, and the Hammer would own Hell before all was said and done."

"The Hammer?" Herin had never heard that name before.

"Old man Tybold. The Hammer, because he just pounds down anyone who stands up to him until they are gone. Bad man to cross, that one. Like as not you'd end up floating in the harbor."

"You didn't name the Magicians Council," Herin pointed out. The man had identified a half dozen other Councils, but not his own.

"Don't own a box, that's why. Them wizards don't mix much in the day to day activities of the city. Guess they're important to have around if we ever need somebody to fight a dragon," the man rocked back and forth laughing at his own joke.

Surprised, Herin filed the information away for later use. How could his Council not have a box if that was a measure of prestige in Kress? It seemed that the Council was more concerned with spells than it was with having power. That seemed a rather glaring mistake to Herin. *Shouldn't the Council have a place with the other power brokers in the city? Surely magicians were more important than merchants. This is exactly what I wrote about in that essay. It seems so damned obvious. Why hasn't anyone else seen this?*

"It won't be long now until the afternoon matches begin," the man assured him. "In fifteen minutes you'll see action."

"Good," Herin told him, "But right now I need to piss."

"To your right out the tunnel," he directed him. "Don't dally. You won't want to miss anything."

"I'll be back in time," Herin promised, making his way up the long, dark tunnel into the main concourse that ran around the perimeter of the stadium. The open space was large enough to hold dozens of booths, selling hot food and drinks, ale, jewelry, icons of the gods and goddesses, and several booths telling fortunes. A hum of excitement seemed to permeate everything, and Herin could now understand why the Games were so popular. For a working man who had no escape from a life of drudgery, this must be like heaven.

A cloth partition walled off a series of long metal troughs bolted to the wall and slanted in such a way that their contents were directed into basins on the ground floor of the Coliseum. Herin didn't care about the engineering behind the set-up. He was more concerned with the relief he felt from emptying his bladder.

Pushing his way back through the crowd, he abruptly found himself face to face with Loki Tybold. Behind him were three of his cronies, the same people Herin saw him with day after day. They were all smiling, though there was no friendliness in their expression. Herin nodded and began to slip past, only to have Loki put a hand on his shoulder and push him back towards the wall.

"Are we going to do this again?" Herin said, shaking his head. "You really don't learn very fast, do you?"

"You're on my ground now, farm boy," Loki sneered. "There won't be any teachers around to save you this time."

To Loki's surprise, Herin laughed. "Save me? From what? You? Don't flatter yourself, Loki. If you have some sort of idea that you and your friends here are some kind of threat to me, you're a stupid ass. Now, get out of my way while you are still able to do so."

"You're about to find out what happens when you take on a Tybold."

"You mean like this?" Herin threw a punch that landed squarely on Loki's nose. He felt cartilage crunching, as Loki reeled away clutching his face, blood pouring from between his fingers. Punching in earnest, Herin landed several blows, but took more than he gave as he was attacked from three sides. Bystanders began taking bets, laughing as they called out advice to the fighters. Herin took shots to his ribs and back, and he could see that it was only a matter of time before his attackers overwhelmed him. If he lost his feet and went down, they would simply kick him into unconsciousness, or worse. That thought gave him a surge of energy, which he turned into a flurry of punches that cleared enough of a space for him to dart into the crowd.

"After him," Loki hollered, using a strip torn from his tunic to staunch the blood streaming from his nose. "Hold him when you get him."

Herin twisted his way through the mob of people who had gathered to watch the fight, then began looking for an avenue of escape, or at least a place where his attackers would be forced to come at him one at a time. The ramps leading downward were all packed with people, so Herin took the only recourse open to him and fled upward. He had no idea where he was going, he just needed some distance between himself and his pursuers.

He hadn't run long before he began to huff and hold his side. *How in the hell did I get out of shape so quickly?* Back home he had been reckoned a swift runner, but he had done no real exercise in the weeks he had been in school. Still, he was in better shape than the pack chasing him, and he gained the upper level a good ten seconds ahead of his enemies.

Herin saw that he had reached the level of the private boxes, and many had armed guards to prevent any outsiders from gaining access. If he got anywhere near the Tybold box, Loki would simply order the guards to detain him. The only piece of luck he had so far was that the Tybold box was on the opposite side of the stadium. Herin could not allow himself to be herded in that direction.

He slid behind a column and watched to see what Loki and his friends would do when they got to the top of the ramp. Loki, bloody and furious, stood for a moment looking in both directions. "Robbo, you and Dolin go that way," he ordered, pointing them away from where Herin was hiding. "Gregor, come with me and we'll cut him off this way."

I didn't think that ass had enough brains for that. Damn! I have to keep moving.

He quickly jogged around the curve of the arena, moving out of sight of his pursuers. It wasn't much of an advantage, but it was all he had. While the groups were split, there was a chance to escape.

Herin could hear the footsteps of Loki and his companion and prepared to act. Waiting behind a thick column, he timed their approach by the sound of their steps, exploding from hiding just as they neared his position.

"Shit!" Gregor yelled. "He's here!"

Herin's first punch caught Gregor below the chin and lifted him off his feet to land on his back with a dull thud. He groaned once, then lay still. Loki backed away, reaching inside his tunic to pull out a knife.

"A knife again?" Herin said with a sigh. "What is it about this city and knives?"

"What are you talking about?" Loki said as he dropped into a crouch.

"Never mind," Herin muttered. "I'm warning you, Loki. Get out of my way or you are going to get hurt."

"You don't get it, farm boy. You're the one who's going to get hurt. You're just going to disappear and no one will ever find your body."

"Talk is cheap. Let's see if you've got the balls to back it up." Herin knew that his best chance lay in taunting Loki into making a foolish move. "What are you waiting for?"

Loki obliged him by making a sudden lunge and Herin chopped down on his exposed wrist. He made solid contact and Loki jerked his hand away in pain, but didn't drop the knife.

"Damn! You fucking bastard! I'm going to make you beg for death."

He came at Herin again, his thrust this time ripping a long slash across Herin's tunic, just missing his stomach but leaving a ragged tear in his shirt. Herin had hoped to resolve the confrontation without using magic, but didn't see any way to avoid it.

Loki made another cut and Herin was nearly skewered. It was time. He activated *Kartok's Defense*, trying to control the power of the spell. It was the most potent protective spell that he knew, and one he had never employed outside of the classroom.

Herin felt the surge of energy that always accompanied magic, and then watched in horror as Loki was thrown backward as if he had been caught in an explosion. With a cry of fear, Loki was slammed against the short restraining wall, his momentum flipping him over the side. He disappeared from sight with a scream that was suddenly cut short by a sickening thud. Herin heard cries from the crowd below and rushed to the edge.

Loki was lying in a spreading pool of blood on the level below. People gathered around the body, and one or two pointed up at him. "You there!" one called. "What happened?"

Herin jerked back, hoping that no one had gotten a good look at him. Without thinking, his feet took him back in the direction he had come, his brain racing as he tried to think of a solution to his predicament. There was no time to consider why he hadn't been able to control the scope of the spell. Later he might have time to think about it, but for now he had only one goal, and that was how to find a way outside the stadium before anyone thought to block the exits.

Luck was with him and he found a ramp that took him down past where the crowds were gathering. Five minutes later he was running down a deserted alleyway, looking fearfully over his shoulder from time to time. Once he was certain there was no pursuit, Herin sank back on his haunches with his back against the rough stone wall of a building and tried to collect his wits.

Herin's first thought was to make his way back to the school, but he quickly realized that would be a huge mistake. *That's the first place they'll look.* If he went back there, it would be a simple matter to pull him from his room and confine him until a trial was set up. The outcome of that trial would be a foregone conclusion. Herin could plead self-defense, but he had no illusions as to how the justice system in Kress operated. As his father had always said, "Kress operates on the golden rule. Those who have the gold make the rules." No, being captured was a death sentence. That meant the school was out as an option.

Where then? Getting in and out of the city wasn't a problem under normal circumstances, but if he was going to leave, it had better be done quickly. Jarl Tybold would no doubt order the gates watched, and Herin might only have a window of an hour or so to get out of the city. *Is that my best chance? Where would I go if I can get outside? Jarl Tybold would have his men on me before I cover five miles. Where can I go where they won't find me?*

Herin began walking down the alley, always checking to make sure he was not being pursued. The alley emptied out into one of the main avenues that connected the harbor with the warehouse district. Even in the late afternoon, it was filled with people, each one jostling their neighbor, the air filled with the murmuring sound of thousands talking all at once. Herin plunged into this river of humanity gratefully, content to let it wash him in the direction of the harbor while he thought over his options. One thing was certain: no one would spot him in this sea of people.

That was it! Where was the last place Tybold would expect me to go? I'll stay here in Kress. They will be looking for me to try to get out of the city. There were millions of people in the capital, certainly enough so that one stranger could lose himself so completely he couldn't be found again. In a few months, when the hue and cry had died down a bit, it might be possible to make his way into the countryside. Going to ground here might buy him time enough to come up with a better plan.

Herin didn't know the city very well, but he did know that the most notorious section of it was located near the harbor, the infamous Pit. Here amongst the pimps, prostitutes, pick-pockets, sailors, thieves, and cutthroats, he might find a temporary haven where he would be safe from Tybold. It was a measure of his desperation that he didn't for a moment consider how he would stay safe from the rest of the denizens of The Pit.

As he moved through the city, Herin began to consider the strange effects of *Kartok's Defense* when he had used it in a real-life situation. *What the hell happened today? I've never had any problems controlling magic before. What went wrong?* He still had no answers by the time he had reached the harbor, a smelly, seething soup of pollution and decay. This was the very heart of The Pit, where it was rumored that with enough money one could have anything one wanted, from a young virgin to a political assassin.

The shock of his encounter with Loki was beginning to wear off now, and Herin realized with a sinking feeling that his dreams had disappeared the moment Loki had flipped over the wall. He could never go back to the school, which meant his eventual entry into the Council was no longer possible either. He couldn't go back to his family since Tybold would certainly send men to search his village. *What can I do? First things first. I'll find a place to stay, some food to eat, then think what to do next.*

Herin thanked his lucky stars that he had grabbed his purse before going out to the Games. At least he had some money, enough to last a few days with care. It meant he could find a room somewhere and get off the streets. Whatever he did from here on out, the road ahead was likely to be short and full of obstacles. This morning he had a bright future. Now, only a few hours later, he was worried about just staying alive.

Chapter Three

Crowds clustered outside the taverns and inns fronting the harbor. In The Pit, warehouses dominated the area near the wharves so that cargo could be quickly recorded and stored. Drinking and eating establishments were grouped together on long streets overlooking the harbor from a slightly elevated position behind these buildings, and cheap inns with rooms for rent were in back of those. Wedged in wherever there was space were the smaller shops offering merchandise and services useful to seamen: sail makers, coopers, rope makers, brothels, pawn brokers, and gambling establishments. The city's biannual census didn't even bother to try to count the people in The Pit, settling for estimates that were wildly inaccurate. Perhaps as many as two hundred thousand people were jammed into an area less than two miles square.

For most of the first day of his escape Herin had wandered the streets, alert for anyone wearing the livery of the Tybolds, but he had gradually realized that he was safe here, at least temporarily. After three more days, he had seen no sign of any sort of pursuit, nor had he heard any rumors of people asking about a young magician wanted for murder. The respite allowed him some time to gather his wits and begin thinking about what his next move should be.

Rooms had proven to be cheaper than he anticipated. He had been able to reserve a dingy attic room for a week. Still, he had to find work of some sort. Herin was going to need steady wages if he hoped to survive here long enough to figure a way out of his predicament. It turned out to be impossible to find a job in a labor market dominated by Councils. In one long, frustrating day, he had been refused positions as a longshoremen, cooper, chandler, blacksmith, baker, and brewer. All of those jobs were held by Council members and the positions were hereditary. The alternatives were odd jobs like cleaning out the latrines or hauling away dead bodies. Herin had no interest in either "profession" but realized that within another six or seven days he might not have any choice in the matter. The future seemed bleak, at best.

He wandered the streets in a black mood. A small crowd gathered just outside one of the inns promised at least some diversion, and Herin ventured over to see what was drawing so much attention. Craning his head to look over a man's shoulder, he saw a street magician doing his act, one of a dozen such performers he had already seen that day. Such men were sleight-of-hand experts pretending to do magic but it was a far cry from the real thing. It might be entertaining enough for the masses, but not for Herin. Such exhibitions never held his attention. Still, this man was more skilled than most, making balls appear to float while at the same time juggling a half dozen knives. The crowd appreciated the show, cheering loudly and tossing coins into the hat at the man's feet.

"I thank you," the man said without missing a beat. "Does my heart good to be appreciated." He had an accent that sounded strange to Herin's ears. The stranger was certainly not a native of Kress. "Still a man's got to eat and I'd count it a real favor if you filled my hat with whatever you can spare. No such thing as a free lunch, as I've found to my disappointment. Eating in some of the places around here I'd say they should pay a man to take the food."

This drew some laughter and a few more coins dropped into the man's hat. "Many thanks, friends," the man said, launching into his next trick, which consisted of making butterflies suddenly appear, their bright colors bringing an appreciative sigh from the onlookers.

It was a slick act, Herin had to admit. He started to leave, and then froze in mid-stride, his eyes widening in surprise.

Cautiously, he sniffed the air to be sure. There was no mistake. Someone was using magic, real magic, and the spells were very powerful. *Magic? Here? The Council!* It was a natural conclusion, and Herin quickly scanned the crowd for evidence that there were magicians present. He saw nothing out of the ordinary, but there was an aroma that told him a spell was being cast, an odor very reminiscent of the rich, earthy smell of springtime in the forest. *Damn, it has to be the Council. Who else could it be? How in the hell did they find me so quickly?*

Herin had discovered long ago that he could not only detect the presence of spells, but could use the intensity of each to determine direction, type of spell, and whether it had been cast recently. Turning his head one way, then another, Herin narrowed his field more and more. He found to his surprise that the smell seemed to be coming from the street magician. *I don't understand. How can this be?*

Herin watched closely and saw that the man was actually using magic to make objects disappear and reappear elsewhere. That was not only shocking, but illegal. No one outside of the Council could legally practice magic. Who was this man?

He isn't a Council magician, and he isn't from Kress. Who the hell is he? How did he learn magic? Maybe he could help me, if I can convince him that I can help him. But how?

Herin waited until the man wrapped up his show with a spectacular flourish, one that surrounded him with miniature fireworks, the small explosions hiding his face. Copper coins rained into the man's hat as the crowd expressed their enjoyment of the act. The man bowed smoothly, and hefted the hat in his hand with a satisfied look on his face.

Herin took the time to examine him closely as the crowd thinned out. The man appeared to be in his mid-thirties, lean and burned dark by the sun. He had long black hair with a neatly trimmed beard to match. *A hard face, but not an evil one, if I'm any judge.* Whoever he was, he certainly looked like a man perfectly capable of taking care of himself.

The stranger was dressed in faded clothes that had definitely seen better days, with numerous patches showing where he had tried to repair rips and tears. His boots were almost worn through at the toes, and his cloak was little better than a horse blanket. All in all, the magician gave the appearance of a man who was somewhat down on his luck.

"A moment of your time?" Herin asked. "I think we might be of assistance to each other."

"Is that so? And what brings you to that conclusion, youngster?" Herin could sense the wariness in the man and tried to put him at ease.

"You don't need to worry about me exposing you," he said with a smile to show he meant no harm.

"Expose me? What are you talking about?" the man snarled, his voice suddenly hard as stone.

"I won't tell anyone you're using magic in your act," Herin explained.

The man looked at him and smiled a bit. "Magic in my act? Just a little harmless fun, boy. Nothing to get worried about. Some tricks I've picked up over the years to entertain people and keep body and soul together, that's all." He turned to go.

"That last spell was a translocation spell," Herin said softly. The man froze, and then slowly turned to face Herin.

"What did you say?"

Herin spread his hands and shrugged. "The last spell. It was the *Song of the Trees*. At least, that's what it's called here in Kress. I don't know what they might call it where you are from."

"Boy, you'd better tell me right now what you know." The stranger's voice was low, but his eyes bore into Herin's with an intensity that was frightening.

"I know you're doing magic," Herin said, bracing himself for a reaction.

"Is that so? How would you know that? What are you going to do with this 'knowledge' of yours?"

"I already told you, nothing. But I can help you," Herin said quickly. "While you're doing your act I could circulate through the crowd and solicit money."

The man shook his head. "I work alone."

"What if I got word to the authorities that you were practicing magic without being in the Council? That would result in jail time at least, something I'm guessing you would rather avoid."

"So much for doing nothing, eh?" The man narrowed his eyes as he whispered something and Herin sensed a change. There was the smell of a spell being put into place. Herin wasn't familiar with the exact incantation, but the aroma identified it as some sort of confinement spell. He could feel his legs trapped as if he was standing in wet concrete and the sensation was rapidly moving up his thighs. Within seconds, he would be powerless.

A quick motion with his hands, a whisper of his own, and the spell disappeared like smoke being blown away by the wind. The man's face was shocked as he dropped back a step. "Who are you?" he asked. "Nobody but a trained magician could have broken that spell and you're just a boy. Are you a shape shifter? Is that it?"

Herin shook his head. "I'm not a boy. I'm twenty years old but I'm not yet a trained magician."

"Bullshit," the man said firmly. "Nobody could break that spell unless they had already mastered some extremely high levels of magic. And I never heard of any twenty-year old who had done that."

"It's true."

The stranger stared hard at Herin, eyes narrowed thoughtfully. "You don't look like a magician. Strange indeed," the man murmured. "How did you know I was doing real magic?"

"I'll tell you later, after we're in partnership together," Herin said with a grin. "Let's just say I have the ability to know magic when I see it. I'm Herin Freeholder."

"How in the hell have you survived in Kress?" the man shook his head in disbelief. "Didn't anyone ever teach you not to give your name to every stranger you meet?"

"I don't normally do that," Herin assured him. "But I saw no problem in sharing it with my partner."

The man smiled crookedly. "You aren't very cautious, but you don't lack for cockiness, I'll give you that. Very well, since we're sharing, you can call me Shadow."

"Shadow? That's not really your name, is it? What kind of a name is Shadow?"

"It's the kind of name that keeps you alive in Kress," Shadow said. "Enough talk out here on the street. I have money for the time being so I will stand you to a meal. I'd like to know more about you and your talents."

"What about here?" Herin said, indicating the tavern.

Shadow shuddered. "I'd sooner eat from a latrine. I know a place just over the hill. Nothing fancy, but the food's hot and the ale's cold. Come on."

The inn turned out to be a small building tucked in between two larger, decrepit structures that were leaning so far to the side that it appeared the inn itself was holding both of them in place. Herin eyed it with suspicion. "We aren't going to have those down around our ears while we eat, are we?"

"Shouldn't think so," Shadow said without looking up. "But if it worries you that much, throw a spell at them and straighten them out."

Herin couldn't tell if he was joking or not. "Here? A little conspicuous, isn't it?"

"A magician with your ability should be able to mask what he's doing. Or is this beyond you?"

Herin wasn't sure if Shadow was serious. *Is he testing me? Fine...he wants a spell, I'll give him a spell.* He raised his hands to start the passes that accompanied every spell, running through various possibilities in his mind. Which one would do the trick?

"What are you doing?" Shadow asked, gripping his arm.

"I'm about to do what you suggested and prop up the buildings," Herin answered.

"I can see that," Shadow said with a smile tugging at the corners of his mouth. "What I really meant was why all the movement with your arms? Planning on conducting the spell like it was a band of musicians, were you?"

Herin was confused. How could you possibly control the spell without following the rituals that had been established over hundreds and hundreds of years? "You have to follow procedure," he said.

Shadow shook his head in amusement. "Is that what they told you at the Institute? Got a campus full of people making wild gestures and all that? I'll grant you, it's showy, but hardly necessary. I can see that you and I are going to have some interesting conversations if I decide to let you stick around." He held up his hand when Herin started to speak. "I haven't decided yet and won't until after we've eaten. Never make a major decision on an empty stomach if you can help it. We'll eat first, and then I'll let you know. Come on."

Inside, the establishment was much neater than Herin had expected. There were perhaps a dozen tables, as well as a handful of booths built against the outside wall. Shadow guided them to a table near the back, sitting so he could face the doorway and have a solid wall behind him. A waitress sauntered over, eyeing Herin with a predatory look.

"Well now, Shadow, this is a new one," she said, smiling at Herin. She was cheerful and she bent low to wipe the table, making sure that Herin had ample opportunity to look down her blouse as she worked. "I'm Gert, what's your pleasure?" she purred, making Herin smile. She reminded him of the tavern girls from his own town.

"I'm thirsty," he said. "Some ale perhaps?"

"Down, Gertie," Shadow said with a chuckle. "We've business to talk about. Go stick your claws into someone else."

She cocked her head at Herin. "He's a big'un, Shadow. He going to be your bodyguard?"

"Piss off, Gert. Bring us some ale and something to eat. Whatever hasn't been spit in this morning."

"Don't tempt me," she called over her shoulder. She returned a few minutes later with two foaming mugs of ale, a large platter of cheese, and a freshly baked loaf of bread. Winking at Herin, she went back to her other customers, leaving them to sip their drinks in silence.

Shadow took the opportunity to look Herin over. He noted the recently repaired tear in the tunic and the nervousness with which the youngster looked about the room. "What are you running from?" he asked, breaking into Herin's thoughts. "And from whom?"

"What makes you think I'm running from anything?"

"First, you obviously don't belong here in The Pit. You aren't a thief or a pickpocket or some kind of flim-flam artist. You claim to be a magician, and you showed that you at least know how to work a spell, so I'll accept that appearances aside, you know magic. Here in Kress, that means some connection with the Magician's Council, probably as a student, given your age. But no student comes down here to The Pit, and you look more like a farmer than a wizard. Your clothes are sporting a rip that looks very much like it was made with a knife. On top of that, you've got a haunted look that makes me think there might be people looking for you. So who are they, and what did you do?"

Given the accuracy of Shadow's guesses, Herin thought it best to put all his cards on the table. He quickly told Shadow what had happened, right from the moment he had entered Kress. Shadow listened in silence, occasionally sipping his ale or chewing a piece of bread, but allowing Herin to finish. When he was done, Shadow sat back in his chair with a look of surprise on his face.

"Now, that's a tale," he said at last. "I've never heard of anyone with the ability to smell magic, but there's more things in the world than any one man could ever know. You marked me right enough, so I suppose I'll have to accept your story." He shook his head. "And killed a man as well, if the rest of your tale is true. The son of the most powerful man in Kress at that. I'll give you this much, you're right to be so jumpy. Tybold isn't likely to let this slide. You've done well to stay free and alive so far. It was a sound decision to hide down here rather than getting out into the open country where you could be tracked easier. Tybold has lots of connections out there in the borderlands so he'd find you soon enough. You might buy a little time here. But why not go back to the school?"

"I already told you. That's one of the first places they'll look," Herin protested.

"Oh, I'm sure they've already done that," Shadow said thoughtfully. "But don't you think the Council would protect you? They won't want to let such a promising pupil get out of their clutches. They must not get one like you very often, maybe never."

"What do you mean one like me?" Herin asked. "I'm just one of a few hundred students."

"Yes, you are. But you are a student who can actually do magic, and those are rarer than you might think."

Now Herin was confused. *What did he mean, do magic? All the graduates of the school could do magic, couldn't they?*

Shadow could read his expression. "It's the dirty little secret of the Council. Most of their graduates can't do more than a handful of very minor spells. The ones who can really handle magic, the true magicians? Maybe one in a hundred students ever shows the potential for that. Most of those will end up at the school teaching. A few are placed here and there throughout the empire, holding positions in the government. Now somebody like you comes along who shows great promise, and suddenly you're gone. They'll be looking for you right enough, count on it. If you trust them, you could go back to the school. They would likely protect you from Tybold."

"What do you mean? I do trust them. But Tybold is pretty powerful. What if he got the Mayor or the Provincial Governor to order them to hand me over? There wouldn't be anything they could do about that."

Shadow laughed. "No one would ever 'order' the Council to do anything. At most, it would be worded as a request. Everyone knows that there would be no way to enforce such a decree, even if they were foolish enough to make it. What I meant was Tybold. Remember, he is ruthless and he has a bottomless purse to use. A few hundred gold pieces in the right hands and you could be delivered up to him like a gift."

"You're suggesting a magician can be bribed?' Herin was shocked.

"Of course they can be bribed," Shadow answered with a laugh. "They might be able to do magic but they are still men. And gold is the real power in Kress, or hadn't you noticed? Tybold might get a gatekeeper to let a team of assassins into the grounds, or open a hidden door, or any of a dozen other ways to penetrate the campus."

"So now you're saying I am lost," Herin sighed. "I'll never be safe from Tybold and I'll never learn to be a real magician."

"Not at all. I'm just trying to get you to consider all of the possibilities. Wouldn't the school be safer than being out here on the streets? It would certainly be more comfortable."

"You make it sound worse than the streets. I'd have to watch my back every minute." Herin turned his mug slowly in his large hands and shook his head. "I think I have to give up my dream of being a really strong magician and start worrying about staying alive."

"Chin up, boy. You weren't going to learn to be a real magician there anyway. All you were going to learn was how to be a court magician, and that's a very different thing."

"Where am I supposed to learn magic if not there?" Herin demanded.

Shadow calmly finished his ale. "There are other ways to learn magic, Herin. Real magic. Practical magic. For instance, I can show you what went wrong with your spell so the next time you need to use it, you'll be able to control it. The Council doesn't have a monopoly on teaching magic. There are other ways to learn and apply it. I never went through the school, and I can obviously use magic."

Herin realized Shadow was right. The implications were obvious; somewhere out there in the world were magicians who had no ties to the empire or to the Council.

"You'd teach me?"

Shadow nodded. "I've made up my mind. As you pointed out, an assistant might be useful. And an ally might be more useful still. But if you agree you will do exactly what I say without any arguments at all. It's my way, or else."

"Agreed." Herin realized that he felt a bit more relaxed, as if a weight had been lifted off his shoulders. He didn't know where this was going to lead, but at least he wouldn't be totally on his own. "What about you? What is your story?"

"You don't need to know anything about me other than I have agreed to be your teacher. I will promise you this: you will be a far more powerful magician when I get finished training you than you ever would have been if you had stayed at that school."

"How long is this going to take? School takes four or five years."

"Is there anything you have more of than time? Your training will move as fast as you can absorb spells and control them. Truth is, I can use a partner who can handle himself, and it seems that you already have some experience in that area. The fact that you can do magic is just a bonus. Where are you staying?"

Herin told him. "Bad location," Shadow decided. "Too near the main avenues through the harbor. Let's go get your things and we'll move them into my building. The landlord was complaining to me just yesterday that he was looking to rent out one of the rooms. Nothing fancy, but it's off the beaten track. You'll be as safe there as anywhere while I train you."

From that day onward Herin's life could be neatly divided into two parts. By day, he circulated through the crowds soliciting donations while Shadow performed. Eventually, he began adding his own touches to the shows, resulting in more spectacular magic and correspondingly bigger hauls at the end of each performance. By night, he was Shadow's pupil, learning spells as fast as he could demonstrate control of them, and in the process also learning quite a bit about the political situation in Kress and the empire. It was a subject that Shadow seemed particularly well informed about, and Herin soon felt like he was somewhat of an expert himself.

After a few weeks of this routine, he still had not figured out Shadow. The man was a trained magician, and an able, if demanding, teacher, but Herin was absolutely certain that he was not from Kress. Just why he was in Kress in the first place remained shrouded in mystery. Shadow never mentioned anything about his purpose in the city, though Herin stayed alert hoping to find a clue as to the background of his companion.

The biggest challenge Herin faced, oddly enough, was his own belief system. He had never given much thought to how or why he had come to believe the things he did, but Shadow was constantly blasting philosophical holes in his mental worldview. It was unnerving. But it did make Herin realize that he was full of misconceptions about magic and how it worked.

One of the first casualties was the simplest, the casting of spells. Shadow commented frequently on Herin's insistence on involving elaborate motions of his hands, arms, and fingers in the process. He told Herin that such things were done for show. Herin insisted that the motions were an integral part of controlling the energies channeled during each incantation.

"Nonsense!" Shadow snorted, snapping his fingers and making several candles suddenly flare alight. "Are you telling me you need to do something more involved than that? Why? Is the point of magic to impress bystanders with the theatre of it all or to accomplish something specific with your spell? There is only one reason you do things that way, and that's because it's always been done that way by the Council. And the Council dictates how magic is used in the empire. They want people to think it's something that's beyond them."

"Well it is, isn't it?" Herin knew from his own experience that very few people could handle magic. Shadow himself had told him that most of the graduates of the Institute would know no more than the barest handful of spells.

"Yes and no," Shadow replied. "A good number of people could probably learn a very basic spell like the one I just used. Not everyone, but probably a lot more than you think. But a real magician has no need of showy tricks. You, my young friend, are going to learn a new way to do spells."

Shadow was as good as his word, and over the next six weeks Herin relearned all of the magic he already knew, becoming adept enough that he could dispense with all but the most basic motions, a mere flick of his fingers to send the spell into activation, but nothing more overt than that. Herin had spent an enjoyable evening practicing this last skill by changing every bowl of food set before the customers in the inn below their rooms, frustrating the barmaids until Shadow ordered him to stop.

Through it all Herin wondered why Shadow was living in The Pit, and what his purpose was in the city. There were times when he would tell Herin he was going to be on his own for a few days and would disappear, only to reappear without any word of where he had been or what he had done. Herin didn't mind so much at first because it got him out of a few lessons. Shadow was easily the most demanding teacher he had ever known. But finally, his natural curiosity got the better of him and he asked Shadow point blank what he was up to.

Shadow had been in the process of preparing another trip, and he pushed back the cloak he had thrown over his shoulders and sat down. His face was guarded and his eyes had the familiar calculating look Herin had come to recognize so well. It always meant that Shadow was about to push him into some new territory and was wondering if he was up to it.

"How do you feel about the empire?" Shadow asked.

"I don't know. It just…is." Herin had never actually done much thinking about the empire at all. He knew that it had come into existence more than six hundred years before, and there had never been a time in his life when he had questioned its existence. "I don't know if I feel anything about it. Why do you ask?"

"Because I'm here to find out everything I can about it and how it operates." Shadow watched him carefully for a reaction.

"Then you're a spy? From where?"

"Relax, Herin, I'm not here to assassinate anyone or overthrow the empire. I'm here to gather information, but that's all. Think of me more as a mercenary than a spy. I work for whoever can afford my services. Just now, I am employed by a country that is a two week sea voyage to the west of your borders. They hired me to look into some things here.

"What things?"

"There is some concern in certain circles in that country that your empire means to extend its power in their direction. Did you know that Kress is building an armada at Nelfheim, out on the coast? Two hundred transports, half that many warships, and a like number of supply boats. Enough to outfit and transport an army of more than twenty thousand men. That worries them, so they hired me to try to find out whether or not their country is the target."

Herin wasn't really all that interested in the political situation, though he found it unsettling that Shadow was a spy. "Why are you telling me? Aren't you afraid I will turn you in to the authorities?"

"Not at the risk of exposing yourself," Shadow replied evenly. "Besides, I think I know you pretty well by now. I don't think you are the kind of person to betray a friend. Am I wrong?"

"No, you're not wrong." Herin considered his options. Obviously, Shadow had a purpose for confessing his identity. There seemed to be no other reason than that Shadow needed his assistance. "Do you want me to work with you?"

Shadow rubbed his hands together and leaned forward in his chair. "You might help me," he suggested. "It would be good practice for you as well."

"Why?" Herin wasn't completely certain he wanted to actually get involved in Shadow's affairs. Wouldn't that make him a traitor, no matter how benign Shadow made what he was doing sound?

Shadow rummaged in the bag he had stored next to his chair and pulled out several small stone containers, along with several wigs. "This," he said indicating the pile, "is how I can move around in the city without too much concern about being identified. Disguise can sometimes be a useful tool, even for a magician."

"Why not use magic to change your appearance?"

"It takes a lot of energy to do shapeshifting spells," Shadow answered. "And because of that they are notoriously unstable. It wouldn't do to have your appearance suddenly revert to normal, just when you could least afford it. This way is safer, and you are going to have to learn to live by your wits as well as your magic if you hope to survive long enough to get out of the city. Or have you forgotten that?"

In truth, there were times when Herin was so occupied that he did forget he might very well have a price on his head. Part of that was because he had learned so many new spells that he felt that he could defend himself against anything Jarl Tybold could throw his way. He had been so busy with all the things going on in his life that he really didn't have much time to devote to worrying about something out of his control.

"Show me how it's done," he asked, and Shadow shifted his chair closer and began to dip into one container after another.

A half hour later, he sat back in satisfaction. "There, now your own mother wouldn't recognize you."

Herin stood to look in the mirror. "You didn't need all the makeup for that," he assured Shadow. "I doubt very much if she would recognize me now anyway. So…?" He froze as he saw his reflection. Instead of the visage of a twenty-year old, the face in the glass looked as if it belonged to a man in his late fifties. In wonderment, Herin reached up to slowly run his fingers over his new face, still unsure he was really looking at himself. "Unbelievable," he laughed.

"See what I mean? Think anyone will recognize you now?

Herin shook his head and continued to finger his face. Shadow had added a gray beard to match the wig Herin now wore to hide his own dark hair. Some fake wrinkle lines had been added under the eyes to give him the tired expression of a man down on his luck and defeated by life. Herin could feel two sticky patches of wax that Shadow had applied to stretch the corners of his mouth downward and dark areas on his cheekbones created the illusion of sunken cheeks in his normally full face. All in all, it was as perfect a disguise as possible.

"Amazing," he whispered. "Can you teach me how to do this sort of thing?"

"Of course. But let's get moving. Our conversation has left me a bit short of time."

"Where are we going?" Herin panted ten minutes later as they moved swiftly through the busy streets of the city.

"To the main gate," Shadow said without slowing the pace. "There's a delegation coming into the city today that interests me. I want to see how Kress deals with them."

The closer they moved towards the center of the city, the more nervous Herin became. He had not been out of The Pit in the weeks since his encounter with Loki, and it seemed to him now that everyone they passed was staring at him. By the time they reached the main gate he was as uneasy as a nun in a brothel.

"What exactly are we looking for?"

"That," Shadow said, using his eyes to indicate the gate. "I wanted to see that in particular."

A party of horsemen was riding through the gate. There were two lines of Imperial soldiers lined up inside the gate itself, standing stiffly at attention with lances held at an angle and every piece of armor polished until it shone like silver. A high-ranking officer and a government official stood waiting at the end of the line. Trumpeters played a flourish with a blast of sound that caused townspeople to stop what they were doing to stare in wonder at the ceremony.

There were perhaps two dozen horsemen in the party entering Kress, all mounted on horses so black they looked almost like shadows. The riders were also in black, and each carried a long lance and had a bow strapped across his back. Herin had never seen such men before, their faces swarthy and bearded. Their eyes had an alien appearance, slightly slanted and rendering their expressions unreadable.

In the middle of the party were three men dressed in robes rather than armor. They looked neither right nor left and carried themselves with the casual arrogance of men who were accustomed to others paying them deference. The party reined to a halt in front of the Kressian official, who began making a flowery speech welcoming them to the city.

"Who are they?" Herin asked quietly.

"Dakarians," Shadow replied. "Dakar is located to the north of here, beyond the mountains. This is an embassy to the empire."

"Seems like a lot of talk just to say welcome," Herin remarked, quickly losing interest.

"Look," Shadow said, jerking his chin upward. Herin looked up to see that many of the nearby buildings had archers on their roofs, arrows already notched. He counted more than fifty.

"What's that all about?"

Shadow smiled grimly. "That's what we're going to try to find out. I just found out about this visit yesterday so my information is a little sketchy right now. But I'd say the empire doesn't completely trust them, wouldn't you? I'll sniff around a bit over the next few days and see what I can come up with."

"What do you want me to do?" Herin asked.

Shadow gave him a long appraising look. "Are you certain you want to be involved in this? It will pit you against the empire. In fact, it's quite likely you'd be doing things that will be considered treasonable and the punishment for that is death."

"If I was to get caught right now, I'd wind up dead anyway, wouldn't I? They can only kill me once."

"True enough, but what about spying on your country?"

Shadow had a point. But the empire had never really existed for him other than as a far-off government that once every two years sent tax collectors through the district to collect the money each citizen owed. More than once while he was growing up, the tax collection had practically beggared his family. Kress claimed the tax was used to keep the roads safe from bandits. But Herin had never seen any Imperial patrols in his district, and every caravan had to hire private guards before moving anywhere.

"My loyalty was going to be to the Council, not the empire," Herin replied. "I'm already an outlaw. At least I trust you."

Shadow nodded and clapped Herin on the shoulder. "I'll do my best not to betray that, and it would be easier to do what I have to do with some assistance. You can begin by nosing around the area near the Palace. That's where any meetings will take place and there are bound to be rumors flying about. Just mingle, maybe strike up some conversations with guards, and keep your ears open. I'll stake out wherever their quarters are and do the same. We can compare notes each night and see if we can't figure out which way the wind's blowing."

And so the routine changed a bit. Rather than working the streets for small change as they had done in the past, Herin and Shadow now spent hours combing the city for information. Herin learned the art of disguise from Shadow and soon came to enjoy the daily forays to the neighborhoods around the Palace. He quickly realized that it wasn't enough just to alter your appearance with paint and make-up. One had to take on a whole new personality to match it, right down to the expressions, posture, mannerisms, and manner of speaking. It meant inventing a new person from the ground up.

Despite the daily trips, he found nothing of importance on these expeditions, even though he had made friends with several of the guards. That had proved to be a simple matter. Herin began to spend his time in one of the taverns near the Palace and stood the guards to drinks once they got off duty. To a man, they held the Dakarians in contempt, dismissing them as outlandish barbarians with no real culture.

"Don't know what they eat," one told him. "But the smells coming from their compound at dinner hour are enough to turn a man's stomach."

"Whatever it is, they can certainly fight on it," added another, to general agreement.

The soldiers told Herin that there had been an altercation between one of the Dakarians and two of the guards, a result of a misunderstanding over where the jurisdiction for each group overlapped. A brief sword fight had taken place, with the Dakarian getting the better of it by far, putting one man in the infirmary and killing the other. The incident had been quickly covered up and new orders issued separating the groups, but the guards were obviously intimidated by the fighting abilities of their guests.

"They's nasty pieces of work from what I hear," the first man added. "There's complaints from some of the inns and brothels in the Pleasure Zone. Whores being beaten and abused, a few knife fights where men got killed. All of it hushed up and gold changing hands to cover the complaints. Don't know what might be going on up there in the Palace, but something sneaky is afoot, mark my words. Still, wouldn't want to meet any of that lot in a dark alley. Not unless I had six or seven of my mates with me."

Herin had filed the information away and decided to wander through the Pleasure Zone that evening to see for himself. The Pleasure Zone was an area set aside for taverns, brothels, gambling houses and the like, clustered so that anyone wishing to be parted with their money would find it easy to do so. The government had found the arrangement conducive to collecting taxes and usually turned a blind eye to what went on there. Hardly a night passed that the streets were not packed to capacity and the revels often went on until dawn.

After dark, Herin wandered the alleys and avenues, winding his way through a half dozen taverns before he found what he was looking for, an inn with three Dakarians drinking silently in one corner. The foreigners sat by themselves, and their faces were expressionless as they drank their ale. Herin noticed that the tables around them were empty, even though men were packed shoulder to shoulder at the bar.

Herin pushed his way through the crowd and emerged with an ale. He settled down at a crowded table where he could see the Dakarians and sat back to watch, pretending to sip his drink from time to time. It was soon apparent that the serving girls were not happy about having the Dakarians as customers. There was none of the usual banter that went on between such wenches and their customers, nor did they linger at the table any longer then it took to replace empty mugs with full ones. They were frightened of the strangers, that much was clear. He could see it in their eyes and wondered why the proprietor allowed the visitors to drink here if it was upsetting his staff so much.

As the night wore on the Dakarians became increasingly belligerent, their voices guttural and harsh as they talked in their strange tongue. Herin wasn't the only one who could see it. His tablemates drained their mugs and left, one commenting that Herin should think about joining them.

"Them foreign devils be quiet enough when the evening starts," the man said as he stood to go, "But they are monsters once they get in their cups. No head for ale, but they drinks it like water. They'll be splitting skulls soon enough, or worse. That'll clear this place out for sure."

The man wasn't exaggerating. As the soldiers became more and more rowdy, Herin watched other groups of men making their way out the door. Within minutes the place held no more than a handful of hard-core drinkers. One of the Dakarians banged his mug on the tabletop, demanding service in a slurred voice. He spoke the Common Language with such an outlandish accent that it was difficult to make out exactly what he was saying, but the intent was clear enough.

A serving girl loaded a tray with three mugs and made her way to the table. She had long black hair plastered to her forehead with a combination of sweat and grease, with a face streaked with ashes from where she had rubbed her cheek. Her eyes were dark enough to match her hair and she moved with a sort of feline grace, though Herin could see the girl was reluctant to be near the Dakarians. Her mouth was tight and she carried herself with a stiffness that was absent when she waited on others.

The girl put down the mugs and quickly collected the empties. Before she could move away, one of the soldiers grabbed her waist and pulled her down to his lap, much to the amusement of his companions. The girl struggled to get free, but she was overmatched. The Dakarian grabbed her wrists in one hand and pulled her arms slowly up over her head, causing her breasts to stretch the fabric of her blouse.

"Let me go, you fucking bastard," the girl cried, squirming in a fruitless attempt to get loose.

The soldier smiled lewdly and moved his hips in time to hers, turning her escape attempt obscene. "That's it," he said in his garbled accent. "Move like the whore you are. Dance for me, my little slut."

The others laughed. Herin remembered Shadow's instructions to stay out of trouble and not get involved in anything he saw, but this was difficult for him to take. He knew from experience that the women who worked in taverns supplemented their income by providing other services to their clients, but it was obvious that this one had no intention of engaging in such activities with the three men.

The Dakarian slipped his hand inside her blouse and casually began squeezing her breasts, turning her so that his companions could watch. The barmaid was weeping in frustration and Herin could see embarrassed looks from the customers who remained, though it was obvious that none was going to go to the girl's aid. Herin saw the proprietor nervously chewing his lip, though he stood rooted behind the bar as if he were nailed to the floor.

The girl was violently thrown back onto the table and her tormentor shifted his hand from her blouse to her skirt, using his legs to force her knees apart and fumbling under the skirt to the ribald encouragement of his companions. She cursed him and was fighting like a wild animal, but it was obvious that she could not avoid the rape that was coming. The other two Dakarians pushed back their chairs and each grabbed an ankle, stretching her legs wide for their comrade.

Herin couldn't watch any longer. He walked to the bar and slammed his mug down, slopping ale on the bar and startling the owner.

"Are you in the practice of letting your girls get raped?" Herin rasped, beyond caring whether he was calling attention to himself.

"Mister, I don't like it but I've got a tavern to run. What do you want me to do about it? Them devils will split me like a pig if I try to do anything. I'll get no help from the city. Already got word that whatever these animals want is to be seen to. If anyone interferes with them in any way they could face charges from the city."

Herin snarled, "Then you are going to have a real problem, friend. Better start thinking up a good story for the authorities."

He turned and walked towards the table, wondering why he was bothering. He knew what went on in taverns, had even availed himself of serving girls on occasion himself. But not as a rapist.

The girl was snarling with rage, her face a mask of fury. As he approached closer, Herin saw that she was a little older than he had thought, probably twenty-three or twenty-four years old. Gathering herself, she spat into the face of the Dakarian who held her down, much to his amusement.

"Let me go, you fucking pig," she snarled.

"When we are done, if you are still able," the man said, reaching down to unbuckle his trousers.

Herin had come up behind the men unseen. He grabbed the shoulder of the man nearest to him and slammed him back against the wall with a thud hard enough to knock the breath from his lungs. Before his companion could react, Herin had picked up an empty mug and smashed him in the face, sending him staggering backward. Herin pulled the rutting Dakarian from the girl and kicked him in the crotch, making him double over, wheezing in pain.

"Fun's over," he said. "Go pleasure each other."

The surprise of the attack had given him a slight advantage, but it was brief and disappeared as the three soldiers pushed themselves to their feet, their faces dark with fury. Spreading out so that they could attack from three sides, each one pulled a long knife as they began circling him like a pack of wolves. Behind him, he heard the girl scramble off the table, but he didn't have time to devote any attention to her. That the men meant to kill him, Herin had no doubt. That he would receive no help from anyone else was just as obvious, as the others in the room backed away from the confrontation as far as the walls allowed. He was alone and whether or not his actions had been wise was now a moot point. He was going to have to fight his way out of this on his own.

"Stupid move old man," one of the men growled. "We are going to skin you alive."

Shadow had lectured him constantly about when and where to use magic, his message mostly being that it should be avoided whenever possible. Shadow's reasons were clear. He was working as a spy and any public use of magic was sure to draw the attention of both the authorities and the Council. But this was different. Herin knew that he had no chance of defeating these three without using it and was already mentally running through his options. Damn the consequences, right now it was simple, kill or be killed.

He had expected that the Dakarians would rush him from several angles at once, but now that he was cornered, one backed quickly away and took his bow down from where it was hanging on the wall, notching an arrow and moving to where he had a clear shot. Herin saw that his time was up. He had to act.

The lessons Shadow had been teaching him now paid off. Had he still relied on making complicated passes he would have been dead before he could get a spell released. As it was, the arrow was already on its way as Herin mouthed the activation phrase for the spell he wanted.

The shaft suddenly bounded backwards as if it had hit a wall. Herin dropped his hands now that the spell was in place and walked to where the arrow lay, crushing it under his boot. "You're next," he said softly, bringing his hands up and this time beginning to make exaggerated passes with his hands and arms, wanting the Dakarians to know exactly what they were up against. He didn't know if they were familiar with magic and magicians. Now he would find out.

The trio backed away so quickly that they stumbled into one another in their haste to get away from him. If he needed any more confirmation of their familiarity with magic, he got it when he saw them making the sign of the horns, the ancient ward against evil.

"He's an Old One," one said. "Get out. We must report this."

Herin was tempted to finish them on the spot, but thought better of it as they rushed through the door and into the night. The onlookers were spellbound, their faces almost as fearful as the Dakarians had been. The innkeeper came out from behind the bar, wiping his hands on a greasy apron.

"Thank you, Lord," he said, addressing Herin in the tone usually reserved for aristocrats.

"I didn't want the girl hurt," Herin replied.

"I didn't mean that," the man said, nervously looking at the doorway. "Thank you for not killing them. If you had, my inn would be taken from me and I'd be ruined. But they can't blame me for this."

"And the girl?" Herin tried to keep the disgust out of his voice. The only thing this weasel cared about was his inn. "What about her?"

"A good point, Lord, we must get her out of here. They will return looking for her, mark my words. It wouldn't be good if she were still here."

"Wouldn't be good for whom? You? You're all heart."

The man drew himself up and stared defiantly back at Herin. "It's well and good to preach when you are obviously a powerful magician. But I have to survive, and to survive you do what you have to do without the benefit of magic. I didn't like what happened, but there wasn't anything I could do about it. Now it's done and I have my business to think about. Ilsa didn't get hurt and she's still alive. She might not have been without your interference and for that I am grateful."

"What about her?" Herin asked. "Where do you suggest she go now?"

The man shook his head. "I don't know, but it isn't safe for her to stay here. Can you take her someplace safe?"

"Where? She isn't my responsibility," Herin said. "I don't have anywhere for her to go that would be safe."

"Anywhere would be safer than here," the innkeeper argued.

"You're right, I'm not your responsibility. I don't need or want your help," came a voice from behind them. "While you two are deciding what to do with me, I'll just be on my way. Rufo, you owe me some money. I'll have it now, with another two gold pieces as well if you don't want me spreading tales that you allow your girls to be assaulted. Try finding help then."

"Ilsa, don't be like that," Rufo whined. "You know I couldn't do anything. I'll give you your wages, but two more gold pieces? That's robbery."

"Go to hell," Ilsa said disgustedly. "Either pay me or wait on tables yourself. Within two days you won't have anyone left to do all your dirty work around here."

While the two argued, Herin took a closer look at the girl. She had taken a moment to wipe her face and her features were more clearly revealed. She would never be considered classically beautiful, but there was a fire in her eyes that drew him. He listened in awe to her mastery of gutter insult, her language harsh enough to make a sailor blush.

Herin was so busy listening and watching the byplay that he had been ignoring a signal that had been trying to worm its way into his head. Now he finally listened to his subconscious, and he drew in his breath in surprise while struggling to hide his shock. Under the smell of garlic, wood smoke, and sour ale, was another more subtle odor. There was no mistake; the aroma of magic was there, overpowered so much by the other earthier smells that he hadn't caught it at first. But it was definitely there. *This girl is a magician? Impossible! Women can't do magic. What the hell is going on? If she is a magician, then how was she able to be so easily overpowered by the Dakarians? There is something strange at work here.*

"They'll be back for you," Herin said, cutting into the conversation. "I know a place where you might be safe, at least for a little while. You should come with me now before they come back with reinforcements."

"I don't know you," Ilsa said. "Why should I come with you?"

"How about because I just saved your life so it's possible I mean you no harm. But you know best. Maybe you can handle them better next time around."

"Listen to the man," Rufo begged. "And do it quickly. Just how long do you think it will be before they're back again? Here, it's all I have right now." He passed Ilsa a handful of coins. "Take it and go."

Ilsa hesitated, then put the money into a small pouch and secured it inside the waistband of her skirt. "Fine, but I hope those bastards come back here and burn your inn to the ground, with you inside it."

"Follow me," Herin said, leading her out into the night. Now that the excitement was over, a new thought struck him. *What will Shadow say when I show up with this girl?* It didn't bear thinking about and Herin pushed the thought to the back of his mind as he led her towards The Pit.

Chapter Four

"Don't be an idiot. Why not try thinking with your head instead of your prick?"

The disgust evident in Shadow's voice elicited an almost automatic reaction from Herin, one that he fought to keep under control. *As always, judging me without listening first. Of course, there couldn't be any other explanation, could there? It has to be a simple case of my own lust getting out of control. He's as bad as my father.*

"I am thinking with my head," Herin's voice reflected his own scorn. "Stop being so judgmental for a second and you might see things the same way I did."

"I doubt that," Shadow answered. He was still seething. "I don't need some complicated story to explain why you violated protocol and security to bring your whore here."

"Fuck you, you stupid bastard!" Ilsa exploded, speaking for the first time. She had held her tongue while trying to figure out the situation, but she would not sit back and let a stranger insult her. "I'm not a whore."

Shadow's expression clearly reflected his doubts about her claim. "Of course not. Obviously, you are an aristocrat out for a stroll."

"Go to hell," Ilsa snarled, starting to get to her feet. She'd sooner take her chances out on the streets. Herin reached out to gently but firmly pull her back down, his expression sympathetic. The fire in Ilsa's eyes burned brightly, but she allowed herself to be settled, though still glaring across the table.

Herin could feel the conversation getting away from him, and a quick glance over one shoulder showed that the interplay between Shadow and Ilsa had not gone unnoticed by the other drinkers in the tavern. *So much for staying inconspicuous.* The thought acted like a bucket of cold water thrown onto a fire, immediately cooling his anger and forcing him to think more clearly.

"Quiet, both of you!" he warned. "We're drawing stares."

"Shit," Shadow muttered, angry at himself for losing control so publicly. "Dammit, Herin, now everyone in here will be telling the story of the argument between me and your wench. This is why you never, ever bring your women back to where you're staying. They probably think we're arguing over who goes first. Damn!"

"We need to go somewhere to talk," Herin insisted. "There is something important you need to know about Ilsa, and this is hardly the place to discuss it."

"Then why did you choose it?" Shadow asked.

Herin shook his head. "I didn't, you did. I just said I wanted to talk to you about this girl I had met and you immediately started accusing me of negligence. Let's go upstairs."

"You are out of your god-damned mind if you think I'm going up to a room with either one of you." Ilsa was still boiling. "Whatever you have to say, say it here."

"I can't," Herin insisted. "And this is important, Ilsa. Look, give me ten minutes and if I haven't convinced you of the importance of what I have to say, you're free to go. No strings attached. I did save your life, remember? I think you can give me ten more minutes of your time."

"Fine, ten minutes and not one second longer." Stiffly, she got to her feet and walked towards the narrow staircase leading to the rooms above the tavern.

Shadow shook his head. "I don't know what you are planning, Herin, but this is a mistake. She should never have been shown where we live. Now, we'll have to move or figure out a way to silence her. Did you think about that?"

"Shadow, for once, just listen. She could be important to us. I'll prove it once we're upstairs."

"Important?" Shadow was openly skeptical. "I'll believe that when I see it."

If Herin had harbored any doubts of his perception about Ilsa's latent abilities, they had been dispelled by her angry outburst at the table. The emotion had apparently enhanced her magical energy to the point where he wondered that it wasn't as visible as smoke from a smoldering fire. The scent was strong enough to make him rub his nose in an attempt to relive the itchiness he felt. "I promise, you'll agree once we're upstairs.".

Once safely in the room, Shadow looked at Ilsa with animosity, a look she returned with equal intensity. He struggled to understand why Herin had brought her back with him. She was coated with layers of dirt and grime and the rank odor of stale ale surrounded her like a fog. Given a bath and the right clothes, she might be pretty enough for one night, but right now all he could see was a security risk. It wasn't the fact that Herin had felt the need for a woman. Both of them had frequented a brothel near their inn from time to time, but he had tried to make Herin understand that security was the most important issue for someone doing what they were doing. To bring the girl to the inn had been a mistake.

"We're all here now," he said, shutting and locking the door. "How does this girl affect us? Do we have a sudden need for a tavern wench?"

"No, we don't," Herin said. "But we might be able to use a third magician."

"What?" Shadow and Ilsa echoed at the same time. Shadow frowned at Herin, and then shook his head. "Are you joking? Magic? A woman? That's impossible."

"What is going on here?" Ilsa demanded. She had followed this stranger to the harbor because he had saved her life, and it hadn't seemed like she had many options. But why would he believe she could do magic?

"You're crazy," Shadow said disgustedly. "Why would you even think such a thing? You've made a mistake."

"I found you, didn't I?" Herin argued. "I used the same method with her."

Shadow turned to her, his expression suspicious and unfriendly. "How about it girl? Care to show me a sample of your power?" Ilsa bristled at the dismissive tone.

"Fuck off," she replied angrily. "You know as well as I do that I can't do any magic. I don't know what he is talking about. Only a magician can do magic, and I'm no magician. I never heard of a female magician anyway."

Shadow turned to his companion. "And neither have you, Herin. So why do you think she can do something no other woman in the history of the empire has done?"

Herin said stubbornly, "She just doesn't know yet she can do it. But I'm telling you she can. Try something with her and see what happens."

"Try something with me and I'll tell you what will happen," Ilsa warned. "You'll be looking for your balls."

"I didn't mean that," Herin said impatiently. "Please, Ilsa, just do what he says and see what happens. You owe me that at least."

"You need to stop playing that card," she warned. "Fine, I'll try whatever you have in mind, just to shut you up with this magical nonsense. What do you want me to do?"

Shadow sighed angrily and said, "I'm telling you this won't work, Herin." He faced Ilsa. "Repeat this phrase, then flick your fingers at that candle over there. *Minn heita, hiti eiga aevi.*"

It was clear from the expression on Ilsa's face that she felt the whole process was a waste of time, but she did as she was asked, repeating the phrase and flicking her fingers towards an unlit candle sitting on the small dresser. A moment later a small flame flickered on the wick for several seconds before going out. Shadow's expression changed from anger to shock, and he looked narrowly at Herin. Ilsa's eyes were wide with surprise. "Did I do that?" she whispered.

"Apparently," Shadow said drily. "The question that comes to my mind now is, how did you do it? Herin, you swear you didn't help?"

Herin shook his head. "I told you, she has the ability. I did nothing."

"How could I do that?" Ilsa asked, still staring in amazement at her fingers. She repeated the phrase and flicked her fingers again. This time the candle stayed lit a few seconds longer, but another small flame caught the edge of the dresser on fire. Herin quickly snuffed it out with the edge of his cloak.

"You aren't ready for anything more yet," he warned. "Don't do spells by yourself."

"Herin's right, don't do that alone," Shadow echoed. "The more often you do it, the stronger the spell will become and you haven't learned control yet."

"You're magicians," Ilsa said, gazing at them with shock and unsuccessfully trying to control the tremor in her voice. All of her life she had heard tales of how powerful the magicians were, stories that did nothing to make her feel more comfortable about being in a room with two of them. Almost as frightening to her was the fact that she apparently possessed the same power, and had been unaware of it until this moment.

Herin looked surprised. "I thought you figured that out back at the inn. What did you think happened to those Dakarians?"

"I didn't see what happened," Ilsa confessed. "As soon as they let me go, I ran back into the kitchen. By the time I got back, they were backing out the door. I never saw what went on."

Shadow held up his hand to cut off Herin's explanation. "I'm not interested in that. You can fill her in on the heroic details later. I want to know how you knew she could do magic?"

"I already told you, the same way I identified you."

"Cut the shit, Herin. I am not in the mood," Shadow said angrily. "I want to know how you could pick out a random girl and know she could do magic. Let's hear it, and this better be good."

"She isn't just a random girl, Shadow," Herin snapped. "It wasn't like I went out looking to find a woman who could do magic. I found her the same way I found you. I could smell the magic on her."

Ilsa protested, "Wait a minute! What's that supposed to mean? Are you saying I stink?"

Shadow ignored her. "Interesting," Shadow mused thoughtfully, pulling at his beard and nodding his head slowly. "I have to admit you were right, though I don't see how it's possible."

"When I caught the scent on Ilsa, I figured she either had to be a magician or had been around one a lot. But if she was a magician, then why was she overpowered so easily by those Dakarians? On the other hand, where would she be around magicians? The only other option that I could see was that maybe she had some magical ability and just didn't know it."

"I don't understand," Ilsa said, still staring at her fingers as if they belonged to someone else. "Are you saying I can do magic?"

"You just did," Herin reminded her, scratching the fake beard he had been wearing all this time. It was beginning to irritate his face and he pulled up one end and ripped it off, rubbing his chin in relief. Ilsa's eyes went wide as he removed the rest of his makeup and tossed the beard onto the dresser.

"You're not any older than I am," she said in wonder, staring at his face. "Is that some sort of magic too?"

"Just a disguise," Herin told her. "What happens now?" he asked Shadow.

"I don't know. I think perhaps she should stick around here for a bit so we can explore this development. What is your name, girl?"

"Ilsa Visskona. What did you mean, you want to explore this?"

"Meaning I'll try teaching you some spells and we'll see if this is just some sort of fluke, or some real talent. It's up to you. I am not going to force you to stay. But if you can do magic, you need to learn how to control it."

"Why not stay?" Herin urged. "Where else do you have to go?"

"You've got a point," Ilsa conceded reluctantly. "I'll stay for a little while. Just to see if there's anything to this."

"And no more spells unless one of us is around," Shadow warned. "It is very dangerous for you to do this unsupervised until you have better control over what you're doing. I'm warning you up front that I don't think it's going to be anything other than a fluky kind of ability. That spell I gave you was one of the most basic ones there is, and even that barely worked. I doubt very much whether you'll be able to handle higher levels of magic."

Ilsa frowned a bit. "You are not a very cheery person, did you know that?"

"Wait until you get to know him," Herin said. "This is one of his good days."

Valgaard stared at the enclosed gardens that surrounded his office, a sight that normally brought him a sense of peace. Today it had no effect at all. His thoughts were a thousand miles away, and his eyes had the vacant stare of a man whose sight is turned inward. Behind the Council Master, Dagmar sat impatiently, a sheet of parchment unfolded on the small desk in front of him, waiting for Valgaard to give him instructions. He had been sitting for more than twenty minutes, and the main thought circulating in his head was how he would have to juggle the schedule, now so badly out of synch. If Valgaard didn't say something soon, it was going to ruin an entire day's planning.

He squirmed in his seat, hoping the noise would jolt Valgaard out of his reverie. "Sit still, you fool," Valgaard snapped without turning around. "I'm trying to think. That doesn't help things."

"My apologies, Lord," Dagmar simpered, "It's just that today is a very busy one and…"

"Damn you and your schedules!" Valgaard thundered, turning and slamming a fist on his desk. "You think that making sure everything gets done on schedule is the most important thing in the world! We have bigger issues in the Council than whether or not you have to rearrange things. Now sit there and shut up before I lose my temper and turn you into a toad."

Sufficiently cowed, Dagmar shrank back into himself and tried to breathe without making even the smallest sound. *What has happened to set Valgaard off like this? Something important...how can I find out what it is?* Dagmar's need to know overrode his impatience and he sat statue-still, every sense alert for any clue as to what had occurred out there in the Empire.

Finally, the magician turned to face him and began dictating orders. Dagmar struggled to keep up with the rapid-fire cadence, so unlike the business-like tones Valgaard normally used. He was writing so fast he didn't really have time to process the full implications of what he was writing until Valgaard had dismissed him and he had gone to his desk to make copies.

Interesting, he thought as he wrote. Valgaard was requesting two senior magicians to come to the capital as quickly as possible. *Now what could that be for?* Another message was to be sent to a shop in the center of the city that was used as a drop for getting messages to the cell the Council used for some of its more undercover activities. The note was going to a man known only as Tempest, and it directed him to speak with an innkeeper near the Palace about an incident three nights earlier that involved an attempted rape by some Dakarians.

That's odd. Why is this rape important? Hardly a day goes by without a report of one of these damned foreigners being involved in some assault. What's so different about this one? The northerners were nothing but barbarians, but Dagmar didn't see why that should concern the Council. His main objective was to see that everything ran smoothly, no matter what was taking place outside the school grounds. Dagmar quickly finished the copies and sealed them before snapping his fingers to summon a page. That done, he turned to his schedule book and began planning on how to fix the day's agenda.

Inside the office, Valgaard continued to stand at the window, lost in thought. The moment he had received the report about what had happened in the inn, it had been a simple matter to draw the logical conclusion. It was obvious that the stranger who had dealt with the Dakarians had used magic. All of the witnesses had concurred on that point. Their descriptions varied, as all eyewitnesses often did, but all agreed at least that it was a man approaching middle age, a common worker by his clothes, but obviously a magician. It had not taken a tremendous leap to conclude that it must be Herin Freeholder.

Who else could it be? No other magician was unaccounted for. As for the appearance, Valgaard thought that easy enough to explain. Herin had obviously used a spell to conceal his true appearance, something they had not taught him but was certainly within his capabilities. The Council had been searching for Herin ever since the accident at the Games, without any success at all. He had disappeared as if he had never existed, and in a city the size of Kress, finding him again had seemed impossible. But if this had been Herin, Valgaard was confident that Tempest would soon find his trail.

He wanted Herin back. The Council needed him back. Students with Freeholder's potential did not come along very often, and Valgaard had no intention of allowing an unfortunate mistake to ruin what promised to be a stellar career. Knowing Loki Tybold as he did, Valgaard had no doubts whatsoever that the fool had initiated the attack. He also knew that Jarl Tybold's agents were searching for Herin as well, with equal frustration. It was important that the Council get to him first.

There was a knock on his door and Dagmar announced Master Mellon.

"We may have found him," Valgaard said when the door closed. "I've sent a notice to Tempest and he will begin sniffing around to see if there's anything to it, but I think it's probably Freeholder."

"Where is he?" Mellon asked.

"I don't know," Valgaard confessed. "But I think I know where he was, and that's a starting point. We need to bring him in and get him under the protection of the Council."

"If we find him, you'll never keep it a secret," Mellon cautioned. "Tybold will hear about it almost the moment he comes through the gates."

"I know, that's why you will escort him to Khartul rather than bringing him here. The Council is strong enough to protect him out there. The Tybolds don't have the connections to threaten him that far away from Kress."

"I can't believe Jarl Tybold is still after him. It's been over two months since the accident."

Valgaard said, "You know he'll never stop trying to get his revenge, and he doesn't think it was an accident. He made that quite clear when he came here demanding we turn Freeholder over to him. All he talked about was the stain on his family's honor."

"Honor? That brigand?"

"I know, I know," Valgaard said, holding up a hand. "But he is rich and powerful, and he is after Herin. We have to find him first."

"I wonder why Herin didn't come back here?" Mellon mused.

"Because he isn't stupid," Valgaard said. "Herin obviously realized that Tybold would be after him even here, and if he came back here he would be a target that would be very easy to find. Some gold in the right places, and even this school could be compromised, and you know it. Herin has been in the city long enough to know it as well. Besides, he probably doesn't even know the whole story and believes a death penalty is waiting for him."

"It's possible," Mellon agreed.

"It's more than possible, it's probable," Valgaard answered. "That's something else Tempest can do for us while he's looking, and it's something I should have done weeks ago."

Mellon looked puzzled.

"Herin probably doesn't know that Loki didn't die that day. If he finds that out, there is still a chance that he'll contact us somehow and save us the trouble of trying to track him down. So while Tempest is looking, I'll have him spread the word that Tybold recovered so the worst thing Herin would face legally is assault."

"Assault." Mellon said disgustedly. "Yes, assault. By that jackass Loki, not by Herin. But that won't matter in a city where the Tybolds have every judge in their pocket."

"He won't face any judge if we get to him first,' Valgaard promised. "Within an hour of him being found, I want you riding for Khartul."

Ilsa slammed her fists down onto the bed in frustration. "I don't see why I have to do the same old spells over and over again," she said. "I've already proven I can do them, why do it one more time?"

"Because I say so," Shadow told her angrily. Herin sat in the corner watching a display he had become all too accustomed to over the past ten days. Shadow was a perfectionist, as he knew well from his own experiences. He wanted everything done just so, and Herin remembered his own early days when he went through the same thing Ilsa was going through now. The difference was that he at least had some background in magic, and was used to the discipline necessary to master it. Ilsa had no foundation with magic at all and didn't even understand what constituted a real magician. To her, it was simply about learning a spell every day, whether or not it could actually be controlled.

The real problem was that she didn't understand what magic was used for. Herin felt like he had been forced to relearn that himself. The sessions with Shadow had taught him that magic was a tool, and a skilled magician knew when to use that tool and when to use another. Wits were as important as skill with spells. Shadow's constant admonition to "Think it through…" had been hammered into his brain so often that he heard it echoing around inside his head every time he went to invoke magic. Shadow had taught him to use his brain to analyze the situation and decide whether magic was the appropriate response.

"Herin doesn't have to do everything over and over again," Ilsa pouted.

"What lessons have you been watching?" Herin interrupted the tirade. "I had to go through the same thing you are. And I still have to do that whenever I learn a new spell. Stop bitching all the time and do what Shadow asks you to do."

She glared at him, her eyes taking on the familiar anger he was so used to seeing. Herin didn't think he had ever met anyone with so much hate bottled up inside. It never took much for her to bristle at some slight, either real or imagined. *God's teeth, she's like some kind of wild animal, just waiting for an opening to attack. I was foolish to bring her here. I should have left her to her own fate.*

"Who asked you?" she spat. "This is because neither one of you think a woman should do magic in the first place. Shadow, you said so the first night. Now that you found out it's possible, you're trying to slow me down so that I never get as advanced as you."

"God's breath, you're a stubborn woman," Shadow cursed. "I've had enough of you for one day. I'm going out and see what's happening in the city. I'll be back in a few hours."

He stomped out of the room and Ilsa smirked as if she had won some sort of contest. "Good riddance," she murmured.

Herin regarded her sourly. "You know," he said conversationally, "If I had known you were this stupid I never would have bothered helping you that night. I should have left you to the Dakarians."

"What's that supposed to mean?" Ilsa said angrily.

"You are going to blow your chance to be somebody, that's what it means. How long do you think Shadow is going to put up with your tantrums? You need to grow up and stop complaining all the time. You're always looking for a reason to be pissed off, and it doesn't take you very long to find one."

"Fine talk coming from you," Ilsa griped. "You don't have to do the same simple things over and over and over again."

Herin shook his head. "Yes I did, just like you're having to do. You just don't want to hear that because it would ruin the 'me against the whole world' thing you've got going on. Why do you always think everyone is out to get you?"

"Because it's true," she said. "My whole life has been one long series of being trampled on."

"Shadow's teaching you magic," Herin said reasonably. "How is that putting you down?"

Ilsa's face was frustrated. "Sure, he's teaching me. At a snail's pace. At the rate we're going, I'll be an old lady before I learn enough magic to do anything."

"I didn't know there was a time schedule we were supposed to be meeting," Herin told her, not the least bit intimidated by her anger, or her arguments. He had experienced too much of both since he had saved her life for them to have any effect on him. "Are you in some sort of hurry? You're learning things that most people would give ten years of their life to learn. And you are the first woman ever to learn magic, according to Shadow. How many spells do you know?"

"I don't know...three or four I guess," Ilsa answered.

"That's three or four more than you knew two weeks ago," Herin pointed out. "You have to understand something about magic, Ilsa. You can't just pick up spells like you're learning how to cook different meals or something. Every spell requires you to be able to control energy, different energies for different spells. Without that control you could unleash a spell that you can't begin to handle, and the result could be dangerous to you and disastrous to everyone else. This isn't some game we're playing here."

"You don't have to do the same simple things," she said sourly. "I just get frustrated because I think I can handle more than he's giving me."

Herin shrugged. "Maybe you can, but Shadow has to be the one to decide that. As you get better and show more control, he'll speed things up. Remember, I have about eight years head start on you. I was taught the basics of magic back in my village, and I got at least a couple of months of real training at the Institute before I had to leave."

She looked at him with a penetrating stare. "Why did you leave? I've heard you and Shadow talk about it a few times, but never any details. What brought you down to this cesspool?"

Herin told her the basics of his story. As he was describing the events at the Coliseum, Ilsa cocked her head sideways, a puzzled expression on her face. Herin noted her reaction and his voice trailed off in the middle of the story. "What is it?"

"I heard about that fight," she told him. "It was all over the city. I mean, Jarl Tybold is pretty powerful and for someone to attack his son…that's news. But you don't know, do you?"

"Know what?" Herin asked.

"You didn't kill him. Tybold's son I mean. He isn't dead."

Herin was stunned. Loki alive? That meant he probably didn't even have a price on his head, hadn't ever had one. For a brief moment, he wondered if Shadow had known and was keeping the information to himself, then rejected that since there would be no reason to do so. "You're certain?"

"Oh yes, very certain. That asshole Loki Tybold sometimes came into the place where I worked. Slumming with the common folk. I think he did it just to throw his position in people's faces."

"Sounds like Loki," Herin agreed. "Damn, he's still alive. Why didn't Shadow or I hear about this on our trips uptown?" he wondered aloud.

"Why should you?" Ilsa responded. "It's yesterday's news."

Herin mulled it over and shook his head in wonder. After a moment's reflection, he realized it really didn't change his situation all that much. Even with Loki alive, the fact remained that he had still attacked him. It was only a miracle that Loki hadn't been killed, although Herin did feel like a great weight had been lifted off his shoulders.

"Let's get back to you," he said, shaking himself out of his reverie. "Shadow is not going to be patient with you much longer," he warned.

"Patient?" Ilsa said. "You call this patient? He's the one who left, remember?"

"Yes, patient. I know him better than you do. You have to stop questioning everything he says. Why can't you just trust him and follow directions?"

She frowned. "Why should I trust him? I don't know what his angle is yet."

"Dammit, not everyone has an angle!"

"Don't they?" Ilsa said, her tone glacial. "That hasn't been my experience. I've seen men at their very worst, so don't lecture me about the milk of human kindness. I know what people are like, especially men. They always have an angle."

"Oh, I forgot, you're the expert on what makes everyone act the way they do," Herin replied. This was a theme he had heard a half dozen times in the past fortnight.

"That's right. Until you've been where I've been you have no idea, so don't sit there and tell me that everyone doesn't work an angle."

"Okay, what's mine then?" he demanded. "Why did I save you that night? What was in it for me?"

"Rather obvious, don't you think?" Ilsa answered. "The same thing that all men are after when it comes right down to it. You wanted to get between my legs. Admit it, if I was some ugly old cow you wouldn't have lifted a finger to help me. But you played the hero hoping that someday you'd get your reward."

Herin stood and stared at her, his face stony with anger. "I feel sorry for you, Ilsa, I really do," he said softly. "It's one thing to be a fool. We all do stupid things from time to time. But to be so willfully ignorant is something else again. I can see that I wasted my time that night. I should have let the Dakarians take you. Is this how you see the world? If so, then you really are just a piece of ass when it comes right down to it."

"You fucking prick," she said, jumping off the bed and pulling her hand back to slap him.

Before she could deliver the blow, Herin shoved her back down on the bed hard enough to make her bounce off the mattress and slam into the wall. She looked up at him in shock. It was the first time he had ever touched her, much less used any kind of force.

"Stay there," he said turning his back. "And you might think about this while you're sitting here soaking in the pitiful world you've created for yourself. You expect to be treated like a whore so you read things into every action. You think all you are to men is some sort of prize. I wouldn't go to bed with you right now if you paid me all the gold in Kress. Maybe you should just do us all a favor and go back to your old life. It would be easier for you, wouldn't it? You'd be treated like you expect there. That should make you happy. I'm done with you."

He left quietly, leaving a thoroughly confused Ilsa behind. She listened to the sound of his footsteps on the stairs, realizing for the first time that she might have misread the situation. She had always subconsciously thought of Herin as someone who sooner or later would want what all men had always wanted from her. She had been prepared to pay her debts in the only coin she had, her body.

Ilsa had started working in inns when she was fourteen, beginning the day after both parents had been taken in one of the frequent plagues that periodically swept through cities. She had little choice; the job market for young girls with no real skills was limited to working in inns or working as a prostitute. The last ten years had shown her how thin the difference was between the two professions. Ilsa had lost her virginity within a week of starting work and had long ago lost track of how many men she had slept with. Once trapped in that life there was no escape and no options.

The contempt that had been on Herin's face as he left chilled her. It certainly wasn't the look of lust that men normally used when looking at her. That she could handle, veteran as she was of a hundred encounters in that arena. This was something altogether different. She might have thrown away her best chance for changing her fate, defeated by her own nature and unwillingness to take anyone at face value. Herin was right; Shadow had lost patience with her.

The enormity of what she had done suddenly overwhelmed her and she felt tears welling up in her eyes. "I'm not going to cry, dammit," she whispered fiercely over and over. It didn't work, and she fell back on the bed, sobbing softly as she finally saw that she might have permanently closed a door that was beginning to open for her. Ilsa had heard priests talking about the fires of hell waiting for sinners. If there was a hell, it must feel like she felt now, devoid of hope. She buried her face in her pillow.

Jarl Tybold sat behind the massive desk that dominated his office. The room was part of a mansion that took up an entire city block in the most expensive neighborhood in Kress. Tybold had commissioned the home ten years before as a way of flaunting his wealth and position, every line of it a purposeful statement that the Tybolds were a family to be reckoned with. For sheer size, it was the largest single dwelling in the city, dwarfing even the Palace of the Mayor. In fact, the Mayor had on more than one occasion used the Tybold mansion for various civic functions.

Tybold had designed the office himself. The size was meant to intimidate any visitor, to make them immediately feel small and insignificant. The desk itself was enormous, as big as a banquet table and kept meticulously clean so that any supplicant who came to see Tybold was forced to face him across an empty wooden space fully five feet across.

The walls of the room contained detailed maps, with multi-colored labels denoting the location of the various parts of the Tybold empire: warehouses, retail establishments, farms, shipping companies, and manufacturing facilities. Shelves held trophies brought back from distant lands, precious art objects, weapons encrusted with jewels, displays of wealth and power with one object in mind: cowing anyone who was in the presence of Jarl Tybold.

At the same time, the office was a place for him to get away for badly needed moments of private time. These moments had always been rare, but lately they had dwindled almost to the point of non-existence as the pressures of running his businesses took more and more of his energy. It was not something he thought much about, accepting it as a price to be paid for being in the position he was in. It had taken fifteen years of hard work to ascend to the top of the Families, a place he had held now for more than ten years. If he felt the first signs of age creeping upon him, he gave no indication, working as long and as hard as he did when he was a younger man.

But Jarl Tybold was a man who always tried to plan ahead. He had been grooming his oldest child and only son, Loki, to take over the business. It was for this reason he had enrolled him in the Institute, not because he thought Loki would eventually become a skilled magician. Even Jarl Tybold could see that his boy had no real ability to do anything other than a few parlor tricks. That wasn't the point. Tybold had been hoping that Loki would make contacts there with students who might one day be occupying important positions throughout the empire.

Tybold was used to success. Failures had been infrequent, but if he was honest with himself, Loki seemed to be one of those failures. He sat looking over the latest report from the school, information provided by his agent on the staff there. Tybold's bleak expression would have told anyone watching that he was not pleased with what he was reading. He reached behind him and pulled a velvet cord connected to a bell in the servant's quarters.

"Sir?" a servant asked, sticking his head through the door.

"Send someone to the school for Loki," Tybold ordered. "I want him here within thirty minutes."

"Yes sir."

While he waited for someone to fetch Loki he re-read the sheet of information from the Institute. It boiled down to this: Loki was an unpopular student who had surrounded himself with a group of cronies made up of all the other Family members who were enrolled in the school. In other words, the same group of young idiots he had been hanging around his entire life.

"The boy's turning into a failure," he said out loud. "It's high time I faced the fact that he might not have the brains he's going to need to run things here. If he doesn't straighten up I'll have to find someone else, one of the nephews or cousins, perhaps. But that's a scruffy lot as well."

School has been a mistake. Loki is wasting his time and my money.

By the time Loki arrived Tybold had decided on a plan of action. He waved his son to a seat and tossed the parchment to him to read, watching his son's expression as he did so. Loki read through the document quickly and tossed it back with a gesture of contempt.

"Well?" Tybold asked.

Loki made a sound of disgust. "Well, what? I don't know where you got that, but it's a bunch of nonsense. Says I don't apply myself. I'm not failing anything there, just ask the registrar. As to whom I spend my time with, I refuse to associate with social inferiors just because they happen to share a desk with me."

"Grow up," The anger in Tybold's voice made no impression on his son. "If you took your head out of your ass for ten seconds you might understand that some of those so-called inferiors will be in a position someday to help this family. Some may even hold posts within the government, with the ear of a Provincial Governor or some other official. They are going to remember you as an arrogant bastard who made them miserable, and they will take that out on us."

"Positions of power? Those nobodies? Impossible." Loki waved off the notion. "My circle of friends will be the ones in power."

Tybold said nothing for a moment, fearful that he would completely lose his temper and with it any chance he might have of fixing the problem. "It's one thing to make a mistake from inexperience; quite another to make it through sheer stupidity," he said through clenched teeth.

"Are you calling me a fool?" Loki asked, his anger at being interrogated now matching that of his father.

"No, I'm thinking that I am one for thinking there was anything in you that would allow you to run this family someday. I see now that it was a delusion on my part. But I will give you one last chance to prove me wrong. You have until the end of this semester to change your ways, or you are out. Out of the school, out of the family, out of the will, cut off from everything. Do you understand? Out."

"That's not fair," Loki protested. "I've done what you asked and gone to the school, even though I didn't want to. I wanted to run one of our businesses to get some experience, but you insisted I go to school instead. It isn't my fault you don't like what is happening."

"That may be so, but you're going to make it right or suffer the consequences. Stop associating with those other idiots you spend so much time with and start cultivating some useful relationships with other students. You already messed up one chance. Don't mess up this one."

Loki was confused and angry. How could his father cut him off from the riches that were rightfully his as the eldest child? "What chance are you talking about?"

"It's obvious that the star pupil at that school was Herin Freeholder. He was someone who would have been highly placed. But you screwed that up by antagonizing him and now he's gone underground somewhere and no one can find him."

Loki was speechless. Why was his own father siding with that rural upstart? "He almost killed me," he shouted, standing so he could lean across the desk.

"Don't raise your voice to me, you arrogant puppy," Tybold said, his eyes hard. "Sit down. If you dare something like that again, I'll have you beaten as if you were a child. It might have been the best thing for this family if you had been killed if you can't show more restraint and sense than you've shown so far. Now listen to me. You have one chance to fix this. There are about eight weeks left in the semester and when I get the next report I want it to tell me that you are cultivating a new group of friends. Here's a list of the students I want you to get close to." Tybold passed over a short list of students his source considered to be the most successful in their studies.

Loki studied the list with distaste. "These are second year students. I can't spend time with students that not only aren't in my social class, but are below me in school as well. I'll be a laughing stock."

"God's blood, you're already a laughing stock," Tybold shot back. "Nevertheless, you will become friends with them or you're done."

"Fine," Loki agreed, though it was obvious he hated the idea. "I'll obey the mighty Jarl Tybold."

"Get out before I lose my temper. One chance, Loki, one chance and you're either in or you're through."

Loki turned to go, and then stopped. "How will you know whether or not I've done as you ask? Do you have spies watching me?"

Tybold could only shake his head in frustration. The boy really was an idiot. "Of course I have spies watching you. How else do you think I get my information? Don't mess this up."

Sighing, Tybold sat and stared at the closed door, struggling to get his thoughts in order. Would this work? It seemed unlikely, but Loki was his son, even if he was a foolish, prideful, immature ass. He owed him at least a chance to turn things around.

Tybold filed the papers from the school before looking over the second message he had received. *So, the Council believes Herin had gone to ground somewhere in The Pit. Perfect.* For years, Tybold had maintained a spy network operating in that area, mostly to keep an eye on the workings of the Longshoreman's Council and any other organizations that might affect his businesses. If Freeholder was down there somewhere, he might be able to locate him before the Council of Magicians did. What should he do with the youngster if he found him first?

On the one hand, it was true that Herin had almost killed his oldest son, and that story was well-known in the city. The Family's honor was at stake. On the other hand, the boy was apparently a very gifted magician, and somebody like that could be very useful to him, very useful indeed. *If I can find him first and convince him to come to work for the Tybolds, will it make me look weak for not punishing him for attacking Loki? Probably not, but the first step is to find the boy, if he was in fact still in Kress. A magician working for me would make me the most powerful man in the Empire. I am going to need more information.*

"Time to pay back my contributions, Dagmar," he said with a grim smile.

Chapter Five

The sun played hide-and-seek with the clouds scuttling overhead as Herin and Shadow lounged against a pile of coiled ropes on one of the wooden docks, watching as longshoremen unloaded and stored cargo. Herin was half-asleep, recovering from a late night at his favorite brothel. His companion was more alert, his eyes missing nothing. Shadow liked to keep track of the ships which were in port, always mindful that it might suddenly become necessary to have a quick escape route from the city.

Having been raised five hundred miles from the nearest ocean, Herin knew as much about ships as the average farmer, which was to say, nothing. He also had a landlubber's natural distrust of any mode of transportation that didn't involve solid ground. Since there no longer seemed to be any pressing concern about leaving Kress, he was enjoying the late autumn sunshine and leaving the task of spotting likely vessels to Shadow.

Shadow frowned sourly at the supine form next to him and dug an elbow into Herin's ribs. "You might at least try to look interested, boy. You do realize that at some point your life might actually depend on knowing which ships are available?"

Herin opened one eye and yawned. "You worry too much, Shadow."

"And you don't worry enough," Shadow said in reply. "Which way will give us the best chance of staying alive?"

Herin sat up, recognizing that Shadow was in one of his "the wolves are at the door" moods. There was just no reasoning with him when a black fit was upon him. Herin had noticed that when things seemed to be going well, Shadow was in his sourest moods. When all hell was breaking loose, he seemed almost happy. "Why do you always look on the bad side of things?" he wondered. "Why can't you ever accept that things are going fine for once?"

"Because everything runs in cycles and the pendulum always swings back the other way at some point. I just want to be prepared for when that happens. The better things are going now, the worse they'll be going later."

Herin shook his head and laughed softly. "You can't enjoy life much that way. You're always looking for something bad to happen. Did it ever occur to you that you might be making bad things happen?"

Could the boy be right? The foundation of any successful spell was that a magician had to first visualize exactly what it was they wanted to happen. The clearer the visualization, the more powerful the spell would be. Logically then, it was the mental part that called the magic into existence. *What if Herin is on to something? Could negative thoughts have that much power? Maybe I am creating some sort of negative energy field that is attracting negative events. That is a troubling concept.*

Herin asked, "See any likely ships?"

Shadow nodded. "Two, the *Swallow* and the *Shark*. Both sail coastal waters so they'll put into port frequently."

"Which is best for us?"

Shadow answered thoughtfully. "The *Shark* sails northeast to Samazar and the *Swallow* goes northwest to Nelfheim. The *Shark* sails in three days, the *Swallow* in five. I'm ultimately headed for Nelfheim, so the first choice for me is pretty obvious."

"So you are definitely leaving?" Herin had known that such a moment was going to come sooner or later. He just hadn't realized it would be so soon.

"There won't be too many more ships sailing from now on," Shadow pointed out. "There's a two week window to get out of here before the winter storm season sets in. Both captains will want to get one last voyage in and that works in our favor."

"Why is that?"

"They won't have time to fill their holds completely," Shadow told him. "Both will just load whatever trade goods are available, which means both captains will be open to taking on some passengers for a little extra gold. We might as well leave while we can pick the time and method instead of waiting for a crisis to force us out."

"What kind of crisis? There haven't been any close calls to speak of."

Shadow looked sideways at him. "Really? Just last week we heard that both the Council and Tybold's men were sniffing around down here asking if anyone had seen a young man fitting your description. You don't think that's a bit troubling?"

"I've been careful," Herin said defensively. "Those men were nothing more than Loki or his family just taking a long shot. They are probably asking the same questions in other sections of the city as well. I'm safe here, don't you think?"

"No, I don't," Shadow disagreed. "It's only a matter of time until gold buys them the information they want. There are people here who would sell their own mothers for the right price, and you know it. It's time to go and if you want to take the easiest way out of the city, it's going to be one of those boats there."

Herin shrugged his broad shoulders. He wasn't bothered by the idea of leaving the metropolis. It wasn't as if Kress was his home. The last few months had been interesting, but it wasn't the life he had planned for himself when he left Chesterfield. If Shadow was leaving the city, he would be content to go with him.

"What about Ilsa?" he asked.

Shadow cocked his head. "Ask her if you want. I've no objections to her coming with us. Whatever you said to her a couple of weeks ago certainly worked. I think she may actually have some real ability once she learns to control that vile temper of hers."

They walked away from the quay and started trudging up the hilly road that led to their quarters, deep in conversation. Neither took note of the two men who left their table at one of the harborside cafes and began to follow.

The men trailed them back to their boardinghouse and took refuge in the shadow of one of the buildings on the opposite side of the street. "Find the others," said one. "I'll stay here and keep watch. Leave that young idiot behind if you can."

"Won't happen," his companion replied. He spat disgustedly. "Not with all of the money he's paying us. He is going to make sure he gets his money's worth."

"The things we do for gold, eh?"

"Best reason in the world to do anything. I should be back in fifteen minutes."

Ilsa was sitting in the main room of their inn making coins appear in one hand, disappear, and then reappear in the other. To anyone watching it would look like nothing more than a normal sleight-of-hand trick. In actuality, she was practicing a minor spell to move an object from one place to another, mostly to amuse herself. When they sat down at the table she put the coins away.

"Where have you two been?"

"Checking out the harbor," Herin said. "There are two ships loading up to leave and we're going to take one of them. Do you want to come with us?"

Ilsa chewed her lip, a habit she had when thinking over a problem. "Where are you headed?"

"I have business on the coast next Spring and thought it might be better to do the trip now rather than waiting here all winter," Shadow told her without elaborating.

"Will you still teach me magic?" she asked. That was the only important part of this, as far as she was concerned. If Shadow said no, there was really no point in going.

Shadow nodded. "There should be enough time to teach you some more before we're done sailing."

Ilsa nodded. "Yes, I'll go. There's nothing for me here but bad memories. I've never been outside the city. I'd like to see something of the rest of the empire."

"There probably won't be much to see other than water. Nothing but a few weeks on board ship, and then another town like this one. One smaller and a lot cleaner, but otherwise more or less the same."

The corners of her mouth curled up a bit in a small smile. "It's a change at least and that's better than staying here."

Shadow nodded. "That's settled then. Herin, why don't you see to our bill here? Make sure we're paid up through the end of the week. Ilsa, you could go start making up the traveling packs. We should have them ready to go in case we have to leave earlier for some reason. I'll find the masters of those two ships and see how much they want for passage. Meet back here in a few hours."

It took only a few minutes for Herin and Ilsa to prepare the travel packs with clothes and food. Shadow had been directing them to horde supplies against such a departure. Herin stole glances at Ilsa as they packed, once more aware of her innate grace. There was no denying that she was an attractive woman. He felt stirrings of something as he watched her move about the room. *Strange, why am I just feeling attracted to her now, after all this time together? We've been together for weeks and there was never anything like this before now.*

Across the street, the man watching the inn saw Shadow leave. He waited a few more minutes, then crossed to the entranceway, peeking through the door and scanning the Common Room for Herin. Reassured that he wasn't present and must be upstairs somewhere, the stranger took the opportunity to sit in a booth and order an ale, content to wait for reinforcements before taking any action. The serving girl who brought his drink confirmed that Herin was staying at the inn.

"Just went upstairs. Had his wench with him," she smiled. "Might be some time before he's down again."

"I'll wait," he told her. "Me and some of his friends are going to surprise him. We've been looking for him for some time now."

The man hadn't long to wait. Before he even finished his drink, five men came through the door and made their way to his table. Four were dressed in dark clothing and carried long knives strapped to their belts. The fifth was dressed in expensive, richly colored clothes, a fashion certain to make him stand out in The Pit.

"Shit! You couldn't leave him behind? He's sure to fuck everything up," The man whispered softly to his companions as they joined him at his table.

"He's also paying the bills. Nothing we could do about it."

Loki Tybold swaggered to the table and loudly ordered five ales, snapping his fingers to get the attention of one of the serving girls.

"What are you doing, you idiot!"

Loki was surprised at the anger in the man's voice. "What am I doing? I'm ordering something for all of you to drink so we can make our plans. Besides, it's thirsty work tracking someone down through all of Kress."

The man blew out his breath and tried to calm down. "We're not going to settle in here for the night. And just so you know for future reference, when you are on a job like this one the last thing you want to do is to call attention to yourself. Although it's a little late to worry about that now, isn't it?

"Sorry."

"You are that. We don't have much time. They are temporarily split up, but we have no way of knowing how long that will last. The youngster is upstairs with his woman. We should take him now before the other one comes back."

"Just remember, he's dangerous," Loki warned. He tossed a pouch of gold to each of the men, the promised reward for finding Herin. Loki knew his father was also actively searching for Herin, so it was vitally important that he find him first. His solution had been to contact the Assassin's Council and hire them to find Herin for him. It was expensive, but to Loki it was money well-spent.

"Don't tell us how to do our jobs," warned one. It was enough to take some of the bluster out of Loki's manner.

"I'm just saying, he is a magician, so make sure you confine his arms right away to keep him from making any passes," Loki instructed. "Gag him as well."

"We have dealt with magicians before," one of the men said, and the others nodded.

"They bleed just like any other man when you stab them," the man promised. "We know all about keeping them from doing any tricks."

Loki quickly apologized, not wishing to anger the men he needed. "I meant no offense. One last thing though. I want to be the one to kill him and I want him to know it was me. Just make sure that you confine him long enough for me to show him who has beaten him."

"You're paying the bills," the man shrugged. "Let's go and get this done."

The group quietly ascended the stairs, the first in line carefully testing each board before committing his full weight to it. Loki, bringing up the rear, was trembling in excited anticipation. This time he would have the upper hand, and by tomorrow the story would be all over school about how he had revenged himself on Herin Freeholder. Loki chortled silently, already anticipating the sweet feeling of sinking his blade deep into Herin's body.

They paused in the hallway, listening carefully at the door. "He isn't alone. The woman is still with him."

"Trantor, you and Belgor take care of her," the leader ordered. "Don't kill her unless you have to. She might be of use to us afterwards." The men grinned and one made a lewd gesture with his hips, much to the others' amusement. "Enough of that! Focus on the job!"

They all pulled their knives and silently arranged themselves outside the door. Loki was already making plans for disposing of Herin's body, his heart pounding as if it was trying to jump out of his chest. He would show that farm boy how things were done in Kress.

The leader kicked in the door, allowing his men to rush into the room. Herin spun in surprise but quickly had his arms pinned by two of the men. They stuffed a rag down his throat and held a knife to his neck, the point pressing hard enough to draw blood. Trantor grabbed Ilsa by one arm while Belgor put his knife under her chin, causing her head to tilt painfully backwards until all she could see was the thick beam holding up the ceiling.

Loki strolled into the room and leaned casually against the dresser, kicking the door slowly shut with one boot and smiling at Herin. "No escape this time, country boy," he drawled. "Now it's time to pay for all the trouble you've caused."

Herin's reply was muffled by his gag and Loki laughed at his frustration. Herin tried desperately to do something, but with the gag in his mouth he couldn't even start a spell.

"As you can see, your attempt to kill me did not work. Mine will be more successful," Loki gloated. "I just wanted you to know who it was that killed you. You've been a thorn in my side for too long. Now it's going to end."

Belgor leaned over to whisper to Ilsa, "As soon as they're done, Kitten, you and I will play," he promised. "Then the others will take their turn. Maybe you can keep us all happy for the rest of the afternoon."

Ilsa's arms were pinioned, but her hands were free and her mouth not gagged, though it was covered by her captor's meaty hand. Whoever these intruders were, they obviously did not think she was capable of much in the way of resistance. That gave her one small advantage, but she would need to take action now. It was obvious that Loki meant to kill Herin. Praying that her actions would work, she bit down hard, causing her captor to recoil in response. Desperately, she chanted, *"Drepa niori Naors helalornari eda andlat."*

Belgor grabbed his bleeding hand, an action that cost him dearly. Ilsa flicked her fingers and he immediately caught fire. It was as if he had been soaked in oil, and he burned and screamed in agony as he was consumed. Ilsa felt the flames licking at her own skin, but was too intent on her other captor to notice. She ignored Belgor writhing on the floor, the flames from his body beginning to lick greedily at the bedclothes. It was only a matter of seconds for her to repeat the spell on Trantor, turning him into a second human torch. While he rolled on the floor in a desperate attempt to extinguish the flames that were killing him, Herin took advantage of the diversion to throw his weight suddenly against his own captor, freeing his arms.

"The bitch knows magic!" cried one of the others as he drew back his arm to throw his knife.

"Kill her!" Loki screamed, desperately trying to retain some control of the situation.

Ilsa raised her hands, fingers splayed out and eyes blazing with anger. *"Rida blasa prumdi drepa!"*

The man holding the knife was struck down by a bolt of lightning that seemed to materialize out of nowhere, leaving behind nothing but a pile of smoking ashes on the floor. The explosion tossed Loki across the bed to slam up against the stone wall on the far side of the room. Herin took advantage of the moment to grab the three packs by the door and pull Ilsa into the hallway.

"Kaerr ergjask bjarg!" he cried, as he slammed the door behind him. It immediately turned the grayish color of stone.

"That will hold them until someone can chisel them out," he said, tugging Ilsa towards the stairway. "We've got to find Shadow and get out of here."

"Who were those men?" Ilsa panted behind him.

"Loki you already know. The others I don't recognize, probably some paid thugs," Herin said over his shoulder. They ran out into the street and sprinted towards the harbor. Herin spared a glance back after they had covered a few hundred yards and slowed his pace to a quick walk. "Okay, there aren't any others," he said. "If Loki had been smarter, he would have left some downstairs, just in case we got away." Herin tore a strip of linen from his tunic and used it to staunch the flow of blood from the wound in his neck.

"What did you do to the door?" Ilsa asked.

Herin grinned. "Combined a closing spell with one used to repair statues," he told her. "It will keep the door shut against anything short of a stonemason chiseling them out. It will be hours, maybe days before anyone can hammer their way through that."

"I don't know that spell," Ilsa said. "What's it called?"

"That isn't really a spell," Herin admitted. "I just put two minor spells together. Wasn't even sure it would work, but it seemed like a time for desperate measures."

"Can you show me how to do it? That seems like a useful skill to have."

Herin shook his head. "I can try. I've never actually done it before. Promise me you won't try something like that until you have more control over your magic. And thanks for not losing your head back there. Without you doing what you did, I'd be dead right now. I owe you my life."

She laughed nervously, the adrenaline from the encounter still in her system. "Let's call it even. We still have to get away."

"I mean it, Ilsa. I won't forget."

"Later, Herin," Ilsa said. "Let's find Shadow."

Herin nodded. She was right. They could no longer risk another night in the city. Herin hoped that Loki had been on his own and not working in conjunction with his father, but it wasn't something he could count on. They needed to leave Kress immediately, without waiting for the ships to sail. They would have to chance the gates. Herin did not know much about Jarl Tybold other than his reputation, but it seemed unlikely that he would have risked his son in a murder attempt. That thought gave him hope that Loki had been working independently, which meant they might still have time to get out of Kress before being discovered.

Herin broke into a trot towards the harbor, pulling Ilsa with him. "We have to get out of the city. You realize we'll have to leave right away?"

She nodded. "What difference does it make? We were going anyway. All this does is speed things up a bit."

"But now we're going to be traveling on foot," Herin explained. "We won't be able to go as far or as fast. We also don't know if we can even get out of the city through the gates. It's possible they are being watched."

"Then we'd better find Shadow," Ilsa said. They disappeared into the crowds of people near the harbor.

Shadow was easy enough to find. He was at one of the popular drinking establishments near the main docks, sitting at a table with several seamen. When he saw them holding up the travel bags as a signal, he quickly stood and hurried to their side. Herin told him what had happened in the barest possible terms, feeling suddenly that each minute spent inside Kress's walls was giving his enemies a chance to find them. Though the rational part of Herin's mind told him that Loki was going to be stuck inside the room for hours, he wouldn't feel really safe until he was outside the city.

"We have to leave now," Herin said quietly.

"Yes, we do," Shadow replied. "Follow me." He slung his pack over his shoulder and led them back out into the street. He set a quick pace away from the harbor.

"Where is he going?" Ilsa panted, running to keep up.

Herin didn't reply, too busy running to answer. Shadow led them through alleyways and streets at a quick trot until they found themselves standing beside a crumbling stairway in a seedy, rundown neighborhood. Ilsa was gasping for breath, bent over and taking deep lungfuls of air in an effort to regulate her breathing. Herin was no better off as he fought down the nausea he felt.

"What the hell are you doing, Shadow?" he gasped. "Why are we running so hard? There's no one behind us."

"You don't know for certain that it was only Loki back at the inn. We need to get out of the city quickly."

"He was alone," Herin insisted. "I didn't see anyone else and we weren't followed."

"You're probably right," Shadow agreed, checking the street to see if it was clear. "But we didn't see anyone when we went into the inn, and they must have been watching the place. Either way, we can't afford to take any chances. We need to get out now, before the word spreads about where we were. I wonder how Loki found you before his father or the Council did."

"Do you want to spend time solving that little mystery, or can we get outside Kress first and then argue about it?" Ilsa panted, still trying to catch her breath.

"Good point," Shadow agreed. "We should get out while we can."

"Where are we?" Ilsa asked. "This looks like an abandoned neighborhood." Many of the houses were boarded up or showed signs of neglect. Several roofs had collapsed and there were two dwellings directly across the street that lacked an entire section of wall, allowing them to see into the ruined and empty interiors.

"It is deserted now," Shadow said. "But it used to be a place where textile workers lived. When that industry moved to Khartul, the workers went with it. Over time this place just fell apart. It does have something we need though, which is access to the top of the wall. The night watch used to maintain a post here, but they gave that up years ago."

Herin eyed the stairway with a dubious expression. "Do you really think that will hold until all of us get to the top?"

"There's a better one a block or so up the street. I'm just giving you two a chance to rest before we move."

"Why don't they still patrol the wall?" Ilsa asked as they walked quickly towards the second stairway.

"Just another thing showing that Kress's best days are behind it," Shadow said, "They've grown lazy and complacent." He led them along the sidewalk, hugging the shadows as much as possible. It was only a matter of a few minutes to gain the steps, and Shadow led them upward until they found themselves on a narrow parapet fully one hundred feet above street level. From where they were standing it was possible to look back the way they had come and see the harbor, crowded with ships but so distant that it looked almost like a painting. Looking away from the water, they could see trade roads in the distance, as well as the dark green smear of the Dark Forest beyond that.

"How do we get down?" Herin said, leaning out to look over the edge of the wall. The surface was rough and much of the stonework had clearly seen better days. It was possible that there might be handholds in those blocks of stone, but to Herin's untrained eye they appeared fairly smooth, and it was a long way down to solid ground. He didn't fancy trying his luck on this.

Shadow went behind a pillar and pulled out a long coil of rope.

"Dammit, Shadow, if you had all of this ready, why were we trying to get onto a boat?" Ilsa asked. "We could have left anytime. Why aren't we just going out the gates anyway? There couldn't have been any alarm yet."

"Maybe not, but why take that chance? Even if we weren't stopped someone might remember two men and a woman leaving by such and such a gate heading in such and such a direction. No, we need to disappear, to vanish as if we were never here at all."

"Why were you keeping this from us?" Herin demanded. "More of your damned secrecy?"

"The truth is, I forgot I had this until we were talking about leaving," Shadow admitted. "But you should always have as many ways out of a place as possible. Plans have a funny way of not working out exactly the way you thought they should. Once down, we'll head for the forest until we're sure there aren't any pursuers from the city. There are half a dozen small villages in there that could provide temporary shelter. Then on to Khartul to wait out the winter. The first storms will be coming along in two or three weeks and we could never hope to reach Nelfheim by then."

Shadow secured the rope to the pillar and they slid down to the ground below. Shadow was the last one down and he laid his hands on the rope, whispering, *"Festr eiga grunnr sjalfr kueoa."* Silently, the rope fell to a pile at his feet and he quickly coiled it and put it in his pack.

"Come on," he said and set off on a path that took them away from the city walls into the sparsely settled countryside that surrounded Kress. The sun had begun to set and the gathering darkness served to hide them from any prying eyes, though the zone they were traveling through seemed deserted.

"How far are you planning on going tonight?" Herin asked Shadow.

"Let's just move as fast as we can for two or three hours and see where we are," Shadow replied over his shoulder.

"Good plan," Ilsa whispered softly, rolling her eyes.

Chapter Six

"You are a damned idiot," Jarl Tybold said, staring at his son. "And lucky to still be alive. Every time I think you cannot possibly be any more foolish, you prove me wrong."

"I wanted to deal with him personally," Loki protested. "It was a matter of face."

Tybold's laugh was derisive. "This is what you call saving face, is it?" Loki winced at the look of open disgust on his father's face. "Making the family a laughing stock in front of all of Kress? How do you propose keeping this latest disaster quiet? Your first encounter with Freeholder was interesting gossip, but nothing more. It's a different story now."

"He would have been a dead man if not for the girl," Loki insisted. "She was the one that messed everything up. I was all set to cut his throat when all hell broke loose and it was her doing. We couldn't have planned for that. Who ever heard of a woman magician?"

"Who indeed?" Tybold said thoughtfully. He had checked through his contact at the school, but Dagmar had no information beyond what Tybold already knew. It had been obvious that the reality of a woman who could handle magic had been as much a surprise to the Council as it was to his son. "How did you find Freeholder in the first place?" he asked, suddenly changing tack.

"I used the Assassin's Council," Loki replied.

"The Assassin's Council? You really are a fool," his father said. "Do you know why I didn't use them? Because they are too expensive for one thing, and because if something like this happens they take you to court to pay a fine for interfering with their business. I don't know what you paid them, but it will cost the Family five times as much to keep them off our backs. Idiot!"

Still, the incident began a train of thought in Tybold's mind. *If there were two magicians out there who were not members of the Council, might there be others? What if I can find some of these others and bring them under my control? The possibilities are far reaching. It would mean that I might become powerful enough to challenge the Magicians' Council on their own ground. That is a goal worth chasing. What could stand in my way if I have my own private army of trained and competent magicians? Nothing, nothing at all.*

"This is going to cost us a hundredweight of gold, maybe more," he complained.

"I'm sure we can afford it." Loki was angry enough to dismiss his father's arguments without a second thought. "Why waste time on that when Herin is the real concern? He could be anywhere by now."

"It's easy to call money a waste when you did nothing to earn it." Tybold's voice was sharp enough to make Loki realize he might be on shaky ground. "Freeholder will obviously be outside the city by now. Only a stupid person would stay inside the walls knowing we were that close to catching him. Being stupid enough to stay here would be something I'd expect from you, but Freeholder strikes me as being smarter than that." Loki held his tongue with difficulty, not wanting to antagonize his father further. He realized he had not yet been told what his punishment would be, and Loki knew he was not going to escape this without something being done to "teach him a lesson".

His father crossed to the large-scale map on the wall, studying it as he considered possible options for the party they were chasing. "Where would they go? Probably Khartul or Samazar since winter won't be far off. Possibly they'll hug the coast and head for Goldar."

"We can cover all of the major roads with patrols," Loki said. "We can set a trap for them."

"*We* aren't going to do anything," his father replied without turning around. "I will take care of this from here on out."

Loki sullenly sat back in his chair, silently vowing revenge on Herin Freeholder. It seemed that every time he went up against the outlander he came out on the losing end, and he could not allow that to continue.

Tybold sat back behind his desk and stared at the ceiling for a few moments, lost in thought. "I'm sending you to Khartul," he said finally.

Loki tried to keep his features neutral. *Khartul? Why there?* He had only visited the city twice, the most recent trip seven years before, as an adolescent. His memories were of a mid-sized city built just below the peaks of the Missark Massif, which meant that at this time of year it was going to be bitter cold.

"I want you to take over our fur trading operations," his father explained. "By next summer I want to see a profit at least twenty percent higher than it was this past season. I've neglected it somewhat over the past few years but it's time to correct that oversight. I'm giving you three years to show me that you can run things there. Do well and I'll have you back here to take over our grain business."

"Three years? What about school?" Loki asked.

"That's over," his father answered. "After this latest debacle you'd be a laughingstock there anyway. You can get a fresh start at Khartul. It's far enough away that this scandal won't mean anything. See that you take advantage of it."

It was obvious to him that Loki needed to be sent away from Kress long enough for this latest incident to become old news. Tybold knew that if his son was ever to take over the family business he would first have to repair his tarnished reputation. That couldn't happen here in Kress, at least not right away. But if he could get Loki out of the city for a few years while he grew up, the boy might just live this down. If Loki stayed here, this story would cling to him like fungus, and Tybold knew his son well enough to know that Loki would react stupidly to the remarks and derision he was certain to face. Better to get him away for a while and let him find himself before exposing him to the pressure of being the heir to the Tybold fortune. And if he failed to live up to expectations, it would cause less of a ripple if Loki was put aside while he was hundreds of miles away in Khartul. Under the circumstances Tybold thought it was the best he could do.

"When do I leave?" Loki showed no enthusiasm for the project, a fact his father chose to ignore for the moment.

"In the morning. The arrangements will be made tonight. It will take the better part of two weeks to get there and that puts you right up against the first of the winter storms. If you can travel faster than that, do so. Otherwise you might be fighting blizzards on the way."

"What about brigands on the road?"

"Don't worry; your party will be large enough that it will be left alone. I'm sending an escort of twenty guards as well as a half dozen clerks and secretaries to help ease you into your new position. At this time of year there aren't many travelers. Any bands of outlaws in the forest have probably already gone into winter quarters to wait for the new season. You'll leave right after sunup so you'd better go get some rest. It's a long trip and you'll need your strength."

Herin stared absently into the flames of the campfire, content to let his thoughts drift. They were three days out from Kress and this had been the first night that Shadow judged it safe enough for a fire. The farmland that surrounded the city was now far behind them, and they were into less settled areas. The land was still fairly level, broken here and there by groves of trees that had been spared the axe. The three of them were safely hidden from view in one of the groves, and with the first hot meal in days sitting comfortably in his stomach, Herin felt a warm glow of contentment.

That realization caught him by surprise. He was cut off from the Council and school, with the Tybold family after him, heading for an unknown future. *Why should that make me feel any satisfaction at all? Everything I wanted is out of my reach now. I should be depressed.* Born and bred in a small village, the teeming crowds of the capital had always made him uneasy. On their first night outside the city he had looked up at the night sky and spotted constellations that he had known since childhood. He hadn't seen them in months because of the nightly haze thrown up by torches and smoke in Kress, and it was like greeting old friends. Every night since then he spent an hour or so just lying on his back gazing at the night sky.

"Where are we going?" Ilsa asked, stirring the fire idly and sending sparks flitting away like fireflies into the darkness.

Shadow sat with his legs crossed, face partially hidden by the dancing shadows thrown off by the fire. "Khartul for now, Nelfheim in the Spring."

"We could go to Samazar or Burberry," Ilsa said. "They are closer than Khartul."

"We could," Shadow agreed. "But I think it best to head for Khartul."

"Why there?" Ilsa asked.

"It will mean less travel when we set off again in the spring."

"I don't care where we go as long as it's somewhere that will let us sleep under a roof when the snows come," Ilsa said. "I don't know much about Khartul, except that it's in the mountains. Can we get there before it snows? Khartul is so far north, it must start snowing there weeks before anywhere else."

"There's still time," Shadow assured her. "If we can make twenty miles or so each day we can be there in three weeks. We might run into a few light snowfalls as we get closer to the mountains, but we should be there in plenty of time to winter over."

"There are more than a hundred thousand people there. You should feel right at home, Ilsa," Herin said, lying back down.

She looked at him with a puzzled expression. "Why would that make me feel at home? And how would you know how many people are there?"

Herin grinned at her. "Just because I grew up in a small village doesn't mean I don't know anything about the rest of the empire. I went there once with my father and some other farmers when they were trying to set up some kind of a trade agreement. I probably wasn't more than five or six, so my memory is a little fuzzy. But it's a big city, even if it isn't the size of Kress. You just never struck me as a small-town type."

"And that's another reason for going there," Shadow added from across the fire. "The bigger the city, the easier it will be to stay hidden. Actually, Herin, you're off by a couple of hundred thousand. There's close to half a million people in Khartul now and it's getting bigger each year."

"Living in a big city is going to be more expensive. Do we have enough money for that?" Ilsa asked.

"No, we don't," Shadow answered. "Enough for a month or so maybe, but then we'll have to work for it. You should be able to find a job in a tavern easy enough, and Herin and I will go back to doing a little street magic to earn our keep."

"The hell with that," Ilsa spat. "I'm not doing that." Herin and Shadow looked at her in surprise.

"What's the problem?" Shadow asked.

"I left that life behind me and I'm not going back to it," she said firmly. "Never again. I'll not be spending any more time pushing some filthy worker's hand out of my skirt. I don't care what you say, I'm not doing it."

"What if we need the gold?" Herin asked. "It's not like you're going back to working full time in a tavern."

"I said no. You have no idea, Herin, none at all about what kind of life that is."

Shadow held up his hand. "I think you're forgetting who you are, Ilsa," he said mildly. "You don't ever have to worry about something like that again. Just put up magical protection. There are a dozen spells you could use to keep men from even wanting to touch you, all without them knowing you're using one. We have plenty of time for you to learn them before we get to Khartul."

Ilsa took a breath to calm herself. "You're sure?"

"I'm sure. Both of you still have a lot to learn about magic, and the winter will give us time to work on that some more. But you won't ever go back to that old life, Ilsa. Once you start using magic, the more you use it, the more powerful you get. That's actually one of the dangers in using it too often, it gets to be more than you can resist and before you know it, your life is consumed with the need to do more and more spells."

Herin propped himself on an elbow. "Is that so? Then why do you use it? How long have you been practicing magic?"

"I don't use it unless I have to," Shadow said. "Especially major spells. There's a reason for that. I've seen more than one magician get so seduced by the power that it's all they thought about. It burns them out, like being addicted to a strong drug. Successful magicians are the ones who learn early on how to control the urge to use magic in every situation they encounter."

"You didn't answer his question. How long have you been practicing?" Ilsa asked.

"It's not important. Remember, you can either make magic your servant or your master. The choice is yours."

Herin shook his head as Shadow talked. *What is Shadow talking about? I've been doing magic for eight years, and I don't feel any ill effects from it. I remember sneaking off sometimes back at home, and doing nothing for four or five hours but spells. It gave me a rush of pleasure, but it never felt addicting.*

"If it's so dangerous then why are you teaching us anything at all?" Ilsa asked.

"A lot of things are dangerous," Shadow told her. "That doesn't mean you don't do them. I just want you two to realize how potent magic is."

"I already knew that," Herin told him. "You still haven't answered the question. How long have you been doing this?"

Shadow stared at him for a moment, and then shrugged. "No reason for you not to know, I guess. It's something you'll have to come to grips with yourself. I've been doing magic for more than one hundred and ten years."

"Bullshit," Herin said, laughing. "My father is fifty and he looks older than you."

"It's true," Shadow insisted. "Doing magic somehow prolongs your lifespan. Nobody knows why. The more powerful you are, the longer you could live. Herin, I guess none of your teachers at the school told you that piece of information. I am one hundred thirty-five years old."

"I can't believe you're a century older than I am." Herin tried to absorb the idea that he might live for hundreds of years.

"Why should I lie?" Shadow asked.

"I don't know, but you do plenty of other things I don't understand."

Ilsa said, "So how long can a magician live? It sounds like almost forever."

"Not quite. Magicians can still fall victim to accidents or attack. It's true that magic seems to somehow keep us from getting ill, but we are subject to the same dangers as normal people. The oldest I ever heard of was eight hundred, but he died in battle so I don't know if anyone has ever figured out the ultimate lifespan. I just know that the more power you can handle, the longer you seem to live."

Herin was silent, turning this new information over in his mind. If he could really live hundreds of years, it meant that all of his family, everyone he had ever known growing up would be dust for centuries before he joined them in death. That was a sobering thought. He wasn't sure he liked the idea.

"We need to get an early start tomorrow," Shadow said. "Let's get some sleep."

"I'm in charge and I say we're changing the route," Loki said angrily. He was face to face with the commander of the escort, a grizzled ex-soldier who had been in the employ of the Tybold family since leaving the army a decade earlier. The man wasn't impressed by Loki's display. He had seen this kind of behavior many times while serving in the legions, always from untrained officers trying to look and sound like veterans. He had marked Loki as just such a personality even before they had left the city. Nothing had happened on the road to change his opinion.

"Be my guest," the man said. "Travel through the forest if that's what you want. The rest of us will stick to the main trade road."

Loki wanted to use one of the minor trade routes that cut through the heart of the Dark Forest, insisting that it would shave several days off their journey. They had been caught in a freak snow shower on the second night out from Kress, and he believed it to be a harbinger of worse weather to come. Loki's only thought was to get to Khartul before a real storm hit.

"Have you looked at the map? It will save us at least fifty or sixty miles if we use the road through the forest." *I hate dealing with people who can't think. Any fool can see the road through the forest would be faster.*

The argument fell on deaf ears. "Maps don't tell the whole story. The woods have only one or two small settlements. What if we do need shelter against another storm? What then? The roads aren't as good either. It won't be faster."

Loki insisted, "If we use the woods we won't have to worry about getting caught out here in the open if it does snow again."

"It will slow us down," the man said stubbornly. "There are a half dozen or more good sized towns between here and Khartul, all conveniently located on the main road. We can use them if the weather turns, and simply pass through if it doesn't. You do what you want. My orders from your father were to carry messages to Khartul and see that the party got there before winter. That's what I plan to do."

"You take orders from me, and I say we're going through the woods." Loki used the same tone of voice he had employed with underclassmen back at the Institute. "Otherwise, the first message to my father will say you abandoned me and left me at the mercy of whatever is out there. How long do you think you'll stay employed then?"

The man cursed silently. Damn the brat, he was right. If they went on without Loki it would make for a more pleasant trip, but when word of that got back to Jarl Tybold there would be hell to pay. The ex-soldier knew that if that happened he would be looking for a new position. Since there weren't many jobs that paid as well as this one, he would just have to put up with the arrogant bastard until Khartul.

"A written order if you please," he said, holding out his hand. "When your father asks me why we went off track I want to show him the reason. If we are delayed in getting to Khartul he will be sure to ask."

"Fine." Loki snapped his fingers and one of the clerks rode up beside him with parchment, pen and ink bottle. The clerk held up the small bottle of ink as Loki furiously dashed off a short message saying it was on his authority that they had changed plans and tossed it to the officer. "Satisfied?"

The man read it quickly before carefully folding it up and securing it inside his shirt. "That will do. Lead on."

Loki hesitated, momentarily at a loss. He had anticipated someone else actually directing the small party, but he had put himself in the position of being in charge, and now it was up to him to choose the route. He had to follow through or lose face. "This way," he said grandly, waving his hand and starting confidently down the closest path. It was barely more than a trail and the rest of the party stayed motionless, the guards looking at their leader quizzically.

He sighed and rode quickly forward to grab the bridle of Loki's horse. "That will take us to the east and we want to go to the west," he pointed out. "Sun's setting over there."

With as much dignity as he could muster under the circumstances, Loki yanked his horse around and headed in the opposite direction. The captain of the guards kept his face carefully neutral, but rolled his eyes at his second in command as Loki rode off.

"Pray to whatever gods you worship," he whispered. "We'll need all the assistance we can get."

Crouched on the edge of a small wooded ridge, Herin and his companions scouted the camp spread out below them. The scent of woodsmoke on the morning air had drawn them to the spot. The camp was in a small clearing and their position allowed them a clear view of the early morning activity. A dozen men and half as many women were in the process of rolling out of their blankets, stretching, and getting ready for another day. Two women were already stirring something in a pot over a small fire.

"Outlaws," Shadow guessed quietly. "They must be pretty certain they are safe if they're cooking over a fire."

The camp had a disorderly air about it, with piles of animal skins and equipment scattered about the clearing. It was obvious the group had no real organization to it. A few rude lean-tos provided shelter against the elements, but the place gave every appearance of being temporary.

"How do they survive out here in the winter?" Herin whispered back.

"They must have a more permanent camp somewhere deeper in the woods. Or maybe they are taken in at one of the villages. You're right though, this isn't where they stay on a regular basis. It's too exposed."

"So now that we've seen them, what are we going to do?" Ilsa asked quietly.

Shadow replied, "We can either by-pass them or go down and see if we can get a meal and maybe some information at the same time. If there is any Imperial activity in this section of the forest, they would know it."

"If they don't slit our throats first," Herin muttered darkly. "Look at them. Have you ever seen a more scraggly lot? I bet they'd just as soon kill us as look at us."

Shadow shook his head. "Appearances can be deceiving. Most of those down there are likely outlaws because of necessity rather than choice. They probably got thrown off their land for non-payment of taxes or some such nonsense. They're robbing to survive, that's all."

"You'd trust them?" Ilsa asked. "What if Herin is right?"

Shadow shrugged. "I'm not dropping my guard completely and just marching into camp with a smile on my face if that's what you mean. They are outlaws, so they could be dangerous if we don't take precautions. But they can't really hurt us as long as we're careful. They won't risk a confrontation if there's nothing in it for them. Face it, we don't really look like rich merchants. They might even mistake us for fellow outlaws if we play it right."

Shadow had assessed them correctly, Herin thought. Ten days of being on the road had been hard on their appearance, and their general air of dishevelment would probably convince the people below that they were not desirable targets. A change in the wind wafted the odor of breakfast their way, and his stomach rumbled in reminder that they had not yet eaten. Whatever the women were cooking down there was going to be more filling than the dried rations they had been subsisting on for the past four days.

"Think they'll feed us?" he asked with a grin.

"There's only one way to find out. Be alert. No hands on weapons but be ready to move if we have to."

"I'm starting a spell already," Herin answered, only half-joking. He was already mentally going through his list of spells to select the ones he could implement the quickest.

"Ilsa, watch behind us to make sure no one is back there when we enter camp," Shadow ordered. "I'll watch the left, Herin you watch right. Sing out at the first sign of trouble and we'll get out. Try to look like people down on their luck."

"That won't be hard," Ilsa said as they left their cover.

Shadow stood so that his upper body was visible over the brush. "Hail the camp!" he called out.

A frenzy of activity energized the people below, with both men and women rushing to fit arrows to bows. Several of the men hefted vicious double-headed battleaxes, spreading out to cover the flanks. Herin noted with unease that the rest were armed with longbows, fearsome weapons in the hands of archers who knew how to use them. He wished he had his own in his hands just then.

Herin, like all of the boys in his village, had been required to spend five to ten hours a week practicing with a longbow, and he knew full well how dangerous the bows could be. As a precaution, he began whispering the opening lines for a protection spell, determined to activate it at the first twang of a bowstring.

Shadow held his hands where they could be seen and led the way out into the open, Herin and Ilsa following. Ten bows tracked every move they made, so they were careful to make their movements slow and unthreatening.

"We mean no harm," Shadow said as they approached the group. "Just three people hoping for a friendly meal is all."

A man with a thick beard motioned two of the bowmen forward. "Search them," he ordered. "See what they carry."

"Little enough, friend," Shadow said, allowing one of the men to rummage through his clothing and pack. "No more than you."

"He's got this, Hawk," the brigand said, hefting the pouch with their money.

"Stealing from a fellow outlaw?" Shadow asked. "No honor among thieves, is that it?"

The man called Hawk stared at Shadow, his swarthy features betraying no emotion. He was a giant of a man, well over six feet tall, broad as a barn, with the thick shoulders and neck of someone who was accustomed to physical labor. An unruly head of shaggy black hair topped a face that was streaked with the sort of ground in dirt that one only attained after living on the run for weeks at a time. He was dressed in clothes that had seen better days, but there was a certain dignity about him that made Herin think he had not always been an outlaw.

"Time enough to talk of honor once we know who you are," he replied in a voice that sounded like it was coming from inside a deep well, the kind of voice that could undoubtedly boom commands.

"You can see what we are," Shadow said, holding his gaze unflinchingly. "All we want is a hot meal and we'll be on our way.

If you have no food to spare, I'll thank you for our money back and we'll trouble you no more."

"How much?" Hawk demanded.

The man who had searched Shadow poured the contents of the pouch into his hand. "Two gold pieces and a handful of copper."

Hawk laughed. "Not very successful brigands are you?"

The other man had continued searching while they talked. He grinned at Ilsa as his hands roamed over her body, pausing at her breasts. "You're carrying some weight there," he said with a leer. "Maybe we need a more thorough search."

"You have a choice," Ilsa told him. "Take your filthy hands off me this second, or I'll gut you like a fish where you stand."

"Your woman, is she?" the outlaw said to Herin. "Well chosen, boy, I'll give you that. A woman with spirit, that's better than gold. This is a filly what will give a fine ride I've no doubt." He winked at her and removed his hand. "Nothing to speak of here, Hawk. A couple of knives is all."

"What brings you to the forest?" Hawk asked.

"I imagine the same thing that brings you," Shadow answered. "A desire to get away from the Imps and all of their laws."

"Is that so? What have you done that would interest Imperials?"

"Running afoul of the First Families will not increase a man's lifespan in Kress," Shadow answered slowly, unwilling to reveal too much information.

"Explain."

"The Tybolds are after me," Herin interrupted. "I almost killed Loki Tybold and they want my head. My friends here helped me escape so they're after them as well."

Looks were exchanged between several of the outlaws, and Hawk motioned for them to put down their bows. "Give them back their money."

Shadow took the pouch back and secured it under his tunic. "What makes you believe us?" he asked Hawk.

The man grinned, his teeth flashing. "Two days ago a party of horsemen rode through the woods near here. Twenty well-armed guards and seven others. They were wearing Tybold livery and they were in a hurry. When did you leave Kress?"

"About ten days ago," Shadow answered. "They were several days behind us, or so we thought."

"Well they're ahead of you now," Hawk said. "Whatever plans you had, you best change them to take into account that fact. Come on and have some of what's in the pot while we talk. I'm curious as to why someone would take on a family as powerful as the Tybolds. That should make for a good tale."

The meal turned out to be a stew laced with meat and a handful of plants from the forest. It was hot and savory and they gratefully ate several bowls as they talked. As Herin had guessed, Hawk was a former blacksmith, now on the run from the authorities as a result of beating a tax collector who had insisted on a bribe in addition to the normal taxes. Most of the rest had similar stories, evictions for back taxes or run-ins because of disputes over what they owed to the empire.

Herin gave a more or less accurate account of his confrontations with Loki, leaving out the part about being a magician in training. Shadow had not mentioned their occupations so he thought it best not to bring up the subject. Hawk and the others listened, shaking their heads in sympathy.

"Too much power in the hands of too few people," one of the men groused, spitting into the fire. "Mark my words, someday it will boil over and everything will be changed. Give some voice to everyone, not just those with money."

"How would you go about doing that?" Shadow asked, and Herin was surprised to see that he was truly interested, not just making conversation to aid their cover story. "You want to throw out the government? Wouldn't that cause chaos and open up the country to invasion?"

Hawk shook his head. "Don't get Wulfsan started," he said with a laugh. "He'll go on for hours. He should have been a philosopher, not an innkeeper. But he's got the right of it, there's too much power in the hands of too few."

Wulfsan ignored the interruption and began talking, hands furiously moving to emphasize each point. "I'm not saying get rid of government, or even taxes. We need an organization to run the big things; to put together an army, look to the roads, build bridges, regulate commerce. But there needs to be some way for the common folk to have a voice as well. Taxes are too high and they go to keeping the rich richer, not to improving the lot of the rest of us. Leaders aren't accountable. Ain't no one here ever even seen the Provincial Governor, much less any other high official."

"A radical idea," Shadow commented. "And how would leaders come to power then?"

"By being chosen," Wulfsan answered. "And not because their father was a leader before them and his father before that. The people would choose. And they'd have a say in the laws as well."

Herin listened in amazement, wondering where the man had come up with his crazy ideas. *Get rid of the aristocracy? Have the common people choose leaders? That would never work.* Herin doubted whether most people were capable of making responsible decisions about who should be in charge. Politics was not something most people ever thought about in any serious fashion.

"See what I mean?" Hawk said, chuckling. "And he's sober now. You should hear him once he's in his cups."

"Why are you in charge?" Shadow asked suddenly, catching Hawk off balance.

"What? What do you mean why am I in charge? I'm the leader." Hawk's expression darkened.

"That's what I'm asking. Why are you the leader?"

Hawk glared at Shadow. "Are you going to abuse my courtesy by coming in here and challenging me for leadership?" He stood and balled his hands into fists the size of small hams.

"Stranger, you are talking in a way that is bound to make your stay here short and unpleasant," Hawk threatened. "We've been on the run for more than two years now and done all right by ourselves. Nobody captured by the Imps, no deaths. We might not be living a rich life, but it's a free one."

Shadow slammed his fist into his palm. "And there's the point! Don't you see it? Has anyone challenged your leadership?"

Hawk snorted. "They'd have no chance. I'd beat them to a pulp."

"What if they all wanted someone else? What then? Do you lead because you've been successful or because you are bigger than everyone else?" Shadow pressed home his point. "You are in charge because they are satisfied with the way you are running things. You are a successful leader. As you said, no deaths, a free life, and for the first time no Imperial staring over your shoulders enforcing some law you don't understand and had nothing to do with approving. But it's their will that keeps you in your position. As long as you satisfy them, you stay the leader."

"You are a troubling man," Hawk said with a frown.

"You don't know the half of it," Ilsa muttered, to Herin's amusement. Shadow ignored the comment and continued his argument.

"Judge them by their acts. If the ruler continues to do things that are not in your best interests, get a new ruler. If he continues to tax you without you seeing some direct benefit from the money collected, change the system. If laws keep you enslaved, overturn them."

"You are saying we should start a revolt?" Hawk asked. The others began talking excitedly amongst themselves. "We're going to overthrow an empire with twenty men?"

"Every revolution starts somewhere, usually by one man with a vision."

Hawk shook his head and the conversation soon passed on to other topics. He invited them to travel with them for a few days, but they declined. Herin spent an hour or so in friendly competition with the bowmen, and was pleasantly surprised to find that he had lost none of his skill. It took him twenty minutes to knock the rust off, then he felt the familiar sensation of the weapon being an extension of his body, as he sent arrow after arrow close to the center of the target.

"Are you sure you don't want to throw in with us?" Hawk asked as he eyed his latest effort. "We could use a bowman of your caliber."

"Thanks all the same, but our paths go in different directions," Herin told him.

They went on their way near mid-day, their packs now bulging with smoked meat and some small loaves of freshly baked bread, a gift from the outlaws. All three now carried bows and quivers of arrows, bought with some of the coins Shadow had in his purse. Herin's skill had convinced him it was a worthwhile investment.

"Were you hexing those last shots?" Ilsa asked.

Herin shook his head. "No magic there," he assured her. "Just hours and hours of practice. I'll show you how to do it when we make camp for the night."

"Show both of us," Shadow added. "This is something that might come in handy if we ever have to fight."

"I still don't understand why we wouldn't just use magic." Ilsa shook her head, puzzled by Shadow's constant reaction to the idea of using magic to escape danger. "What is the point of knowing how to use magic if you never actually do use it?"

"You never know. There might be a time when magic is impossible," Shadow told her.

"What kind of situation?" Ilsa wanted to know.

"I don't know, that's why it's always good to be prepared for the unexpected."

Herin asked, "What was all of that back there about leadership and the people? Do you really believe that band of ragamuffins can overthrow the empire?"

Shadow shook his head. "No, but it is true that every revolution starts with an idea. If they do start even a minor sort of revolt against the way things are done, who knows what might happen? Why not plant the seed and see if it takes root?"

"I think you're seeing something in them that isn't there," Herin said thoughtfully. "Do you really buy into what you said back there? Leaders are only leaders because the people they are leading are willing to accept them as leaders?"

"Yes, I do. It is the way things work, even though most people don't think about it. Why do you ask?"

"Oh, just a thought," Herin grinned. "What do you think, Ilsa? Should we change leaders?"

"Absolutely," she said. "Yes, it's time to get rid of the tyranny we've been living under. Get some new blood in there I say."

"My thoughts exactly," Herin agreed, smiling at Shadow's scowl. "Now, the question is who should be in charge?"

"Very cute," Shadow said. "Anytime one of you two want the responsibility of taking over, just let me know."

"A shoe doesn't always fit comfortably when it's on the other foot, does it?" Ilsa said sweetly, as she and Herin laughed. Shadow turned away and walked quickly ahead. They quickened their pace to catch up.

Chapter Seven

Loki's face held a look of disgust as he gazed around the central marketplace of Khartul. He compared it to the Great Market in Kress, famous throughout the empire for the variety and quantity of its goods. The rustic nature of the square brought home to him just how much his life was going to change now that he had been exiled to this isolated backwater. The market consisted of rudely constructed booths hawking produce and homemade goods, most of which would have been rejected out of hand by the sophisticated consumers back in the capital. If this was an example of what life was going to be like here in this barren provincial city he knew he was in for a long, unpleasant exile. Loki had hoped the city would have at least some pretensions to culture, inasmuch as Khartul was the capital of the Northern Province and the home of the Tenth Legion, stationed there to protect the borders. He could see now that he had been overly optimistic.

"I'm going to see to my men," the captain of the escort told him, anxious to be rid of this fool he had been following for the past two weeks. The rest of the guards shared his attitude. It had taken all of his persuasive powers to keep them from outright mutiny over the past four or five days. "If you need us for anything, send a messenger to the servant's quarters on King Street." He was familiar with the layout in Khartul from his days in the legions. It would be good to look up a few of his ex-mates and talk over old times while enjoying a few mugs of ale.

"I am going to our offices to see what needs to be done here. Make sure the horses are unloaded and the supplies stored. I will contact you when I need your services. It may take me a few days to get the lay of the land before I take over everything here."

The man rode away shaking his head. *Take over? Take over what? It is winter for god's sake, and the snows will be here in earnest before too many more days are out. Nothing's going to happen here until spring thaws out the roads again. Unless Tybold plans on building snow forts, this idiot won't need me or my men until spring. Thank the gods for that. Another day or two with this spoiled rich brat and I would kill him.*

"Follow me," Loki arrogantly ordered the clerks who remained with him, kicking his horse into motion. The small party rode slowly toward the center of the city looking for the Tybold offices. Loki knew the address of his family's main office; what he didn't know was where he was in relation to that address. He hadn't been paying attention when his party left the marketplace, with the result being that he now found himself completely lost. Compared to the relatively orderly layout of the streets back in Kress, the streets here twisted and turned like pretzels, following the ups and downs of the terrain. Buildings crowded in on every side, so that there wasn't an inch of undeveloped space anywhere, resulting in a hodge-podge of styles, shapes, and sizes.

Behind him the clerks dutifully followed, although it was soon apparent that they were wandering aimlessly rather than going to a specific destination.

"God's balls, did this idiot lose us again?" one whispered to another. "How many times is that since we left Kress, five or six?"

"Quiet, you fool," his companion warned. "He may be an idiot, but he's an idiot that can break you if he hears your talk."

"I don't give a damn, this is crazy," the first man said. "Any fool can see we're nowhere near the business section now. We missed the turn about three streets back." He kicked his horse into a trot and caught up to Loki. After a short conversation, the party retraced their steps to the turn and went off in a different direction.

The Tybold offices were located less than fifty yards down the new street. The party gratefully dismounted, happy the trip was over. Loki walked inside, standing for a moment in the doorway while his eyes adjusted to the slightly gloomy interior of the stone building. He waited to be noticed, but all of the clerks were focused on their work. Loki's expression reflected his disappointment, but he would deal with that soon enough. *Things are going to change now that I am in charge.*

Flurries were beginning to dance in the crisp mountain air as they entered the main gate of Khartul. Herin saw that its walls were perhaps half as high as the ones at Kress, no more than twenty feet in height, but they were well-constructed of huge marble blocks and mortared in place with cement. Passing through the gate, he estimated the stones to be at least ten feet wide at the base, tapering gracefully to the catwalks for the guards on patrol along the walls. The construction gave the appearance of both great strength and great beauty, most unlike the more utilitarian aspect he was familiar with back in the capital.

"Looks crowded," he remarked to Shadow as they pushed their way through a market square just inside the gate. "Shouldn't it be getting less crowded this time of year?"

"You're thinking like a Lowlander," Shadow laughed. "It gets cold so early and stays that way so long up here that people don't regard the weather the same way folks do down in the flats. What down there would be called a heavy snowfall won't keep people inside here. But I am a little surprised to see so many people out midweek."

"A holiday you suppose?" Herin asked, though no celebrations were evident, nor were any sort of street decorations in sight.

"Probably some caravan just arrived," Shadow guessed. "I wouldn't think there would be too many more this season, so maybe everyone just wants one last chance at some goods before the roads shut down for the winter. Let's find someplace to stay."

"Where should we look?" Herin assumed that Shadow would have knowledge of the city layout. His friend had not come right out and said that he had spent time here before, but Herin was assuming this to be the case, content to follow wherever he led.

"Working class inns are clustered on the west side near the wall," Shadow told him. "We'll try that section first and get a feel for prices. Shouldn't be too many people looking to winter over here so we'll find a good deal someplace."

"Prices might be higher than you think," Ilsa suggested. She had lagged behind to check out some of the merchandise on display in the marketplace, and noted how the costs compared to the goods in Kress.

"What makes you think that?" Herin asked.

Ilsa tossed an apple to him, and Herin turned it over in his hand with a puzzled look on his face. There wasn't anything remarkable about the fruit. "I don't understand."

"You can get three of those for a copper in Kress," Ilsa told him. "Here they are two coppers apiece.

Shadow frowned. "That's going to make money tight. We'll have to work, and we'll have to make sure we know where Tybold is so he doesn't cause us any problems."

"Can we at least get out of the cold first?" Ilsa asked, blowing on her hands to warm them. "Let's find these inns you were telling us about and get a fire going."

It was a simple enough matter to locate a suitable place, though the price was higher than Shadow would have liked. They piled their belongings in their rooms and then met in the common room for mugs of hot cider, sitting before a welcome fire as they talked over their possibilities.

"There's plenty of inns," Ilsa said, relieved by the knowledge that she could work in one without worrying about the unwanted attentions of customers.

"Pick one of the middling establishments," Shadow suggested.

"Why not one of the better places uptown?" Ilsa asked. "I'd make more in tips that way."

"And increase the chances that it would be a place that Tybold uses," Shadow answered. "His type would never stoop so low as to use a working man's place. The money might not be quite as good, but the danger would be lessened."

"I assume you and I will do our street act?" Herin said, his voice lacking enthusiasm.

"Afraid you'll freeze your ass off every night?" Ilsa laughed.

"You can laugh all you want, but that's exactly what I'm thinking," Herin told her. "You'll at least get to stay inside somewhere nice and warm."

"I'm sure you'll survive."

"Maybe, but will we make any money? Who is going to come out with the temperature well below freezing?"

"I don't think you need to worry about that," Shadow assured him. "People here are used to the cold. They'll be out, just like in any other city. We can find a likely spot tomorrow, but you need to figure out where Tybold hangs out as well. Don't take too long. I don't want any surprises before Spring."

The new routine was much like the old one back in Kress. Part of the time Herin and Shadow performed their old street act outside one of the inns while Ilsa served tables inside. She found that Shadow had been correct. She took a moment to put a protective spell into place each night before beginning her shift, and no hands ever touched her, a welcome change from her former life. The set-up also allowed them plenty of free time to roam the streets, and Herin took advantage of the idle hours to memorize the twisting maze of alleyways and roads that sliced through Khartul. Unlike the grid pattern so common in Kress, the roadways looked as if they had been designed by a drunken surveyor, doubling back on themselves, leading to cul-de-sacs, or making loops that re-connected with streets they had already left. It was obvious that the designers had simply taken advantage of every open space they could in a city that was growing more and more crowded each year. Khartul had half the area of Kress, but with two thirds as many people. It made for conditions that were perfect if someone wanted to lose themselves, as he did.

It had taken Herin and Ilsa less than a day to locate the main offices of the Tybold family, and they spent one entire afternoon waiting in the shadows across the street from the impressive marble building. Finally, an hour before sunset, Loki had emerged, pausing on the top of the wide stairway until a carriage pulled up. The driver quickly dismounted to open a door on the side so Loki could hoist himself into the padded seat.

"Look at that idiot," Herin muttered to her. "A carriage can't get you through these streets any faster than walking, it's just a way to show that you have money."

"Don't complain," Ilsa said in reply. "It makes him easier to follow."

They soon discovered that Loki spent most of his time in his offices and frequented the same tavern every night.

They all worked steadily for the next month, watching their meager stack of coins grow, until Shadow announced that they could cease working at all. "We've got enough now to see us through the rest of the winter, with plenty left over to buy supplies for the trip to Nelfheim. We might as well stop while our luck's still good. The longer we do the act, the more chance that Loki discovers where you are."

"Come on, Shadow, I told you that's probably almost impossible," Herin said, though he was happy enough to stop working. The nights had turned bitter cold, and while Shadow's prediction that the weather would not affect the actions of Khartul's citizens had turned out to be accurate, he was not used to the frigid conditions. It often took several hours in front of a fire before he was thawed out from a night's performance.

"Almost impossible isn't the same thing as impossible," Shadow shot back. "I know as well as you do that it's unlikely he shows his face down here with the working people, but why risk it at all if we don't have to? If we start to run short, we can always pick it up again, can't we?"

Herin nodded. "I suppose you're right. So, what do you want to do tonight if we aren't working?"

Shadow looked at him with a small smile, and Herin realized his friend had some sort of plans of his own that didn't include him. "I'll fill you in later," Shadow said. "But there's something I need to look into, and it would go smoother if I do it alone. At least for now."

"It will be nice not to have to work," Ilsa said happily. "I'm owed my wages for this week. Herin, want to come with me to collect them?"

Herin shrugged. "Why not?" She was right, it was going to be nice to have free time for the rest of the winter.

Shadow stood motionless in the darkness, his hood pulled down far enough to keep his face invisible in the dim light. He didn't really anticipate trouble, but he hadn't survived for this long without planning for the possibility of something going wrong.

It had been a chance meeting several days earlier that led to his presence now near one of the old tunnels servicing the sewage systems of the city. Even in the winter season, Khartul had open markets which sold furs and clothing. Shadow had taken to visiting these marketplaces, and was sometimes rewarded with rumors of events elsewhere in the empire. Merchants were usually the first to hear any rumors, and Shadow had learned long since to cultivate relationships with as many of that caste as possible.

The day had begun innocently enough, as he had wandered from booth to booth, finally stopping to finger a fur on a table out on the very fringes of the square.

"You won't find better than that, friend," the shopkeeper had told him, "Not even in Kress itself."

"I've seen better," Shadow answered automatically, knowing very little about the quality of the piece he was holding, but familiar with the ancient procedure for bargaining.

"Hardly better, now, hardly better," the man replied. "Rub your hand this way and see how the fur holds its shape. No rain or wind will get through it, that I will guarantee. If it doesn't live up to expectations, bring it back here and I'll give you twice your money back, no questions asked."

"Is that so?" Shadow answered, appearing interested just to keep the man talking. He had always made it a policy to interact with merchants as much as possible. They often had a truer feel for what was happening in a city than any other group. "I've been sold furs a time or two before that didn't fare well once they had a bit of wear on them. They were only made for the rich to wear to balls and such. I need something to keep me dry on the road. My line of work takes me out in all sorts of weather. I can't afford to waste my money on something that won't do the job. I'd be better off buying a wool cloak. That at least will keep me warm."

The merchant looked pained. "Wool? Surely not, sir, not someone who obviously has the discriminating taste to see and appreciate good fur. This will hold up, I swear on my sainted mother's life. Yanico, sir, from the Missark Massif itself."

Shadow kept his face neutral, but his mind began racing. *Yanico? How is that possible?* The Yanico fur trade was rigidly controlled by the Furrier's Council in Kress. Yanico, the goats which lived in the highest peaks of the mountains, were virtually inaccessible to anyone but the hardy mountaineers who also lived there. The frigid conditions in which the animals thrived had evolved a creature with very high quality fur, thick and warm. When it was sewn into cloaks, the material was also water and wind-proof and very, very expensive. Shadow's understanding was that there was no trade done without a license granted by the Council, and such licenses were costly and hard to come by. It was unlikely that one would have been given to a small-time peddler like the man in front of him. Shadow ran his fingers once more through the fur, giving the appearance of looking over the quality, but in actuality looking for the stamp that would show it had been passed by the inspectors of the Council. There was none, which led to two possibilities. Either this wasn't really Yanico fur, or the man was a smuggler who had somehow by-passed the normal routes for obtaining the item.

A swift examination of the man led him to lean toward the latter explanation. Shadow thought he recognized the type well enough after years of living in The Pit. The man's eyes were just a bit too hard for a merchant's, his hands a bit too calloused for someone who supposedly spent their life behind a counter. It seemed likely there was more to the merchant than met the eye.

That line of thought led him to another. *If this man has Yanico furs to sell this late in the winter season, he must have obtained them recently. Otherwise they would have been gone long before now. There hasn't been a caravan through here in weeks, not since the snows started. That means this man has a source outside the city. And it also means he must have a method for getting in and out of Khartul that doesn't involve going through the main gate.* If the man had some other way to get out of Khartul, it was something to explore. Shadow always liked to have an escape route ready for emergencies.

"Yanico, is it? Where from? There aren't any caravans coming in this time of year."

The man had glanced quickly to the right and left, then motioned Shadow forward to speak quietly. "Not through the gates, mind you. I've got a private source."

"Is that so?" Shadow answered. "So you're a man who can get ahead and isn't afraid to skip around the Imperial rules? I've some experience with that myself. I admire a man who can cut through all that bullshit so he can make some money."

The man looked Shadow over keenly and smiled. "There's always room for a man with ambition," he said carefully. "Providing they don't mind cutting a few corners or ignoring a law here and a law there."

"Laws protect the rich," Shadow said. "For us, they're obstacles."

"Like that is it? Might you be interested in making a little money now?"

Shadow had replaced the fur and nodded. "I'm always interested in making money. What did you have in mind?"

"You look like someone who knows a thing or two," the man said, winking and laying a finger beside his nose as he grinned at Shadow. "Would you be able to leave the city for a few days? I'd make it worth your while."

Shadow had not needed to feign reluctance; the thought of traveling in the bitter winter weather was not a welcome one. "Leave in this weather? To go where? Will the guards even let me leave?"

"I told you I have my own way in and out. The Imps won't know anything about it," the man had assured him. "You won't be going far. Just a few miles up into the hills to meet some people. I'd go myself but the authorities have been paying far too much attention to me lately. You'd be doing me a great service by going in my place."

Fifteen minutes of haggling had resulted in Shadow agreeing to meet Hagarth, as the man was called, at his exit route. He now waited impatiently at the site, his thoughts running into new channels as he considered the possibilities being presented to him.

The trip offered more than just finding an escape route, it also raised the possibility of tapping into an already existing network of people outside the city. Shadow assumed he would be meeting representatives from the mountain people. They would know how to move through the mountains quickly, and also how to avoid the places patrolled by the Imperial troops. If he and Herin ever did have to leave Khartul hurriedly, avoiding Imp patrols was likely to be as important as getting outside the walls in the first place.

Hagarth emerged from the darkness, extending his hand with a smile. "Well met, Rollo," he said, using the name Shadow had given him. "Come, and I'll show you something of interest."

Two hours later found Shadow sitting in an inn thoughtfully sipping a mug of warm cider, hoping to get some circulation back into his body. Hagarth had led him through a series of underground chambers that eventually emptied outside the walls to the plateau upon which the city was built. The route had been bone-numbingly cold, the passage lined with stone walls that gave off frigid air like the breath from some invisible creature.

The opening led to a path that wound its way down the hillside to a river, mostly frozen over now. It was a rough, but certainly serviceable route. After a short negotiation Shadow had agreed to be Hagarth's agent with the Yanico hunters who lived in the peaks above Khartul. His first trip was to be in three days. It was nothing more than a meeting to confirm the upcoming yearly contract. But it would give him the chance to familiarize himself with both the escape route and the hunters. There were still two months or more of winter, time enough to go back several more times to cement the connection with them.

Now he was struggling to get some blood circulating. By the time they had re-entered the city, Shadow had been chilled right down to the bone. If he was going to travel up into the peaks, even for just a mile or two, he would have to get some warmer clothing. The traveling clothes that had served coming from Kress would be of no use high in the mountains. *Maybe I can get Hagarth to throw in some Yanico furs as a bonus. If the tunnel was any indicator, the mountains are going to be brutally cold.*

He was practically sitting in the fire itself, working on his third cider, still feeling as if someone had dropped him into a snowbank and left him there to freeze. But he had what he wanted, which was all that mattered. He drained his mug and tossed a few coppers on the table. He needed to tell Herin and Ilsa of the change in routine. As always, Shadow felt better when he was anticipating trouble and developing avenues for dealing with it if it came.

Loki leaned languidly against the marble mantle of the ornate fireplace gracing the main room of his residence, smiling smugly as he gazed at the swirling couples moving about the dance floor. If attendance was any measure of the success of a party, this one would certainly top any other put on this season. Every important person in the city was here, from the commanding general of the Legion to the Provincial Governor. Council Masters, rich merchants, high ranking government officials, even the Prefect of the Church were rubbing elbows as they enjoyed his hospitality. It was gratifying to find that even here the Tybold name carried some weight.

"Fantastic turnout, Loki old boy," said a voice at his elbow. It was the Lieutenant Governor of the Province, a man just a few years older than himself. Loki wasn't completely sure of the man's name. Grundfeld, Gerfald, Garfound….something like that.

"Thank you. I'm so glad you are enjoying yourself. Is the Governor having a good time?" The whole point of throwing the ball had been to make connections. It was very important to see that the men who pulled the strings here were satisfied.

"You have ample wine, so he will most definitely be happy," the man said, sipping his own drink. "This must have set you back quite a bit."

"Money well spent if everyone is enjoying themselves," Loki said, waving off the compliment.

"What brings you to Khartul, if you don't mind me asking?"

"My father wanted me to get some experience running one of our branches," Loki replied, sticking to the cover story Jarl Tybold had given him. "He wanted my expertise here to run the branch more efficiently and increase our profits."

"I see. That certainly makes more sense than the rumor I heard." The man sipped his wine slowly, enjoying the expression of curiosity on Tybold's face. "There is a story circulating that you had some sort of run-in with a fellow student back at the Magician's School in Kress and had to leave the city to avoid further embarrassment. I must admit that story seemed a bit far-fetched to me. I never gave it a moment's credence. I knew there was nothing to it. We must get together soon, and you can tell me all about what is going on back at the capital. We are so cut off out here in the provinces."

Loki watched him go, seething inside and struggling to keep his features under control. Suddenly the evening lost a good bit of its luster. *Does everyone here know the rumor? I have to assume so. They must all be laughing at me behind my back. But how did the story spread here? Certainly my father wasn't the source of the leak. Damn! I thought things were going so well.*

He took another glass of wine and drained it in one long swallow.

Across the room the Governor watched with a small smile on his face. "Did you deliver the message, Gordon?" he asked his second in command.

"Yes, your Excellency," the Lieutenant Governor replied. "Judging from the expression on his face, I'd say the rumors about Tybold are true. Some sort of scandal chased him out here."

"As I thought. That young bastard needed a strong dose of reality. Thinking he could come in here strutting like a peacock and everyone would fall at his feet as if he were a god. The nerve. I can see why his father sent him here. The boy has no tact, no sense of propriety at all."

"As you say, sir," Gordon replied. "But he does have something we value all the same, doesn't he?"

The Governor smiled and clicked his glass against Gordon's. "To the Tybold family fortune. May it find a worthy new home."

Herin relaxed in a comfortable chair by the fire, while Ilsa dozed on the bed. They had walked around a bit after collecting her wages, long enough to feel both tired and cold, so that the warmth of the room was a welcome luxury.

The sound of boots slowly climbing the wooden stairs broke his train of thought. Herin quickly crossed to the door and threw it open, watching with some concern as Shadow painfully pulled himself up, using the railing for support. He was moving so slowly that Herin immediately assumed he had been injured.

"Were you attacked?" he asked, coming to his side to support him.

"I'm fine," Shadow told him, refusing his help. "Just a little stiff."

"You were outside all this time? In this weather? You are either crazy or you were up to something, and knowing you, I'm choosing the second option."

"Let's get inside and I'll tell you both all about it." Shadow hobbled into the room and collapsed into the chair Herin had recently vacated. Ilsa examined him with a critical eye.

"You look like Death," she said finally. "What did you get into this time?"

"It's nice to know that you two have such a high opinion of my ability," Shadow groused, holding his hands over the fire to warm them.

"Well, we do know you," Herin said, pulling another chair closer. "Are you going to tell us where you've been and what you've been up to?"

As Shadow thawed, he told them what he had discovered. "I will be going out of the city for a few days, but once I get back I will take both of you to see the tunnels. If anything happens that's the spot to use as a rendezvous point."

"How long will you be gone?" Herin asked.

"Shouldn't be more than two days, maybe three at the most," Shadow told them. "I'm just going up to make contact with the mountaineers so that they know me better. They could be a resource for us if we ever have to leave Khartul in a hurry. We might even find sanctuary there in an emergency."

"Likely freeze to death trying to find them," Ilsa said, glancing out the window at the icy peaks visible over the looming walls of the city. "You are welcome to the mountains. I will stay here in the city where I am warm and safe."

"You never know how things might change in a heartbeat," Shadow cautioned. "Anyway, I am going to put a traveling pack together. I'm getting some sleep, then I'm off. We can talk again when I get back."

Herin knocked on Ilsa's door early the next morning. She answered, rubbing sleep from her eyes, her hair hanging loosely around her shoulders. She was dressed in a long shirt that silhouetted her slender figure against the light streaming through the window behind her.

"I was going uptown to see what was in the market," Herin said, fighting unsuccessfully to keep his eyes from roaming over her body. "Want to come with me?"

Ilsa snapped her fingers, causing Herin to look up, startled. "Are you talking to me or my tits?"

"Sorry. You just look different dressed like that." On the trail Ilsa had slept in her clothes each night, as had Herin and Shadow. "Do you want to come with me?"

"Why not? I've nothing else to do. I don't know though," she said teasingly. "Can I trust you not to push me into some alley and try to have your way with me?" She posed with a hip cocked seductively, running her tongue over her lips.

"God's balls, Ilsa, have you looked outside?" Herin laughed. "There is still a foot of snow on the ground and it must be a good twenty degrees below freezing. Anyone trying something like that in this weather is liable to have his prick snap off like an icicle."

She smiled. "Give me five minutes. I'll meet you downstairs."

After hot mugs of tea, they set off uptown. Even through the heavy layers of clothing they were wearing, the cold cut like a knife. At least there wasn't any wind, a rarity in Khartul given its close proximity to the mountains. Their breath hung around them like fog, lingering in the air long after they had moved on. They walked quickly, trying to get some circulation going.

Despite the weather, there were hundreds of people moving about the street. Herin had been surprised to discover that the citizens of Khartul treated the winter as nothing out of the ordinary, no matter how severe it seemed to him. Back in his village nothing much got done in the winter. Farmers generally used those months to see to their equipment, or to spend long hours in the inn talking and drinking. Here, life went on as usual, with businesses open, people running errands, children playing, and all the other normal activities that went on in warmer seasons. As a Lowlander it still seemed so cold he could feel it in his bones.

"Where are we going?" Ilsa asked through the scarf wrapped around her face, her voice muffled.

"Nowhere in particular," Herin answered. "I just wanted to get out and see what's going on. Now I'm sorry I thought of it. I don't know how these people can stand this year after year."

"Put your mind on something else," Ilsa advised. Herin avoided her eyes. In truth, his mind had been on "something else" ever since she had opened her door, leaving him still sorting out his feelings.

Don't be such an ass, he told himself. *I've felt something for her for some time now but was afraid to act on it for fear of breaking up the partnership.* As cold as it was, he felt a flash of heat when he thought of her standing in the doorway in nothing more than a shirt.

"Why are you so quiet?" Ilsa asked, interrupting his thoughts.

"No reason. Just thinking about things, I guess."

"You are strange this morning, Herin," she said with a laugh. "Even stranger than usual if that's possible."

He pulled her off to the side of the pavement, sheltered under an overhang festooned with long, sharp icicles. Her eyes held a puzzled expression, but she made no effort to pull away.

"What is going on?" she asked, wondering at his behavior.

"I don't know when it happened, or even why it happened now, but I can't stop thinking about being with you," he said, unwrapping his scarf so he could talk easier.

"You're with me every day," Ilsa pointed out.

"You know what I mean," Herin insisted. "I was with you every day in Kress as well and I never felt this way. I thought of you as a companion, but nothing more. Something happened over the past day or so to change all of that. I can't explain it, but I can't deny feeling it either."

She unwrapped her scarf and he saw that she was smiling. She gently laid a hand on his arm. "When was the last time you had a woman? Did you ever stop to think that might be it? I'm here and you are just feeling the need for a woman."

"That isn't it," Herin insisted. "If I just wanted that I know a half dozen places to go to fix the problem. I've been trying to figure out what changed this morning, but I don't know what it was."

"Why tell me?" Ilsa asked sharply. "What exactly did you think was going to happen?"

"Hell, I don't know. I just wanted to tell you how I was feeling. I don't even know what I expected, but I thought you should know how I felt in case you felt the same."

"Happily ever after, is that it?" Ilsa asked. "Another fairy tale that ends well? That isn't real life Herin, believe me. You haven't lived where I've lived; your background is nothing like mine. Do you know of anyone who had good relationships past a few months?"

"Yes I do," he replied, surprise in his voice. "In my village most marriages last for decades. I think the people are fairly happy. At least they appear so."

"In public maybe," Ilsa conceded. "But I'll bet that behind closed doors it's a different story."

"I think people can be good for each other if they are the right two people," Herin insisted. "Look, I don't want this to be an issue between us. I am perfectly capable of controlling myself if the feeling isn't mutual. I just thought I should tell you what I was feeling. If you don't feel the same way, we just go on as before. Who knows, maybe you're right. Maybe I am just a bit out of sorts and all I need is a night with a woman. But maybe it's more than that."

"I appreciate your honesty," she told him. "Let's just enjoy the day and let the future take care of itself."

"Meaning you don't feel the same way," he said, re-wrapping his face against the cold.

"Meaning I don't know," she answered. "You just dumped this on me out of the blue. I hadn't thought of you in any way other than as a part of the partnership. Give it time. That's not so much to ask, is it?"

Ilsa was right; he had thrown this at her unexpectedly. "Okay, let's go finish the walk. I don't think I can stand here any longer or I'll freeze to the pavement."

They set off towards the marketplace, Herin struggling to keep his emotions on an even keel while Ilsa was lost in thought. She linked her arm through his, and she could feel the tension go out of him as he relaxed against her. Ilsa was wiser in the ways of men and women than Herin, given her background. She knew that despite the way they had left it, things could never be the same now. She didn't know if they would be better or worse, but they would be changed.

The markets were crowded, as they always were on sunny days, with people strolling slowly through the stores and the booths. All of the booths were surrounded by large tent walls with small iron stoves inside to keep patrons warm. In fact, once inside it was necessary to take off scarves, gloves and hats or risk being bathed in sweat, a dangerous condition once back outside.

Herin pushed back his hood and stuffed his gloves in his pockets, helping Ilsa to unwrap herself as they moved away from the doorway. The dozen or so booths on this side of the plaza had linked their tent walls to form a passageway that allowed access to each booth without the necessity of going back into the cold. The heat from the combined stoves was enough to let them loosen their inner garments as well.

"Warm in here," Ilsa commented, fanning her neck as she loosened her blouse.

"It's probably only about ten degrees above freezing, but I think we're getting used to the weather. If we were still living in

Kress, we'd think this temperature was frigid. I guess you can get used to anything if you're exposed to it long enough."

"I'd rather get used to someplace that's sunny all year round," Ilsa shot back with a smile. "But this is bearable and it's certainly better than spending the day cooped up in those rooms back at the inn. Let's see what Khartul has to offer this time of the year."

They spent the better part of the next two hours strolling slowly from booth to booth, only bundling up when it was necessary to cross the open space between sections of the plaza. They were leaving the last booth and Herin was in the process of wrapping his scarf over his mouth, when he was bumped violently by someone entering the tent. "Hey, watch it," he said, turning to see who it was. He found himself face to face with Loki Tybold.

Herin reacted first, shoving Loki back against the side of the tent, causing it to pull three of the support poles down and collapsing a large section on top of him, temporarily pinning Tybold underneath. He pulled Ilsa through the opening into the plaza. There were a half dozen armed guards wearing Tybold livery just outside, moving towards the tent entrance to help their employer. Herin lowered his shoulder and bulled his way through them, knocking two off their feet and causing two others to get tangled in their legs.

"Stop them!" ordered the officer in charge. "On your feet!"

"Shit!" Herin cursed. "Come on, this way." They began running across the plaza, headed for the tangled web of streets that led deeper into the city. If he could get out of the marketplace they should be able to lose their pursuit in the maze of streets and alleys.

Loki had untangled himself and rolled from the canvas. "Get them! I want them alive! Go!"

Herin heard his order, sparing a moment to glance over his shoulder to see that the guards were now in full pursuit. "Hurry!" he panted. They sprinted down a blind alley, hoping it would lead them out into a broader street. The snow still on the ground hampered them, but it was an obstacle that would hold back their pursuit as well. The alleyway was little used and the snow was deeper than it had been in the plaza. It came up past their ankles and made footing treacherous. The snow also clearly showed where they had gone. Even if they could shake their pursuit, the guards would still be able to track them without any problem.

As they turned a corner, Herin almost crashed into a brick wall, skidding to a stop right against the freezing cold barrier. He stood for a moment looking dumbfounded at the obstacle, which stretched a full twelve or thirteen feet over their heads, far too high to jump. They had trapped themselves in a cul-de-sac, with no escape possible. Herin looked around frantically for a door or window they could use, but saw nothing but bare bricks on three sides. He could hear the stomp of the boots in the alleyway behind them. They were not going to be able to go back the way they came.

"Dammit," Herin cursed. "Who builds buildings without doors and windows?"

"These are warehouses," Ilsa panted beside him. "None needed. What do we do now?"

He looked at her. "Nothing to do but use magic. But that means someone will get hurt."

Ilsa shook her head. "Bad plan, Herin. Gets the authorities involved."

He looked at the opening to the alley. It would be a matter of only a moment before their attackers were on them. "I'm open to suggestions."

"Cloaking spell," she said, gulping air into her lungs. "Hurry, link up with me."

Cloaking spells were notoriously hard to maintain, but Herin could see no alternative. They only needed the spell to hold for a few minutes, long enough for the pursuers to leave. If they could make themselves invisible, maybe the guards would leave after a few minutes and they could get away.

He shook off his glove and motioned Ilsa to do the same. Skin to skin contact seemed to increase the energy available to them. Her hand was warm in his, and the current running through his body made him feel as if he might actually be glowing.

"The Seventh Veil," he said, squeezing her hand. "You remember the words?"

She nodded and they began to chant in unison as the guards rushed around the corner.

"Fela austrvegr likami hlif andskoti blindr syn skjotr".

They instantly vanished from sight as Loki and his escort skidded to a stop in surprise. He stared furiously at the empty space. "Where are they?" he demanded.

"They disappeared," a guard reported in an awed voice. "Here's their tracks, and there's no way out of this place." The rest of the guards looked uneasy. "You didn't tell us you was after a magician," he said accusingly.

Loki waved him off. "He isn't a master magician. He learned a couple of minor spells at the school in Kress. He still has to be here somewhere."

The guard had spent the better part of his life in and around Kress, and he knew powerful magic when he saw it. "We didn't sign up for this," he said, shoving his sword back into its scabbard and motioning his men to do the same. "I'll protect you, as is my duty to your House, and I'll fight any man you order me to, but not a magician. We can't fight magic."

"You'll do as you're told," Loki fumed.

"The hell I will," the man insisted. "You want to fight a magician, find another magician."

"Where am I supposed to do that out here?" Loki snarled.

The man looked at him in wonderment. How did this fool get lucky enough to be born to a powerful family? "Where else? Go to the Council of Magicians here in the city. Maybe they will help you."

The Council, Loki thought excitedly. *Of course!* "Put up your swords and follow me," he said as if it was his idea all along. They left the alley. Moments later, Herin and Ilsa popped back into view, dropping the cloaking spell.

"Now the Council will get involved?" Ilsa asked. "That can't be a good thing."

"No, it can't," Herin said softly, looking down the alley. "It can't be good at all."

Chapter Eight

Shadow peered over the edge of the boulder, his face hidden by a thick scarf. It protected him from the worst of the frigid mountain weather, while also hiding the tell-tale mist of his breath. He hadn't thought of that as being important before, but he had never had to move silently through the woods in the middle of winter.

Beside him crouched three of the Yanico hunters he had met when he left Khartul. They were dressed in white outer garments to blend in with the snow that coated the mountain and everything on it. All of them carried short bows and quivers of arrows, the shafts painted white and fletched with snowy goose feathers to complete the camouflage. From ten feet away they were virtually invisible. Added to that was the fact that they could move like ghosts through the mountains. Shadow had come to realize what an effective guerrilla force they would be if given the leadership of an experienced officer. But that could only happen if someone could find a way to get the scattered groups to drop their clannish loyalties long enough to band together against a common foe.

His hosts had awakened him before dawn with excitement in their eyes, anxious to show him what they had discovered. Shadow had already been stranded up in the high passes for the better part of a week. What he had hoped they were taking him to see was a clear passage back down to Khartul, but in that he had been disappointed.

Instead, he was now looking at a vast camp of thousands of soldiers, dressed in the characteristic black armor that identified them as Dakarians. The camp looked as if it were a temporary one, with the soldiers housed in tents rather than more permanent wooden barracks. He wondered how they had managed to move so many men through the passes with snow already on the ground.

He sank back down out of sight. "How long have you known about them?" he asked.

Mikita, the headsman of the village that was hosting him, held up two fingers. "Two day," he answered in the simple Common Tongue he used. "Scouts find and track. We think you see, tell Lowlanders."

"Tell them what? What are they doing up here in the middle of the winter?" Shadow asked. He thought it odd that the hunters wanted him to deliver a message at all. In his short time up here he had learned of the long-held antagonism that existed between the empire and these people. The mountaineers were willing to deal with individual smugglers because it brought them badly needed supplies and gold, but they had no love for the empire as a whole. "Why do you want to warn them?"

"Lowlanders problem. But problem we know. We deal with problem. Dragon people devils. Drive out ancestors. Their land once our land. We see, we kill. Now too many to fight so need Imp help."

Shadow nodded. So the Dakarians had once driven these people from the valleys and plains on the far side of the mountains? How long ago must that have been? From the perspective of the mountaineers it certainly made sense to seek help from the empire if the Dakarians were going to be here in force. The clans numbered no more than five or six thousand people, with only thirty or forty percent of that total being men of fighting age. They couldn't hope to resist any sort of large force.

"Why do you call them Dragon people?"

"Always call that. Legend say they use dragon magic. Evil people. You tell them below?"

"How do I get back?" Shadow asked, wondering what dragon magic referred to, but more interested at the moment in getting out of the mountains. "The passes are still blocked. What are the Dragon people doing in the mountains?"

Mikita shrugged. "They dig their way. Got many hands, use them. No hurry. Imps not expect attack in snows."

It made sense he supposed, if one was willing to chance losing a large number of men to frostbite, avalanche, or exposure.

With thousands of men they might eventually dig their way through the passes, but it would take weeks, if not months. On the other hand, as Mikita had suggested, the Imps would certainly not be looking for any sort of attack during the long winter months. Once the Dakarians had broken through the passes, they could use the element of surprise to hit Khartul. If they moved quickly enough, they might catch the garrison unprepared for a fight and be able to capture the city. It seemed a long shot however, given the size of the force he saw below. Shadow risked another peek over the shielding boulder. He saw no more than a few thousand men down below, certainly not enough for a siege of a city.

"There aren't enough men down there to capture Khartul," he said.

"More come. One more group like this to west. These dig, others follow. Scouts find. Black soldiers come like stars in sky. You warn. Lowlanders get ready for fight."

Shadow considered the information. So these weren't attacking groups, merely labor for clearing the way for a larger force to come through once the passes were cleared.

"How long before the passes are open enough for more soldiers?"

Mikita conferred briefly with one of the other hooded figures. "Two sevens of days, maybe less. Seven more days to get army through, then attack."

Three weeks then, if the information was correct, and Shadow was willing to bet it was accurate. *That's plenty of time for me to warn the authorities in Khartul about an attack, but there is still a problem. There isn't enough time to send word back to Kress for reinforcements and have them get here before the attack begins. They'll call in the outlying garrisons, but that's probably less than half a legion all told. Six thousand men at best. Shitty odds, no matter how you look at it.*

That raised the question of why Dakar was attacking the empire at all. Shadow considered the possibilities. *Was this a probe or was it a full-scale invasion?* Apparently, all of the diplomatic maneuvering had been nothing more than a diversion to hide Dakar's true motives. Shadow might not love the Empire, but he had to get down to Khartul to warn the authorities all the same. It simply would not do to have the Dakarians ransack the city, with all the bloody carnage that would entail, while he and the others were still living inside the walls. Perhaps they could use the tunnel to escape Khartul before the Dakarians were able to besiege it.

"How do I get past them?" he asked, pointing at the army below.

"Scout take. Not show way before. Dangerous. Now no time be safe, time warn Lowlanders. Clans gather. We kill Dragon People, but not enough. Lowlanders be ready. You go?"

Shadow nodded. "I'll go. The sooner the better. I've got friends in the city that need to know."

"You get out, you come here," Mikita said. "We have place for you, friends. You come here."

Shadow was surprised by the offer. After all, he had only known these people a short time, and taking in strangers was not something their culture seemed to do on a regular basis. "Thank you," he said. "We may have to do that. Why would you take us in?"

Mikita looked him in the eyes. "You not like others. You not Lowlander. You not try to cheat us. You ..." he struggled to find the right words. "You listen, respect Elders. We know you now. Trust you, trust your friends."

Shadow nodded. "Get me down below and we'll see what happens. I may be back or we might be forced another way."

"Fate has path for every man," Mikita answered. "We see, not see, all same thing. Walk your path, I walk mine."

"We'd better get moving," Shadow said, seeing that the activity in the camp below had increased. The force looked like it was getting ready to move, and when they were on the move they would be harder to avoid. The sooner he started, the more time he would have to make a plan to deal with this new variable. "How long to get to Khartul?"

"Two days if no more snow."

"Let's go then." The small party crawled away from the boulder and made their way back in the direction of Mikita's village.

Loki waited impatiently in the outer office of Master Renfeld, the Council Master for the magicians in Khartul. He had rushed to the building as soon as he had left the area where Herin Freeholder and his woman has escaped. That had been almost two days before. Every time he came for a meeting the Council Master had always been "busy". Loki fumed at the delays. He was coming to realize that his name didn't mean as much out here in the west as he had thought. In Kress, he would have been given an immediate appointment, he was certain of it.

I don't know anything about Council Master Renfeld, but he will be like any other official, always looking for more power. And more power comes from having more gold. I have the gold, now it's just a question of making sure the Council sees how finding Freeholder would be in their interest. I'll have to be careful. If Herin was once more taken into the Council, Loki would at least know where he was, and the bastard might relax his guard enough to make assassination a viable alternative. Herin was now aware of Loki's presence and would be taking precautions, which would make retribution more difficult.

Although he had been careful to hide it from his men, Loki had been deeply shaken by Herin's display of magic. *Where in the name of all the gods had he learned such power? I know damned well the Council isn't teaching their students spells like that one. I've never heard of anyone being able to do it, so how did Herin? That had to be the same woman with him who had been in the rooms back in Kress. I just don't understand how he got so powerful.*

"Master Renfeld will see you now," a secretary announced, leading Loki into the inner offices. He emerged fifteen minutes later with a smug smile on his face, certain that he was a step closer to his revenge. Renfeld had snapped at the bait like a hungry fish, thanking Loki for the information. Perfect. Not only would Herin be picked up now, but Loki himself would look like a saint for assisting the Council in its work. He silently congratulated himself on a slick piece of manipulation. In his mind, it was even worthy of his father. Puffed up with self-satisfaction, he bounced down the marble steps of the Council Hall and headed to the Tybold offices, certain it was going to be a good day.

Across the city, Herin sat on the edge of the bed, shaking the snow from his boots as he stretched his feet towards the fire. As the warmth penetrated his soaked stockings, he sighed with pleasure.

"How can you be so calm?" Ilsa asked, peering out the window for the fourth time since they had returned to the room. "The Council could be outside our door any minute."

"Why would you think that?" Herin asked in surprise. "We've scouted the streets the last two days and haven't seen any indication that Tybold has any idea where we are. Relax before you send yourself into a panic. We don't have anything to worry about just yet. We might not have anything to worry about at all."

"What do you mean?"

Herin rubbed his toes to help get the circulation flowing again. "The Council hasn't found us yet in all the months we've been here. I'm sure they were told to look for me. Just because Loki tells them he's seen us here doesn't mean they'll be any more successful in finding us now. How can they find us unless we let our guard down or something unlooked for happens like it did the other day?"

Ilsa let the curtain fall back into place and sat beside him on the bed. "That's just it. What if something happens like that? What then?"

Herin shrugged. "I don't know. We'll just have to cross that bridge when we come to it. Why look for problems when there aren't any?"

She gave him a hard look, clearly exasperated that he wasn't taking the situation more seriously. "You were at school for a few months. You don't seem to think much of the magicians teaching there."

"I did when I first got there," Herin told her, pushing his boots closer to the fire to dry out. "But that was before I met Shadow and found out that there are other paths to magic besides the ones they teach. There really aren't that many good magicians in the Council, and the good ones will all be back in Kress. Being sent out here would be a pretty clear indicator that you weren't a top-flight magician. Trust me, both you and I are more powerful than anyone I met while I was at school, with the possible exception of Thorsson Valgaard himself. Together, we might even be a match for him, so stop fretting so much."

"I still think they could be trouble," Ilsa insisted.

"I'm not ignoring that possibility. But there really isn't much to be done before Shadow gets back."

"When will that be, do you think? He's been gone a lot longer than he thought."

Herin finished taking off his wet outer garments, draping his coat over a chair and pushing it towards the fire. Steam curled lazily from it as the heat began to melt away the icy coating that covered every inch of it. "Probably got caught in the blizzard," he said. "The passes must be impossible to get through now. I wouldn't be surprised if it takes him three or four more days to get back down here."

"Three or four more days is a long time to just sit here with the Council breathing down our necks," Ilsa muttered.

To her annoyance, Herin laughed at her. "God's teeth, Ilsa, you are in a mood this morning. The Council is hardly breathing down our necks. Why worry about something that hasn't happened yet?"

She shook her head without answering and began to move about the room, straightening the furniture, pulling the quilt on the bed so that it was tight again, finally neatly folding her shawl before placing it on the dresser. Herin watched her with one eyebrow cocked in puzzlement. *What has gotten into her?* Seeing that no conversation was forthcoming, he shook his head and walked to the door, his feet leaving wet spots on the floor.

"I'm going to see about getting a hot bath," he told her. "Come over to the room later if you feel like talking."

Ilsa watched him go without comment, before sinking into a chair by the window, staring sightlessly down at the street below. Herin was right, there wasn't any immediate danger. The Council wouldn't suddenly materialize in the hallway outside. If they were careful there was little danger from that quarter.

It isn't the detection itself that is worrying me, it is what might happen afterwards. What if Herin and I are separated, what if the Council takes him back and we're apart? What then? I would be left with...what? It was the uncertainty that haunted her.

"Damn!" she cursed softly under her breath as she thought the whole thing through. She realized that she really didn't know Herin well enough to hazard a guess as to what he might do if given an offer to rejoin the Council. She didn't think he would just abandon her. *But there is always a chance. Herin went to Kress to become a member of the Council. What if they want him back? Will he turn down his life's dream? Shit! I wish I could really trust him.* Ilsa hated having to depend on someone else for her well-being.

What if he took the offer, where would I be then? Shadow could always go back to his own country, or just go back to operating on his own as he had always done. That would leave her with the possibility of being the odd one out, left to fend for herself.

How can I be sure of him? she wondered. It did not take long to come up with an answer, especially considering Herin's confession to her earlier in the week. She tried to push it away as sneaky and unworthy, but it was a thought that refused to be denied, hammering at the doorways of her mind like an unwanted guest. There was a sure method to cement him to her with an unbreakable bond, if she was willing to act upon it. Once, not all that long ago, she would not even have hesitated.

She knew that she had the skills to make it work for her. Herin might not be a virgin, but he still had an idealistic way of looking at things. Ilsa held a colder, more critical view of the world, and it was that side of her that was going to control her actions.

"Shit," she muttered sadly, getting to her feet and crossing to the cracked mirror over the dresser. She pulled a hairbrush from the drawer and began to slowly untangle the snarls in her hair, studiously avoiding meeting her own eyes in the mirror. She believed that her actions were necessary to safeguard her own future, but it didn't mean she had to feel good about them.

Finishing, she shook her hair from side to side so that it fell past her shoulders. The brushing had removed most of the tangles and it glowed in the firelight. Ilsa stared at her reflection. "You are a cold-hearted bitch," she told it, getting to her feet and moving to the door.

Ilsa moved down the hallway to a stone-lined room at the end of the corridor that was used as a laundry area, or for the rare guest who required a bath. Steam seeped from under the door, and the soft sound of Herin humming was audible through the wood. Taking a deep breath, she quietly opened the door and slipped inside.

Herin was soaking in the huge iron cauldron that doubled as a laundry tub, his arms hanging loosely over the side and his head resting on the rim. His eyes were closed as he softly hummed a drinking song, his face a mask of contentment, while the heat of the water slowly baked the chill from his muscles. The temperature in the room was a good twenty degrees warmer than the hallway. Ilsa could feel the sweat begin to trickle down her neck after just a few moments.

It was odd, but this was the first time in all the months they had spent together that she had seen Herin naked. His back and shoulders bulged with muscles from his years working on his family's farm. She steeled herself for what she was about to do, pushing down the small voice of conscience that was telling her it was wrong, a calculated and ruthless use of his feelings for her. This was survival, a bet against a possible future where she might need

Herin bound to her by more than friendship. What could it hurt? He wasn't a virgin, he had experienced this before. But she knew this would be more than just a dalliance to him, it would mean something.

Herin heard the door open, but assumed it was one of the serving girls fetching more hot water. Without opening his eyes, he murmured, "No more water, thanks. It's hot enough."

"It certainly is," Ilsa said, kneeling behind him to massage his shoulders.

Herin jerked his eyes open and turned to look at her. "What are you doing here?"

She smiled and reached one hand over his shoulder to trail her fingers down his chest, leaving a path of tingling energy in its wake. "Relax, Herin, I won't bite," she whispered seductively. "Not too hard anyway." She crawled to the side of the tub, her hand slowly moving down his stomach.

Herin stared into her eyes and started to lean forward, but Ilsa used her other hand to push him gently back against the side. Her eyes held his as her hand dipped under the water to grasp him, stroking him into a state of arousal. "Ilsa..." he whispered.

"Shhh," she said, putting her finger to his lips. "There's no need for talk now. Later, but not now."

"Now," he said firmly, moving her hand out of the water. "You said you didn't feel anything for me, and now you're here. Why?"

"I guess the run-in with Loki made me realize that our time together might be short and we shouldn't waste any of it," she lied, hoping Herin could not see the truth in her eyes.

"And that's all this is?" he asked.

Ilsa chose not to answer. Herin watched as her hands went to the ties on her blouse, teasing him by pulling the garment partly down from her shoulders to reveal the swelling of her breasts. Herin stared hungrily at her, his eyes afire.

Ilsa lifted the garment up and over her head, shaking her hair loose and tossing the blouse aside. She kept her hands at her sides and allowed Herin to gaze at her. Slowly, he reached out and began to arouse her body, touching her stomach with light, feathery strokes. She was a bit surprised to find that he was gentle and unhurried in his approach. Knowing that he had experienced women before, she had expected a more direct approach, with no foreplay. It was what she was used to in her own encounters, quick and violent couplings that were over almost before they began.

"God's breath," he whispered, "You are beautiful."

Ilsa could feel her emotional control slip a bit as Herin continued to stimulate her. She untied her skirt, letting it fall to the floor. Herin sat up straighter in the tub to allow her room to step in with him, his eyes worshipping her in a way she had never seen before from any of the men she had been with. She moved gingerly into the water, gasping at the sudden heat as she slowly sank down to straddle Herin, her legs wrapped around his hips. It was difficult to move in the confined space, but neither of them noticed at the moment.

"How can you stand it this hot?" she panted, as the sweat began pouring down her body.

"It feels good," Herin murmured absently, his hands moving her hips into a more comfortable position. He shifted slightly, lifting her so the length of him slid inside her like a sword returning to its sheath. She gasped softly, settling against him as he began a steady motion, slopping water over the sides of the tub and onto the floor.

Ilsa wrapped her arms around his neck and kissed him, softly at first then more passionately as her body responded to his. This was not what she had experienced in the past, nor had she expected anything like it when she had entered the room. There was an energy that transfused her, a connection that went beyond the physical. She surrendered to it, allowing herself to be carried wherever it would take her. Herin held her tighter, his arms supporting her weight, his hands on her waist lifting and moving her to a rhythm he controlled. She felt as if she were somehow outside her own body, experiencing and watching at the same time as they came together.

Neither could have said how long it lasted. Ilsa broke off kissing him to groan loudly, her body taking on a frantic movement as she felt herself being lifted up away from the physical plane into some other place. Herin matched her. The walls echoed with their cries of pleasure, muffled only when Herin laughingly put his hand over her mouth, breaking the feeling and causing her to begin giggling, still carried away by the waves of pleasure coursing through her body. She sagged against his shoulder, playfully biting his skin before resting her head against him.

"My God," she said with a forced laugh. "What the hell did you do to me?"

Herin made small movements that sent ripples through her, a reminder of what she had just experienced. His hands stroked her back as he rested his cheek against her shoulder. "What did you do to me?" he asked in return. "I've been with women before, but it's never been like that for me."

"Really?" Ilsa pulled away so she could look into his eyes.

He nodded. "Not like that. A kind of….I don't know, a feeling like something else was in charge of my body. I don't know how to describe it. It was as if I had no control over anything."

She sank back down, her face troubled a bit as she tried to work out what had just occurred between the two of them. *Why should this be any more powerful than any other coupling I've ever had? Why was it any different with Herin? Is it the magic? Did that have something to do with it? Did our work doing spells together somehow bind us in a way that goes beyond normal human relationships?*

There had been many, far too many former partners for her to dwell on, and given the purpose of her visit here, this act should have had all the passion of a business negotiation in the marketplace. She had counted on Herin being so aroused he wouldn't know she was faking passion, but she had found herself being swept away on a flood of emotion unlike anything she had ever felt before.

Neither was anxious to move but the tub was cramped and uncomfortable now that the passion was beginning to dissipate. Ilsa gave Herin a quick kiss and pulled herself free, trying to disentangle their limbs enough so she could get out. It was far harder to break apart than it had been to join together. They were soon laughing as they bounced various parts of their bodies against the iron sides of the vessel.

"No...move your leg...now to the right," Herin said between laughs. Suddenly Ilsa felt herself lifted up in his powerful hands and practically thrown from the cauldron. "Damn!" Herin cursed, his face suddenly twisted in pain.

"What's wrong?" Ilsa asked, putting her hand on his arm.

Herin stood gingerly, water dripping from him and a sheepish look on his face. "Sorry," he apologized. "I got a cramp in my leg."

"You must not be as limber as you were when you were younger," Ilsa teased. "Getting old are you?" She glanced down at his crotch and shook her head in mock wonder. "Not too old I see. You couldn't possibly have the energy for a repeat performance already."

Herin snorted in amusement. "It does have a one-track mind, but I really think that session will hold me for a while. At least until dinner." He grinned at her and stepped from the tub, reaching for a towel to dry himself. "Turn around," he ordered, using the cloth to dry her back, pulling her to him so that she could feel the heat of his body against her own. "Only one towel," he whispered, his hands giving lie to the idea that he had exhausted himself.

"I'll make do," she said, taking it from him to dry her front, then wrapping it around her like a robe. She looked up when she was finished to find him standing in front of her watching every move she made with a look that made her uncomfortable. Lust she had anticipated. But she saw something much deeper than that. It awakened guilty feelings that she had been successfully ignoring up to this point. That there were some answering feelings boiling inside her helped a bit, but there was no avoiding the inner knowledge that she had seduced him for her own purposes, a selfish motive no matter how she felt now. Ilsa looked away and began walking slowly past him.

"I'll bring you another towel," she promised as she opened the door.

"Don't bother," Herin told her, reaching to the pile of clean clothes he had brought with him to the room. "I'll fetch one myself. Meet me downstairs and we can get something to eat."

Ilsa nodded, turning so he would not see the confused look on her face. Walking swiftly to her room, she shut the door behind her and leaned against it for support while she tried to sort out her emotions. *There really isn't anything for me to feel guilty about, is there? Herin seems like he has accepted this for what it is, just two people attracted to each other who have just had an enjoyable encounter. Yes, it was strangely powerful, but Herin didn't make any mention of anything romantic once we were finished. No flowery talk of love, no promises of eternal devotion, none of the things I half-expected to hear from his lips. So why do I feel uneasy? Maybe I am overanalyzing the situation.*

There was one thing she knew for sure. She would have to be careful when she talked to Herin so there wouldn't be any negative repercussions from this. Delicacy would be required, and Ilsa knew she wasn't all that experienced in that particular area. In her experience, a long-term relationship was one that lasted more than one weekend. This was something altogether different, and she felt a bit lost as she considered how to approach him.

Herin was already sitting in the taproom, two mugs on the table. He smiled at her and pushed one across as she sat. "I ordered some food already."

She drank while she considered her options. *What can I say to him that won't drive him away from me, but also won't make him think this is some kind of permanent relationship? I just need to know he won't abandon me for the Council.*

Herin suddenly put his mug on the table to stare at her, eyes squinted in concentration. She was caught by surprise. "What is it?" she asked as he leaned closer. His expression had changed to curiosity. He looked at her as if she were some sort of interesting specimen he was examining in a laboratory.

"You're different," he said in a tone of wonderment, sinking back into his seat. "You smell different."

Ilsa didn't misinterpret him; she knew he wasn't making a comment about her perfume. "Different how? Stronger or weaker than before?"

He shook his head. "Stronger. Much stronger. Can't say exactly what it is that's different, but the smell has definitely changed from what it was earlier. It's…I don't know how to express it. I haven't detected anything like this before."

"What does magic smell like?" Ilsa had never thought to ask before.

"It depends on what the spell is," Herin answered. "Any sort of growth or fertility spell sort of reminds me of how woods smell in the spring, kind of flowery. Containment spells smell like hot metal. Protection and beautification spells tend to all smell like baking bread for some reason. And the intent colors it as well. When I first met you back in Kress, the smell was so faint that I wasn't altogether certain I really smelled it at all."

Ilsa's face showed her astonishment. "But you seemed so sure," she said.

Herin grinned. "As soon as I saw you do the flaming spell I knew I was right. Shadow knew it too, but he sometimes can be mule-headed about things. Anyway, as time went on your own particular scent got stronger and more recognizable. That's another thing I found out about my gift. I can identify individual magicians by their scent."

"What was mine like?"

Herin looked thoughtful. "It has an earthy sort of feel to it, something like grass after a summer rain. No matter what spells you do, that signature smell is part of it. I really think I could follow you through the city like a bloodhound. But now it's different."

"In what way?" The serving girl brought a steaming platter of meat and some vegetables. They stopped talking until she was safely out of earshot.

"It's still your scent," Herin said, chewing his meat slowly as he spoke. "But there's something added to it now that wasn't there before. More powerful, that's for sure, but a new scent all the same. And the original scent is still there."

"What about you?" Ilsa asked. "Is yours any different?"

Herin shook his head. "I can't tell. I can smell spells as I do them so I know if I'm on the right track, but I've never been able to sense any odors about me at other times, so I don't know. I guess I'd have to find some other magical freak to do it for me."

"More powerful you said. Do you think it has something to do with our...um, our..."

Herin laughed. "I swear Ilsa, you'd think you were a blushing virgin. Lovemaking? Sex? Coupling? Fucking? Screwing? I've heard the words before. And to answer your question, I think that most certainly had something to do with it. I've had time to think this over while I was waiting for you. Do you realize that we are breaking new ground here, you and I?"

"What do you mean?"

"You never spent much time with Shadow talking about magical theory, did you?"

Ilsa cocked an eyebrow. "In case you hadn't noticed, Shadow and I are never on the best of terms. I always thought he was more interested in the novelty of having a woman who could perform magic than anything else. You were his protégé."

Herin didn't bother to contradict her. "Before you met us, and even more so afterwards, he and I had some long talks about magic and magicians working together. Even Shadow and I were something of a rarity. When we used to do that street act I could supplement what he was doing with some complementary spells of my own, but it wasn't like what I feel with you. He told me that even something that basic almost never happened."

Ilsa was a bit confused. "What do you mean? What never happens?"

"Two magicians being able to do magic of any kind together," Herin told her. "From what Shadow told me, most of the time the energies of two magicians tends to cancel each other out if they try to do a spell together. Sometimes it even results in turning the spell into something destructive. Nobody knows why. His theory is that each magician has their own particular kind of energy that is theirs and theirs alone, so those energies usually don't mesh without years and years of slowly working together to learn how to do it. A place like the Council of Magicians can pull it off because the instructors are there for decades at a time, but two individual practitioners who just met probably couldn't."

"Why can we do it if it's so rare?" Ilsa remembered the power of the cloaking spell they had done together.

Herin shrugged. "Who knows? Shadow cautioned me many, many times about having a physical relationship with you. The more powerful you became, the more worried he was about it until he saw that there was nothing going on between us."

"Why?" Ilsa asked.

Herin popped a piece of meat into his mouth and slowly chewed it as he considered his answer. "Shadow said he had never heard of a woman magician, so he didn't know what might happen if we were to join physically. How it would affect our magic, he meant. This is all new. I think he was worried we might explode or something and maybe take out half the city." He laughed.

"We don't really know how it does affect the magic part though, do we?" Ilsa asked. "We haven't tried it yet."

"I know. I was going to suggest we try a few simple spells to see what happens."

"Do you think something bad is going to happen?" she asked, concern in her voice. She certainly didn't want to lose her magic.

"It doesn't feel like that," he said reassuringly. "Who knows, it might be easier now."

Ilsa looked down at her hands and bit her lip. "Let's talk about that," she said, avoiding his eyes. "Where do you see this going?" She needed to know what Herin had made of their lovemaking. Ilsa suddenly realized that the seduction was a double-edged sword; if the relationship didn't work out, a rejected Herin might be even less willing to concern himself with her future.

"I forgot to tell you. I've already sent a messenger for the local priest. I thought we could take some time this afternoon and make it official."

Ilsa looked up with shock, only to see Herin laughing at her. "You bastard!" she spat.

"I wish you could see the expression on your face," he told her, untouched by her anger. "What did you think I was going to do, faint away at the thought that you might be madly in love with me? You're either overestimating yourself or underestimating me, I'm not sure which. I made it clear to you the other day that my feelings had changed. You said yours didn't go beyond friendship. I accepted that, even though I was disappointed. But it takes two people to make a relationship, not one dragging the other into it. It hasn't escaped my notice that you are hardly the shy, helpless type that would let a man do that anyway."

"What are you saying?" Ilsa asked, truly puzzled.

"I'm not saying anything," Herin replied. "But we almost get killed and the next thing I know you're jumping into the bath with me. Why? Was it because you suddenly realized just how empty this world would be without me in it? A view I heartily subscribe to, by the way."

He took a long drink of ale before continuing, leaning back in his chair to gather his thoughts. When he began speaking, he spaced his words carefully. "Maybe the fact that Loki mentioned going to the Council had something to do with it? That changed the stakes, didn't it? It's more dangerous now. So maybe you just wanted some insurance that I'll stick around, and sex seemed like a good way to do that. I won't pretend I'm not interested since you already knew I was. But I have no illusions about us, if that's what you are worried about. I'm willing to enjoy this, whatever it is, for as long as I can. How long that might be, only time will tell, won't it?"

"So where do we go from here?" she repeated.

"Wherever our paths take us," Herin answered levelly. "I'm not going to lie to you. I enjoyed today and I'd like to enjoy it again. There was a powerful energy moving through that room. I really do want to see what effects it might have on any magic we do together. But I won't force myself on you. I have enough pride not to do that and enough respect for your power and your personality to know it wouldn't be very effective anyway. Finish up while I settle the bill, then we'll go see what we can still do."

Ilsa watched him go, glad to have a few moments to herself to try to sort out the situation. She was floundering; it was as if she had pushed against something expecting resistance and found none. She would have to re-think her views about Herin, that much was certain. He had surprised her in a way she hadn't thought possible.

"All set," he told her, returning to the table. "Let's go see what happens."

Council Master Renfeld paced back and forth in front of the three most senior magicians in Khartul. All of them had been with the Council for decades, but it had been some time since they had done any field work. Most of their time was spent experimenting or writing long treatises on various aspects of magic. Working in a lab as opposed to practicing out in the real world were two very different things. None of the trio was very enthusiastic about the project their Council leader had laid before them.

"What makes you think we can find him?" one asked.

Renfeld whirled on him angrily. "We are the most skilled magicians in the city. If a Council magician can't do a simple task like locate someone in a city this size, then perhaps they aren't Council material after all. Gentlemen, Master Valgaard himself is taking a direct interest in this. All Council Halls were told to be looking for Freeholder, and Tybold confirmed that he is in the city. Finding him could be a great coup for us."

"He is skilled himself if that young Tybold's report can be believed," said another. "An invisibility spell? That is very advanced magic. Any student who can do something like that at his age is someone we have to worry about. What else might he know?"

"What difference does it make?" Renfeld responded, increasing his pace. "He can't possibly fight four skilled magicians. What I want is for each of us to take a quarter of the city and scan it for any magical activity over the next week or so. If we sense anything, we can narrow the search within that area. Besides, we aren't trying to overpower him, we just need to know where he is."

The three looked openly skeptical. "I don't know if that's going to work," the first protested. "Dividing the city up into quadrants means we each have a very large area to cover. Any scan we try on an area that size will likely leave large parts uncovered."

"What do you suggest then?"

"All of us together should cover each quadrant instead of assigning one to each of us. It might take longer, but it will be more accurate. Once we find out where he is, we can decide what to do next."

The others nodded their heads in agreement. "Very well," Renfeld conceded. "We'll do it your way. Remember we want him unharmed. The object is to get him back into the Council, nothing else. Do you all understand? Good, then let's get started."

Chapter Nine

Shivering violently and slapping snow from his cloak, Shadow entered the main room of the inn just as the early morning diners were leaving it for work. He saw Herin and Ilsa coming down the stairs, heads bent together as they shared a laugh. Shadow's eyes were knowing as he stamped snow from his boots, and a small smile tugged at the corners of his mouth. While Ilsa crossed to the bar to order breakfast, Herin caught sight of Shadow.

"You certainly popped up out of nowhere," Herin said, helping Shadow beat snow from his cloak. "We wondered when you'd get back."

"The passes are closed for the most part," Shadow answered, hanging his wet garment over a peg. "I need to get something hot inside me."

"Well, your timing is perfect," Herin said. "We're just getting ready to eat ourselves. Come on over by the fire and tell us what's happening up there. I've got some news for you as well. It's not good, but not a disaster."

"What I have falls more under the disaster category," Shadow said grimly, making his way towards the fire.

"What's wrong?" Herin asked as they sat at an empty table. Ilsa joined them, setting down two steaming cups of hot tea.

Shadow warmed his hands over the fire before motioning them closer. He said quietly, "Khartul is going to be invaded, almost certainly within the month. There are thousands of Dakarian soldiers up there clearing out the passes so the invasion force can sweep down on the city. My guides thought perhaps as many as five to ten thousand soldiers could be committed to an attack. I don't know how reliable their figures might be but it's going to be a substantial force, and they are going to be here before winter ends."

"Why?" Herin asked. "I thought when we left Kress there was a treaty in place."

"So did I," Shadow agreed. "Maybe they negotiated as a smokescreen to hide the fact that they were planning an invasion. Maybe something went wrong with the treaty. I don't know. But I do know that there is going to be an army on its way here in a matter of a few weeks."

"Can the city hold them off?" Ilsa asked. "They wouldn't be able to stay out there for very long in the middle of winter would they?"

Shadow looked thoughtful. "You're right, they can't. There's no way to supply a good-sized army in this weather. It's going to be difficult enough to move men through the passes, even when they get cleared. Moving enough supplies to keep them in a siege for any length of time would be almost impossible. But my friends up there were certain that a large force would be coming."

"Maybe this is just a test of the defenses of Khartul," Herin guessed. "If they can somehow break through quickly, they take the city. If not, they know how strong it is so they can plan another attack for later in the spring."

Shadow shook his head. "That loses the element of surprise, which is the main advantage in an attack like this one. If they failed now, the city would be that much more prepared in the spring, making the chances of success then almost zero. No, they must have something that makes them confident they can take the city now."

"What? Some kind of weapon with the power to knock down the walls or something?"

"Or something," Shadow murmured, lost in thought. A serving girl placed bowls of thick porridge on the table, and he took the opportunity to order a pot of tea for them all.

"What I don't understand is what they are after. A force of that size won't be large enough for a siege, even in good weather,"

Shadow said at last. "It is barely large enough to control the city as an occupation force even if they capture it, and I don't see how they hope to capture it with that few soldiers."

"What could bring the walls down fast enough that the Dakarians won't be caught in the cold?" Ilsa asked as she ate.

Herin stopped eating as the answer suddenly hit him. "Magic?" he asked and Shadow nodded.

Shadow said, "They must have magicians with them. The tribesmen said they called the Dakarians "The Dragon People" because they practiced dragon magic."

"What's dragon magic?" Herin asked.

"I have no idea," Shadow replied. "I don't suppose they've actually figured out a way to create dragons, so it must be a term for the type of magic they use."

"What are we going to do?" Ilsa asked. "Obviously you think this is going to affect us, or you wouldn't have brought it up. Are we going to leave the city before it's surrounded?"

"That's one option," Shadow said. "But if we do that we're going to have to worry about spending time out in the worst of the winter, and we'd be miles from any safe spot. If the Dakarians do mean to contain the city, they will also send patrols out into the surrounding countryside for supplies. We'd have to get a good forty or fifty miles away before we would be safe. I don't know of any large towns that would give us adequate shelter out there. All things considered, we might be better off in here."

"Doing what?" Herin demanded. "If you are suggesting we use our own magic to help save this city, I have to tell you what happened since you left." Quickly, he filled Shadow in on the events of the past week. "You'd have the Council down on us in a minute, with Tybold not far behind. We'd be exposed."

"What if we stayed out of sight and threw our help into the fight?" Ilsa asked. Seeing Herin's expression, she laid a hand on his arm. "I'm just putting it out there for us to think about."

"That might be possible," Shadow conceded. "But Herin's point is valid as well. If we use magic we leave a signature for other magicians to follow, like a dog following a scent."

"If that's so, then why haven't we been picked up already?" Ilsa questioned. "We've been doing spells off and on for months now."

"No one was looking for us for one thing," Shadow said. "We've been doing small enough spells; they wouldn't leave much of a trace. The larger ones we've mostly done outside the walls of the city. But the size of the spells we'd have to use in this situation would make it obvious that powerful magicians were somewhere close by. It would leave a big clue as to our whereabouts."

They ate in silence for a few minutes, each lost in their own thoughts. Herin realized that he had been enjoying the last few days. With Shadow gone there had been nothing much to worry about other than making sure Loki wasn't following them each time they went out. He and Ilsa had made love several times, with each session becoming more and more intense. Whatever was going on between them seemed to have opened up some sort of valve for their magic, and Herin was coming to believe there was no spell too powerful for them to work, providing they were linked.

The flip side, however, was that both of them were unsure how to deal with the physical joining, which increased in power each time they were together. It was a bit unnerving. It was so powerful they were almost afraid to indulge themselves again. By mutual agreement, it had been several days since their last session, and Herin, for his part, was trying to figure out how he felt about the whole thing. He hadn't quite figured out a way to bring the topic up in conversation with Ilsa.

"What if we stop them before they get here?" Ilsa said.

Shadow looked interested. "What did you have in mind?"

"I don't know exactly. But you said the Dakarians are digging their way here, right? If they do have magicians, then why not just use magic to clear the passes? The Dakarians must not have the ability to control the weather."

"Or maybe they just don't want to give away their position by using a powerful spell that might trigger some sort of alarm with the Council here in the city," Shadow countered.

"That's possible. But we could delay them if we closed the passes again, right?" she asked. "What if we could shut them down so the Dakarians would have to push back the attack?"

"Why not just send word to the army that an attack is coming?" Herin asked.

"I plan on doing that," Shadow told him. "But there's no guarantee they'll believe it. I can't take word in person or they will want to know how I got the information. That would lead to the discovery of the tunnel leading out of the city. We need that route now more than ever, just in case things go wrong. The same holds true for contacting the Council. We can send word, but how to make them believe it?"

"Ilsa's plan might delay an attack long enough for spring to get here so the Imps could reinforce the city," Herin mused. "No surprise attack then. It might give the Council time to prepare defenses. The question is, do we stay or go?"

Shadow let out a breath slowly. "I just don't know what the right decision would be. I'd hate being caught out in the open in this weather, but I also hate the thought of being trapped inside a city that might be occupied. A better question might be, can we close down the passes?"

"Herin and I can do it," Ilsa said confidently.

Shadow studied her closely. She was sincere. "You've never tried anything even remotely of that magnitude before," he pointed out. "I do respect what you two can do, but I don't know if you can take on a job of this size. It would require spells of immense scope and control. You'd be dealing with elemental forces of nature. Those energies are very dangerous."

Ilsa was unmoved. "We can do it if we work together. I know we can."

"It isn't like we have a lot of options, do we?" Herin added. "Not if we want to stay in the city and have the passes closed off to invaders. You're probably right about the army and the Council. The only way to really convince them would be to go in person and reveal that we are magicians, and I don't think any of us are willing to do that. So it leaves us with option two. Shadow, we've been working closely together since you've been gone. I think we can pull it off."

Shadow laughed softly as a small smile flashed through his beard. "Yes, I was aware of your 'close work' the second I saw you. I warned you about possible consequences. How has it affected your magic?"

Herin glanced at Ilsa before answering. "It's made it stronger, I think. That's why I think we could do this if we need to."

"The sooner the better, too," Ilsa put in. "Because if it doesn't work, we want time to come up with something else before it's too late."

Shadow nodded. "All right, I'll send word as best I can to the army and the Council. Hopefully, it will cause them to at least begin making some preparations in case the attack comes. I'll also need to send a message to my smuggler friend so we don't have him interfering at the wrong time. I'll meet you at the tunnel mouth in...let's say an hour. No sense in delaying, is there? We'll go well outside the walls and find out if you two are right."

Two hours later found them huddling against the walls outside of the city, trying to stay out of the wind as much as possible. The air was bitingly cold, so frigid that Herin felt as if he were being physically attacked. He clutched his arms to his sides while he burrowed deeper into his thick outer coat. Here the full force of the winter gales hit them unchecked, the wind strong enough to force them to shout in order to be heard.

The clouds above the peaks were pregnant with snow, their undersides black and threatening. Glancing upward and squinting his eyes against the wind, Herin wondered if all of this was even necessary. From the look of things, the weather might very well take care of closing the passes without any help from them. He leaned closer to Shadow and said as much, pointing upward to emphasize his point.

"Just as likely to dump the snow down here rather than up on the peaks," Shadow shouted against the wind. "All that would do is hamper any reinforcements trying to get to the city."

"Did you send the message?"

Shadow nodded impatiently, clearly not in a mood to try talking more than was necessary. "Let's try to get up into the mountains a bit!" They trudged for the better part of an hour, but were only able to advance a few hundred yards. Seeing the futility of exhausting themselves any longer, Shadow pulled Herin close enough to yell at him over the wind. "Try it!"

Herin nodded and moved closer to Ilsa. She was shivering uncontrollably, her teeth chattering and her hands and arms wrapped tightly to her sides. Herin moved so that he could talk directly into her ear without shouting, his lips almost touching her. "Are you ready?"

She nodded, shedding a glove so she could take his hand. Herin did the same. They had agreed beforehand which set of spells to try, starting on a hill just opposite where the tunnel exited the city. If they could start a small-scale avalanche there, they could then try it on something much larger.

Herin could hear his own voice in his head, but had to turn to see Ilsa's lips moving to make sure they were in synch. There was no chance of hearing her in this wind.

"Snaer missa mynd bregoa liki vatn
verda sker veggr vardi landnam sigr stjarna illr"

It was a complicated spell, one of Herin's own devising. It combined three distinct spells into one. The first was for making a solid object into a liquid, a simple enough spell by itself. The second turned that liquid back into a solid again, molding it into a rock-hard barrier. The last part put a charm on the wall that would resist any magic used against it. Shadow had been skeptical that it would work, urging instead a less complicated spell to merely shake the snow loose and let gravity do the rest. Herin had argued that if there were magicians with the Dakarians, they would simply use their magic to remove the obstacle. While he and Ilsa had crouched in the tunnel waiting for Shadow, he had spent his time trying various combinations until he got one that had the right smell and feel to it.

Whether it would actually work in real life was another thing. Herin knew it would take every bit of power he had just to try to get the various energies in harmony. He was counting on the boost that Ilsa provided when they worked together to harness the power to send the spell outward. If everything went as he hoped, the snow on the hillside would move down the slope as if it were water, then immediately turn into a solid wall of snow at the bottom. It should look like a natural avalanche, but anyone attempting to move the mass out of the way would find that it was impossible to penetrate. That was the plan at any rate.

As Herin completed the phrase that would finish the incantation, he felt a rush of energy shoot through him and out through his fingertips. It was as if every hair was standing on end, crackling with electricity. He forgot about the wind and cold in the euphoria that always accompanied any magic he and Ilsa did in tandem. A glance to his side showed him that Ilsa was feeling the same thing, and he turned to watch the hillside to see what effect it had on the snow banked up on the slope.

For a few seconds, it looked as if nothing was happening. He had focused his attention on the middle of the snowpack, trying to concentrate the force of the spell in that spot. The snow began to oscillate up and down as if some giant was trapped underneath trying to dig his way out. Small cascades of snow broke free in several places, mini-avalanches that rolled down the hillside before dying out. He squeezed Ilsa's hand as a signal, and when she looked over at him, he shouted "Again!" They repeated the spell.

A bigger section broke loose this time, a sheet fully as large as the marketplace in the city behind them. It started to slowly slide down the hillside, then picked up speed while appearing to change in shape and composition, until it looked more like a white river of water rather than snow. Gathering momentum, it took down several large pine trees as if they were nothing more than matchsticks, breaking them off and burying them in the flood. At the foot of the hill the snow changed appearance again, instantly transforming itself into a wall ten feet high and twice as long. It looked as solid as the stone masonry of the wall surrounding Khartul.

They waited five more minutes but nothing else happened. Herin looked at the wall and shook his head. The spell had partially worked, but only a small portion of the snow had actually moved. There was still plenty of room to go around the barrier, even in the narrow confines of the path below. In one of the wider passes of the mountains it wouldn't even slow the Dakarians down at all.

Shadow jerked his head back towards the tunnel and they willingly followed him inside. Even though it was well below freezing in the opening, once they were out of the wind it seemed almost balmy in comparisons to the outside.

"No good," Shadow said, uncovering his face and pushing his scarf aside. "I was afraid you took on more than you could handle."

"It wasn't the spell itself," Herin argued. "That worked. It's just the scale of the thing. I think you'd need a dozen or more magicians to pull this off. It might not even work trying a normal avalanche. There will still be openings to get through."

"Do we really need to bring down the whole mountain?" Ilsa asked, slapping her arms against her side to try to restore some circulation. She blew on the hand that had been exposed. "What if we could just dump enough snow on what they already cleared to make them have to do it all over again? That would cost them a few more weeks and might give the city time to get ready."

She saw Shadow's look. "I'm not an idiot," she snapped. "Don't be so surprised a woman thought of something useful."

He laughed. "I wasn't thinking anything like that at all. I was thinking it was a good idea and might be possible. The mountaineers said they were working on two passes. If we split up we could cover both."

"I don't think one person is going to be able to do much on their own," Herin replied. "It took everything Ilsa and I had just to get that result. Even if we ignore everything other than just moving the snow it's going to be a big job. It might even end up taking all three of us throwing power at it just to get any snow moving at all. We might have to try to hit them in turn, if that's possible."

Shadow considered it, his eyes wandering over the snow wall below them. "Ilsa? How do you feel power-wise right now?"

"A little drained," she admitted. "Not exhausted, but I can feel the strain. I could probably do a bit more magic if I had to, but it would take all I've got. I think Herin might be right."

"That's not going to work," Shadow said, shaking his head. "It's going to take days just to get to the closest pass. I was thinking we'd be cutting it close as it was. If we all three have to do it, we'd never get both passes closed in time."

"So let's do what we can," Herin said. "Even if we only close one of them, it might help when the attack comes. Who knows? Maybe we'll get lucky and hit the pass that is going to have the magicians and bury them under tons of snow."

"I don't think that will do much good," Shadow answered with a shake of his head. "But I really don't see much in the way of alternatives. Let's get back now and start getting some supplies together. We'll head for the nearest pass, the one I used when I returned here. At least I know the way there. If we have time for another we can worry about that after we take care of the first one."

"Any way you look at this, it is going to be a problem if the army and Council don't believe your messages," Herin reminded him.

"That's out of our hands for the time being. Let's deal with the first pass, and then we'll see what the city is doing when we return. It's two days out and two days back, so the sooner we get started the more time we'll have if we need an alternate plan."

They began climbing over the rubble that had collected in the tunnel over the years and slowly made their way back into the city. Shadow paused at the entranceway, scanning the street in both directions before motioning them out. They quickly brushed the dust and debris from their clothing and walked quickly away from the opening.

"Renfeld, I have something," one of the magicians said, opening his eyes and turning in his chair.

"What is it?" the Council Master asked.

"Some sort of spell was just used on the north side, near the walls. I don't know what it was, but it was powerful. It's gone now, but it was definitely there. It has to be Freeholder."

"Send some men over to that area and see if they can find anything more concrete," Renfeld ordered. "The rest of you, shift your attention to that spot. We'll go house to house and room to room if that's what it takes to track him down."

He went into his office through the connecting door and was surprised to find his secretary already waiting.

"What is it?" he asked gruffly. "It had better be important."

"This came a few hours ago but you were already in session with the others," the man said, handing over a paper.

Renfeld snatched the parchment and quickly scanned the message. "Dakarians in the mountains waiting to attack? Impossible! Nobody could survive up there in this weather. Who brought this?" he demanded.

"I don't know," the secretary admitted. "Just a man. He handed it over and said he had something he thought the Council Master might be interested in."

Renfeld frowned and read the note again. *It couldn't be true. Why would they attack? And why attack Khartul?*

"This must be some sort of joke," he said.

"You would know best, sir," the secretary said. "Should we inform the army, just in case?"

Renfeld considered the consequences if this turned out to be a legitimate warning and he did nothing. What if he told the commander of the Tenth that the disturbance they detected was part of a possible Dakarian attack? The man certainly couldn't afford to ignore that threat, and Renfeld would get the soldiers he needed to assist in rooting Freeholder out of hiding. This message might grease the process considerably. He still put no credence in it, but whoever had brought it may have done him a favor.

"Bring me parchment and ink," he ordered. "And get a runner ready to take this to Legion Headquarters."

The man rushed out and Renfeld began to consider how best to word his communication.

The officers looked grimly at the figures being passed around that showed the state of readiness for the army in Khartul. Commander Bjorkenberg, the general in charge of the Tenth Legion, waited until everyone had been given the opportunity to thoroughly absorb the information.

"We have five thousand, eight hundred men ready for duty," he said, opening the meeting. "There are one hundred thirty rated sick or disabled, with another seventy who are home on leave. The ones in that last group all live within ten miles of the city or in the city itself, so they will be fairly easy to retrieve if this warning is accurate."

"Do you think it is, sir? Accurate?" asked one of the junior officers.

Bjorkenberg clasped his hands behind his back and began to pace back and forth on the small stage he used when having full meetings. "I don't know," he said at last. "It seems pretty far-fetched. On the other hand, we haven't been sending any scouts out because I thought there was no reason to expose men unnecessarily to winter weather."

"But sir, surely this is some sort of joke," protested another. "Dakarians in such numbers coming at this time of year? That's impossible."

The general shook his head. "Impossible or not, it isn't a threat we can ignore. If we mobilize the men and nothing happens, at least we will have worked on that exercise. If we don't prepare and there really is an attack, the consequences would be fatal. We have no choice but to treat this as a very real threat." He paused and pointed to the next item highlighted on the agenda. "Which brings me to my second point. We don't have enough men to man the walls in anything like adequate numbers."

"If we call in the outlying garrisons we would add another six or seven hundred men to our force," one of the more senior officers pointed out.

"Actually, only five hundred and seventy-five," Bjorkenberg said, referring to a piece of parchment. "I've already sent riders calling all of them in, which is going to leave the countryside unprotected. That means that we can also expect a large number of villagers to come in with them. Even in this weather, those who are close enough will move inside the walls, which will give us another few hundred mouths to feed. Fortunately, food doesn't seem to be a problem at the moment. The commissary estimates we have enough to feed the city for three to four months. No siege will go on for that long, not at this time of year. I think we can forget about those concerns for the moment and focus on the manpower issue."

He paused for thought. "How many men do we need? With reinforcements, we'll have almost seven thousand. If we activate the city auxiliaries, it will give us another two to three thousand. Will that be sufficient? That is the question before us."

"Barely sufficient right now," a senior officer answered. "What happens when we start getting casualties? Once we lose four or five hundred, even if they are only wounded, it will put parts of our defensive positions in jeopardy. We need to be thinking about how to plug those gaps now before it happens."

"Why not use townspeople?" offered the junior officer who had spoken first, earning him looks of contempt from the more senior members of the council.

"Use for what? Target practice for the Dakarians?" one growled. "The auxiliaries are bad enough, but at least they have some training. You can't put raw recruits on the walls and expect any kind of performance from them. The whole idea is ridiculous. It takes a good three to four months of intensive training to produce a good legionnaire."

"They'll be fighting for their homes and their own lives," the younger man protested. "Surely that will count for something. There must be two hundred thousand men of fighting age here in the city."

"Two hundred thousand useless bodies you mean," the older man snorted. "You're welcome to them."

Bjorkenberg slammed his fist down on the table, effectively ending the argument. "Must I remind you that I hold control of these meetings? General Laird, you have made your opinions known for quite some time as to the advisability of using non-military personnel in the army. There is no need to bring them up at every opportunity."

Laird grumbled under his breath but said nothing. Bjorkenberg stared at him for a moment, deciding to forgo a full-blown confrontation for another time, once the emergency had passed. In a situation like this, enthusiasm and vision might be just as important as experience. What Laird was overlooking was that anyone they drafted into service would be fighting defensively only, manning the walls without being expected to conduct themselves like soldiers on campaign. There was a huge difference in fighting behind stout walls and fighting on an open battlefield.

"Lieutenant Leslie, you have brought up a good point. I am going to put you in charge of recruiting and training a force of ten thousand men to be used on the walls of Khartul. You have three weeks to get them enough training so that they can be of use to us. Choose ten officers you trust and let them act as commanders of a thousand men each while you hold overall command. As of today, you will be bumped in rank to Adjutant Commander."

"Thank you, sir," Leslie gushed. The older officers exchanged looks which did not go unnoticed by their commander.

"We must change our approach to meet this threat," Bjorkenberg told them. "The army has become too rigid, and the situation here does not call for open battle. There is another issue. I met with Renfeld, the head of the Council of Magicians. He claims there is some sort of magical component to all of this. He has requested a hundred men to help him search a section of the city where the magic was supposed to have occurred."

"Magic?" one asked in wonder. "If it's magical, then what can soldiers do about it? Why can't the Council handle their own affairs?"

"Renfeld was a bit vague about what the threat was," Bjorkenberg replied. "But I gave him the men anyway. It will keep them busy. That isn't the point. Renfeld also claimed the Dakarians will be bringing magicians with them to aid in their attack. If there is any sort of magic coming our way, we might need the Council's help. If magicians come to you with a reasonable request, honor it. Make sure to tell the men our magicians are working with us on this. Knowing we have the Council backing us up may make them a bit more relaxed. If the stories of a Dakarian attack are accurate, then it is likely enough that they used something other than simple human muscle to clear those passes up there. Questions?"

There were none. Nodding, Bjorkenberg continued. "All sections to go to Alert Level Two. Beginning tomorrow morning we will be using a rotation to have the walls fully manned at all times. In the meantime, start spreading the word to the civilian population in your sector about the real threat of attack so they can prepare themselves. Each house should have food stored in case they get cut off from the marketplace. I'm depending on you to have your own sectors in order before anything happens."

"Any chance of reinforcements other than the garrisons?"

Bjorkenberg shook his head. "I had Renfeld contact his Council Master in Kress. I've sent messenger pigeons as a backup, but even if word is already there it would be close to two months before a force could get within twenty miles of Khartul. By then we'll either be successfully defending ourselves or be invested to the point where they couldn't break through and help us anyway. We are on our own and must move forward with that thought in mind. Gentlemen, see to your men."

Shadow moved to the window, and glanced at the sky with concern, noting the threatening clouds that hovered over the city like a cat readying to pounce on a helpless mouse. The storm could make their journey the next day much more dangerous, and if it began snowing before they left they might not be able to leave at all. There was also the danger of the snow coming once they were already in the mountains, stranding them far from shelter. Either way, the risks increased with every hour they spent in Khartul.

They had planned on leaving the city just before first light, when the streets would be most deserted. This would at least reduce the chances of anyone seeing them walking through the streets with loaded packs, an activity guaranteed to attract attention. An additional benefit was that it would give them the maximum amount of daylight hours to start working their way upwards into the mountains. The closer they were to the pass, the more effective the magic would be. Or so they hoped.

To guard against the possibility of being caught in a storm, they had loaded their packs with enough supplies to see them through at least a fortnight. That would give them time to find a village if need be, where they could procure food and shelter.

There had been some evidence over the previous two days that Shadow's messages had been given serious consideration. Preparations were undertaken making the city ready to repel an attack, and the citizens appeared to accept the possibility with a surprising calm. One unforeseen problem had been the army rounding up "volunteers" to man the defenses. Not willing to depend solely on the patriotism of the men of Khartul, the army had resorted to the tried and true method of filling ranks quickly by sending press gangs roaming through the streets to gather up enough bodies to fill their quotas. Shadow and Herin had to exercise care whenever they walked the streets so they could avoid the press gangs.

Suddenly nervous, Shadow left the window, grabbing his cloak from the chair and settling it around his shoulders as he walked quickly into the hallway. He just needed to get out of the inn for a bit. It wasn't normal for him to feel this way and it unsettled him. Before a mission, Shadow experienced the same tension as any man, but once involved he had always been able to function with a calmness that had kept him safe and under control. Now he could feel that control fraying a bit at the edges and hungered for activity the way a drunkard craved drink.

He knocked on Ilsa's door. It was opened by Herin who asked, "Why are you dressed already? I thought we weren't leaving for hours yet."

"We aren't," Shadow confirmed. "I'm going to walk around for a bit and clear my head. I also want to check and make certain nothing has gone wrong with the plan in any way. I'll check the tunnel to make sure it's still open. I might not be back until very late, maybe not until first light, so don't be concerned if you don't see me before we leave tomorrow. Is everything ready?"

Herin nodded. "We're set. You look worried. Is something wrong?"

Shadow forced a smile. "No, just couldn't stand the thought of staying cooped up in the room. Get some sleep, you'll need it."

"What about you?" Herin shot back. "Sounds like you aren't planning on hitting the bed at all tonight."

"I don't need much sleep," Shadow assured him. "I'll see you in the morning."

Ilsa laughed after Herin closed the door. "I never figured Shadow for the nervous type."

Herin was staring thoughtfully at the door. "Neither did I," he said slowly. "And that concerns me."

"Everything will be fine," Ilsa assured him.

"I hope so. But I've seen Shadow in every kind of mood. He's never acted like this. Something must be wrong."

"All right, now you're making me nervous," Ilsa replied. "Look, Herin, we've done all we can to prepare for this. Fretting about it is only going to make you jittery tomorrow. You'll wind up tossing and turning all night and be exhausted in the morning. Spells work better when we're at full strength. We know this is going to take everything we have, so for god's sake relax tonight and let tomorrow take care of itself."

"You're right." Herin shook himself like a dog coming in out of the wet. "I guess I'm a little nervous myself. Up until now, I've only used magic in an emergency, when I didn't have time to think about what I was doing."

"You wanted to be a magician," Ilsa reminded him. "What did you think you would be doing with your life if not using magic in real life situations?"

Herin laughed a bit self-consciously as he sat back on the bed. "When you put it like that, there really isn't an answer, is there? Do you want to go downstairs and have a few drinks before we call it a night?"

"No, I'm going to go to bed," Ilsa said. Herin nodded absently, and left the room, his expressions still distracted. Ilsa realized that she was no longer able to read Herin's emotions. She had thought that once they were lovers that part of their relationship would become easier, but if anything it had grown even more difficult. *God's teeth, I wish I had more experience with this kind of thing. I just don't know how to deal with something that might turn into a more permanent relationship.*

Twenty minutes later she was still lying wide awake in bed, unable to sleep. For the first time, she really started to think about what was going to happen in just a few hours. To this point it had been nothing more than plans, and in a sense they hadn't seemed real. But now things were really ready to start happening. They were going to leave the city and climb up into the mountains in the middle of winter. Forget the Dakarians; they could easily get in trouble just from a combination of weather and terrain.

"It's Shadow and all of his doom and gloom, dammit," she said, hoping to blame her mood on his uneasiness, but she knew it to be a lie. The truth was that this had nothing to do with what they were going to do, and everything to do with her and Herin. The uncertainty of not knowing where the relationship between them was headed made her uneasy, an emotion she would rather dispense with given what they were going to try in the morning.

There was a soft knock at the door and she called out." Who is it?"

The door pushed open and she could see Herin silhouetted in the light from the guttering torches in the hallway. "Herin? Is something wrong?"

He snapped his fingers and one of the candles lit, allowing enough light for her to see his face. "I can't sleep."

She sat up in bed and met his eyes. "Neither can I."

She watched as he slowly walked towards her, their eyes never leaving each other. Time seemed to stand still. The part of her brain that was questioning why this was happening was silenced as she allowed herself to stop thinking and just feel.

"Ilsa…"

She pushed back the cover as he walked to the side of the bed, staring at her in the soft glow of the candlelight. "Are you getting in or not?" she asked, trying to keep her voice from shaking. Maybe talk wasn't what was needed, maybe it was time just to act and worry about the consequences later.

Instead of taking her up on the invitation, Herin sat on the bed, reaching out to gently stroke her hair. "I've been thinking about what's been happening between us," he began, his eyes looking away from her as he talked. "It was so different from anything I ever felt before. It was different from what I thought I'd feel if I was ever with you. It sounds odd to say it like this but it was…magical."

Ilsa propped herself on one elbow, searching his face for any sign of jest or sarcasm. She saw none. "You don't mean magical as is in it was special, do you?" she asked quietly. "You're talking literally."

Herin nodded. "Yes. Something really weird is happening between us, don't you think? Don't you feel it as well? A kind of energy that is different from just plain lust or even what I thought love might feel like. Hell, if this is what love is like there would be more people talking about it."

Ilsa had to laugh, breaking the mood a bit. "That is true. I feel it each time too. It's sort of like doing a spell, but not exactly."

"That's why I haven't pressured you the last few days," Herin continued, now looking at her. "I don't want you to think I am using you as some kind of magical experiment to see what kind of power we can summon up."

"Why would that bother you?" Ilsa asked softly.

"It wouldn't be fair to you for one thing," Herin explained. "It would make you like one of the lab animals we used to practice spells on back at the school, not a partner. I wasn't comfortable with that so I've forced myself to keep my distance."

"And now...?"

"I don't know," he confessed. "I meant to go to sleep so I could try to rest up for whatever we might be facing up there. But something kept niggling at me, telling me that you and I might need whatever it was that has grown between us, that it keeps getting more powerful the more we're together. I still don't know what it is, but I do know what it does."

"Is this just you asking if I'd be willing to have sex with you again in case we need the power?" Ilsa asked. Herin was right; they might very well need to be able to summon up that energy again, but if that was what he was asking, she wasn't interested. Something inside her had changed and the idea of sex for nothing more than a casual joining no longer held any appeal for her, not even with Herin.

"No, it's me asking you if you want me," he said with a rueful smile. "I think that Shadow's mood made me nervous, and I guess I could use a little human contact tonight. We don't have to do anything but sleep, but I am wondering if I could share your bed. And I want you to think about whether or not you are willing to explore the rest of it."

"What happened to loving me?" Ilsa teased.

Herin looked at her seriously. "I've never been in love, Ilsa. I finally realized I don't know the first thing about being in love. I don't know what I should be feeling or not feeling. I do care about you, that hasn't changed. Is that love? I don't know."

Ilsa sat up in the bed, pushing her hair from her eyes. She took a breath before she began talking, glancing down at the covers because she didn't want to see the expression in his eyes. "There is something maybe you should know first. I came to you in the bath because I was afraid you might be tempted to go back to the Council if they ever found you, and there's no place for me there. It was just a way to try to bind you to me so I wouldn't be alone in case that was something you'd want to do. I know it was selfish, but that meeting with Tybold and his men threw me a little."

"We already talked about that, didn't we?" Herin said softly, putting his hand under her chin to force her to look at him. "I told you then, and I'll tell you again now if you need to hear it, I didn't blame you. What is important is what we are feeling when we are together." He leaned forward to brush his lips against hers, a gentle caress that sent shivers down her spine.

Herin slipped off his shirt and trousers before sliding in beside her, his body so warm it was like lying next to a fire. A snap of his fingers extinguished the candle, leaving the room to be softly illuminated by the moonlight streaming in the window. Herin settled himself so that he could cradle Ilsa against his chest, one hand slowly tracing a path from her hip to her shoulder, leaving behind a tingling energy that was a reminder of what had built between them. "I think you were just doing what you had to do to make yourself feel safe," he said, causing Ilsa to turn her head so she could see his expression. "Seriously, Ilsa. From your point of view, it was probably the logical thing to do. But you aren't giving me very much credit. You were just assuming that you meant nothing to me other than a quick fuck. At least give me a chance to be better than a bastard before you label me one."

She laughed. "Fine, but you'd better not turn out to be one."

"Time will tell," he said, turning her so that their bodies were together. He wrapped his arms around her so that she could feel his body's response. His arousal was both immediate and obvious. Ilsa ran her fingers lightly over his back, making him sigh with pleasure.

"What is tonight, then?" she whispered.

She could feel him shrug in the darkness. "Who knows? Let's just see where this takes us and go from there."

"Let's," she said, giving herself to him.

As soon as they embraced, Herin felt as if her body was a flame against his. He instantly became lost in a world bounded by Ilsa's touch, her kiss, her legs moving over his, her hands roaming over his body, and he allowed his own control to go, giving himself completely to whatever it was that was moving them. It was a sweet surrender. When he finally did slide into her it was as if he was being torn from his body and sent to another level of existence. He was swallowed up in her, body and mind gone, a more primitive, powerful force taking over as it drove them both towards some unknown destination.

It was so intense that it frightened him. He began to pull back, only to have Ilsa desperately grab him, as if she were a drowning victim and he her rescuer. She clutched him to her, arching her back to bring their bodies into tighter contact with each other. Herin was distantly aware of her legs trapping him against her. They moved together in what seemed to be almost a dance, but much more powerful and irresistible. After what seemed like only moments, she cried out, a primal scream of release and animal joy. Herin felt Ilsa's intense shuddering as she climbed higher and higher, until finally she managed to cross the threshold between pleasure and pain and go over the peak. Herin was only seconds behind her, racing to a finish that his body craved, lost in his feelings. He groaned loudly as he collapsed on top of her, their bodies slickly coated with sweat, their breathing ragged and loud in the sudden silence of the room.

"Okay," Ilsa said with an audible tremor in her voice, "You can stay."

Herin laughed, but there was an edge to it that bordered on panic. Whatever was happening between them simply was beyond the normal feelings between a man and a woman. This time had been even more powerful than the last, and both were thinking the same thoughts. Where would it end?

"God's balls, that felt like I was being hexed," Herin panted. "It felt like something else was controlling my body. I'm not even sure if I liked it or not."

Rather than being offended by the remark, Ilsa sighed and nodded. "I know what you mean. It was like being sucked into a whirlpool, like we were just two leaves or something just picked up and carried along."

"It's a good thing it didn't last all that long," Herin murmured. "I don't know if I could have kept it up longer than a few minutes."

"I know…" Suddenly he felt Ilsa stiffen against him. "Oh my God! The window," she whispered.

Herin glanced over at the window. What he saw caused him to shoot to his feet in shock and surprise. The first fringes of pink light were just below the horizon, evidence that dawn was no more than an hour off.

"What the hell happened to us?" he asked. Apparently, they had been involved for more than seven hours rather than the handful of minutes it had seemed. "Didn't it just seem like a few minutes to you?" His voice was shaky.

She dumbly nodded, unable to speak. Ilsa's eyes held a terrified look. Herin reached out to pull her closer, trying to gentle her as he would a spooked horse. It was made more difficult because he was fighting down the same feelings himself. He was certain their joining had taken no more than ten minutes, perhaps even less. He hadn't fallen asleep. But the evidence was irrefutable. Whatever had happened between them had taken them away for hours and hours.

"Bet you won't forget me now," Herin said, attempting a feeble joke.

Ilsa laughed a ragged laugh, taking a deep breath to pull herself together. "No, I don't suppose I will at that. I don't know what is going on, but it's more powerful than just two people wanting each other."

Before they could discuss it further, there was a hard knock on the door and Shadow's voice echoed harshly from the hallway beyond. "What are you two doing in there?" he hissed, agitation apparent in his tone. "Have you taken leave of your senses?"

Puzzled, Herin hexed a candle into flame and crossed to the door, pulling on his trousers before opening it. There was no point in trying to hide anything, but he didn't know why it would upset Shadow so much. As he cracked open the door, Shadow roughly pushed his way inside, closing it quickly behind him.

"What in the world do you two think you are doing?" he snapped. "Don't you realize how dangerous it is to use magic now inside the city? Tybold has put the Council on your trail, yet here you are casting spells so powerful a blind man could find them."

"What are you talking about?" Herin asked, tugging his shirt over his head. Ilsa pulled her clothes to her, wriggling into them under the blankets before leaving the bed to slip on her boots.

"I'm talking about you two practicing spells up here," Shadow said, clearly livid. "I could sense them from halfway across town for God's sake. What the hell were you thinking? You're leaving a trail that could bring every magician in the city down on top of us."

"We didn't do any spells," Herin said, his eyes flicking to Ilsa's.

"Don't fucking lie to me." Anger shot from Shadow like sparks from a fire. Herin half-expected to see bolts of lightning flying from him. "I felt them, dammit!"

"What did you feel?" Ilsa asked from her chair.

"What?" Shadow shot back, distracted. He rubbed a hand over his face, making a visible effort to control himself before continuing. "It was like somebody was shining a torch on my face," he replied. "I first thought that one of the magicians from the

Council was trying some sort of containment or seeking spell, although at the time I thought it strange that it was directed at me since they don't know anything about me. Then I realized it wasn't anything like that, it was just a sense that some great spell was being performed somewhere fairly close by."

"I didn't know you could sense magic," Herin said. Shadow glared at him.

"I can't," he snarled. "At least I've never been able to. But this was so strong it was hard to ignore. I was near the tunnel, so I got away from there as quickly as I could to find out what was going on. Everywhere I went I could feel it touching me like sunlight on a hot summer day. I thought about coming here to get you two in case this meant we had to leave sooner than I thought. And what do I find? There is so much power coming from it that the inn should be glowing. This is the center, no doubt about it. I need to know just what you've done."

Herin crossed to look out into the streets. Other than a handful of early morning laborers on their way to their jobs, the road was deserted. "It doesn't look like anyone else noticed," he observed, his mind whirling as he tried to make sense of what was happening.

"Unless they are magicians they won't feel anything," Ilsa guessed. "Right?"

"Who knows?" Shadow snapped back. "You two are still avoiding the issue. What spell did you do here to soak this place in so much magic?"

Herin said, "No spell. We didn't do any magic. We had sex. I swear that was it, just sex."

Shadow looked from one to the other. Ilsa nodded to confirm Herin's story, causing Shadow's expression to change from anger to worry. As far as he could tell, they were not lying. "Are you telling me that this came from you two having sex with each other? What the hell have you tapped into?" he said at last.

"I don't know," Herin admitted. "We were just trying to figure it out ourselves when you came. We started well before midnight and we thought we had spent no more than ten minutes or so …"

"And?" Shadow said.

"And it was more than seven hours apparently," Herin replied. "Whatever happened was something totally beyond our control. We don't know what it is, but it isn't something either one of us thought would happen."

"The magic, do you think?" Ilsa asked. "Herin and I doing spells together created a kind of magical bond that gets activated somehow?"

"How the hell should I know?" Shadow answered irritably. "I've never heard of anything like this happening before. Of course, I never heard of anyone smelling magic before or someone reaching adulthood without knowing they can even do magic. Both of you are unknowns, so what happens between you is going to be unknown as well."

"Do we need to leave now?" Ilsa asked. "Do you really think the Council might be headed this way?"

"It's time to go anyway," Shadow answered. "I don't know how fast the Council can work, but there's no sense taking chances."

Herin pulled on a thick coat and picked up his pack, tossing it to Shadow. "I'll go down to the alley. Toss these to me."

Shadow cocked a questioning eyebrow at him.

"Do you really want people downstairs to see us walking through the common room dressed for travel and carrying loaded packs?" he asked. "Don't you think that might make people wonder just a bit, especially when we disappear for a few days?"

"Good point," Shadow admitted.

Minutes later, they were moving quickly towards the tunnel. The populace was just beginning to stir, but it was still easy enough for them to make their way unnoticed to the hidden entrance. They had taken the precaution of covering the opening with loose masonry, so that it appeared there was a large pile of rubble in the alleyway rather than an opening to one of the old sewer drains.

"Watch for anyone noticing us," Shadow commanded. Herin and Ilsa made certain no one was watching them, as Shadow used a simple lifting spell to move aside a few of the bigger pieces to reveal the entranceway. They quickly scampered through it, and he sent the stones back into place once they were safely inside.

Torches were conveniently stored on a ledge near the entrance. Herin groped in the darkness until he found one, setting it alight with a basic spell. He handed it to Shadow before lighting another for himself.

"We have some time now," Shadow said, holding Herin's arm when he would have headed deeper into the tunnel. "Now, tell me again exactly what happened last night."

Herin filled him in as best he could, while Ilsa added details from her point of view, their stories similar enough that it was obvious both had experienced the same thing. Shadow's eyes took on a thoughtful look as they finished.

"I don't know what to say," he said in response to their looks. "When you get a chance to do your spells in the passes, pay attention to what you are feeling. This might be something that makes you much more powerful. If so, we should use it."

"Except for one small detail. We didn't have any control over it," Ilsa reminded him. "Which means it might not come when we want it, or it might come and take the spells right out of our hands. Who knows what that would do?"

"There's only one way to find out," Shadow said, setting off down the tunnel. Herin and Ilsa fell into place behind him. Herin squeezed Ilsa's hand, giving her what he hoped was a smile of reassurance, although he thought his face probably looked a bit like hers, scared and uncertain. He decided to look on the positive side of things. As odd as the experience had been, it seemed to have left no negative aftereffects. For one thing, he felt as energized as if he had slept for days. Maybe this would somehow enhance their ability to use magic. The control part of it might come in time, providing they were willing to keep putting themselves in a position to experience the energy.

"What are you thinking?" Ilsa asked him as they clambered over pieces of wall that had fallen.

He helped her over a slab of concrete before replying. "I'm wondering how we can learn to direct that energy. It was pretty powerful."

"I felt like I was losing myself in it. I don't know if I want to do that again or not," Ilsa said. "Maybe a better question is whether or not we can do the physical part without the magical part taking over. That would at least be the beginning of control. We need to pay attention when it happens again."

"Horny again already?" Herin joked. "Can't you think about anything else? You need to get your mind out of the gutter."

"In case you hadn't noticed we are in the gutter, jackass," Ilsa shot back. "Be serious, Herin. If we can't control the magic, I don't want to do that again, not ever. This is getting to be too much. Each time is more powerful than the time before, and tonight was the most powerful of all. If the next time is even more powerful, there might not be anything left of us. We'd be consumed, used up. Is that what you want?"

"Of course not. But why assume that it would destroy us? Do you feel destroyed? I feel like I am bursting with energy, like my body can barely contain it all."

Ilsa shook her head and rolled her eyes. "That's exactly what I'm talking about. What if the next time our bodies can't contain all of the energy and it just burns us out?"

"But that hasn't happened. I know we can't control what is happening to us while we are together, but when we are done we are still in one piece," Herin answered. "And the magic keeps getting stronger and stronger when we do linked spells. I think if this was some kind of negative experience, it would affect us differently." This was certainly not something that had been covered in his classes back at the Institute.

"I have an idea," he said suddenly, grabbing Ilsa's arm. "What if we try creating a magical space to do it in? Maybe that could contain the energies."

"Do 'it'? How romantic. You certainly have a way with words, Herin Freeholder." Ilsa waved off his reply. "Let's just try to get through today in one piece, and then we can concern ourselves with what to do next."

Chapter Ten

Herin had never been so cold. He had thought the weather was fierce enough sheltered in Khartul, but the bitterness of the winter here in the mountains was on a scale totally beyond that. It seemed impossible that an army was trying to move through weather this frigid, much less planning to attack a city. He was shivering uncontrollably even under three layers of clothing that included a heavy padded jacket as well as two thick woolen shirts. He blew on his fingers to try to get some feeling back in them, wondering if magic would even function, given that he couldn't feel his extremities. Ilsa shivered against him, her body trembling and her breath coming in ragged gasps.

"I can't feel my damn feet," she complained gruffly. "This is ridiculous. We're going to die up here if we stay out much longer."

"The Dakarians are doing it," Herin reminded her.

"Fuck the Dakarians," Ilsa's teeth were chattering. "I'm worried about us."

"Too late to worry about it now," Herin answered, putting his arm around her to pull her closer so they could share body heat. They were sheltered, if that word applied in weather like this, in a small hollow formed by two huge boulders. The rocks shielded them from the worst of the wind, but what did find its way into their space was funneled through a small crack between the stones so that it increased in power, cutting through their clothing with ease.

Shadow had left them here while he reconnoitered, warning them that if any mountaineers came upon them, they should do nothing threatening. He had now been gone for more than a half hour. Long enough for Herin to have serious misgivings about following his instructions about not lighting a fire. *Who would see it up this high? The mountaineers? What difference would that make? They aren't our enemies, and they probably know better than to be caught out in weather like this. The hell with it, I'm warming us up.*

As if reading his mind, Ilsa shouted, "Can we at least try a spell of some kind? A shielding spell? Fire? Something?"

Herin nodded. "Let me try something alone first and see if it works," he yelled back. "If not, we can try something together."

She waved at him to get on with it, moving back a bit to give him more room. Herin mentally ran through his repertoire looking for something that might work on both the wind and the cold. A few seconds thought was enough to convince him of the futility of trying something of that magnitude. Perhaps just blocking off the wind would make it more bearable.

"Dveljask vedr fram fell har

Flytja ykkarr ver beida"

The wind disappeared as if it had never been blowing at all. It was as if someone had suddenly plugged the gap between the stones with a wall. It was still frigidly cold, but without the wind ripping at them, it seemed almost warm by comparison. Ilsa sighed as she unwrapped the scarf from her face. "God's balls, I felt like I was being suffocated in this," she said, pulling the thick wool away from her neck. "Whatever you used, worked. Nice job."

"Thanks," Herin said, his eyes scanning the snow field blocking the pass in front of them. "But I'm starting to get a little worried about Shadow. He should have been back by now."

"By now? You don't even know how far he had to go, or what kind of conditions he would find. We don't have any idea how long he's going to be. Just sit down and be patient."

She took her own advice, scooping snow away from the surface of a flat rock before settling herself upon it, basking in the weak winter sun. Herin spared one last glance for the pass before joining her, looking over his shoulder from time to time to see if he could catch any sight of Shadow.

He was rewarded ten minutes later by a black speck moving quickly, almost recklessly down the mountain. "Shit," he muttered. Whatever had happened up there, it seemed they were about to be in the middle of something dangerous again. He shook Ilsa's shoulder. "Get ready," he ordered, taking off his gloves, waiting impatiently for her to do the same. As they touched they could both could feel a tingle running from their hands up their arms and into their chests. "Start the chant, but don't finish it until I tell you."

Ilsa had also seen the figure. Whatever Shadow had seen up in the pass was causing him to descend at a dangerous rate. Without another word, she began a slow chant, outlining the beginnings of the spell they had decided to use. They had never practiced it together, but it was simple enough in concept that they both felt comfortable it would work.

Shadow slid into their hiding spot in a cloud of powdery snow. "They're in the pass," he panted. "They might have seen me. Do it now."

Herin didn't waste any time on a reply, focusing instead on the task. Ilsa's hand was trembling, but the steady and familiar rush of magic remained unchanged. They chanted together and he felt something powerful awakening, moving through him and around him at the same time. It was the oddest feeling, as if he were part of the magic yet separate from it all at once. Sparing a glance at Ilsa, he saw that she had her eyes closed and her lips half-parted, already deeply invested in the spell.

One last word and it was done. Both he and Ilsa pointed their free hands towards the distant peaks. A ball of fire as big as a house shot from their bodies, speeding towards the snow that was packed high above them in the pass. It took perhaps five seconds for the ball to reach its target, but when it did, it exploded with a crash louder than fifty thunderstorms, echoing and re-echoing off the surrounding heights. A snow cloud was thrown more than a hundred feet into the air, looking like some sort of gigantic fountain. When the snow had settled, Herin saw that the glacier was scorched as black as a log in a fireplace. There was a pit that looked tiny from this distance, but Herin realized that it must be hundreds of feet wide to even be visible from where they stood. Herin met Ilsa's eyes in wordless wonder at the power they had generated, far more than either of them could have hoped to accomplish alone.

"Let's go!" Shadow said, pulling them with him as he began descending the path they had used to bring them this high.

"What's the hurry?" Herin panted as he tried to match his long strides.

"You saw it work," Shadow told him. "Do you want to sit around until you're swept away by the avalanche? The noise of the explosion alone could be enough to start things rolling. Come on!"

"There isn't an avalanche," Ilsa pointed out, struggling to keep up with the quicker pace of the two men. "Just a big hole."

"Maybe not yet," Shadow answered grimly. "But there will be. And if we don't get moving, we're going to be buried under it."

They had covered three or four hundred yards at a quick trot when they were aware of a quiet rumble coming from the pass behind them. Shadow shot a look over his shoulder and Ilsa saw his eyes widen in shock and fear.

"God's teeth, it's coming faster than I thought. Hurry up!" He began running as fast as he could, ignoring the danger of a fall. Herin turned to grab Ilsa's hand, before speeding after him. In the brief moment when he had turned his head he had seen what Shadow had seen; a solid wall of snow more than thirty feet high moving swiftly down the mountain. Whoever was in the pass was going to be buried under tons of snow. They would share the same fate unless they could stay ahead of it. The mass was still six or seven hundred yards behind them, but it was picking up speed as it slid further down the mountain.

They could feel it now, a deep vibration through the earth, sounding in Herin's ears like the growl of a wild beast. It was almost as if the mountain was roaring out defiance against the magic they had used, wanting to crush them beneath tons of snow, like an angry god whose territory had been violated. Herin knew it was just his imagination, but he was unable to shake the very real feeling that they were being pursued like prey.

"In here," Shadow cried, diving into the cave they had located earlier that day before climbing to make their assault. Their packs were stacked against the back wall. They had planned on spending the night there before heading back to Khartul. Now it was the only thing standing between survival and death.

Herin shoved Ilsa in ahead of him, sparing one brief moment to look back the way they had come. The snow was roaring down towards him like an ocean wave, now less than fifty yards away, moving faster than a rushing river. The wall was fully as tall as the city walls of Khartul, and was so wide and destructive that it was breaking off trees as if they were mere sticks.

"Move back!" he yelled frantically as he dove in after Ilsa. He desperately invoked a blocking spell on the opening. There wasn't time for anything complicated, and Herin prayed it was strong enough to protect them. The cave was only fifteen feet deep, and they pushed themselves flat against the back wall as they awaited the avalanche. Seconds later, snow blotted out the sunlight completely as it covered the entrance to the cave, but Herin's spell seemed to be holding. It was like being behind a waterfall as it cascaded over a cliff. The sound was muted by the snow already blocking the opening to the cave, but it went on for many minutes before it was silent again.

"Well, that worked well," Herin said cheerfully in the darkness. "I can hardly wait to try it again."

There was a flash of light as Shadow hexed one of the torches they had stored in the cave alight, allowing them to examine their shelter in its sputtering flame. Snow completely blocked the entrance to the cave, lowering the temperature inside the shelter so much that it was almost as cold as being on the exposed mountainside. The opening itself was now a solid wall of white. They were safe enough from detection, but there remained the task of getting through the snow that now entombed them.

"I guess the pass is blocked now," Herin said lightly, while trying to control his shaking hands. Now that the adrenaline of the moment had passed, his body was trying to bring itself back to equilibrium.

"Dammit, just stop it," Ilsa scolded, shaking even more than he was. "This isn't funny. We might not be able to get out of here. Did you even think of that?"

"We'll be fine," Herin assured her. "Why were you running?" he asked Shadow.

"Dakarians," Shadow replied. "I ran into a patrol that was in the pass. I think the invasion might be closer than we thought. They didn't bother to chase me, so either they sent someone back to the higher ups to report, or more likely just assumed it was one of the mountain people so they didn't have to worry about it. It doesn't matter much now. That camp will be under tons of snow. That was excellent work by the way."

"Congratulate us when we're safe," Ilsa said. "Right now, we're trapped in here."

Shadow shook his head. "Right now, we're safe. We've got our packs and supplies with us so we don't have to worry about food. Relax. Let's eat something first, and then we'll figure things out after we've got a meal in us."

They ate in silence, each lost in their own thoughts. The meal was simple and basic, consisting of strips of dried meat and hunks of dark bread, plain enough but filling. Food would not be an issue. Neither would water, as melted snow would provide ample liquid.

The torch Shadow had lit began to sputter as the atmosphere inside the cave took on a decidedly stuffy nature. "We're using up the air," Ilsa said. "Are we going to have to choose between freezing to death and suffocation?"

Shadow walked to the edge of the cave mouth, poking at the snow with his walking stick, a thick pole a bit taller than he was. The stick sank into the snow as Shadow continued to push until his arm was covered up to the elbow. He pulled it back out in a shower of snow. Herin could see that he had penetrated perhaps ten feet into the blockage without breaking through into daylight.

"Thicker than I thought," Shadow mumbled, brushing snow from his sleeve. He tossed the stick aside. " *Hniga austrvegr stigr leita ljas,"* he whispered. There was a whirling sound like a drill working its way through wood, followed by a rush of cold air. Shadow stepped back with a satisfied nod. Herin and Ilsa could see that he had created a tunnel through the snow, perhaps four or five inches across, which was letting in fresh air as well as a bit of light. The tunnel looked to be at least fifteen feet long, packed solidly now that the snow had settled. From the nature of the light coming in, it appeared to be nearly dark.

"That will work well enough for tonight," Shadow said. "We can worry about digging ourselves out of here in the morning."

"I suppose a fire is out of the question," Ilsa said.

"Why?" Shadow asked. "It's unlikely there will be anyone out there wandering around in the dark. That slide more than likely wiped out all of the Dakarians in the pass. I don't see how they could have survived. I'm willing to chance a fire. Otherwise, it's going to be awfully cold in here by morning."

Fortunately, foresight had caused them to take the precaution of storing a goodly supply of wood when they had first located the cave. Herin piled some of those sticks together now, using a fire spell to set them ablaze. The warmth and light made their shelter seem a bit less claustrophobic, and the flames dancing off the stone walls of the cave made the small space seem almost cheery.

Shadow rolled himself into a blanket and tried to find a comfortable position on the hard floor, as close to the fire as he dared. "I'm worn out," he mumbled. "If you two are going to talk, try to keep it down so I can get some sleep. We'll need our rest tomorrow."

"I can't keep my eyes open," Ilsa admitted, following Shadow's example and grabbing her own blanket. "There's plenty of time to talk tomorrow, but right now I feel like I could sleep for days. That spell took something out of me."

Herin realized that he was feeling more drained than usual as well. He pulled his own blanket around him, lost in thought. *Why did this spell tire me out so much? Ilsa and I never felt that before, so why now? Maybe it wasn't the spell at all. Maybe it was from running like hell down the mountain.* He hoped that was the case, but regardless of the cause, he needed a nice, long, uninterrupted sleep. Reaching a hand to the pile of wood, he threw a few more sticks onto the fire before closing his eyes.

He awoke to a dimly lit cave, the air well below freezing. The fire had burned down to a few glowing embers, giving off very little light and even less heat. Herin stretched, his muscles protesting against a night spent on a rocky floor. Gathering what was left of the wood they had collected, he tossed it on the glowing remnants of the fire. In no particular hurry, Herin chose to stir the embers to start the fire rather than using a spell. After the drain of yesterday, he thought it best to conserve his energy, just in case the drain had been from the magic rather than the exertion of escaping the avalanche. When the wood had safely caught, he walked over to the vent Shadow had created, squinting along its length.

Through the small patch that was visible, he saw the dark blackish-blue that always painted the sky just before dawn. There was a chilly draft pouring down the opening that made his eyes tear, and he quickly turned away to warm his face by the fire.

"What time is it?" Ilsa asked, struggling out of her blankets.

"Maybe an hour until dawn," Herin replied, holding his hands to the fire to get some blood circulating in his fingers. "We might as well start now if we can. Once we're out, we've got a couple of hours yet before we're in the city. After yesterday, I am frozen straight through. I could really use a hot meal."

"What I tried last night is about the extent of what I can do by myself," Shadow told them, emerging from his cocoon of blankets. "I might be able to eventually widen the hole until it's large enough for one of us to crawl through, but it's going to take hours."

Ilsa shook her head irritably. "We all know the best chance of getting out of here quickly is if Herin and I do something together."

"I don't know if that's such a good idea," Herin told her. "The spells seem to be getting more and more powerful. This is a pretty small space. If something goes wrong, we have nowhere to hide."

"Scared?" Ilsa challenged.

"You're damned right I'm scared," Herin told her without embarrassment. "And you should be too. That last spell brought down the whole mountainside. What do you think is going to happen in this little cave?"

"We were trying to bring down the mountainside," Ilsa argued. "So the spell did exactly what we wanted it to. This is a different situation altogether. We just need to get the snow away from the opening."

"A repulsion spell maybe?" Shadow thought out loud. "Or one for opening secure barriers?"

"Destruction spells are out of the question," Herin added thoughtfully. "They are just too powerful and I wouldn't feel comfortable trying one in here."

They discussed several other options, walking to the base of the vent to check on the condition of the snow around the cave entrance. During the night, it had settled. The snow was now as thick and solid as a stone wall. Ilsa watched them in growing exasperation for a few minutes before bending over to pick up a flaming stick from the fire.

Without a word, she whipped the burning brand back and forth to increase the size of the flame before shoving her way between the two men and holding the makeshift torch to the snow. The flames began licking at the icy sheet. Within seconds, the wall began to drip water to the floor of the cave. She turned to them, shaking her head. "Why complicate things? Fire melts snow. Fire is an easy spell to use and control, so we use it."

Herin watched the melting ice before turning to her with a smile. "That just might work. And it would be far safer than anything else."

"You might think about asking my opinion next time," Ilsa replied, acid dripping from every syllable. "Instead of thinking you have all of the answers."

"Let's try it," he said, moving back to the far wall of the cave.

Ilsa tossed the burning stick back onto the fire. Shadow moved to Herin's other side, idle for the moment, but preparing a spell designed to snuff out flames, just in case. He doubted it would do much good if things went awry, but at least it made him feel useful.

"The first spell you were taught, do you think?" Herin asked. "Remember what happened when you tried it in the room that first night back?"

"That will do for starters," Ilsa agreed. "If it doesn't do anything, we can always try other ones."

Ilsa and Herin joined hands, quickly whispering the phrase to unleash the spell, pointing their fingers at the solidly packed snow that was sealing them in. A jet of flame fully five feet wide shot from their hands, eating away at the snow. It melted it so quickly that the floor of the cave was soon awash in icy water that rose ankle-deep.

"Keep it up," Shadow urged. "I'll deal with the runoff."

He activated a spell to gouge out a shallow basin in the stone floor, three feet deep and wider than a man's reach. The water began to drain into it, allowing Herin and Ilsa to focus all of their attention and energy on the task before them. The wall was melting away as if the summer sun had suddenly been transported inside the cave.

Within fifteen minutes the worst of the snow was gone, clearing the entranceway but for a drift perhaps a foot deep. They hefted their packs and gingerly climbed out of the cave, cautiously testing the surface when they were clear. The snow was now hard enough to walk on, although it was unsettling to be moving about on something that only a handful of hours before had been a heaving mass of destruction.

"I'm not sure I trust this," Herin said, kicking at the snow with his boot. "How stable is it?"

"It should be stable enough now that it's settled," Shadow assured him. "Besides, it's not like we have a choice. This is the only way down."

"What now?" Ilsa asked. "Do we head back to Khartul, then right back out again to the other pass?"

"Khartul first," Shadow said. "We might as well see if the situation has changed at all since we left. This should have effectively eliminated one of the attacking forces, or at least prevented them from joining their comrades."

"Whatever we do, let's get moving," Herin urged. "The sooner we're off this mountain and inside somewhere warm, the happier I'll be."

Shadow led the way, setting as brisk a pace as he dared on the still treacherously slippery snow. Herin periodically checked behind them, more from habit than any fear they were being followed. The mountainside was deserted, but their footprints were clearly visible in the snow. Anyone who wanted to track them could do so easily. A simple spell took care of that, and the marks from their boots vanished as soon as they were created, leaving nothing behind but a pristine surface. *Good thing we had picked out the cave ahead of time. Otherwise, we'd be buried under this somewhere. If we try the other pass, we'll need a safe shelter before we start.*

Bjorkenberg was holding onto his temper by the barest of threads. Dealing with various city officials all morning had worn his patience thin. Accustomed to the iron discipline of the regular army, where giving a command meant it would be done at once, he was not prepared for the world of political give-and-take. It had proved impossible to get cooperation from the city officials without first going through long explanations about how that cooperation would benefit particular factions, an action he found both frustrating and wasteful. The simplest of requests could turn into hour long discussions of the whys and wherefores of the order. After several days of that, Bjorkenberg had declared martial law to eliminate the delays and give him enough time to get the city's defenses prepared before a possible attack.

The elected officials had been bad enough, but at least they had the saving grace of being used to a hierarchy. Once it had been established that the Legion Commander was at the top of that pyramid, the career bureaucrats fell into place. But the merchants proved to be more problematic. Many of them saw the present emergency as a chance to reap huge profits, and they had every intention of taking advantage of that leverage. Others were those looking to use the emergency as a springboard to greater power within the city.

Loki Tybold now stood arrogantly before Bjorkenberg's desk, demanding to be given a commission in the defense forces. That he lacked military experience did not faze the youngster in the slightest, the commander noted with disgust. Loki was confident his request was reasonable. He was already picturing himself leading a heroic defense of the city and collecting medals afterwards. *That will show my father I am worthy to take over the business.*

"Out of the question," Bjorkenberg snapped. "You have no experience leading men or have even the slightest military training. What makes you think you deserve command of anything?"

"I've ordered people around plenty of times," Loki said. "I know how to do that."

"There is more to commanding men than ordering people around," Bjorkenberg replied.

"It wouldn't be right for the son of Jarl Tybold to be without a commission."

The general fought back the urge to slap sense into Tybold. *This stupid son of a bitch thinks he can just walk in here and be given a command because of his father's reputation? What an ass! I ought to send him out on a patrol and rid myself of his presence for good.* "Do you have any idea what we might be facing?" he asked. "We could very well be facing a prolonged siege, and if that turns out to be the case, I will need men in command who can act calmly under pressure, and who know what they are doing. Neither of those attributes applies to you."

Loki argued with the commander for twenty minutes, but in the end left the office frustrated and without a commission. *Damn the man!* Loki had already prepared a letter to his father describing his anticipated new position, but now he had nothing to report. As he stomped down the marble steps fronting the building, Loki briefly considered the advisability of leaving the city before any attack. He certainly didn't want to be cooped up inside with all the rest of the sheep, being ordered around by men who would more than likely be his social inferiors. But what choice did he have? His father had ordered him to Khartul, and unless he could come up with a really compelling reason to leave the city, here he would stay.

The leader of his escort met him outside the commander's office. One look at Loki's face told him what he needed to know, and he allowed himself the comfort of an internal sigh of relief. The gods only knew what kind of mischief this young idiot could have gotten into if he had been put in command of fighting men. "No luck, sir?" he asked with false solicitousness.

"No, the fools couldn't see what they need to see. Who else has the prestige to raise enough men to fill the levies they want?"

"Oh, I'm sure you're right," the man said, turning to the two other guards who had accompanied Loki on his errand. Loki had taken to having an armed escort in full armor and livery accompany him everywhere he went. He had hoped in this way to imprint on the minds of those making the decisions that he was a man of importance, someone to be reckoned with who could command men in battle. It galled him a bit to realize the effort had been in vain.

"Let's go you two sluggards," the ex-legionnaire ordered. "Get out in front of us and clear a path."

"Too bad, my lord," said one to Loki as he walked in front of him. "They should respect a man who has enough money at hand to equip an entire cohort."

"What did you say?" Loki snapped, jolted out of his cloud of disappointment.

"I was just saying you were rich, and they should use you to help them raise men," the man mumbled, catching the look of disgust on the face of his own leader as he stood behind Loki.

"Yes...why not?" Loki said. "Why not? Who could stop me? I'm just doing my part to help defend the city in its time of trouble. It's brilliant...it's even noble. Perfect." He picked up his pace. "Let's go; I have things to do."

The leader of the escort grabbed the young guard by his tunic and growled, "You ass, now look what you've done! When Tybold forms up his little army, I am going to make sure that you are in the front line. When will you learn not to put ideas in that fool's head?"

"I was just making conversation," the man whined, trying to free himself from the iron grip on his shirt.

"Sucking up is what you were doing. I've had my eye on you for weeks now. Every time our esteemed leader is around, you are so far up his ass you can tell what he had for breakfast. Now you're going to get some of us killed. Do you really fancy going into battle with Tybold in command?"

"That wouldn't affect you," the man said, jerking himself free. "Just tell him you're too old or something."

"Hah! As if that would stop him. No, now you've forced my hand, and I'll make you pay for it one way or the other."

"What are you going to do?"

The leader spat on the ground. "You can bet everything you have that Tybold will get a troop together and volunteer to do the most dangerous assignments available just because he thinks it will bring him glory. Which it might, but it will be because of the men he gets killed."

"You're exaggerating."

"You just keep thinking that right up to the moment you catch a spear or arrow in your chest. If I'm going to have to fight, I'm at least going to do it where I have the most chance of survival. I'm putting in my resignation today so I can re-enlist with the Tenth. I still have connections there, so they'll take me back with open arms. But it means giving them five more years of my life. I'm of a mind to take every single one of those days out of your hide before I leave."

The younger man could see that the threat was real and hastily backed away, trotting to catch up with the other guard escorting Tybold. The ex-solider let him go, shaking his head. The last thing Khartul needed was Loki Tybold taking potential soldiers away from the Legion. There would be plenty of men willing to fill the ranks of whatever private army Tybold had in mind. The fool certainly had coffers deep enough to double or even triple what they would get paid by the Legion, with the added bonus of not having to fill the five-year enlistment requirement that was part of the regular army's policy. In a battle you were only safe when you fought with discipline, which meant that his chances of survival were greater with the Legion than with Tybold and whatever rag-tag force he put together.

The veteran knew what would happen. Loki would have his factories make uniforms, manufacture his own weapons, and then put out flyers advertising top wages to enlist in his force. The unemployed would flock to him, riff-raff from the streets and gutters of the city. This was actually the same labor pool that the Legion drew from, but with the crucial difference that the army had centuries of experience in turning such scum into good soldiers. Loki did not. The result would be a motley group of badly trained men with weapons, really little more than a mob. He didn't want to be around to get sucked into that.

Rather than following the others, he turned back to the building that housed army headquarters. *Might as well take care of this part first,* he thought. *Once I'm back in the army, Tybold can't touch me.*

Herin stretched painfully, slowly bending over to pull off his boots, placing them near the fire to dry out. It had taken them the better part of a day to make their way back into the city, where they had arrived footsore, cold, and tired. The combination of the cold and walking through deep snow, combined with the stress of their experience had made all of them crave the warmth of the inn as a drug addict craved narcotics. Shadow had remained behind in the main room to fetch up some hot food, while Ilsa and Herin had headed straight for their rooms to get out of their wet clothes.

"I'm not looking forward to having to do that again," Herin said as he peeled his shirt off, hanging it over a chair to dry. It was soon joined by the rest of his clothes. Ilsa followed his example. Still shivering, she pulled dry clothes from her pack and began to dress.

"Maybe we won't have to," she said. "Without half of the attackers, the Dakarians might call everything off."

"Maybe," Herin conceded, as he pulled a new shirt and pair of trousers from his own pack. "But you know Shadow, he's all about finishing what you start. Mark my words, he'll say we need to do the other pass, just to be sure."

"I still don't see how this is our fight," Ilsa commented. "I know, I know, we're stuck here in the city, so we're part of it. But why not just sit tight now and see what happens? We've cut off one invasion path. Won't that be enough to make an attack impossible? Do we have to close both passes?"

Herin shrugged, crossing to the fire, letting its warmth wash over him, reveling in the feeling of being both warm and dry, something that had eluded him for the last two days. "I don't know. I guess we'll take at least a day or two to sniff around to see what kind of preparations are being taken. It looked like more activity than usual in the streets. We must have passed three or four patrols. That's new. The streets never had any patrols before. Maybe we can just sit it out here."

"God, that would be wonderful," Ilsa sighed softly, as she spread her clothes to dry.

A few moments later, Shadow entered with a tray of food that included a pitcher of something hot, the steam curling lazily in the air. He shut the door with his foot before placing the tray on the table. He shed his cloak and hung it on a peg behind the door, but otherwise made no concession to the fact that he was still wearing the same clothes he had traveled in. Picking up a mug, he poured himself a drink, sipping it with a small sigh of pleasure.

Herin and Ilsa sat at the table to eat. It was a simple enough meal, but seemed like a feast after the travel provisions they had been subsisting on. Herin slapped a thick slab of warm meat between two pieces of black bread, handing it to Ilsa before creating a similar meal for himself. "Speaking of which," he said, "Just how much time do we have? Are we heading back out again anytime soon?"

Shadow shook his head. "We can't right now. The army sent patrols out and at least two of them were headed in the direction we'd have to take. For better or worse we'll have to sit tight for a few days to let events unfold."

"I can't say I'm disappointed," Ilsa said as she chewed. "This room might not be much, but it certainly beats sleeping on a cold cave floor. What happens if the Dakarians do attack?"

"I don't know," Shadow admitted. "Maybe nothing, as far as we're concerned. It may be that the army will be strong enough to beat off anything the Dakarians can throw at them. It may be that we will be forced into lending a hand. Secretly, if possible. We'll just have to be flexible."

"All I care about is that we won't be going back out anytime soon," Herin said. "I feel the chill right down to my bones. I think I need a good long soak in a hot bath."

Ilsa caught his eye and winked. Herin hid his answering smile in his sandwich.

The sentry slit his eyes against the glare, scanning the area outside the walls. Work details had cut back the foliage for more than two hundred yards around the city to provide a killing zone in the event of an attack. It provided a good view, but the fact that the ground was clear also allowed snow to accumulate where once had been trees. The effect of that change was that anyone on duty during the daylight hours ran the risk of an acute case of snow blindness on any sunny day. As a result, most of the guards began to spend less time scanning the surrounding area for possible threats, and more time looking into the city to watch activity in the streets below. It meant they didn't have to battle the splitting headaches that were often the companion of the burning blindness.

In reality, it didn't matter since there was no way to see under the trees no matter how long one stared at the woods. That was unfortunate for the guard on duty. He never saw the black arrow flying from the shadows to suddenly sprout from his throat like some exotic and deadly flower. Clutching his neck in a vain effort to draw air into his lungs, he toppled from the battlements to land twenty feet below, sprawling lifelessly on the cobblestones of the street. Women screamed as a crowd gathered, although the soldier was far beyond any earthly help.

Above the furor, his partner carefully peered in the direction of the woods and saw a long line of black clad soldiers slowly emerging from the cover of the trees. Their numbers were hard to estimate with any certainty, but it looked to the soldier as if there were several thousand. The long anticipated Dakarian attack was now a reality. Racing to the end of the platform, he began to frantically ring the large bell hung there for just this purpose, alarming the rest of the city.

The peals had barely died away before men were scrambling for their posts, the whole city as frantic as a disturbed anthill. People rushed to their houses, merchants closed up their shops, the civilian levies shouldered their shields and spears before manning their assigned posts. Everyone who was in the regular defense force reported to their pre-assigned rally point. It was obvious that the city had been drilling for weeks for this situation. Despite the suddenness of the attack, the defenders moved with efficiency. Within a few minutes, the walls of the city bristled with archers waiting for the order to loose their arrows.

The Dakarians paused just outside the treeline to straighten lines that had been disrupted by moving through the forest. Men continued to come from the woods until it seemed that the trees must be dropping them like fruit. To the veterans on the wall, there was the usual nervousness before battle, but all of them were happy to be behind stout fortifications rather than out in the open. The Dakarians formed their long battle lines, and then stood silently watching the city without further movement.

"What in bloody hell are they waiting for?" a soldier growled, keeping an eye on the lines of Dakarians.

"Fucking barbarians, no telling what they be thinking," answered his companion. "Sizing us up, most like, or trying to get inside our heads. I wonder if they can be reached from here?"

"What are you thinking?" his friend asked.

"They shot Arod didn't they? If'n their bows can reach here, reckon ours can do the same to where they be sitting."

"Good thinking. What about officers though? Nobody gave an order to fire."

"The officers can kiss my ass," the soldier growled, notching an arrow. "Besides, who's to say just who shot? Must be two hundred archers or more in this section alone. How would anyone know who shot? Be a shame to waste all those nice sitting ducks, now wouldn't it? I wouldn't mind killing me a Dakarian."

His companion risked a peek over the wall. It might work. The Dakarians were drawn up in four long straight lines, not moving, just standing as still as if they had been turned to stone and no more than two hundred yards away. With the masses of men drawn up on the plain outside the city, it would be difficult to miss if an arrow made it that far.

"What the hell, give it a shot," he agreed. "Eye for an eye and one less bastard to worry about when they hit the walls. I'll watch for officers."

The archer carefully sighted the ranks of enemy soldiers, staying undercover to make certain he wasn't going to be a target himself. The Dakarians were just beginning to stir.

"Hurry up," his friend urged. "It looks like they're getting ready to move."

The archer stood, pulled the bow back to its fullest length and let fly, ducking back below the wall as soon as he had loosed the shaft. It arched upwards in a graceful parabola, seeming to pause momentarily at the apex of its flight, before diving down at the Dakarians like a hawk after its prey. The arrow struck a solider in the second rank, taking him in the neck just above his breastplate. He clutched at the arrow before sinking slowly to his knees, blood running down the front of his armor. A ragged cheer went up from the soldiers on the wall who had witnessed the shot.

Atop the tallest tower in the city, Bjorkenberg watched the arrow fly out from the wall. He noted the cheering echoing from the legionnaires on the wall. While he was a believer in iron discipline, sometimes it was best to turn a blind eye to such an act. Especially when it was successful. It was an opportunity that should not be wasted.

"Order volley fire immediately," he told his aide. The man obediently hoisted the proper flags on the tall pole built to signal orders to the defenders.

Within thirty seconds, a volley of arrows was flying towards the enemy line. Before the first volley had hit home a second was on its way, with deadly effects. Some arrows fell short of their target, but hundreds more found homes in the flesh of soldiers, causing holes to suddenly appear in the Dakarian line. As the bowmen found their range, far fewer arrows fell short.

Dakarian bodies began to litter the ground, but if the defenders had hoped the carnage would discourage an attack, they were disappointed. The air was filled with a sudden blast of trumpets, sending thousands of soldiers streaming towards the city walls, an ebony ocean of men rushing to battle. Scaling ladders were carried by pairs of men in the front ranks of the attackers. As the first wave reached the walls, Bjorkenberg saw small catapults being wheeled out of the woods, setting up just clear of the trees. Soldiers as well as men dressed in dark robes clustered around the machines.

"How did they carry those damn things over the mountains?" his aide asked, watching with dismay as they began to throw heavy stones against the walls of the city.

"Carried them in pieces most like," Bjorkenberg answered, his attention on the attack. "Makes no difference. Get down there and tell the closest section to focus their arrows on the crews. Maybe we can put them out of commission before they do too much damage."

The boulders were chipping large chunks of masonry from the walls. It didn't seem possible for such small machines to throw such large stones, or that those missiles could do so much damage when they hit. Something had to be done before a breach appeared in one of the walls. Even as Bjorkenberg watched, a stone hit squarely on one of the walkways, causing a hole ten feet wide which dropped a half dozen men to the street. He saw that even though the Dakarians were much closer now, for some reason his soldiers' arrows were not doing the amount of damage they had accomplished at a longer range. It was as if there was some kind of protection around the Dakarians that kept them from harm, and the implications of that were obvious.

"Get someone here from the Council," he ordered another runner. "Go to Master Renfeld and tell him we need their help right away. Hurry!" The young officer sped down the ladder and sprinted through the streets in the direction of the Hall. Bjorkenberg berated himself for not thinking of this sooner. He should have had a magician with him right from the start, just in case they needed any sort of assistance. Too late to worry about it. Now he had to figure a way to keep the city walls intact until one arrived. He hoped that was possible.

Chapter Eleven

A huge explosion rocked the city, shaking pieces of concrete and masonry loose and showering pedestrians with rubble, sending them sprinting for cover. The inn where Herin, Shadow, and Ilsa had taken rooms was built right against the wall. With each thud of a boulder hitting the battlements, shock waves reverberated throughout the building, coating the three with dust from the rafters as their shelter shuddered from the force of the bombardment.

"We need to get out of here," Herin urged as a pitcher crashed to the floor and splintered into fragments. "I'd rather take my chances out in the open."

"You might be right," Shadow said in the silence between attacks. They had learned that the boulders came about five minutes apart, the time it took to reload before sending the next flight towards the city. "Let's head for the center of the city. I think that's probably out of range. We might get a better read on the situation from there."

"Take everything," Herin added. "Just in case we don't come back here."

"Hurry," Ilsa said, grabbing two packs and rushing for the stairs. She was doing her best to control her fear, but every bombardment pushed her closer to the breaking point. Each time a shot hit the walls, she was certain the inn would come tumbling down, trapping them in the ruins. Being cooped up inside the small room had not helped. She wanted to feel the cold wind on her face, away from the constant pounding from the siege engines out on the plateau.

Herin and Shadow picked up the remaining pack and their bows before following Ilsa down the stairs and out to the street. She set a brisk pace towards the city center, keeping well away from the buildings to lessen the chance of being hit by any shrapnel from the missiles. The streets were teeming with people: civilians seeking shelter, soldiers rushing to reinforce the walls, and hundreds of people who just seemed dazed by the turn of events and were milling about, uncertain where to go. Screams of fear and cries for help mixed with the shouted orders of officers to create a maelstrom of noise and confusion.

Shadow and Herin moved ahead of Ilsa to shoulder a path through the throng, making it easier for her to follow. Now that she was outside, her mind began to work clearly again. First, they just needed to get away from the danger zone. Once that was done, they could make further plans. But it seemed obvious to her that this attack was going to be a serious problem. You could read it in the body language of the soldiers and in the voices of their officers. Perhaps it would be best to take advantage of the tunnel to get outside the city.

As they left the area under attack, the traffic thinned enough to allow them to walk abreast. Behind them, smoke rose from a dozen fires and the cries, though muted at this distance, told them that the stones were accurately finding targets within the city. The Dakarians had switched their tactics after just a few volleys, aiming to shoot more of their missiles into the city itself as opposed to attacking the thick, sturdy walls. The result was a huge amount of what the army called collateral damage, the cumulative effect being that it occupied men that would have been better employed on the walls defending the city.

"How can they be so accurate?" Herin asked as he saw one stone clear a wall before landing squarely on a three-story building, bringing a huge part of it crashing to the street.

Shadow stood watching the attack with a frown on his face. "That's a good question," he acknowledged. "It is strange. Hardly a boulder that clears the wall fails to find a target and that is beyond coincidence. It could be that they infiltrated the city with spies long before the attack. This is obviously part of some well-timed plan. They negotiate to get the Empire to relax its guard, and then launch an attack on one of the most important cities. They must have been planning this for more than a year."

"So the treaty was a sham," Herin said. Shadow nodded.

"It certainly seems that way. It was just luck that put me in the mountains in time to see them coming. Otherwise, this might have worked."

Another boulder appeared briefly above the rooftops surrounding the square they were standing in, seeming to pause momentarily before crashing down on buildings just a block or so away.

"They're coming closer," Ilsa said, eyeing the damage that was within their view. "We should move farther back."

Herin stood still, his eyes closed and his head cocked slightly to one side. Shadow looked at him in puzzlement, then grabbed his arm and gave it a shake. "No time for dreaming, Herin," he said as another rock landed within twenty yards of where they were standing. "We have to take cover."

Herin came out of his reverie and shook his arm free. "Of course! They're using magic, Shadow. Those stones have some sort of spell on them. That's why they're carrying so far."

"You're certain?" Herin stared at him. "Sorry," Shadow apologized. "Do you recognize the spell? Is it something we can counteract?"

"I don't recognize it," Herin told him. "I need to get somewhere high enough to let me see over the walls so I can get an idea of what's going on out there."

"They won't let us on the walls themselves, "Shadow said. "That much is sure."

"What about that church tower?" Ilsa suggested, pointing to the tall stone spire that shot more than a hundred feet into the air. A pall of smoke wreathed it now, but the tower would give an unparalleled view of the surrounding countryside.

"That will work. Hurry!" Herin sprinted towards the building, Shadow and Ilsa in his wake. A spiral stone staircase just off the entranceway led to the belfry. Herin took the worn steps two at a time. The passageway was narrow enough that he could feel the cold stone rubbing against both shoulders. The stairway opened out into a small open air bell tower, barely four feet across, crowded now with all three of them on it.

They were more than a hundred feet above the level of the pavement, easily high enough to see over the walls. Catapults were clearly visible on the edge of the forest just a few hundred yards from where they now stood watching. They had barely had time to catch their breath before another dozen boulders flew into the city, their impact causing additional damage.

"It's there," Herin confirmed, smelling the air. "I can't tell where the magic is coming from out there, but it's on every stone being shot at the city."

"Must be at the catapult site," Shadow guessed. "See those men in robes? They must be magicians."

"And pretty powerful ones if they can make the boulders get this far so accurately," Herin agreed. "Catapults that small don't normally have this kind of range, do they?"

"No, they don't. Is there any chance of intercepting the missiles while they are in flight?"

"That's going to be tricky," Herin said. "Even if I can do it successfully, I'd have to stay at it the whole battle. I would rather just stop them once and for all and get out of here."

Ilsa had been leaning on the wall of the tower, shielding her eyes with one hand and staring at the launch sites. "Herin, the mountain was farther away than those machines," she pointed out.

Herin followed her gaze and nodded. "You're right. Let's try it and see what happens."

"Someone will see," Shadow reminded them. "This will have to be quick."

Herin raised his eyebrows. "Who's looking up here?" he asked. "This is the only place high enough to let us see what we're aiming at. I think we just have to chance it, but I'm willing to listen to a better idea."

"I don't have one," Shadow admitted. "Go ahead."

Ilsa took Herin's hand. "Which spell do you want to use?"

"Let's try the one we used on the mountain and see what happens," he suggested.

"Fine." It took only a few seconds before they felt the powerful energies they had become familiar with moving through them. A fireball shot from the tower, headed for the catapult site. It exploded with a huge roar and a flash of light. The echoes of the explosion were muted by distance, but the suddenness of the counterattack caused the Dakarians to stop their assault for a moment, milling about in confusion. As the dust settled from the explosion, it was obvious that the catapults themselves were untouched.

"What the hell happened?" Ilsa asked.

"A counterspell of some sort," Shadow said tersely. "See?" He pointed to a large crater twenty yards in front of the catapults. "They must have wards of some kind out to deflect any kind of spell that might be used against them."

Herin was rubbing his chin, lost in thought. "If we can't break through it, we'll go around it," he said at last.

"What do you mean?" Ilsa asked.

"They have to be using a tremendous amount of energy to maintain that barrier and to charm the missiles at the same time. I'm betting it's just in front of them. After all, why guard their rear? That's their weak spot."

"What did you have in mind?" Shadow asked.

"Combination spell," Herin told him. "We mix a manifestation spell with a destruction spell, then materialize the spell right behind the catapults. It won't have to go through the barrier that way, just appear behind it."

"Do you think that will work?" Shadow was clearly skeptical. "I never heard of anyone combining spells like that before."

"I'm sure," Herin said. "Trust me."

"This is going to take a tremendous amount of energy," Shadow frowned. "Have you thought of that?"

"With our combined power, there's no problem," Herin assured him. "We seem to get more energized every time we work together."

"If Herin thinks this will work, I'm fine with trying it," Ilsa said. "What do I need to do?"

Quickly, Herin repeated the phrasing for the two spells he had decided on using, making Ilsa repeat it several times until he was sure she had the words memorized in the correct order.

Shadow watched as the spell was activated. They had barely finished the last words when a tremendous explosion rocked the battlefield. This time when the smoke had cleared, he could see that Herin and Ilsa had been successful. Catapults lay in ruins, some on fire, with others tossed about as if some giant had used them for playthings. It was difficult to tell through the smoke, but Shadow estimated there were more than two dozen bodies strewn about the wreckage, including all of the Dakarian magicians.

"Damn, I don't understand what you two have going on, but it seems to work, whatever it is," Shadow commented. "How do you feel?"

Ilsa looked at her hands, turning them slowly back and forth. "I actually feel like there is energy coming out of me still."

"I suppose that's to be expected," Shadow replied. "You two are becoming more and more magically compatible. We'd better get down before someone takes it into their head to check out the glow coming from the church tower. That spell was fairly conspicuous."

Herin took one last satisfied glance at the results of his spell before turning for the stairway, being careful to find the first step before moving forward. The stairway was dark, making it easy to take a tumble and roll the entire way down to the bottom. As he began to make his way down, he heard voices coming from below.

"Quiet!" Herin hissed, halting and straining to hear.

"I want them alive. Do you understand?" The voice was one he recognized.

Herin shook his head. *Again? How in the hell did Tybold find me this time? Dammit!*

Herin could hear the sound of booted feet trying to climb the stairs stealthily. He pushed Shadow and Ilsa back to the tower platform, warning them quietly of the new threat.

"Loki?" Shadow whispered. "Are you sure that was him?"

"I'm sure," Herin confirmed. "Now what?"

"This is too small a space to use the concealment ruse you used before," Shadow said. "I see no other choice but to either use magic or try to fight our way down. We're going to have to kill some people to get out of here."

"Maybe not," Herin said, quickly stringing his bow and notching an arrow. "There isn't much room on those stairs. They can't come up here quicker than one at a time. Follow my lead."

"Even if you kill one, we'll still be stuck up here in the tower," Shadow pointed out.

"Fuck it, Shadow, I can only deal with one problem at a time," Herin shot back. "Even if we use magic we're still stuck in the tower, right?

Ilsa peered over the edge of a tower window to the square below. "There are eight or ten more down there," she reported.

Herin cocked his head and listened closely to the sounds coming up from the stairwell. "Come on Shadow, get ready."

"I hope you know what you're doing," Shadow muttered, stringing his bow and pulling an arrow from his quiver. Ilsa followed suit and they waited tensely just out of sight of the last turn in the spiral staircase. Neither Shadow nor Ilsa had handled a bow since they had arrived in Khartul, but they could hardly miss at this range. Herin hoped they could somehow make their way out of here without having to kill anyone. They might be in Khartul and not Kress, but he was certain that Loki Tybold would have much more influence here than they would if it came to any kind of trial. If this resulted in bloodshed, it would definitely mean a trial.

The first man poked his head cautiously around the corner and froze with one foot raised to take the next step as Herin stepped forward, an arrow already in place and pointed at his chest. "You have a choice," Herin told him quietly. "Back down those stairs and live, or refuse and die. Choose wisely and choose quickly."

The man's face paled and he swallowed nervously. He knew that if he so much as twitched a muscle he was a dead man. He didn't know much about this group they were after other than Tybold had ordered them attacked, but one look at Herin's eyes told him the young bowman was serious.

"I'm going back," he said, lowering his sword and dropping his hands to his side. He turned and called over his shoulder to the men behind him, hidden by the curve of the stairs. "Back up. Hurry up, get back."

"What's going on?" a voice called from behind him. "What's happening? We can't move in this god damned tower."

"Figure it out!" he called frantically, seeing Herin raise the bow to eye level and take aim. "Hurry!"

There was the sound of scuffling feet accompanied by the scrape of metal weapons against the stone walls, allowing the man to slowly begin backing his way down the steps. Herin followed, staying close enough to keep him in sight but far enough away that the man could not try to grab the bow away from him. He needn't have worried. The would-be attacker had enough to keep him busy trying not to lose his footing on the narrow, twisting stairway as he carefully reached behind him with every step to find the next one.

"We'd better keep our bows ready," Shadow whispered to Ilsa as she descended ahead of him. "We're going to need these again once we're off the stairs."

"I hope he knows what he's doing," Ilsa whispered back.

They were perhaps halfway to the ground floor when Loki's voice echoed up the stairway, indignation apparent in his tone. "What the hell is going on?" he cried. "Get your asses back up those steps now. Cowards! Get back up after them or I swear I'll have you flogged alive."

There was a mumble of confused voices. Herin craned his head around the corner but could still not see the bottom. He motioned with the arrow and the man in front of him continued to descend the stairs. Herin could imagine what was happening down at ground level. Loki would be furious as more and more of his men came back to mill around the entranceway to the church. He would almost certainly order an attack of some kind the moment Herin and his companions left the cover of the stairwell.

It was time to figure out the next move. They had an advantage only while they were on the stairway. Once out in the open, Loki's superior numbers would shift that advantage. Herin spared a glance out of one of the narrow windows that allowed light and air into the tower. They were still perhaps fifteen feet from ground level, and he could see armed men standing outside the church doors, apparently waiting for orders.

"Far enough," he said to the man. "Stop there for a moment." He looked around the corner of the tower and could see the barest edge of the stone floor that marked the entranceway. "Loki!" he called. "Loki Tybold! Can you hear me?"

"I hear you, Freeholder," Loki called back. "You can't get out."

"Shut up and listen. I want you and all of your men outside the church where I can see them."

"Why should we do that?" Loki called back. "You can't get out of here."

"Don't be an ass, Tybold," Herin cried angrily, the stress of the situation eroding whatever patience he might have had. "If it comes to it, we can just destroy all of you where you stand. I'm giving you a chance to get away with your lives."

"Liar. You can do nothing against this many men."

"Are you really that big a fool?" Herin asked, switching tactics and aiming his words now at Loki's men. "Do you really think this will be a challenge after we've already killed three times that many Dakarians, and destroyed a half dozen of their magicians to boot?" Herin had no idea of the true casualty count from their spell, but he also knew that Loki wouldn't either.

"Shit," the man in front of him quietly cursed, his eyes mirroring his fear. Herin hoped his words were having the same effect on his companions outside.

"You're bluffing," Loki blustered, aware that his men were beginning to mutter amongst themselves. "Stay where you are," he ordered them before turning his attention back to Herin.

"Are you willing to bet your life on that?" Herin answered. "I'm going to count to ten and if the church isn't cleared by then we'll start clearing it our way. One...two...three...four..."

Herin hadn't given Loki any time to negotiate, sensing that the longer this confrontation went on, the more the momentum would shift away from him to Loki. If Loki had learned anything back at the school, it should have been the limitations of magic. The hole in Herin's argument was that he couldn't possibly use a spell like he had on the Dakarians without destroying the church, with himself inside. He was afraid that if he gave Loki time to think he might realize that. Right now, the control was in Herin's hands, and he intended to keep it there.

Behind him Ilsa looked out the window. "They're moving away," she reported.

Herin gestured with the bow. "Start moving," he told his prisoner.

The man was only too happy to comply, taking the steps two at a time in his haste to get away. It wasn't bad enough that he had an arrow pointed at his chest, but the man holding it was also apparently a magician. He reached the ground floor, turning to go. His companions had already cleared the church, moving swiftly back from the door.

"Hold it," Herin ordered. Slowly, he emerged from the protection of the stairway. Cautiously, he glanced around the foyer. The wooden doors to the church itself were closed, leaving only the doorway out into the square. "Put your sword away. Easy!" The man obeyed, keeping his hands out in front of him where they were plainly visible.

Herin maneuvered him so that his back filled the doorway, blocking the view of those in the square. He glanced over the man's shoulder to see Loki's men surrounding the steps, but most had their swords in their scabbards. Loki stood with his arms folded, his face a mask of fury. Shadow and Ilsa came down the stairs to stand behind Herin. "Check the doors, Shadow," Herin ordered. He wanted to make certain Loki had not tried to leave any surprises behind.

"Bolted tight," Shadow reported, after tugging on the handles.

"Move back farther," Herin called to the men outside. Loki waved them back. The group moved until they were twenty yards or so from the steps. Herin put his arrow against the man's chest and pushed him outside the door, keeping him in front of the group as a shield. "Ilsa, Shadow, cover Loki."

They quickly aimed their bows at Tybold, a movement that caused him to order his men farther back without being told. "Back, all of you! Move back to the other side of the square." He faced Herin, anger etched into his face. "I've moved them back. Now let my man go."

"Not just yet," Herin told him. "Come here."

Loki hesitated, and then moved forward until he was standing ten feet away. "Going to take me hostage now?"

Herin shook his head. "Tempting, but no. I just want you to get away and leave us alone. You can only lose, Loki. Why keep trying?"

"I'm not going to be made the laughingstock of Kress," Loki answered angrily. "I won't have people gossiping about how a Tybold was bested by some farm boy from the Grasslands."

"Stop being such a stupid damned idiot. I'm not just some farm boy, I'm a magician. The more you try to beat me, the more foolish you are going to look. So leave it, before you end up getting yourself and your men killed. I'm giving you a chance, Tybold. I suggest you take it. I've nothing against these men you employ, but if I ever see anyone wearing your colors coming near me again, I'll kill them on the spot."

That part of the speech was for the benefit of his prisoner. He knew the man would repeat it to his comrades the moment he returned to them. Hopefully, it would make Loki's hired men much less willing to look for them in the future.

"Someday I'll find a way," Loki vowed.

"But not today," Herin told him pointedly. "Get your men out of the square completely. Order them back to wherever their barracks are."

Loki complied with ill-concealed distaste. His men melted away down one of the streets radiating off the square. Herin waited until the last one had left before indicating that the remaining mercenary could leave as well.

"My thanks for not killing me, lord," the man said, with a grateful nod in Herin's direction.

Herin watched him go before turning his attention back to Loki. "You need to move on, Tybold. You have nothing I want or any reason to ever have contact with me other than this childish quest you've set for yourself. Give it up. I'm serious about what I said. If you send anyone after us, not only will they end up dead, but then I will come after you, if only to stop the game."

"Are you done?" Loki asked disdainfully. "I don't take orders from my inferiors."

"As if you could find any," Ilsa muttered, making Loki glare at her before turning his attention back to Herin.

"This isn't over, Freeholder. I'll find a way to make you pay. You, your whore, and your partner."

Herin put out a hand to hold Ilsa back. "Get out of here while you still can, Tybold. I tried to warn you. If you choose to ignore it, it will be on your head. Go."

"What an ass," Ilsa spat as he walked away.

"We'd better not linger," Shadow said. "You know he is going to be back just as soon as he gets his men reorganized."

"I doubt they'll be too enthusiastic about chasing us," Herin replied. "But we probably have to get out of the square. And we need to think about what to do next. Do we stay here in the city or get out? That's twice Loki has managed to find us. I don't want to keep running into him."

"How did he find us?" Ilsa wondered.

"Maybe he saw the spell we were using, maybe he just happened to see us passing on the street," Herin answered. "It doesn't really matter. What matters now is that we find someplace where we can plan what to do next."

"Where can we go for the night where he won't find us?" Ilsa asked. "He'll be sending people to every inn and boardinghouse in the city after this."

"We can't take cover in the tunnel," Shadow said. "Unless we're willing to freeze our asses off. We also need to find out what your spell did to the attack. Maybe the Dakarians will pull back so we can leave."

Herin considered the possibilities, and then his face cleared. "There is a place where he won't look. There." He pointed back to the church. "He saw us with packs so he'll surely figure we're on the move. That could buy us a day or two."

"Good idea," Shadow agreed. He turned up the stairs, using an opening spell on the locked doors.

"So now you're in charge?" Ilsa teased quietly, slipping her arm through his.

"What?" Herin was surprised. "Why do you say that?"

"Just saying, that's all," Ilsa told him. "Come on, let's get inside."

"If it wasn't you, then who was it?" Bjorkenberg demanded.

Master Renfeld faced him across the commander's desk. The attack on the city had been beaten off easily once the catapults had been destroyed. Bjorkenberg had seen the explosions himself, and made the natural assumption that magic had been the cause. He had called Renfeld to his office to thank him for his assistance, only to find that the Council's magicians had not yet been in place when the explosions occurred. They had fenced back and forth for a few minutes, the atmosphere growing more and more strained as it became obvious the Council Master either didn't know, or didn't want to tell, who was behind the spell.

From the moment he had heard of the attack, Renfeld had been certain that Herin Freeholder had been responsible. Once he had seen the destruction, his desire to get Herin back into the Council had doubled. Only a magician of the first rank could have possibly pulled off a spell that powerful. He doubted whether any of the magicians in the Council could even come close to it. Renfeld was determined to keep his knowledge from the army if he could. The last thing he needed now was for the army to try to assume jurisdiction over Freeholder.

Bjorkenberg was determined to find out who was responsible. He was growing more and more frustrated with the obvious reluctance of his visitor to divulge information about the activities of the Council. *Why won't this stubborn fool just tell me which one of his magicians beat off the attack? I want to thank that man.* The attack had withered after the destruction of the catapults and there had been no further attacks, although the Dakarian army was still encamped within sight of the city. He was grateful for the respite. It had given them time to repair most of the damage done to the city and to re-organize the defenses so they would be more prepared the next time. But he still wanted to know that he had this same power at his disposal in the event of another attack, and that meant finding out who was responsible.

"I'm waiting," he said, drumming his fingers on his desktop.

"I am not at liberty to give you that information at this time," Renfeld said, meeting him stare for stare.

"Why not? Whoever was behind that spell saved the city. If it wasn't for that, the Dakarians would have kept battering the walls until they made a breach somewhere. Or they would have destroyed so many buildings that we would have been too busy digging out survivors to be able to defend the city properly. It would have created a panic that would have made it impossible to keep them out. If they come again, I need to know that I can count on that same kind of help."

"You can," Renfeld replied, keeping his face impassive. "In the event of another attack, I promise that you can depend on such assistance as is necessary."

"Very reassuring," Bjorkenberg said sourly. "But you know what would be more reassuring? Having the person who did this sitting in that chair so I could talk to him and find out how to best use his talents. Now, which of your magicians was the one behind this, and why won't you let me speak with him?"

Renfeld's mind was scrambling to find an explanation that would satisfy the commander while keeping Herin's identity a secret. It certainly wouldn't do to allow the army to find out that the city's savior wasn't even a member of the Council. As long as the army believed the Council was behind the act, they would be treated with deference and respect. But, if they found out differently, the Council would lose face as well as political influence. He had to find Freeholder and bring him back into the fold as quickly as possible.

"Commander, you must know it is necessary at times to withhold information even from your most trusted officers. I am not trying to be difficult, but you have to understand that I cannot divulge Council business to outsiders without authorization from my Council Master in Kress."

"Then get it. I assume you have some way of getting messages back and forth faster than by carrier pigeon. Some sort of magical connection? Then use it and get his permission. I will expect to have your full cooperation in this. How long will it take?"

"These things are not as easy as outsiders assume," Renfeld answered, on familiar ground now. It was never difficult to keep the public in the dark as to how magic actually operated. "It can be done of course, but it takes time. I may have an answer in…say two day's time if Master Valgaard replies promptly."

"I will hold you to that," Bjorkenberg told him, terminating the interview. "I'll expect a name on my desk by noon the day after tomorrow. I'll let you get busy on your communication now."

Renfeld bowed and made his way out of the office slowly, his mind racing. He had bought himself forty-eight hours to find Herin Freeholder. At the end of that time he was going to have to either produce him or confess that he didn't know where he was, which would be to admit the Council had nothing to do with what happened. He had to get the resources of the Council to work on this problem.

Herin stretched to work the soreness from his muscles. They had spent the first night after the attack sleeping on the hard wooden benches of the church, the second night in an abandoned house on a nearly deserted side street. The house was a bit isolated, which served their purpose for the time being, but it lacked certain amenities, among them a proper bed. They had spent the night on the floor. Herin's muscles were protesting the lack of a mattress or something soft to lie on.

Ilsa came in shivering from the cold, shoving the badly hung door to get it to close against the wind. "Whew!" she exclaimed, crossing quickly to the fire to get some warmth back into her body. "It's cold enough out there to freeze your fingers off. Next time let's find a house with an indoor privy. Where's Shadow?"

"You know him, he's never happy until he sniffs around to see if there is any danger," Herin replied, steeling himself for his own trip outside.

By the time Herin returned, Ilsa had started a pot of porridge, their normal morning meal the last few days. It wasn't much, but it did warm a body, an important thing in weather this frigid. Herin glanced around at their refuge with a critical eye, and realized they couldn't spend another night there. Gaping holes in the wall allowed cold drafts of air inside, making the interior of the dwelling barely warmer than outside. The roof had shingles missing as well.

Fortunately, the previous night had been clear, but it appeared that another snowfall would shortly be on its way. They had to find snugger quarters before that evening. Herin considered the problem.

Maybe we're being foolish. Loki can't really do anything to hurt us. Why spend another night out in the cold?

Shadow came in slapping his arms against his body to get some circulation back, his face red from the wind chill. "Find anything?" Herin asked.

"There haven't been any more attacks anywhere," Shadow told him. "I covered the entire city and there wasn't any word anywhere of another fight."

"So they're gone?"

Shadow shook his head. "No, that's the strange thing; they're still there. I heard a couple of soldiers talking about it in one of the taverns. But they're just sitting out there not doing anything."

"That seems silly," Ilsa said as she began doling out porridge in wooden bowls. "Why just sit there if you aren't going to attack?"

"Could be they're waiting for reinforcements," Herin guessed, taking his bowl and spooning the hot cereal into his mouth. "Maybe more magicians are on the way, maybe more soldiers, maybe both."

"Could be," Shadow agreed. "It might be that they just don't want to seem like they were beaten off so easily so they're going to force the city to withstand a siege, even if there's little chance of getting inside. But we've a grace period for however long it lasts."

"What does that mean to us?" Ilsa asked, as she sat and began eating. "I don't fancy the idea of spending another night here."

"I agree," Herin said. "Let's move to an inn. With a little caution, we should be able to find rooms that are safe."

"That's fine for the short-term," Ilsa said. "What about long-term? Are we going to stay here in the city?"

"It's going to be hard to leave with all those Dakarians out there," Shadow pointed out.

"Are you still planning on going to Nelfheim?" Herin asked.

"It's why I left Kress," Shadow confirmed. "I still need to get a closer look at that armada out there."

Herin ate in silence for a few minutes. It was the answer he had expected, so it didn't come as much of a surprise. *What about Ilsa and me? There isn't anything for either of us here in the city, except more trouble from that ass Tybold. Even if the Dakarians were to leave right this minute, we'd still have to look over our shoulders all of the time to see if Loki was on our trail.*

"What's the weather like in Nelfheim this time of year?" he asked.

"Cold, but not as cold as this," Shadow answered. "There's a warm current that passes just a few miles offshore. Keeps the harbor clear of ice and the city warmer than other places in this season. Rarely snows, and even freezes are few and far between. Must be…oh, ten or fifteen degrees warmer on average than here. Why?"

"Just a thought," Herin said as he stared into the fire. "But it might be worth a gamble leaving here if things look like they're taking a turn for the worse. We might have to travel through some bad weather, but the closer we get to Nelfheim the better it should be. Right?"

Shadow rubbed his beard thoughtfully. "I suppose there's something to that," he said judiciously. "But that zone only extends maybe fifty miles from the city. There's a range of hills, almost small mountains, about fifty or sixty miles from Nelfheim. On the far side the weather will improve, but this side of the hills is still pretty cold. And climbing them in the winter is going to expose anyone doing so to weather that is colder still."

"But it's possible," Herin pressed.

"Yes, it's possible if you are desperate enough," Shadow answered.

"Why would you want to do that in this weather?" Ilsa asked. "Are you seriously suggesting we leave Khartul in the winter, with all those soldiers camped right outside the walls?"

"I'm not saying it's the best option," Herin protested. "But we might have to try that if Loki becomes a nuisance. If the

Dakarians were to withdraw, it would make it more feasible. The winter will be over in two months or so. Leaving here in two weeks wouldn't be that much of a gamble. By the time we hit those hills spring would almost be here."

"Maybe, maybe not," Shadow said. "Spring might just be a wet season in the Lowlands, but in the higher elevations winter hangs on for weeks, sometimes months, longer. We might get lucky and get weather warm enough to make travel feasible, but we might just as easily get up into those hills and be stranded by sudden blizzards."

"It was just a thought," Herin said as he scraped the remains of his porridge off the sides of his bowl and gulped it down. "But right now, I want to find somewhere better to sleep tonight. Let's split up and check out some places. Meet back here at midday?"

Shadow and Ilsa nodded their agreement. They quickly finished their meager breakfast and wiped the bowls clean. "Watch your back," Shadow said as they wrapped scarves around their faces and prepared to venture into the cold. "Loki is still sniffing around out there somewhere."

"You watch yours," Herin replied as he bundled up and pushed the door open. "Meet you back here in a few hours."

Chapter Twelve

Loki leaned back in his chair with a satisfied smile, hands locked comfortably behind his head. His visitor peered inside the leather bag Loki had placed on the desk, his eyes reflecting the sheen of gold from the coins which filled the pouch to the top. Retying the bag, he placed it inside his tunic.

"It's all there?" he asked.

"Two hundred gold pieces, just like we agreed," Loki replied, enjoying a feeling of triumph as he reeled in his informer. "And another two hundred when you finish the job. Quickly, Master Bjarni, quickly. And quietly if you please. There can be no obvious connection between us. Do you understand?"

Bjarni waved off the question. "I will send word as soon as I hear anything."

"Don't delay," Loki warned the man. "It's important that my men and I get to wherever they need to be before the Council can act."

"I know," Bjarni told him. "They're already out looking for him. Don't worry. You'll know within fifteen minutes of me hearing anything."

"Good. Get back there and keep your ears open." Bjarni bowed and closed the door softly behind him, leaving Loki alone to gloat over his coup. He had finally realized his mistake when dealing with Freeholder, so he had simply applied one of his father's old sayings to the situation at hand: "When money talks, no one is deaf." It had been a relatively simple matter to find someone inside the Council of Magicians who could use four hundred gold pieces.

It was worth it to rid himself of Freeholder once and for all. He had plenty of money, so why not let the Council do his dirty work for him? A win-win situation and the real beauty of it was that he would not have to dirty his hands in the slightest way. Bjarni would find out where Freeholder was because the Council was already looking for him. Once the farmboy was located, Loki would put the rest of his plans into operation.

"You're as good as dead, Freeholder," Loki said gleefully, swinging around in his chair. "You've been a pain in the ass, but you're going to be nothing more than a bad memory before the week is out."

At that moment, Herin was checking out boarding houses and inns on the western side of the city. Only a few sections had been hit here; the rest still stood intact. He began the process of finding out what the going rates were for rooms.

"Not much call for them right now," one innkeeper declared in a voice that was several levels past despondent. "Let you have the best rooms in the house for a copper a week."

That price was only a fraction of what rooms had fetched just a few days before. "Why so cheap?" Herin asked suspiciously. "What's wrong with the room?"

"There's nothing wrong with the room. It's just that there isn't anyone to rent it," the man replied testily. "Too many men either got killed in one of the attacks or are serving with this force or that force, so they stay in the barracks. There's no market. Now, do you want the rooms or not?"

Herin considered his options. He really should consult the others, but this was just too good a deal to let pass. The main objective was to get off the streets, and these rooms were more than reasonable. Impulsively, he agreed. "I'll take two rooms for two weeks. The two at the very back of the inn."

He pushed across two copper coins and the man handed over two huge iron keys, the largest Herin had ever seen. Noticing Herin's expression, the man said defensively, "Don't look so surprised. We have the most up to date security system in Khartul.

You won't have to worry about your valuables while you're here, no sir."

Herin made no comment and quickly climbed the stairs to inspect what he had just rented. He found two fairly spacious rooms, complete with simple furniture and colorful curtains covering the windows. Herin crossed to one and carefully scanned the alley outside. The inn itself was on a side street just off one of the major thoroughfares connecting the banking houses with the merchant Council Halls. The back rooms would be secluded, but close enough to the heart of Khartul that they could keep an eye on things. The only drawback as far as he could see was that it was only a few hundred yards from the Tybold compound. He justified that by convincing himself that Loki wouldn't think of looking so close to home for them. *He'll never think of looking for us right under his nose, not in a million years.*

As Herin left to find the others, he failed to notice a man sitting in the shadows near the door. The stranger waited for Herin to get well down the street before sliding out of his booth and exiting the building. He broke into a trot once outside, heading straight for the Magicians Hall.

Ilsa waited impatiently for the others, trying to keep warm by walking quickly up and down the sidewalk. She glanced at the sky, seeing the familiar gray cover that made her feel like she was trapped in a world that never knew sunlight. It had been a week or more since the last clear day, and although nothing more than a few scattered flurries had hit the ground, the weather was oppressive all the same, dampening her spirits, and making her feel depressed. Spring couldn't come quickly enough.

Shadow turned the corner and joined her, blowing on his hands to keep them warm. "Herin?"

"I haven't seen him yet," Ilsa told him. "Did you find anything?"

"Dozens of places," Shadow answered. "It seems we can have our pick. Business is down everywhere, and the innkeepers are lowering prices to try to entice people back. I guess they think if someone is staying there they might spend additional money on food and drink."

"Where in the hell is he?" she wondered aloud. "Do you suppose he got into any trouble?"

"I'm sure he just got side-tracked somewhere," Shadow assured her. "See, there he is now." Herin had just entered the far end of the street and hurried over to them.

"Sorry I'm running late," he apologized. "I was checking out some really good rooms and lost track of time."

"You said midday and that was more than an hour ago," Ilsa said sharply.

"I couldn't help it," Herin told them. "I found rooms with such a good rate that I went ahead and rented them already. They're perfect, bigger than anything we've stayed in so far and only a couple of coppers." He pulled one of the keys from his pocket and tossed it to Ilsa. "We can go there now."

Ilsa turned the massive key back and forth in her hand. "Am I supposed to use this on the door or as a weapon? And what happened to all of us making decisions together?"

"I just thought it was too good a deal to pass up," Herin replied defensively. "I didn't think you would mind."

"Where is this perfect place?" Shadow put in.

"I don't know why you sound so angry," Herin answered. "It's located on Peddler's Alley."

"Peddler's Alley?" Shadow repeated. "Not five hundred yards from the Tybold compound? Have you taken leave of your senses? Not only is Tybold nearby, but so is the Legion Headquarters as well as the Council of Magicians. Why not just walk up and turn ourselves in?"

"Don't you see, that's the beauty of it," Herin explained. "Loki will never look for us that close to where he is. The Council will be searching near where the attack came from. We don't know that the army is interested in us at all. They would never think we'd live right under their noses. And it will let us keep an eye on them as well, won't it?"

"It makes a kind of weird sense," Ilsa said, not really caring about where they went as long as it was warm.

Shadow was unconvinced. "It's dangerous, Herin, and something we all should have talked about before making any decisions. For one person, your argument might make sense, but for three people it increases the odds that one of us will be spotted. Loki has seen all three of us together, so none of us is safe."

"You're getting soft in your old age," Herin joked. "Believe me, I thought about all of that before making the rental. Anywhere in the city could be dangerous now. We know for a fact we've got Loki and the Council both looking for us. Come on Shadow, we know enough magic between the three of us to stay safe there until we can leave the city."

"It's against my better judgment," Shadow said sourly. "I say we look elsewhere. We've been successful so far staying in the more crowded sections, haven't we?"

"I don't care where we go as long as we go," Ilsa piped in. "Let's just get out of the cold and get something hot to eat. I vote we go to these rooms."

Shadow seemed on the verge of saying something, but realized he would only be prolonging an argument that was already decided. Acquiescing as gracefully as possible, he shrugged his shoulders to show he was not going to argue any longer. "Just stay alert you two. I'm hungry and cold as well, but I'd rather be hungry and cold than dead."

"It will be fine," Herin promised, turning and heading down the street the way he had come. "You'll see."

A few hours later even Shadow was willing to concede that it might be an acceptable choice. The rooms were everything Herin had promised, and a filling meal had lifted their spirits as it filled their bellies. Now, seated before a small fire, they were able to relax for the first time in days. Shadow checked the windows before taking a seat, gratified to find that the alley behind the inn was not well traveled, making it easier to spot any possible danger. He was still a bit uneasy, but Herin might have been right. The rooms were well-proportioned and the food outstanding. They could have done worse.

"That's the first time I've felt satisfied in ages," Ilsa smiled, sinking back in a wooden chair near the fire. She sighed contentedly.

"I told you," Herin said, patting his stomach placidly. He was now inclined to close his eyes and sleep like a hibernating bear, lulled by the warmth of the room combined with a full stomach.

"We should talk about what's going to happen over the next few weeks," Shadow reminded them.

"What is going to happen?" Herin asked, one eye closed as he dozed off.

"Pay attention!" Shadow snapped, kicking him sharply to jolt him from his semi-slumber. "Just because we're in a nice room and full of food doesn't mean there aren't people out there who would like to see us all dead. Don't ever forget that. The sooner we can get out of the city, the better."

"Don't the Dakarians have something to say about that?" Herin retorted, stung by the tone of Shadow's voice. "We can't go anywhere with them still camped outside the walls."

"They'll be gone soon," Shadow predicted.

"Based on what?" Herin wanted to know. "What makes you think they'll suddenly disappear?"

"Do they have a choice?" Shadow asked. "They were obviously counting on their magic to enable them to get inside the city. That option no longer exists so it means they'll have to take on the city the normal way, besieging it to starve out the inhabitants. That won't work. That meal we just ate confirms that food is not going to be a problem here. If supplies were short, we would never have eaten something that filling. When spring arrives, they know a relief force will be coming with it. They can't get in, so either they leave or they'll be caught between the forces inside and the ones coming from Kress."

"If there are actually forces coming from the capital," Ilsa reminded them. "We don't really know what's going on out there, do we?"

"No, we don't, but there will be reinforcements sent as soon as word gets to the capital, and I'm certain the commander here has already sent that message," Shadow insisted. "Count on it, the Dakarians will be gone soon, one way or the other."

"That's still just a guess on your part," Herin argued. "They might have reinforcements of their own on the way. Did you consider that? Any ideas on how we might find out for certain?"

Shadow nodded. "One. Ilsa could try a Viewing."

"I'm willing to try, but I can never hold the vision long enough to make any sense of it. Maybe I don't have enough power yet."

"Power? Seems to me you have access to all the power you'd ever want." Shadow inclined his head in Herin's direction.

Ilsa's face showed her surprise. *Why not? It might work with Herin helping.* "It's worth a try. Will you help?"

Herin nodded. "Tell me what to do."

Ilsa chewed on her lower lip as she considered how best to set it up. "A sacred space would be helpful."

Shadow interrupted. "You two can channel a lot of power. You've already shown that much. Why not try using it to first construct a safe zone for the spell, and then see what you can do with the Viewing?"

Ilsa cracked her fingers to loosen them up. She moved to a space near the fire, pushing furniture back to create room for them to work. Three rugs piled one atop the other provided them with a soft place to kneel. "Take my hand," she ordered. Herin sank down beside her, willing to add his energies to whatever spell she tried.

Ilsa focused on a mental picture of a space around the fireplace, protected by magic so that no outside influences could invade while they were working. She began whispering the same spells that they had used to ward their campsites, figuring that what had worked outside might serve a similar purpose inside, especially when Herin's assistance would lend more power to the magic. There was a pause after the last syllable had been uttered before she felt the welcome whoosh of magic moving through her body and out into the surrounding room.

Shadow could see the air shimmering between the pair, and reached out tentatively to see what he could feel. He lacked Herin's ability to smell magic of course, but he could feel a tingle on his skin as it approached the border of the spell, evidence enough that they were in some sort of magical field.

"It's up," he reported. "Or at least something's in place. Try looking into the fire."

Ilsa settled herself, clearing her mind of everything but the flames. She was dimly aware of Herin's touch, but her focus was on the fire itself. She allowed her consciousness to slip deeper and deeper into the blaze, letting the bright oranges and reds become her whole world. After a few minutes, she realized physical sensations were leaving her, as her mind floated free of the world of the normal senses, connected by the thinnest of invisible threads to her body. It was an unsettling sensation. Getting herself under control, she concentrated on letting the flames serve as a backdrop for whatever information she could conjure up to help them.

Ilsa slowed her breathing, letting all conscious thoughts fall away like droplets sizzling on a hot griddle, evaporating away the instant they appeared. She felt a peaceful lassitude creep over her, and held onto the feeling as she began working her way toward a vision. Where to start? Ilsa allowed her mind to roam, trusting that the magic would show her whatever was important.

With a suddenness that surprised her, the fire seemed to drop away and fade in intensity, to be replaced by a growing circle of spectral light superimposed on top of it. She took a few deep breaths to steady herself, allowing her mind to relax even more, and the vision immediately firmed up so that she could see that it was a forest clearing, the ground covered in snow.

Huts were scattered about the edges of the clearing, grayish smoke curling lazily from the stone chimneys. It was a camp of some sort, and her consciousness was pulled towards one cabin in particular. Without effort, her perception shifted inside, the point of view somewhere near the ceiling, as if she were hovering over the room itself.

The center of the cabin was taken up by a large wooden table, its surface now covered with a map. Hawk and half a dozen other outlaws were bent over the map, discussing various features in low tones. Ilsa saw that it contained a series of notations in red ink, and appeared to show the area between the forest and Kress itself.

"Damned Imps," one of the men muttered. "May they rot in hell."

"Concentrate," Hawk growled. "If we didn't already feel that way we wouldn't be doing this, would we?" He looked around the table. "No one's seen Wulfsan? He should have been back hours ago."

As he finished speaking, the door flew open to admit Wulfsan, his face caked with frozen snow, his eyelashes and beard frosted like some sort of cake. He went directly to the fire, his face so close to it that Ilsa thought for a moment he was going to thrust his head directly into the flames. He blew out his breath before turning back to the others, his beard dripping water and his face flushed from the heat.

"Sorry, lads, but I've been thinking of little else but that for the past five miles." He looked directly at Hawk. "Talked to the council at Pembertown. They're in. It didn't hurt that the Imps came through not two days ago and cleaned out almost all of their excess grain. That took all the fence sitters off the fence right enough."

Hawk leaned down to the map and made a notation. "That's six towns will support us," he said. "We need more."

"It's a start," one of the men said. "Be spring soon and we can begin."

Hawk nodded. "That we can."

Ilsa tried to hold onto the vision, but it began to shimmer in and out of focus like a reflection in a pool disturbed by ripples. She fought to keep the vision intact, but it finally slipped away from her, leaving her to slowly become aware of her surroundings. It had been a good first effort, she thought. She had been able to create and hold a vision for several minutes, long enough to actually get real information from it. Apparently, the outlaws were planning some sort of attack on Imperial forces in the spring, as unlikely as that sounded. She needed to tell Herin and Shadow. Would this affect their plans in any way?

She took her hand from Herin, moving her shoulders to loosen them after staying still for the vision, de-activating the wards without thinking. "Interesting events going on out there," she began.

"We know," Shadow told her. "We saw it in the vision. The outlaws are up to something."

"You saw it?" Ilsa was surprised.

"Took up almost the whole wall," Herin confirmed. "It was really impressive. I almost thought I was in the cabin with them. Why didn't you tell us you could do that?"

"Mostly because I didn't know I could," Ilsa answered.

"As interesting as that was, it didn't really help us much," Shadow reminded them. "Any chance of finding something more pertinent to us right now?"

Ilsa nodded. "Let me just rest for a few minutes, and then I will try again."

Herin was lost in thought. It had sounded very much like the outlaws were planning something other than robbery. "That didn't interest you?" he asked Shadow.

"Why should it?"

"I think they were talking about some sort of revolt, not planning to hold up caravans come spring. Didn't you?"

"They were more than likely just lining up places that would shelter them if they needed it when the authorities made the forest too dangerous. The Imps periodically go through and clean it out once the travel season is on."

"I'd like to see more," Herin argued. "I think it was more than that."

"Even if it was, what difference does that make to us?" Shadow asked. "They're hundreds of miles away, and we've more pressing things to concern us right here."

"Don't you want to know what the army and Loki are up to?" Ilsa added. "Or the Council? We might need to know what the Dakarians are doing too, don't you think?"

Herin waved his hands in defeat. "I know, I know," he said. "But something is telling me that what we saw could be important. Why else would you have been drawn to it?"

"Maybe we can come back to it later," Shadow said. "Right now, I'm more interested in what is going on here in the city."

Ilsa rested a few more minutes before she indicated she was ready for another session. She went through the same steps as before, but this time even with Herin's assistance, it was difficult to get any vision that lasted for more than a few seconds. They got a brief glimpse of Loki in conference with what looked like a magician, although the scene disappeared before they could tell who it was. A slightly longer vision showed them Bjorkenberg in conference with his officers, discussing the possibility of breaking the siege with an attack of their own on a weak spot they had located in the Dakarian encirclement. Ilsa managed to keep that one open long enough for them to at least see and hear that a strike was going to take place.

"That's all I can do," Ilsa gasped as the scene faded. She would have slumped to the floor if Herin hadn't caught her by the arms and eased her against the wall. Sweat matted her hair to her face. Her breath came in ragged sighs as she struggled to regain her strength. "I can't hold it any longer than that."

"That was still enough," Shadow said encouragingly. "We know the army thinks the siege is losing ground and are planning a breakout. They wouldn't do that unless they had very good reason to believe it would be successful."

"What's changed?" Herin wondered.

"Maybe nothing really," Shadow replied. "We knew all along that the Dakarians didn't really have enough men to batter their way inside. Apparently, they were planning on having an edge by using magic. You and Ilsa took care of that."

"What does it mean for us?" Ilsa wanted to know. She sipped greedily at a mug of water Herin had poured for her, wiping sweat from her forehead with her sleeve.

"We didn't hear when this might take place," Shadow said as he paced the room. "If we want to leave, this attack might provide us with cover. We could get outside the walls right before the attack, wait to see if the confusion creates a hole in the line, and then we could slip through. Reinforcements will be here from Kress quicker than from Dakar."

"Maybe, maybe not," Herin mused.

"What do you mean?" Shadow asked.

"What if what we heard in the first vision really was the beginning of some sort of uprising? What if there was enough of a resistance to delay or even turn back any reinforcements sent here? What if Kress is too busy with its own problems to worry about Khartul's?"

"That's a lot of 'what ifs'," Ilsa said with a laugh.

"Yes, it certainly is," Shadow said sourly. "That's a pretty flimsy set of ideas, Herin. Certainly not enough to base our future on. They're just a bunch of outlaws. They weren't organized well enough to attempt any sort of resistance movement. That takes years and years of careful coordination to pull off."

"In your opinion," Herin argued. "Maybe they don't know any better."

"I've done that sort of thing before. It isn't easy, and those people back in the forest have no training in how to make it work. It just isn't possible for them to have put something together so quickly. I know I planted the idea in Hawk's head before we left, but nothing of substance could have happened so fast. Revolutions take patience and planning."

"Maybe he isn't as patient as you," Herin shot back, unwilling to be talked out of it just because Shadow said it was so.

"What do you want to do, stay here because the empire is about to fall?"

"I'm just pointing out that it should be a factor we consider in making our plans. That's all."

"I still say it isn't important." Shadow's face was hard.

"You say?" Ilsa caught the edgy note of anger in Herin's voice and tried to head off what she knew was coming.

"Come on you two, let's calm down," she said.

"I am calm," Herin said sharply. "But I'm not a child who has to listen to his elders because they know everything. Tell me, Shadow, why is your opinion any more valuable than mine? Or Ilsa's?"

"I'm not saying mine is more important, but you're chasing after something for which you have no proof. And now is the time where we need to make some plan to take advantage of a situation here. Here in Khartul, not hundreds of miles away in god knows what section of that forest with a bunch of men with prices on their heads. How many times have we gone over the concept of thinking things through?"

"Fine, let's hear your plan then," Herin said, holding on to his temper with difficulty. "I'm sure it will be thought through."

"The first thing we need is more information. Ilsa can't hold those visions for more than a few minutes, so it will be impossible to pick the exact moment for her to listen in on a council session. We'll have to do this the hard way. Hit the streets to see what rumors are floating about. Something like this can't stay secret. There will be signs that something is about to take place. We keep our ears open and try to put together pieces of information until we have a clearer picture."

"What about Loki?" Herin said. "If we're out wandering around the streets, won't it increase our chances of being discovered?"

Shadow refused to be drawn into another side argument. "As you pointed out yourself, we need to stay alert. We have no choice. If there is going to be an attack, it will be happening soon or they wouldn't be discussing it. We won't have to worry about it for long. But we do need the information."

Ilsa stared at Herin, watching his expression. It was clear that he was still angry. She wondered if he now knew what she had already seen. *Herin is no longer willing to act like an apprentice. I wonder if Shadow knows that? What will this mean for us? What about the relationship I have with Herin? Will this affect it? Will it make it harder to keep everyone together?* The last question troubled her. Ilsa had no more experience in a long-term relationship than Herin did. She was treading unfamiliar ground, and it made her uneasy.

"Let's get it over with then," Herin said flatly. "I'll take the section near the barracks. Ilsa, why don't you take near the Council? They don't know you there so that should be less dangerous for you. Shadow can handle the business section. Especially Tybold's."

"Fine," Shadow agreed, pulling on his cloak. "Let's meet back here at dinner time and we can compare notes." Without another word, he left the room and they heard his boots on the stairs leading to the common room.

"Be careful, Ilsa" Herin said, pulling on his own cloak. Ilsa tugged at his arm, forcing him to look her in the eye.

"Don't do something stupid just because you are angry," she warned. "Shadow is just used to giving orders, that's all."

"Fuck that," Herin spat. "He's going to have to get used to listening to what we want."

We, is it? It's we now? Then why haven't you said anything to me, Herin Freeholder? "Give it time. If you want this to work that is."

"What do you mean?" Herin frowned.

Ilsa said, "I just think that maybe you are feeling like you want to be on your own, making your own decisions. You could do that now if that's what you really want. Shadow hasn't taught you anything new in months, so you don't need him for that any more. Maybe you should be thinking about what you do need him for, and whether or not you want to stay with him."

"What about you?" Herin demanded. "What are you going to do?"

"If you are asking something…then ask. I'll give you a straight answer to a straight question. But you have to ask the question."

Herin opened his mouth to say something, and then just as quickly shut it again. "We'll talk later tonight when we get back. I need to think some things over."

Ilsa stepped back and nodded, watching as he left the room. *Where does that leave us, Herin? Do you want me with you or not? I can't tell what you are thinking anymore. You used to be so easy to read, but now it's like you are a stranger. I thought I meant something more to you than just a quick fuck or two, but now you are closed off and impossible to decipher. What happened to us?* They had all changed so much since that day back in Kress, so slowly as to be almost undetectable until one stepped back and remembered how it had once been. She grabbed her own cloak and left the room, taking the time to place a protection spell on it to prevent anyone from entering before they returned.

Chapter Thirteen

"You're absolutely sure?" Renfeld carefully scanned the man's face for any signs that he might be lying. If the information was accurate, it might mean he could finally return to Kress. *Let it be true, by all the gods,* he thought.

"I am sure, Master. I worked in the library back at the Institute before they sent me out here. Freeholder came in there nearly every day for tutoring. It was him, I'm sure of that."

"You've been very useful," Renfeld assured the man. "I will not forget."

The informant bowed and scuttled off. Bjarni saw the man leave the office and intercepted him in a deserted hallway. One gold piece was enough to buy him the information he needed, and a message was quickly dispatched to Loki Tybold telling him where his adversaries could be found. Bjarni was a bit shocked at the audacity of Freeholder going to ground so close to the Tybold complex. But it was gutsy, he had to admit.

Renfeld lost little time in gathering his men. In less than an hour, they were stationed outside the inn. Each magician would work to construct an energy web to trap Herin inside once he returned. The field would only last for a few hours, but he hoped that would be of sufficient duration to do what was needed. Renfeld was optimistic that he would be able to convince Herin to go back to Kress willingly and assume his membership in the Council.

Renfeld quickly walked around the building to confirm that everyone was in place. It was only a matter of time now.

Loki smiled, a smug look of satisfaction crossing his face as he tossed the message from Bjarni into the fireplace, watching as the flames turned the parchment to ash. So, Herin was staying nearby, practically in the next building. "Pretty damned clever, Freeholder," he said to the fire. "I never would have looked there. But not nearly clever enough. I've got you now."

Loki wanted more than a mere death. He intended to make Herin pay for the humiliations he had endured. Loki looked to the flames as if they held answers for him, thinking over his plan. *What is Freeholder's weak point? The girl...she is the bait I need. He dotes on that whore, bringing her all the way out here from the capital. We just have to be careful capturing her. She's the way to get to him.*

"What now, boss?" asked one of his bodyguards.

"We will use Freeholder's bitch to draw him into an ambush. We'll take her off the street. He'll soon figure out that something happened to her. Hopefully, he'll come rushing after her without thinking and I'll have him at last. I want nothing more than to watch his face as I sink my blade into his guts. That bastard has humiliated me for the last time."

The man looked a bit uneasy. "But she's a magician, isn't she? Isn't that dangerous?"

"Not if we take the proper precautions," Loki assured him. "We just have to get her arms secure and her mouth gagged. Don't worry. This is foolproof. Nothing can go wrong. This time I have Freeholder, once and for all."

Ilsa stood in the shadow of a storefront, blowing on her hands in a vain effort to get her circulation working. She had been watching the entrance of the Council House for more than an hour, and only four men had left in all that time. No one else had entered or left since, turning her assignment into a study in boredom. *Ten more minutes*, she promised herself, *then the hell with this.*

The ten minutes passed as slowly as the previous ninety had done. She pushed herself away from the wall, intending to head back to the inn. The wait had been tedious, but that wasn't what had her upset. The real problem had been that it had given her far too much time to think and the direction of her thoughts had not been pleasant.

Ilsa had managed to convince herself that Herin might decide to go back to Kress without her. He certainly wasn't the same youngster she had first met so many months before. Ilsa could see that Herin would have a tremendous amount of leverage if he decided on that course of action. He was no longer an unknown Provincial hoping to learn some magic. Instead, he would be one of the more powerful members in the Council. Which, after all, was what he had wanted in the first place. It was the reason he had come to Kress all those months ago.

Ilsa tried to slow her thoughts down and think without so much emotion, but it proved impossible. *What do I do if Herin asks me to go with him to Kress? Do I want to stay with him? What is there for me back there in the capital?* She didn't want to lose what she had, but she could not see a clear future either.

He is still attracted to me. I think he is still attracted to me. But why did he hesitate when I asked him about the future? I wish I knew what he was thinking. Stop being so foolish. Of course he wants to be with you.

Lost in thought, she turned a corner and was violently pulled into an alley by two men. Waiting in the alley were four more. Ilsa felt her arms being cruelly yanked behind her back, her wrists secured with rope. The suddenness of the assault made it impossible for her to effectively resist, though she thrashed about wildly. A gag was tied over her mouth as one of the men yanked her head back by pulling on her hair.

"No tricks," he snarled in her ear. "We know all about your power. You're ours now." He cuffed her on the cheek, the sting of it making her eyes water. "Bag," he ordered and a sack was pulled over her head, cutting off the light and rendering her helpless.

She continued struggling to free herself, lashing out with her feet, making solid contact with one of her kidnappers. He cursed and then punched her hard in the pit of the stomach. Unprepared for the blow, Ilsa gagged, sinking to her knees as she fought to get air into her lungs. With her mouth covered, it was hard to breathe, making it difficult for her to remain conscious.

"Stop it," the one in charge growled. "Time enough for that later. Get her into the cart."

She was lifted into a vehicle, while a tarp of some sort was thrown over her. Two of the men got into the cart with her, one sitting on her legs while the other pricked her ribs with a sharp knife.

"No trouble now," he warned, leaning down to whisper in her ear. "Do what you're told and you might just live through the night."

Ilsa tried to think calmly, but it was difficult to master her fear. The suddenness of the attack made the whole thing seem as if she was in a waking nightmare. She struggled to get her thoughts under control. *It's Loki, of course. The men have to be Loki's. But how did he know where to find me? It's obvious that they were waiting for me. What about Herin and Shadow? Would they be waiting for them as well? How do I warn them?*

She tried desperately to figure out Loki's intentions. *The fucking bastard is going to kill me, I just know it. I have to stay calm. Herin will find me. Herin will find me if I can make even the smallest spell to leave a clue.* He might be able to trace her without one, but it would be far more difficult and time consuming, and time was something she might not have. If she could find a way to do some magic it might help lead him to her. It was a long shot, she knew, but the only card she could play in her present circumstances.

Using her tongue, she pushed the gag as far out of her mouth as she could, gaining a small breathing space. It loosened slightly, allowing her lips a bit of movement. Hopefully, it would prove enough.

"Fylgja minn ljos," she whispered softly so as not to alert her captors. *"Fylgja minn hugr. Hitta ykkar sal."*

Nothing happened. The familiar feeling of energy flowing through her did not occur. Ilsa knew with a sinking feeling that her magic would be of no use to her unless she could get her hands free as well. Shadow had constantly been pushing her to learn how to activate spells with less obvious passes, and it was a lesson she now heartily wished she had learned. With magic denied her, she was going to have to depend on her courage and toughness to survive.

The cart jolted to a stop, causing her to cry out as the motion threw her painfully onto her wrists. The gag effectively muffled her cries. Her captors roughly dragged her to her feet, dropping her from the cart into the waiting arms of a man who hustled her down a set of stone steps, his hand squeezing her arm to keep her upright. She heard him hammer on a thick wooden door, and there was the sound of rusting hinges creaking open. Her guard shoved her roughly down the steps, causing Ilsa to stumble into the cold, musty dampness of a warehouse. The moldy smell told her that the place was not used very often. She stood still, senses alert to pick up whatever clues might be available as to her whereabouts.

It sounded like five or six people were with her, judging from the shuffling of feet and whispered conversations. Suddenly, the bag covering her head was jerked off, making her squint as her eyes were exposed to the brightly lit room. Ilsa blinked rapidly to try to clear her vision. When her eyes had adjusted, she saw that she had guessed correctly. Around her were crates piled higher than a man's head, but with a thick coating of dust on every surface, a sure indication that they had been stored there undisturbed for quite some time. Loki Tybold was standing right in front of her, a cruel smile playing across his face.

The room was lit by torches set in iron brackets. There were no windows, and the walls themselves were constructed of stone, giving the impression of great thickness. *A Tybold warehouse,* she thought. *I'll get no help here. Where in the hell are we?*

"Tie her," Loki ordered, and two of his men undid the binding on her wrists before dragging her to two wooden beams that served as supports to the cellar. They pulled her arms up over her head and shackled her to iron rings set in the poles. Ilsa tugged futilely, knowing it was useless, but somehow driven to make the effort. She glared at Loki, causing him to smile complacently back at her.

If I can get my hands free for a second, you're a dead man.

"Save your strength," he advised, stepping to her and running a finger softly along one cheek. "You don't want to use it up needlessly. Believe me, you will find other uses for it soon enough." Without warning, he struck her a stinging slap across her cheek, snapping her head against the pole and making stars explode behind her eyes.

Loki gave her no time to recover, launching a series of blows that flung her head from side to side, leaving her cheeks red and burning with pain. After a dozen slaps he stopped, stepping back as if admiring his work. Ilsa's face was already beginning to puff up, her cheeks flaming and bruised. Over her gag her dark eyes were full of hatred, which did not go unnoticed by Loki.

"I'm sure you're asking yourself what I hope to accomplish by this," Loki said with a laugh. "No doubt you're thinking that if you could get free you'd turn me into an insect or something like that. You probably could. We know you can do magic. I don't know how you can do it, being a woman, but it's apparent that you are some sort of freak who can use that power. But we're not going to allow you to free your hands or to speak, so it won't matter. It's tempting to remove the gag so I can hear you scream, but it's far too dangerous."

He walked back and forth as he talked, his men lounging against crates, but with predatory looks on their faces that made her very uncomfortable. Whatever Loki had in mind, she steeled herself to endure it, trying desperately to believe that Herin would find her in time to make this monster pay. She had to hang on until he found her.

"You are unimportant," Loki continued, his hands clasped behind his back, and his head tilted upwards as if he were a professor lecturing to a class of students. "Unimportant except for one thing. You have a close connection to Herin Freeholder, and that makes you a key part of what I have planned. You are going to be the bait that traps that upstart once and for all. I could ransom you, I suppose. I'm sure Freeholder would find a way to come up with whatever payment I ask, but I don't need money. I've got plenty of that already. I just want your lover dead and you are going to help me do that."

Ilsa shook her head, causing Loki to laugh. "You have no choice, slut. Your fate was decided the day you let that farmboy into your bed. You may survive this, but he won't. But you won't have to worry about that for a long, long time. For now, he probably doesn't even know you are missing. We have to find some way to pass the time while we wait. What to do? Gentlemen, perhaps you have some ideas?"

He perched on the edge of a packing crate, taking an apple from inside his tunic and polishing it on his sleeve. His men eagerly unbuckled their sword belts, piling their weapons neatly on the floor before slowly advancing towards her. There were four of them, their eyes lit by lust, their faces showing their bestial natures perfectly. They surrounded her, hands on her body, their breath foul and putrid as they whispered in her ear what they intended for her. Loki bit into his apple, wiping the excess juice from his face with one hand, grinning at her efforts to get away.

"Don't damage her too much," he warned his men. "We'll need her alive."

One of the men reached into the neckline of her blouse, ripping it down and off in one motion, baring her breasts. The men pawed at her, pinching and groping as they abused her. Ilsa screamed into her gag, but it served no purpose other than to make the men laugh at her squirming.

"The dress," one directed and another ripped her skirt from her, leaving her naked and defenseless. She could do nothing but throw her head back, screaming in muffled rage. Two of the thugs grabbed her ankles, levering her off the ground and pulling her legs apart. She felt the first attacker brutally enter her, snorting like a beast. Ilsa fell into a hellish world of pain and degradation, her mind ripped away as the assault on her body began. Loki calmly finished his apple, tossing the core away before wiping his hands fastidiously on his pants. He wondered what Herin would do when he found out what had happened to his woman. No doubt it would make him berserk, and that was exactly what Loki wanted.

There was some danger in that, but it also meant that Herin wouldn't be thinking straight; he would rush to find the woman without thinking over the possibility that he might be walking into a trap. Loki was counting on that. He wanted Herin out of control, so mad that he could think of nothing but revenge. When he came to get it, Loki's men would be ready. Herin might be a powerful magician, but even magicians could be killed if they weren't careful.

His men switched places while the assault continued. Loki watched for a few moments, but soon grew bored. "I'll be outside," he told his men. "Come and get me when you are finished. Remember, have your fun, but she is not to be killed."

"We understand, Lord," said one over his shoulder as he held Ilsa's hips in his grubby hands. "We won't be long."

Loki waved his comment off. "Take your time. I'm in no hurry." He walked up the steps leading from the cellar to the street and took a breath of air as he gazed at the starry sky. It was going to be a nice night. A very nice night indeed.

Herin wandered back towards the inn, lost in thought as he tried to figure out what the next step should be. It seemed that Ilsa's vision had been pretty accurate. It was obvious that there was some sort of operation being planned. He hadn't been able to get into the army compound itself, but even what he could see through the gates had shown a fairly frantic level of activity, far too much for an army that was doing nothing more than simply resisting a siege. Something was going to happen very soon, perhaps even the next day. If that was so, they would have to be ready to move quickly.

A quick glance skyward told him that there was less than an hour of daylight left. Shadow and Ilsa must be back at the inn already. Herin had cooled down considerably since the argument that afternoon. Given the chance to think things over, he had seen that Ilsa had probably been right in her assessment. Something had been niggling at him for days and days, just out of his sense of conscious awareness. He hadn't been able to pin it down, but her suggestion had cleared a path for him. Shadow was acting in a way that reminded him very much of his father, and that was a memory he'd rather forget.

Lately, his interactions with Shadow were creating a similar situation, one where it seemed as if his companion felt that he couldn't think for himself, or that his ideas were just plain foolish. The plain fact of the matter was that Herin was no longer willing to follow him blindly. Either their partnership took on a more balanced division of power, or they would have to break it off to go their separate ways. It would depend on how much Shadow was willing to bend.

Ilsa was a different matter altogether. Herin didn't fool himself about what she was implying back in the room. He had been too wound up from his argument with Shadow to want to address that at the same time. *I wish I knew for sure what she felt.* It was strange, but the physical coupling, something he had wanted and had thought would draw them closer, had changed things in ways he hadn't anticipated. Before they had become lovers, he would have thought the physical part very important. Now that they had passed that threshold, it had forced him to look at her in a whole new light. The fact that their lovemaking seemed to increase their magical abilities when working together was just another facet he had to consider.

I wanted her. Now…I don't know what I want. The magic is interesting but having Ilsa as a lifelong companion is a different matter. Is that what I want? Is she right, is it impossible for people to be happy forever? Herin pushed such thoughts to the back of his mind. Getting safely out of Khartul had to be their first priority.

He saw Shadow on the far side of the street, frantically waving him over. "What's wrong?" he asked, a sinking feeling in his stomach.

"Trouble," Shadow replied. "There were all sorts of rumors floating around over at Tybold's. Seems he went out today with some hired bullies. The feeling was that he was up to something. No real details, but everyone there seemed to know that something was planned for today."

"I haven't seen anything even remotely suspicious," Herin answered. "If Tybold was going to try to take me, where would he have gotten the information about where we are? I've been careful."

"Maybe it isn't you he wanted," Shadow mused. "Have you seen Ilsa yet?"

Herin hoped that Ilsa was already at the inn, but his stomach had suddenly turned into knots. "Let's go check," he urged, an icy barb of fear stabbing at his guts.

"Carefully," Shadow cautioned. "If she's there already we have no reason to hurry. And even if she isn't back yet it's not quite dinnertime, so she might still be out sniffing around. Let's not just walk into something."

"There's only one way to find out. Come on."

Herin set a brisk pace, staying near the cover of the buildings, pausing before crossing any alley or open street, and carefully checking to see that it was clear before venturing into the open. At the intersection where Peddler's Alley met the main road, he stopped short, grabbing Shadow by the sleeve and pulling him off the street.

"What's wrong?" Shadow asked, eyes shifting to look around them in every direction.

"Magic," Herin said bluntly. "Down the street there. Strong magic."

"The Council," Shadow said, shaking his head. "It has to be. Now you know how Tybold knew where we were. We thought that they might be working together. If they're waiting down there somewhere, then it's likely Tybold found out from them."

"Why would they tell him?" Herin asked.

"I don't know, but we can worry about that later. The question now is whether or not Ilsa tried to go back inside yet."

"How do we find that out without alerting them?" Herin asked, looking around the corner and down the street to try to locate the magician. Magicians, he corrected. The odor was too mixed to just be one. He carefully sniffed the air once more.

"They've got some kind of containment spell set up down there. If we had gone a little farther, we would have tripped whatever alarms they set up."

"That means trying to use magic to sense her is out," Shadow said with a worried look. "And we can't just go walking down there ourselves. Any suggestions?"

"I've got an idea," Herin said. He fished a gold piece out of his pocket.

"What are you going to do with that?" Shadow asked.

"If we can't use magic, we'll do what everybody else does and buy information," Herin told him. "Wait here."

Shadow watched him walk into a tavern, emerging a few minutes later with one of the establishment's serving girls. Herin had an embarrassed look on his face. The girl listened to what Herin was telling her with an amused expression of her own. She laughed and nodded, then set off down Peddler's Alley in the direction of the inn.

"What did you tell her?" Shadow asked, as Herin rejoined him.

"I told her I was supposed to meet a woman, but I thought maybe her husband would be waiting for me instead. I asked her to go to the inn to see if a dark-haired woman had checked in, and to tell me if she saw a man with black hair and a beard."

"Every tavern in this city has a man with black hair and a beard," Shadow commented.

"I know, that's what will make the story seem real. I don't want her getting suspicious. The important thing is that she'll find out if Ilsa has checked back in yet. She should have by this time."

"Pretty clever," Shadow conceded.

The girl came out a few minutes later. Herin met her outside her own place. He passed over the coin, and quickly trotted back to Shadow. One look at Herin's face was enough to tell Shadow the news was bad.

"She hasn't returned," Herin confirmed.

"The Council obviously doesn't have her," Shadow said. "There's no reason for them to take her. It's you they would be after."

"Which leaves Tybold," Herin said.

"Which leaves Tybold," Shadow agreed. "Let's start with that idea, and see what we can find. Come on."

They were soon swallowed up in the growing darkness.

Ilsa sagged against her bonds, her hair matted with sweat, one eye swollen shut and bruised a deep purple. Blood dripped slowly from her nose, creating a small puddle beneath her, drop by drop. Her ribs ached painfully. She was sure at least one of them was broken. There was no way for her to estimate how long the assault had gone on; hours certainly, although it felt like days. Loki's men had used her viciously, until they were satiated, leaving her bruised, battered, and broken.

Ilsa had long since stopped trying to figure out an escape plan, focusing on merely staying alive and surviving the ordeal. Loki had come back to the warehouse, where he sat idly through most of it, watching with a look of satisfaction as she suffered at the hands of his men. Her body was a mass of bruises and every breath was painful. She was having difficulty breathing with the gag in her mouth. Her hopes for a rescue by Herin had faded long ago. Now, she wondered how much longer Loki was going to play out this charade. Her mind was too filled with pain for much else to penetrate.

Loki boosted himself from his seat, strolling slowly to her, lifting her head with his finger, turning it from side to side as if inspecting a piece of fine art.

"Not quite the pretty maid who came in here with us," he commented. "Not that you were ever a maid anyway, but not as pretty nonetheless. How are we holding up?" He let her head fall back down. Ilsa hung helplessly in her chains.

"Give me a bucket of water," Loki ordered, and dashed the contents on her. The icy liquid shocked her into movement, causing her to groan as her ribs protested the suddenness of the motion. "Ah, you're still active. Good, very good. We wouldn't want you to give up before your partner figures out what's going on. Do you think he's figured it out by now? It's a few hours after dark, certainly long enough for him to get worried, don't you think? But where could you be? Who has you? That will take a bit longer for him to discover. I have faith in him. I'm sure he'll eventually find out. If you can hold on long enough you can watch me kill him."

If Ilsa had her mouth free she would have filled the air with the strongest curses she could find. As helpless as she was, there was little she could do other than glare at her tormenter through one good eye. But his calculated nastiness had one effect he hadn't counted on. Adrenaline surged through her system, driving away some of the pain, lighting an anger in her that made her stand straighter in her bonds, daring him, taunting him with the knowledge that he hadn't broken her.

Loki was surprised enough to step back out of range in case she should try to lash out with her feet. His face for the first time registered just a hint of uncertainty. Ilsa suddenly realized that he was afraid of her. That was the reason for the beatings and the gag, to break her so she couldn't bring her powers to bear. It wasn't much of an edge, but it was something to hold onto. She cradled the thought to her as a beggar would clutch a gold coin he had suddenly found in the street. *You'd better be afraid of me, you son of a bitch. If I get free there won't be enough of you left to mop up with a rag.*

Loki sensed the change in her and stepped back farther. "Again," he commanded.

His men did not obey immediately, milling about, exchanging uncertain glances. They shared quick looks, and Loki angrily turned on them, his face flushed with rage. "I said again," he snarled. "What's the matter with you? Get started. I want her broken quickly."

"Fuck that. You do it," the leader snarled. "You wanted her picked up to give some sort of message. We did that. But if you do any more of this she will die. Rape's one thing, beating a woman to death is another. You want her dead? You kill her."

"I'll have your heads for this," Loki threatened.

The man stepped towards him and Loki shrank back a step. "Save your threats and pay us the money you owe us you slimy, little bastard, or there will be a dead body on the streets tonight and it won't be hers." Quickly, Loki reached inside his tunic to grasp a pouch of gold, passing it over without another word.

The thug waved his men up the stairs. "Don't send anyone after us, you little prick," he warned, pausing on the top step to face Loki. "You do that and one of us will find you."

Ilsa watched them go, forcing herself to continue to stand straight, even though the fire from the adrenaline had burned out, leaving only the pain behind. There was still a chance she might get out of this. Loki stood rooted where he was, his face blank and shocked, his mind awhirl. *What happened? I don't understand. My plan was foolproof.*

Gathering himself, he swiftly went to the door to push it closed. This changed things a bit. If Herin was to find him now, unprotected, it would mean death. *I have to get some more men here, men I can trust to carry out my orders without question. My mistake was in trusting criminals. I should have just ordered some of my men to do the job. But will they do it? I might have the same problem I had with those thugs. There has to be a way out of this, there has to!*

With his hired men gone, Ilsa now became a double-edged sword. He couldn't very well release her, not after what had been done to her that night. *But if I kill her, I lose a bargaining chip with Freeholder, and I might need her now to trade for my life. Shit! How did things get so mixed up?* Ilsa saw the uncertainty on his face, and it gave her a new surge of strength. She nodded her head slowly, taunting him as best she could under the circumstances. The gesture did not go unnoticed by Loki.

What if I got my defense force to think she was a spy? That could work. They might hang her right on the spot, and that would be perfect. Herin is eventually going to figure out where she is, and when he finds her body dangling from one of these rafters, he'll go berserk. How can I explain to them her being here tied and gagged in the first place? I'll plant some evidence, that's what I'll do. A few drawings of the defenses, and a list of defenders should do the trick. She needs to die before Freeholder finds where she is, and he's sure to be searching by this time. Damn!

He glanced upward and a smile crossed his face. There were support beams running across the ceiling. Crossing to a pile of old barrels, he found a long rope and tied a brick around the middle to give it enough weight to flip over the beam. Whistling to himself, he undid the brick, then fashioned the end of the rope into a noose.

"I could do this myself of course," he told Ilsa as he worked. "But I'm going to need help disposing of your body so I'll need to go get some of my men. I'll convince them that you are a Dakarian spy. It might take a little time to come up with the evidence of your spying, so I might be gone for an hour or so. But don't worry, we'll all be back here soon and this will be over. Now, don't go anywhere."

As emphasis, he crossed to where Ilsa hung to deliver a sharp blow to her stomach, making her sag in her bonds, her breath all but gone. She panicked for a moment as she fought unsuccessfully to get air into her lungs, her respiratory system temporarily shut down. Her vision faded, blackness creeping in at the edges of her consciousness as her mind began to flee. With an effort, she finally drew a ragged breath, snorting desperately to keep her nose open enough to take in more. Breathing in quick gasps, she was able to finally start her lungs up again, barely holding onto her awareness.

"You still serve a purpose," Loki promised. "I'll make sure your lover hears about the Dakarian spy that was found, and when he sees you hanging here like a piece of meat, I'm sure it will send him the right message. He'll learn once and for all what it means to take on a Tybold."

Ilsa was helpless to do anything other than endure the pain in her midsection. Loki extinguished all of the torches but one, which he took with him as he left the cellar. The door swung close, leaving her in the dark. There seemed to be no hope, but she clung onto the thought that she had somehow bought herself another hour or more in which Herin could find her. It wasn't much to cling to at this point, but it was all she had.

Herin was frantic with worry. It was all he could do to keep from running headlong down the streets of Khartul crying out Ilsa's name. He and Shadow had come up with nothing, not a shred of anything tangible that might give them a clue as to her whereabouts, or whether she was still alive. With each passing moment that possibility grew less likely. Shadow, watching his friend's growing concern, knew that if they did not find Ilsa soon, it might be too late. The chances were good that it was already too late.

He had suggested that they could cover more ground if they split up, but Herin had been of the opinion that it wouldn't take all that long to pick up Ilsa's trail, and he wanted Shadow with him in the event of a confrontation with Tybold and his men. Now that the time was slipping away from them, this decision was a further source of anguish to him. Herin cursed silently under his breath, his emotions beginning to boil over.

"Stay with me, Herin," Shadow urged, gripping his shoulder in support. "Don't give up hope. Stay focused."

"Shadow, she's out there somewhere and I can't do a fucking thing to help her," Herin said, the misery clearly etched on his features, his eyes tortured by his helpless rage. "When I find Tybold, there isn't a power in heaven or hell that will keep me from destroying him in the most painful way I can."

"Time enough for revenge when's she safe," Shadow reminded him. "Let's try to think this through a little bit more. Running around hasn't helped us so far."

He pulled Herin to the side of the street, shoving him roughly up against a building. Herin shook his head, focusing on Shadow with difficulty, his eyes haunted and bleak. Shadow shook him violently, until he began to struggle to free himself. "What the hell are you doing?" Herin snapped.

"Trying to get your attention," Shadow told him. "Now shut up and listen to me. We believe Tybold has her. If it was the Army, there would have been soldiers waiting for us back at the inn. You know it isn't the Council. It would be far too much of a coincidence to think that she should be just snatched off the streets randomly. So we work with the idea that it's Tybold and see where that leads us."

"I don't understand."

Shadow leaned closer, compelling Herin to look him in the eye. "Put yourself in Tybold's place," he said. "Think! Where would he take her? You know him better than anyone else. What place would he use to do whatever it is he has in mind?"

"How the hell should I know? Somewhere private? A warehouse or something like that? He probably doesn't want word of this getting out. Kidnapping and maybe murder? No, he'd go to ground somewhere so that he could have the privacy to do whatever his screwed-up mind is telling him to do."

"That's how I read it as well," Shadow affirmed. "Do you know where his warehouses are located?"

Herin nodded. "Maybe. When Loki almost caught Ilsa and I we ran into some alleys and up against warehouses. There were dozens of them over on the north side of the city, right off the marketplace."

"Let's start there."

"Follow me," Herin ordered, taking off in a sprint in the direction of the main market district.

He ran with grim determination, promising himself that Loki would pay the ultimate price for this. Herin thought of the times he had that rich bastard in his hands and had let him escape, spending precious minutes berating himself for that lapse before realizing that thinking like that would do Ilsa no good. *I know I'll sense her when I'm close, I know it. I have to. Otherwise we're going to have to search every fucking warehouse in the cit,y and there must be fifty or sixty of them. She could be anywhere. Tybold, you're going to die like the worthless piece of shit you are.*

His boots pounded out a rhythm on the cobblestoned street, each step jolting him as they weaved their way towards the North Gate. Turning a corner, he came to a stop and took a cautious sniff of the air, certain he had caught a whiff of Ilsa's scent. *This is her, I know it. They passed this way.*

"You have something?" Shadow asked.

"I think so. Faint, but I think they passed this way. We're going to have to go a little slower now or I'll run right past any more clues. I almost missed this one."

"Which way?"

Herin slowly quartered the street, searching it section by section, his eyes closed and all of his concentration on the clues he was picking up through the aromas coming to him. It was difficult to tell exactly where the scent was from. *There's another way. Our magic has connected us somehow. I need to trust that connection to lead me to where she is.* "This way," he told Shadow, setting off down a side street.

Ilsa was shivering in the icy cold of the warehouse, her body reacting to the darkness and the hopelessness of her situation. She had stopped twisting in the iron shackles, realizing that it was doing nothing other than making her wrists bloody. She had little time left before Loki returned. She needed to do something before he came back. Otherwise, she was as good as dead.

Panic began seeping into her consciousness. While she was being raped, the pain and degradation she was undergoing had dominated her mind, making her live second to second. Now, with time to imagine what was next for her, she was frightened. Ilsa wasted several precious minutes fighting back the wave of terror that was welling up from deep inside, shaking and trembling in her bonds, shivering from terror rather than the cold. Even though it was pitch black in the cellar and she could see nothing, the image of the waiting noose was burned into her brain. Ilsa had no doubt that Loki would do exactly what he had threatened to do once he returned. Her whole life was now distilled down to what she was able to accomplish in the few short minutes allowed to her before he came back.

She heard the scrape of a metal key in the door to her prison. Torches suddenly lit the room, causing her to shut her eyes against the intensity. When she re-opened them, she saw Loki with a half dozen men in some sort of military uniforms. They were dressed better than his previous group had been, but any hope that this would signal a change in her treatment was quickly dashed when one of the men walked forward to spit in her face.

"That's right, Enrico, give the traitorous slut what she deserves" grinned one of the others.

"There she is, just as I promised," Loki said boastfully, climbing to stand on a packing crate in order to elevate himself above his men. "I came upon her making these drawings." He held up a clutch of papers in one hand. "These are sketches of our defenses, along with a list of how many men were manning each one, and a schedule of when the watch changes. Obviously, she was collecting information for the Dakarians in order to help them get into the city."

There was a dangerous undercurrent in the room now. Ilsa sensed the animosity emanating from the men like a foul odor. She knew instinctively that any hope she might have harbored of mercy was nothing more than wishful thinking. Loki smiled wolfishly, and continued to talk rapidly, whipping his men into the proper frame of mind so they would do what he wished without resistance or unwanted questions.

"She's a spy and there's only one sentence for a spy," he cried.

"Death!" came thundering back at him, causing him to nod solemnly.

"Death," he repeated. "We will act as judge, jury, and executioner.

"Shouldn't the Army talk to her?" asked a man, causing the others to nod in agreement.

"Give her to them," shouted one. "They'll find out what she knows." They were all staring at her now. Ilsa realized that she had one slim chance and took it, hoping it would work.

She purposely widened her eyes in feigned terror, shaking her head vigorously from side to side as if she were frightened of the prospect of being given to the authorities. "She's scared shitless," one of the men said gleefully, yanking on her hair, leaning close enough for her to smell the garlic on his breath. "Afraid of the Legion, are you?" he laughed. "Well, you should be. They'll break you soon enough."

"No, we don't need them," Loki cried desperately, trying to bring the group back under his control. "We have the means of her death prepared already. I just need a couple of strong men to pull her up and we'll be done with the Dakarian bitch."

It was no use. His words were ignored as the men began taunting Ilsa with what would happen to her once the Army got her into its clutches. She continued to play her part to the hilt, pulling away from them and trying her very best to give the impression of abject horror at the prospect.

"Timmons, go fetch a patrol from Legion Headquarters," ordered a man. One of the soldiers sped off, much to Loki's dismay.

"That will waste valuable time," Loki protested. "We must deal with her ourselves here and now. For all we know she has confederates in the city looking for her."

"An excellent point, my lord," the man said, and Loki breathed a sigh of relief. Finally, the fools were coming to their senses. "Enrico, you and Serge go watch the street to make sure we aren't disturbed. The Legion will be here soon enough. Then we can take credit for handing over this spy to them for interrogation."

Loki screeched at the remaining men. "I'm ordering you to kill that woman this instant! You take your orders from me."

"Don't worry, my lord, she will certainly get what's coming to her. Keep those papers safe so we can hand them over when the soldiers get here. They'll find out everything she knows. You will be a hero for saving the city."

Nothing he said made any sort of impression on the men. Loki finally sank back onto a crate in frustration. He looked bitterly at Ilsa, who met his glare with one of her own. She stared defiantly at him for just a moment, before turning her attention back to the others. She was certainly not out of danger by any means. It was more than possible that Loki's faked evidence might be enough to convict her if the Army believed his story. But she at least had a fighting chance now.

Within twenty minutes the messenger was back, accompanied by a squad of legionnaires and a centurion. He quickly sized up the situation and crossed over to Loki. "You're Loki Tybold?" Loki nodded glumly.

"Your man said this woman is a spy you caught. Where's your proof?" Loki handed over the papers he was holding, and the officer thumbed through them quickly. "Where did you find her?"

Loki outlined the cover story he had concocted while he waited, outlining how he had seen Ilsa skulking through the streets, describing how he had decided to follow her to see what she was up to. After watching her make drawings of the defenses, he had captured her, bringing her here to his warehouse for interrogation. The officer listened to the story in silence, his hard eyes betraying nothing.

"Why is she so bloody?"

"I was trying to get information out of her," Loki explained.

"That's our job," the Legionnaire told him. "You should have turned her over to us right away. We'll take her to headquarters and see what we can find from her. You'd better come along as well. Bring your men too."

"They played no part in the capture," Loki quickly explained. "I did that on my own. They're just here to help guard her."

"Very well, they can be dismissed. But you come with us. Cut her down and cover her," he ordered.

"Better keep her gagged," Loki advised. "She tried to incite the crowd on the way over here. We don't want any trouble."

"True enough," the centurion agreed. "Make sure the gag is tight. A man on each side, and if she tries anything run her through."

Ilsa had no intention of trying anything. She was confident that once in the clutches of the Army, Loki's story could be exposed for the pack of lies that it was. All she wanted at this point was to be taken away from her captor.

"I'll help your men," Loki suggested, moving as if to be by her side, planning to deliver a knife between her ribs at the first opportunity.

"Won't be necessary," the officer replied curtly. "You walk with me and give me more information. If the Dakarians have a spy network active in the city we need to root it out quickly. Let's go."

The party marched out of the cellar and into the streets, gathering their share of stares from pedestrians, but setting such a swift pace that no one had time for anything other than a quick glance. Within minutes the street was empty.

Chapter Fourteen

Herin slid to a sudden stop in front of a warehouse. Shadow could see nothing to distinguish it from the dozens of others they had passed already, but Herin sniffed the fetid air and nodded confidently to Shadow. "Here," he said.

Shadow cautiously pushed against the door, which swung noisily open to reveal a space that was obviously deserted. Picking up an old piece of wood, he charmed it into flame, holding it high over his head to illuminate the interior of the building. Herin entered behind him, pushing the door closed after checking to see that no one was paying any attention to what they were doing. When he caught sight of the noose hanging from the beam his face paled. Slowly, he walked to the spot and stared helplessly up at the rope.

"No," he whispered, shaking with a combination of fear and anger. "Damn him to hell, Loki is going to pay for this. I'll destroy his entire family."

Shadow pulled a crate over so that he could stand and examine the rope more closely under the light from his torch. "I don't think they used this, Herin," he called down from his perch. "It doesn't look like there are any marks on it. If they had hung someone, there would be abrasions from them struggling."

"You're sure?" Herin said.

"I'm not one hundred percent certain, but I don't think it was ever used."

"Then why put it there?" Herin asked.

Shadow nimbly hopped to the floor. "A threat maybe, something to mess with her head a little. Who knows? Maybe they meant to use it but never got a chance."

"It still isn't a good sign," Herin insisted. "Let's go back outside. There's nothing more to see here."

"Which way now?" Shadow asked him once they had regained the street.

Herin turned his head to one side, then the other, his eyes closed. "This way," he said.

As he led Shadow through the streets of the city, Herin tried to piece together what might have happened based on the little they already knew. He was certain Ilsa had been taken off the street and sometime in the last few hours had been in that warehouse. *But why take her there and then leave? Obviously, Loki had intended to hang her, or he wouldn't have gone to all the trouble to set it up in the first place. What had happened? Why had he taken her from a place of absolute security, where he knew he wouldn't be disturbed? And where in the hell is he now?*

Shadow was caught by surprise when Herin began sprinting, and it took a few moments before he could catch up to him. He grabbed Herin's arm and yanked it so violently that it sent them both crashing against the support beam of one of the stores, bouncing them around in a staggering dance that brought Herin face to face with Shadow.

"What in the hell do you think you are doing?" Shadow demanded angrily. "We're trying to find Ilsa without attracting attention to ourselves, and you just take off without a word? What are you thinking?"

"She's been this way, I know it!" Herin shouted, pulling his sleeve from Shadow's grasp. "The scent is stronger! If we hurry we might catch them."

"Keep your voice down, you damned fool," Shadow ordered. "Do you want everyone in Khartul to know what we're doing? Look where we are!"

For the first time, Herin became aware of his surroundings. He had been so focused on just following Ilsa that he hadn't really paid much attention to the area. He saw now that they were standing on one of the main avenues cutting through the heart of the city. People were starting to gather in groups to stare curiously at them. He nodded to Shadow and they quickly gained the safety of the sidewalk.

"Good, now you're starting to think again," Shadow approved. "But you see my point? From here it is about the same distance to the Tybold compound and offices, the Council, or even Army headquarters. We don't know who has her or where she might be kept."

"Loki is the only one who has anything to gain from having her," Herin argued.

"Oh, Loki took her all right," Shadow agreed. "And he does have the most to gain by having her. But that doesn't mean he still has her. I'm betting he doesn't."

"What? Why not? What are you basing that on?"

Shadow pushed Herin along the sidewalk so that they were moving as they talked. "If he had her, they would still be back at that warehouse. She was there at some point. Why go to all of the trouble to kidnap her, take her away from this area to torture her, then bring her back to the same area? It doesn't make any sense. I think somebody else got to her and took her away from Loki."

"For what purpose?" Herin demanded. "Who else benefits from having her as a prisoner?"

"That's what we have to find out," Shadow answered. "You're sure she was brought this way?"

Herin nodded. Shadow said, "Then let's keep going and see where it leads us. We'll track her like we're on a hunt. With caution and some thought to what to do once we find her. Are you under control now?"

Herin was a bit calmer, reassured by his friend's reasoning. Shadow was right, it would do no good to just rush down the street and run into something unexpected. "I'll be fine," he assured his companion. "Let's go."

Within fifteen minutes, it was apparent to Herin where Ilsa had been taken. The odor led him to Legion Headquarters, its broad stairway flanked by two armed sentries. He halted twenty yards from the building, leaning wearily against a wall out of sight of the sentries.

"She's in there," he said, and Shadow narrowed his eyes thoughtfully. He rubbed his beard while he considered the possibilities.

"How lucky do you feel?" Shadow asked.

"Not very lucky at the moment," Herin replied. He turned from watching the sentries to search Shadow's face. "What do you have in mind?"

"I think any kind of magical assault would be ill advised," Shadow answered. "We don't really know why they have her in custody. It's safe to assume that the men on guard duty don't know all of the details surrounding her arrest. Will you follow my lead?"

"I don't know what your lead is," Herin reminded him. "But if it will get us inside, I'm all yours. What do you want me to do?"

"Just play along with me. Come on, the longer we wait, the harder it will be for her."

Shadow left the refuge of the building, walking straight down the middle of the street, his long legs setting a quick pace. Herin quickly caught up to him and they rapidly approached the guards, who eyed them warily. One lowered his spear so that it was pointed at the middle of Shadow's chest.

"Far enough," he said flatly. "What's your business here?"

"The girl that was just brought in a few minutes ago," Shadow replied. "I have information about her."

"What information?" asked the sentry.

"It's for your officers," Shadow answered back. "I need to talk to whoever is in command here."

The man eyed the pair with outright disbelief written on his features, causing Herin to begin trying to think of another way to get inside the building. "State your business with me first, and I will decide whether it warrants notifying an officer or not." The guard's face was suspicious and wary.

Shadow snorted. "Is that the way things are done in the Army? It's no wonder we're cooped up here inside the city if they let the enlisted men make all of their own decisions. Fine, be like that. It doesn't bother me a bit if your superiors learn what I know about your prisoner or not. It won't affect me in the slightest. What it does for your career once it becomes known that you did not pass on valuable information is anybody's guess. Come on." He turned Herin around and they began walking away from the steps.

"What are you doing?" Herin hissed. "I thought the object was for us to get inside the building."

"He'll come for us," Shadow whispered beside him. "He's not going to let us walk away, just in case we do know something important."

From behind they heard the pounding of boots against the cobblestones and the clank of arms. "Hold up there you two!" the guard said, running to catch up to them. "Not so fast. You're coming with me."

Shadow sneered at the guard, knowing that he needed to push him as far as he could. "I thought you weren't going to let us inside?"

Herin decided to follow Shadow's lead and push the man further. "Come on, let's get out of here. We don't have time to deal with underlings like this."

"That's enough," the guard snarled, grabbing Herin by the arm. "Both of you come with me. If you know about the prisoner, maybe you are in league with her. Fantor! Come give me a hand with these two."

The other guard hurried over and took Shadow in custody. They resisted just enough to appear to be protesting against the rough treatment, but not so much as to be arrested themselves.

The soldiers led them down a long hallway into a large open room. There was a huge desk with four men working behind it, initialing forms, writing out orders, and organizing paperwork. The guard took them to the oldest of the four, a man with a face that looked like an aged piece of leather. He turned bored eyes on them and sighed the sigh of an official who knows he is about to have to fill out one more piece of paper.

"Well?" he asked, impatience etched on every feature. "Who are these people, Olaf?"

"This one here says he knows something about that prisoner they brought in about twenty-five minutes ago," he said, jerking a thumb in Shadow's direction.

"Is that so?" the clerk asked in a tone that clearly communicated that he didn't believe it and didn't care. "And his friend here?"

"He can corroborate my story," Shadow said.

"Oh, no doubt, no doubt," the clerk said with a thin smile. "I'm sure he can. Very well, Olaf, I'll take it from here." He eyed the pair suspiciously. "Well?"

Shadow shook his head. "For the officers in charge only," he insisted. "It's too important to trust to anyone else."

"Is it now? Very well, I'll send you to the proper person. But under guard mind you. And you should know that if you are wasting our time you will be dealt with severely. Is that understood?"

"I understand," Shadow said. "You think I like being here? I wouldn't have come if I didn't think it was important. Don't worry. Your superiors will thank you for your efficiency."

"That will be the day," the man muttered, filling in a form and ringing a small bell on his desk. A clerk instantly appeared and waved them towards a door behind the desk.

"This way," the man said, leading them into a long corridor that ran towards the back of the building. Herin started to say something, but Shadow shook his head and held a finger to his lips. The corridor was narrow and dimly lit, making Herin feel as if he were being pushed down a chute towards the light that shone at the far end. There was an oppressive feel about the space, a combination of decades of residue from the torches blackening the walls, mixed with the odor of ancient leather, all combined with the sweat of the thousands of soldiers who had passed through the hallway over the years. It was overpowering. Herin rubbed his nose violently, unable to shake the sensation of having it coated inside and out with the invisible cloud that seemed to hang everywhere in the building.

As they neared the open doorway at the end of the passage, he smelled the one odor more important to him than anything else in the world at that moment. Shadow felt him stiffen beside him and glanced over quickly, to see Herin's nod of satisfaction. They had found Ilsa.

The clerk stopped at the entrance to the room beyond, temporarily blocking their view.

"Two people to see you sir," the man announced. "They claim to have information about the prisoner."

Herin heard a voice order them into the room. He didn't immediately absorb the details because his eyes went straight to Ilsa. She was dressed in a seedy piece of linen, once white but now stained in dozens of places and faded to a dull gray. It covered her from shoulder to mid-thigh, leaving her arms and legs bare. Her hands were tied behind her, and she had been gagged with a leather mouthpiece. Her hair was matted and filthy, hanging in straggly bands that were partially stuck to her cheeks with sweat.

There had been enough time since her ordeal for her bruises to develop fully, making her face look mottled and raw. One eye had swollen completely shut, the puffiness streaked through with ugly purple and yellow markings. The part of her arms that were visible sported bruises of their own. Angry splotches ran up both legs. Ilsa had to be in pain, but she seemed to be handling it, judging from her defiant posture and glaring eyes. She hadn't turned to look at them, her attention fully focused on the officer seated before her behind a large wooden desk.

"Ilsa," Herin said before Shadow could stop him. Every eye in the room turned towards the door. Ilsa's face registered her surprise and relief at seeing Herin and Shadow.

"You know this prisoner? Guards!"

They were immediately surrounded by the sharp spears of the guards, herding them over to stand next to Ilsa in front of the desk. "How do you know her?"

Shadow met the man's glare with a calm stare. This was an area he had some expertise in, and he hoped Herin had enough sense to allow him to handle things without making the situation worse. "She is the reason we are here. To whom am I speaking?" Shadow asked, ignoring the demand.

"I am General Bjorkenberg, commander of the Tenth Legion here in Khartul. Now, who are you, and how do you know this spy?"

"Spy?" Shadow feigned surprise. "She's no spy. She belongs to me. I heard she was abducted off the street, and we came here looking for her. I congratulate you on your efficiency in finding her, but I am wondering just how she came to be so…damaged. She is a valuable piece of property. Was this the Army's doing? If so I will be filing a formal complaint and asking for compensation."

Bjorkenberg was put off balance by Shadow's approach. It did not seem at all like the behavior of someone with something to hide. He stared thoughtfully at the two for a moment before waving them to seats in front of the desk, a move that Shadow interpreted as one indicating his willingness to listen. All well and good so far, but there was a long way to go before they could all walk out of the building freely.

"Perhaps you can explain how these came to be found on her person," Bjorkenberg asked, pushing the sheaf of drawings towards him with one hand. Shadow looked through them quickly before tossing them back onto the desk.

"These have nothing to do with Ilsa," he announced. "If these were found on her, they were planted there by someone. Did she actually have these in her possession?"

"They were handed over at the same time as the prisoner was taken into custody," Bjorkenberg answered carefully.

Shadow shook his head. "If she were a spy, why would she keep such drawings? Besides, she is illiterate. Whoever wrote the names and figures on that paper, it wasn't her. Do I look like the kind of man who is stupid enough to own a slave who can read and write? Those kind are nothing but trouble. Besides, how would she pass this information out of the city? I believe you have all of the gates well-guarded, do you not?"

"She might want to have copies to send out of the city somehow while she remains here to gather more intelligence."

"She might be able to fly too, but I think it highly unlikely," Shadow said with a tone of amusement. He spared a look at Ilsa. "Why is she tied and gagged? Surely you aren't afraid of one woman in a room full of trained soldiers?"

"We were warned that she is a magician," Bjorkenberg said. "This is just a precaution."

Shadow stared at him as if he had grown another head. "A *magician*? A woman magician? Really, commander, I have to say I thought better of the Army. Who ever heard of a woman magician? Who told you such a tale?"

"That isn't important," Bjorkenberg replied stiffly, but Shadow could see he was wavering.

"I should say it is very important if that is why you are holding her in such a condition. She looks like she's been beaten half to death. If she truly was a magician, she certainly would have prevented that from happening, don't you think?" He paused to shake his head. "A woman magician. Quite a story, General."

Bjorkenberg pursed his lips and nodded to one of the guards. "Untie her, but leave the gag. If she makes any movement at all, kill her."

"If she was a spy and a magician, then what need would she have of drawings in the first place?" Shadow asked. "Surely there would be some magical method that would allow her to gather what she needed without being detected. I really think you have been badly misled."

"That remains to be seen," Bjorkenberg replied. "You say you know this woman and that she was abducted. Why would she be taken?"

"If it's who I think it is, it's a business rival," Shadow answered smoothly. "One Loki Tybold. He has dogged our heels for years. The woman is unimportant, being mostly a diversion for my young partner here. But Tybold believed she had access to some of our inner secrets, and judging from her appearance, he hoped to beat them out of her. Why he gave her to you, I cannot even guess. Perhaps it was to hide his crime. But I am gratified to get the wench back. She cost us a pretty penny. But I am not surprised that Tybold tried to get the Army involved. It is the sort of manipulative thing for which he is famous."

Bjorkenberg drummed his fingers on the desktop as he sifted through the story. The man in front of him looked less like a businessman than an outlaw, but many merchants skirted with the edges of legality and often were but one step removed from being brigands themselves. It was quite possible that he was telling the truth. It certainly made more sense than the story told to him by Tybold.

He asked, "What sort of business are you in?"

"Import and export," Shadow answered, knowing that Bjorkenberg would correctly assume that meant smuggling. It was a profession that was illegal, but also one that was impossible to eradicate. Bjorkenberg had been in the Army long enough to know how the game was played; smugglers and officers often came to understandings that proved financially beneficial to both parties. "When you have dealt with this Dakarian unpleasantness, I would be happy to sit down with you and discuss how soon my business can get back to normal." Shadow was taking a bit of a risk and he knew it. It was possible that Bjorkenberg was one of those officers who took the letter of the law very seriously. But it was also something that a "merchant" would do, and Shadow knew the importance of playing a role to the hilt.

"That remains to be seen," Bjorkenberg answered. "We will set that aside for now until we get to the bottom of this. You still haven't answered my question. Why would Tybold believe this woman would know things about your business?"

"Because the man is an idiot," Shadow snorted. "As you must know if you've met him. He obviously thought that my partner here would tell his slut business secrets. As if he would discuss such things with a woman. Maybe that is how Tybold conducts his affairs, but I assure you we know better. She is skilled at what she does and we used her from time to time when we had clients in the city on extended trips. Entertainment, you understand. She helped us secure many a deal in just such a manner. More than paid me back for the initial outlay I can assure you."

It was vitally important that Bjorkenberg look at Ilsa as nothing more than a common whore. It would be far easier to talk her out of captivity if he thought her a piece of merchandise rather than someone capable of being a spy. Bjorkenberg was probably doing him a favor by having her gagged. Shadow doubted very much if Ilsa would have willingly played this part without protest.

"A pleasure slave?"

"A very good one indeed," Shadow answered. "Or at least, she used to be." He frowned. "That brings me to another point. She is now damaged goods. It will be weeks, perhaps months, before she can be used again. And maybe never if some of those bruises leave permanent marks. I will be demanding compensation for the damage. Do I collect from the Army? You are the ones who have her now in this disgusting state."

"We received her in this condition," Bjorkenberg protested, and Shadow knew he had won. Rather than continuing the line of questioning he had begun, the officer was now on the defensive. It was time to press his luck.

"Received her this way from Tybold?" Shadow snarled, trying to convey righteous anger.

Bjorkenberg nodded, and Shadow slammed his fist on the desk. "I knew it! That piece of dung has interfered with me for the last time. I demand you do something about this outrage!"

"You demand?" Bjorkenberg said coldly, his eyes hardening.

"A thousand apologies, sir," Shadow said with humility, acting the part of contrite petitioner perfectly. "I didn't mean to lash out at you, I just lost my head. I meant to say I would regard it as a great favor if I could take my property and go. I will deal with Tybold on my own."

"If by dealing with him you are suggesting there will be a physical reckoning, I better not hear of anything like an assassination attempt or a murder. If so, I will know exactly where to place the blame."

"Will you arrest him then?" Herin spoke for the first time. "Will you put him in custody?"

Bjorkenberg considered the possibilities if he took such a course. He had no use for Tybold, having sized him up as a braggart and a fool. Tybold might be an idiot who had involved the Army in what could turn out to be a serious civil situation, but he was also the son of the richest man in the empire. Bjorkenberg knew that if he was to throw Tybold into prison there would be political repercussions that might adversely affect his career. It wasn't worth the risk.

"I have nothing to hold him on other than your word," he said. "You'll have to pursue any legal action on your own."

"But that's not..." Herin sputtered angrily.

"...Going to be a problem," Shadow finished smoothly, squeezing Herin's arm under the desk to warn him to curb his temper. "We will, of course, take your advice. Nothing but legal actions from our end. The girl?"

"I never caught your name."

"Leif Thagsson," Shadow replied smoothly. "You'll find my shop on Merchant's Row near the main marketplace."

"I will release the girl into your custody for now, but I want you to report back here the day after tomorrow at noon for a hearing." He indicated that Ilsa's gag should be removed.

Shadow nodded in gratitude. "Promptly at midday. Will Tybold be here as well?"

Bjorkenberg nodded. "Yes, I think it will be instructive to have all parties present."

"Very well, we will see you the day after tomorrow," Shadow replied, standing and shaking Bjorkenberg's hand. "Fetch your woman," he ordered Herin, not even sparing a glance in Ilsa's direction. Hopefully, Herin wouldn't ruin the charade by an overt demonstration of emotion.

He needn't have worried. Herin asked brusquely, "Can you walk, or am I going to have to haul your sorry ass home myself?"

"I'll walk, my lord," Ilsa said through gritted teeth, fighting to hold onto her consciousness until they were safely away from the building.

Herin turned to the closest soldier. "Do you have a spare cloak I can cover her with? It would be just my luck to retrieve her in one piece only to have her catch a chill and die on me."

The man laughed and pulled off his own cloak, a garment that had seen better days and carried with it the aroma of every place the man had been, reeking of cooking fires, sweat, blood and god only knew what else. "Here, use this. It's about done for anyway. Now I can requisition a newer one."

"My thanks," Herin said, casually tossing the garment to Ilsa. "That should hold you until we get back home. Dammit, come on, step lively. We've already wasted enough time fetching your worthless carcass back. And you are going to pay us back for the time. Let's go!"

Shadow led the way back down the corridor, Ilsa staggering behind him, and Herin bringing up the rear. It was all Herin could do not to reach out to hold her, wincing at every stumble or gasp of pain that fought its way out of her throat. They were almost free. He wanted to make certain that nothing they did would arouse suspicion in any of the soldiers before they could regain the safety of the streets.

Their exit caused no commotion. Even at this time of night there was activity going on, with men walking briskly from one room to another, or squads of soldiers being employed as runners, dashing off down the street carrying messages to distant officers on the walls. Shadow took note of all of the activity, concluding that the rumors of an impending attack from inside the city were accurate. They didn't have much time.

He paused on the top step to pull his cloak tighter against the cold, shrieking wind that had blown up while they were inside. "This way," Shadow said, quickly descending the stairs and turning the corner, letting Ilsa and Herin pass him by while he looked back to make sure they weren't being followed. "All clear," he reported. Herin caught Ilsa just as her strength deserted her, picking her up and cradling her to his chest.

"We've got to get her out of this," he said to Shadow. "We can't go back to the inn now."

"We don't have much choice," Shadow answered grimly. "She needs immediate care and we can't do it out here in the open. We need a warm room and plenty of food. And we need our supplies. We'll have to chance it. Besides, I doubt the Council means you any harm. More likely they're looking for you so they can try to get you back."

"You don't know that for certain," Herin answered, moving down the street as he talked. Ilsa was content to allow herself to finally release consciousness and she drifted into a deep and dreamless state of sleep. "They might be working with Loki. It's obvious he has the Army helping him. I'm a little surprised they let her go so easily."

"It's an exaggeration to say he has their help. Let's not forget that Loki has a real talent for pissing people off," Shadow replied. "The commander didn't seem to regard him too highly."

"Then why not arrest him?" Herin wondered.

"Family connections, what else?" Shadow answered. "Bjorkenberg might not like him, but he isn't foolish enough to throw his career away over what must seem like a trifle. He released Ilsa. Don't expect any more help from him after that."

"You're not really planning on appearing at that hearing, are you?"

"Of course not. It's just fortunate for us he didn't want it tomorrow. No doubt the press of getting this attack ready. But it gives us an extra day to try to heal her before leaving the city. Our path is pretty clear now; we must get out by tomorrow evening at the very latest."

"If she can travel," Herin said, looking at her battered and swollen face. His anger began to boil up again. "If I find that pig before we go, I'll leave him splattered over every inch of this city."

"She has to travel, Herin, even if she isn't completely well. Don't you get it? We can't go to the hearing and take the chance that some of Loki's charges stick. If we don't show up, the army is going to come looking for us. It would behoove us to be long gone by the time that happens. If Ilsa were healthy, I'd say we leave here within the hour. Since she is not, we must do the best we can for her between now and this time tomorrow night. But tomorrow is the deadline."

"Can we heal her in time?" Herin asked, his face grim and worried.

"I don't know what we can do in the time we have," Shadow admitted. "We'll just have to do our best and hope it's enough. It's a good thing she's such a tough woman or we wouldn't have been in time to save her."

"Save her?" Herin repeated miserably. "I didn't save her. Look at her, she's been beaten to a pulp and had god only knows what else done to her."

"She's alive," Shadow reminded him. "And that's all you have to hold onto now, so I suggest you take what you've been given. I'm sure she was raped as well as beaten. That seems the kind of thing Tybold would do. He obviously meant to use her to get at you. But she is going to be very fragile for awhile, and she'll need somebody to help her through that. It sure as hell isn't going to be me, so you're elected. It isn't going to be easy. For either of you."

"Let's get back to the rooms first, then we can talk about what she'll need."

Shadow paused when they approached the last bend before the inn. "Give her to me," he said, taking Ilsa from Herin. "Sense anything?"

Herin cautiously stuck his head around the corner of the building, taking several experimental sniffs. There was definitely a faint odor of magic lingering, but it seemed that it was at least several hours old. The intensity wasn't strong enough to make him believe any magicians were actively maintaining the spell or working any kind of magic at the moment.

"Something's there all right," he reported. "But it's not a fresh spell. Smells more like some sort of warding spell but it's at least several hours old. It's so weak I can barely sense it at all."

"That makes sense," Shadow nodded. "They probably got tired of standing out here in the cold waiting for you. Maybe Tybold did us a back-handed favor by making us chase him all over the city. Otherwise, we might have run into the Council here."

"So now what?" Herin asked. "We can get into the inn, but someone could be watching, or even be waiting inside."

Shadow nodded. "Here, you take her. I'll create a little diversion outside the inn. You slip in the side entrance and get her upstairs while everyone is involved. I'll slip in later and we can try to start healing her. We won't be able to leave the rooms again until we're ready to go, but I think it's likely we can get her inside unseen. Now go, and be ready to move."

Herin moved out of the shadows, carrying Ilsa to the small door used for deliveries. It had the advantage of opening onto a side street, which was deserted at this time of night. He eased the handle to make sure the door was unlocked, sighing in relief as it cracked open a bit. He didn't know what kind of diversion Shadow had in mind so he simply pulled the door shut again and waited.

It didn't take long. He heard shouts from within the inn, accompanied by sounds of benches being shoved back from their tables. Easing open the door to peek inside, he saw the patrons rushing about in confusion. Through the open front door, he saw flames leaping high from a wagon filled with straw that was sitting in the street right outside. Men were shouting for buckets, hastily forming a line to pass the containers from one of the water troughs to douse the flames.

Herin quickly slipped through the door, taking Ilsa upstairs as fast as he could, wincing with every creak of the stairway. It didn't matter. Everyone was either fighting the fire or watching the people fighting the fire. Herin carried Ilsa to the bed, where he gently laid her down, covering her with a blanket before going back to the door to stand guard.

There were footsteps on the stairs followed by a soft knock. "It's me," said Shadow, and Herin quickly let him in, locking the door behind him.

"Nice work."

Shadow smiled. "I didn't really have to do much. Seeing that wagon right there in front of the door made it almost too easy. That should keep everyone occupied for a few minutes. No one saw you?" Herin shook his head. "Good, then let's see what we can do for her."

Shadow pulled back the blanket and slowly unwrapped the cloak, careful not to touch Ilsa any more than necessary. He didn't think she would feel anything. It appeared that she had fallen into a sleep so deep it was almost a coma, as her body began the recovery process. That would at least make their work a little easier. "Hand me your knife," he said to Herin and used the blade to carefully cut away the tunic the soldiers had given her to cover her nakedness.

When Herin saw the damage to her body he began cursing softly, the heat of his anger washing over him like a roaring fire. "That does her no good now," Shadow said, bringing him back to his senses. "Ilsa is going to need your full focus. You'll have plenty of time to think about revenge later. Right now, concentrate on her."

"Sorry," Herin apologized, taking a few deep breaths to get himself under control. "What do you want me to do?"

"She looks like she's in a pretty deep sleep already," Shadow said. "We probably don't need to waste any energy on a spell for that. Try any healing spells you can think of for wounds, and I'll try any I can think of for grief and emotional damage."

For the next twenty minutes both men tried a series of spells, dredging up every healing charm they could think of to help Ilsa recover. Herin was on more solid ground than Shadow. Any skilled magician was well versed in minor healing spells, the sort used on wounds or bruises, and Ilsa had need of these charms in profusion. Herin was confident that her physical damages would heal cleanly and fairly quickly. As he applied each spell, he was careful to check its aroma, trying to match the smell of each one with the feel of the wound.

I can feel our connection. It's still there, and that saved her tonight. Loki Tybold is a dead man. I'll flay him alive and make him eat his own guts.

Shadow's task was more difficult. He was reluctant to try anything too powerful or intrusive, fearful of doing more harm than good if he started manipulating her consciousness. He limited himself to laying down soothing charms, the sort that could be used to relieve anxiety and fear. It hardly seemed adequate given the circumstances, but he thought that Ilsa's recovery would depend more on her own inner strength than anything he and Herin could do. He just wanted to create a healing atmosphere around her so her own energies could work more efficiently.

He sat back when he was finished, softly blowing out a deep breath. "That's all we can do at the moment. We'll just have to let her rest for now."

"What if she isn't up to traveling tomorrow?" Herin asked, a frown of worry creasing his brow.

"A bridge we don't have to cross yet," Shadow reminded him. "Besides, you already know the answer. Even if we have to take turns carrying her, we are leaving tomorrow. I'd like to go check on the tunnel, but it's too risky leaving this room before we need to. We will just have to have faith that it's still open and undiscovered. In the meantime, get everything ready to go in case we have to leave quickly."

Herin busied himself gathering up their meager belongings and piling them near the door. "If we get stopped...?"

"We use whatever means necessary to get away," Shadow confirmed. "We have to get out of Khartul. We can't have the

Army, the Council, and Tybold all looking for us. Sooner or later one of them will find us. We hit the road until we can find a place where we can rest up until Ilsa recovers completely."

"I know a place," Herin said. "It might work. Three days, maybe four from here. And we can stay there as long as we need to."

"Where?"

"My home," Herin said in a voice that made Shadow stare at him curiously.

"And they'll take us in? No questions asked?"

Herin laughed harshly. "Oh, there will be questions. That's the one thing you can count on, the fucking questions. But at least it will be shelter, and it's far enough off the beaten path that we might be safe there for a bit."

Shadow didn't have a better alternative. The roads were going to be difficult for weeks still, but they needed somewhere other than Khartul for Ilsa to rest and recover from her ordeal. Herin's suggestion might work. He didn't know much about his friend's background, but from the little Herin had shared, Shadow knew that he had come from a small village that probably didn't appear on any Imperial maps. Herin had shared enough about the tense relationship he had with his father that it was entirely possible that they could be refused shelter, despite the fact that it was still winter.

They took turns watching Ilsa. By the time daylight brightened the room, they were both stiff and a bit tired. Ilsa had barely stirred all night. Shadow felt her forehead, bending close to listen to her breathing.

"No fever and she seems to be breathing normally. That's a good sign. I think all she is going to need to heal her body is some rest. We won't know what else she'll need until she wakes up."

"Should we renew the spells?" Herin asked.

"Probably won't do any harm," Shadow agreed. It only took a few minutes to lay down more magic, repeating what they had done the night before. Herin sniffed the air and nodded. "Seems right," he reported. "What are we going to do about breakfast?"

Shadow dug in their pack, tossing Herin some hard crusts of bread they had packed for the road. "For now, this is breakfast. We have enough food here for two days. We'll need to get more on our way out tonight. Unless you think we can make your village faster than three days."

Herin shook his head. "Maybe in dry weather, but not this time of year. Four days might even be too optimistic. It might take a week. I don't know what kind of shape the roads are in, and Ilsa probably isn't going to be able to move very quickly."

"Then we will need some more supplies before leaving the city. Let's get as much rest as we can. We're going to need it."

The day passed with excruciating slowness, so that it seemed each minute was hours long. Ilsa slept until late afternoon before finally stirring, moving gingerly as she tried to shift to a more comfortable position. Herin quickly kneeled by her side, taking her hand and forcing a smile.

"About time you woke up, lazybones," he teased.

"How long was I asleep?" Ilsa asked.

"Last night, all morning and most of the afternoon," Herin told her. "Maybe seventeen or eighteen hours. How are you feeling?"

"Like I was run over by a herd of cattle," she said weakly. "I thought I was going to die. I kept hoping you would find me."

"I'm sorry," Herin said. "I should have been there sooner."

"That would have been fine with me," she said, closing her eyes for a moment.

"What happened?" Herin asked. "It was Loki, wasn't it?"

Ilsa nodded. "He was planning to leave me somewhere that was very public. He hoped you would lose your head and come after him so he could set up an ambush. At least the trash he hired wouldn't beat me to death." She laughed, a horrible sound that bordered on hysteria. Concerned, Herin touched her cheek to bring her awareness back to the room, away from her memories.

"Sorry…anyway, they wouldn't do that. I guess they had some scruples. He decided to try to fool his soldiers into thinking I was a spy. He was going to hang me right there in that building, then throw my body in the street where you would find it. He had it all planned out."

"Luckily for all of us, he remains an idiot," Shadow said from over Herin's shoulder. "There is no way he would be able to sneak a body into the street, not with all of the activity from the Army while it's preparing to attack. He would have been arrested."

"That would not have made much difference to me, would it?" Ilsa asked. "But his men thought the Army should handle everything and there was nothing he could say to change their minds. The next thing I knew, there was a squad of soldiers taking us all to the Legion headquarters."

"And…?"

"Give me some water," Ilsa requested. She greedily drank from the mug Herin handed her. "We got there and they started asking Loki questions. I was too far gone to follow too much of what they said, but I got the impression the officer didn't really believe the whole story. Tybold lost his temper and began shouting that the people would hear of this outrage, that the Army was not doing its duty, things like that."

"See?" Shadow said with a soft laugh. "Tybold pisses everybody off."

"Pissed off the officer enough that he threatened to throw him in the dungeons," Ilsa said. "Tybold was taken away under guard. I don't know what they did with him."

"Probably just tossed his ass into the street," Shadow said.

"You two showed up and that's pretty much the last thing I remember. The rest is sort of foggy. You talked them out of keeping me?"

Herin grinned. "Shadow's doing. He told them you were my pleasure slave and a valuable purchase that had been damaged."

"When I feel better I'm going to be really offended," Ilsa promised wearily. "Right now, I just ache all over."

"Ilsa, we're going to have to leave here tonight," Shadow told her. "Are you going to be able to walk? We bought ourselves a day, but we're supposed to be back at headquarters tomorrow for a hearing. We leave tonight."

She pushed herself up in bed. "Help me up," she told Herin, grasping his arm for support.

She stood stiffly with his help, gazing in wonder at the bruises on her body. "Shit, no wonder I hurt," she muttered. Taking a few tentative steps, she reached for the blanket and pulled it around her. "I don't think I can walk very fast, but I guess I can hobble along a bit."

"We'll see," Shadow told her. "I think it might be a better idea for us to rig a litter of some kind so Herin and I can carry you as much as possible. You won't be able to heal very quickly if you're still stressing your body."

Herin was eyeing the bed frame. "We can break some pieces off of this and stretch the blankets between them to make a stretcher."

"Let's wait a few more hours before we do anything. Ilsa, you might as well rest as much as you can. Even being carried, this isn't going to be easy for you."

"It won't be as hard as last night," she shot back, but she did as Shadow asked, sinking back in the bed. "Maybe a quick nap wouldn't hurt." Within seconds she was back asleep.

Herin looked down at her with concern. "Shadow, do you really think she can make it? She was only awake for ten minutes, and I've never seen anyone fall asleep that quickly."

"I'm a little surprised she was up at all. She is stronger than I thought," Shadow assured him. "Might as well get some rest ourselves. We'll leave in about four hours."

Night fell quickly. Two hours after sunset, Shadow decided it was time. They gathered together their packs, with Herin taking both his own and Ilsa's so that she wouldn't have to carry any extra weight. Herin headed for the door, but Shadow's hand stopped him.

"Not that way," Shadow said, shaking his head. "The Council might have decided to come back to renew their watch. We can't risk it. We must get away cleanly and buy as much time as we can before we're missed."

"How then?" Herin asked.

Shadow first blew out the candles in the room, then sat on the windowsill and looked upward. Satisfied, he ducked back inside. "The roof. We can take that route to get us a few buildings away before coming back to street level. If there are wards or watchers around this inn, they won't have covered that way out."

"You hope," Herin said. "Because if they have, we'll be stuck up there with no room to maneuver. And how are we going to get Ilsa to the roof in her condition?"

In answer, Shadow dug in his pack and came out with a coiled rope. "Get ready to catch this," he said. "Tie it securely." Without another word, he boosted himself to the opening, stood on the sill, and jumped upward. His lower half stayed in sight for a moment as he caught a handhold, before disappearing as he hoisted himself to the rooftop. Herin stuck his head out the window to watch his progress. Ilsa leaned against him, resting her head on his shoulder.

"He's handy, you have to give him that," she said weakly.

"Are you going to be okay?" Herin asked.

She shrugged. "I don't know, but we have to leave, so it's a moot point."

"I still think that I should have been there sooner," he said.

"I'll tell you the truth, I wouldn't have turned that down," Ilsa said weakly. "But what's done is done and I'm here. Forget about what should have happened, and let's focus on getting out of this place."

As they spoke, Shadow's whisper came from the roof. "Catch!" followed a moment later by the coil of rope. Herin caught it neatly, giving it a good hard tug to make sure it was secure.

Satisfied, he looped the rope under Ilsa's armpits, knotting it in front of her chest to form a rough sling. "Use the rope as support and walk your way up the wall," he advised. "Shadow will be pulling from above to help you."

He put his hands on her waist to ease her out of the window, making sure her feet were firmly planted before letting her go. Ilsa held the rope in both hands and began working her way up the wall a step at a time, inching her way to where Shadow waited on the roof. Herin watched her closely to make certain she was strong enough, but saw no signs to indicate she was in any immediate danger. With Shadow hauling on the rope from above and Ilsa doggedly making her way up the wall, they soon had her safely on the roof. Shadow tossed the rope back down so that Herin could fashion a similar sling, using it to work his way swiftly to where the others waited.

Shadow took a moment to coil the rope around his arm, and then stowed it neatly back in his pack. "Stay low," he cautioned. "No silhouettes. We'll go over four or five buildings before we check the street."

"Don't be a hero," Herin whispered to Ilsa. "If you need to rest say so."

She nodded and they set off. Shadow seemed to be able to pick his way across the rooftops as swiftly and effortlessly as if he had been walking over his own carpet. Herin occasionally tripped over some unseen piece of rubbish, but Shadow never seemed to stumble. It took them about ten minutes to work their way to the fifth building from their own. Shadow located a set of wooden stairs, which they used to gain the street.

"Everyone okay?" he asked as they hit the pavement.

"Stop worrying about me," Ilsa shot back. "If I can't go on, I'll tell you."

They gained the tunnel entrance without incident. Ilsa was breathing hard and holding her ribs, still feeling the effects of her beating. Shadow noticed and said encouragingly, "Just a little farther and you can rest a bit."

Ilsa nodded, saving her strength to focus on keeping up. Her body was protesting every movement now, making her wonder if she would really be able to endure the rigors of travel, even for a few days. Gulping deep breaths of air, she plowed forward, determined not to slow down her companions any more than necessary. Shadow led them fifty or sixty feet into the tunnel, far enough to get them around a bend and out of sight of the opening. He fumbled in his pack, bringing out a short torch he had carried with him and setting it alight.

"We can rest here for five minutes. Then we have to be moving."

Ilsa sank gratefully to the ground, her head hanging limply between her knees. Herin watched her, his face creased with worry. It certainly didn't look like she would be able to keep up. If she could not move quickly enough it would seriously jeopardize their plans. He thought they could still make it outside the city without undue problems, but once in the open they really needed to be able to move with as much speed as possible. It would not be a good thing if it took them nine or ten days to get to his village.

"I'll be back," Shadow promised, slipping off into the tunnel, leaving his torch in Herin's hand. Herin had no time to wonder where he was going; he was more concerned with Ilsa.

He sank down beside her, jamming the torch into a crevice so that both hands were free. "Give me your hands," he said. She was cold so he rubbed them to restore a little circulation. "I'm going to try to do some quick healing spells to see if that helps a bit."

Ilsa nodded, her face pale, sweat beading her brow. Closing his eyes and taking a few deep breaths to calm himself, Herin tried to recall all of the healing spells he had been exposed to in his training so far. It didn't take long, since he only knew a half dozen or so. Healing had not been his focus, a lack he regretted now, but one he could do little about just then. He promised himself that when he had the time, he would try to find out more about that aspect of magic.

"*Logn sasi barn annask austregr mein,*" he chanted, feeling the energy course through him and into Ilsa. "*Enda ogleoi angan taufr hlifa varda illr.*" He sniffed the air to make certain he had put the spell together correctly. "Anything?" he asked.

Ilsa's face had regained its normal coloring, and some of the brightness had returned to her eyes. "I felt it," she said with a tone of surprise. "It was like a hot wave washing over me, and when it was gone, so was a lot of the pain. What did you use?"

"Just some low-grade charms," Herin answered. "I was hoping it would ease some of the pain, so I put an extra part in to try to give you a bit of protection. But it wasn't really a powerful spell."

"It sure seemed pretty powerful," Ilsa said, tentatively moving her arms and legs. She shook her head and smiled. "Whatever it was, it removed almost all of the pain. I feel a little stiff, but it's nothing worse than you might feel after a long walk."

"That shouldn't have happened," Herin said a little uneasily. "I'm no healer."

"Maybe not by yourself," Ilsa reminded him. "But I'm conscious now. Maybe that makes a difference. We can worry about this later. Right now, let's go find Shadow and get moving."

He helped her to her feet and they set off down the tunnel, picking their way over the rubble in the corridor. They found Shadow coming back their way with two long pieces of wood he had found somewhere.

"What are those for?" Herin asked.

"I got them so that we can make a litter to carry Ilsa,' Shadow answered. "We're going to have to pick up the pace, and it's obvious she won't be able to do that just yet."

"Wrong," Ilsa said, stretching her arms to the side and twisting her shoulders to loosen them. "I can move almost as fast as you can. Throw those things away and let's get going."

"How in the hell...?" Shadow asked in confusion.

Herin shrugged. "I don't know. All I did was to use a small healing spell. Ilsa claims all of the pain is gone."

Shadow looked at him strangely, shaking his head. "I think when we do get to your village, we need to really take some time to explore what you two can do together. I've never seen or even heard of anything like it."

"We need to get to the village safely first. Let's go."

Quickly making their way through the tunnel, they emerged onto the barren hill outside the city. The walls stretched high above them, soaring hundreds of feet above the river. The bulge of the cliff itself hid the path they were using. Shadow pushed loose bushes back into place to hide the entrance to the tunnel before setting off down towards the riverbed. The going was made doubly difficult by the snow, which was still packed on the path. More than once, they had to grab a tree to keep from sliding all the way down to the frozen river below. Herin checked for signs of pursuit before deciding he was being foolish. *Who would be following us in this weather?*

Shadow paused when they reached the foot of the path, gazing out at the silvery frozen surface of the river. He tossed a large stone out onto the ice, watching as it bounced off with a crack, leaving a small mark behind before sliding to the other side.

"Do you think that's thick enough to hold us?" Herin asked.

"I don't know," Shadow answered. "It's been pretty cold the last few weeks so it shouldn't have started to thaw yet. Stay spread out to distribute our weight and try to walk exactly where the person in front of you stepped."

"Why worry about it?" Herin asked. He focused his attention on the icy surface and whispered,

> *Logr fastr soma herda sker*
> *Halda lofa til stiga.*

The ice creaked for a few moments, and then took on the appearance of stone. They found it solid and were able to walk easily to the far side of the river.

"I hate leaving any way behind us for people to follow," Shadow said. "Do you think you and Ilsa can conjure up some sort of melting spell?"

Herin looked doubtful. "I'm not sure. I don't know if we can counteract the spell I just laid on it."

"It's worth a try," Ilsa said. "If it doesn't work we're no worse off than we are right now."

"Fine," Herin said, still unsure. "Let's just try the fire spell first to see what happens."

Joining hands, they quickly recited the proper phrase to create a fire. A solid sheet of flame burst from their hands to slide across the ice like a film of oil, quickly burning its way through the frozen surface and allowing water to suddenly explode like a fountain through the hole that was created. A space fifty yards wide appeared, and floes were sent crashing downstream, flinging shards of ice into the air.

"Try it again farther upriver," Shadow urged. They repeated the spell with the same results, clearing another fifty yards of river, which made an even more powerful flow as the water washed out of the opening and over the still frozen parts downstream.

Shadow shook his head. "Amazing," he said in wonder.

"Will that be enough?" Herin asked. "We didn't clear the whole river."

"This might work even better," Shadow said. "The water on top of the ice is going to flood all of the lower elevations as we work our way down towards the flatlands. When the legion attacks, it will pin the Dakarians between the flood and the city walls. The Dakarians will be too busy to worry about anything other than escaping annihilation. It should make it easier to slip by their camps. Come on, we still have a lot of ground to cover before daybreak."

Their tentative plan was to travel by night and rest during the daylight hours until they had cleared the Dakarian encampments. Once past, they would try to move as quickly as they could to Herin's village.

As they moved downstream, the flooding river forced them higher and higher onto the bank, making them struggle through thick underbrush. They had to clamber over ridges of rocks, pushing their way through the closely clustered mountain pines. As a result, they had not quite gained the flatlands before first light.

Shadow had hoped they could clear the Dakarians before daybreak, but finally he had to admit defeat and make the best of it where they were. From their vantage point he could see the winking campfires of the invaders, surrounding the city in a circle of lights.

They were safe enough for the moment, but still too close to the invaders to risk any sort of fire.

"What now?" Herin asked, squatting beside Shadow. "We can't try anything with all those Dakarians still out there."

"Stay here today and try again tonight I suppose," Shadow told him.

"We'll be missed soon," Herin commented. "Not that they can do anything about it now, but Loki will certainly know we're gone."

"That won't do him any good until the Dakarians leave," Shadow replied.

"If Bjorkenberg is half the general he's supposed to be, they'll drive the Dakarians away," Herin mused. "They should be attacking tomorrow."

"If they do, we'll have to move quickly to take advantage of the diversion," Shadow said. "We need to get well out onto the plain. Ilsa, how are you feeling now?"

"Tired and sore, but the pain is still fading," she answered from where she was laying, her head propped against her pack. "Whatever Herin did worked pretty well."

"Let's get some sleep," Herin urged. He pulled his pack next to Ilsa's and lay down beside her. "We're going to need it."

"I'll watch for a bit first," Shadow said. "We need to be ready to move tonight."

Chapter Fifteen

Shadow roused them just before sunset to gulp down a quick meal of water and hard rolls. It wasn't much of a breakfast, but it would sustain them for a few hours at least, which would hopefully be long enough to get past the Dakarians and well out into the flatlands. Herin stretched his arms to work the kinks out of his protesting muscles, taking a moment to step behind a screen of trees to relieve himself. In so doing, he found himself looking through an opening in the branches, which gave him a perfect view of the Dakarian encampments below.

Spread out in a semi-circle around the city, the camps appeared as if they stretched all the way to the horizon fifty miles away, though he knew that was an illusion. The sight was impressive.

"I feel like I've been sleeping for a week. Whatever you did certainly worked," Ilsa remarked to Herin as they set off.

"This is unheard of," Shadow said. "Whatever force drew you two together is obviously growing more powerful every time you interact."

"We'll have time enough to worry about it if we can make it safely to my village," Herin reminded him. "But for now, we have all those Dakarians to worry about."

"Let's give them a wide berth," Shadow said. "It might add a few hours to our trip, but it will get us safely past them into the open country. I think the Legion will be attacking them before too long."

"Then let's move," Herin urged, and they picked up the pace, walking as quickly as they dared while still maintaining caution. Shadow seemed to have a good idea of where he wanted to go, never hesitating when the trail forked and offered multiple choices to them. Ilsa was once again placed in the middle, with Herin bringing up the rear. They were descending at a rapid rate, and within the first hour of travel they had climbed down out of the mountains onto the flatlands below.

Shadow stopped at the edge of the tree line, staying well-hidden while he scanned the area they would need to cover. With the full moon and snow still on the ground they would make easy marks for any eyes turned their way. Herin and Ilsa stood beside him, both a bit nervous now that the time had finally come to leave cover.

"It looks awfully exposed," Ilsa said softly.

"The Dakarians shouldn't be looking in this direction," Herin said with a confidence he didn't quite feel.

"You hope," Ilsa reminded him.

"It seems clear enough," Shadow said, after carefully scanning the path ahead of them. "We can't wait here until we're one hundred percent sure it's okay; we'll just have to trust to luck until we're well past the camps. They are more than a half mile away, so there shouldn't be many patrols in this direction. They should have all of their attention focused on the city."

The clearing they were crossing was perhaps five hundred yards wide and they were less than halfway across when the sound of metal on metal froze them in their tracks. The clanging was accompanied by the shouts of men and the sound of horses. Shadow listened for only a moment before grabbing Ilsa by the arm, pushing her ahead of him.

"The legion is attacking now!" he cried. "This is our chance! Move your ass!"

The need for secrecy no longer necessary, they sprinted as best they could for the safety of the trees, their boots sending showers of snow up into their faces to cling to their eyebrows and lashes, and sting their exposed cheeks. It was difficult to run full speed in the snow, but they pushed on as quickly as they could, their breath fogging the chilly night air. Shadow caught up to Ilsa, leading the way along a path that twisted through the trees.

"We're okay now," Herin panted from the rear. "Why are we still running?"

"Move!" Shadow shot back over his shoulder. "Save your breath and run!"

Herin did as he was directed. They pressed on until they had covered close to a mile from the clearing. When Shadow finally halted, Ilsa bent over with her hands on her knees, gulping in huge breaths of air. Herin leaned against a tree, his chest heaving, his face hot and flushed despite the cold. Shadow faced back the way they had come, his head cocked as if listening for something. After a few moments, he turned to the others with a look of satisfaction on his face.

"What was that all about?" Herin gasped. "Why the hurry?"

"With the Legion attacking there was always a chance they'd send cavalry swinging around the encampments to try to cut off any retreat. Or they could just be chasing stragglers through the woods. We needed to get as far away as quickly as possible."

"How far should we go before we can feel safe?" Ilsa asked, straightening and wiping the sweat from her face.

"Once you two get your breath we should take off again," Shadow said. "We need to keep up as quick a pace as possible for as long as we can. If the Legion was successful, they're going to be flooding the whole area around the city looking for any Dakarians that broke away from the main attack. They'll send mounted patrols out for days, and there's really no way we can stay ahead of them on the main roads. We're going to be cutting cross country so the faster we get to that point, the more chance we have of slipping through any pursuit."

"How long do you think they'll send out patrols?" Herin asked.

Shadow shook his head. "I have no idea, but I should think for as long as they think there might be groups of Dakarians to round up. They've also undoubtedly found out that there is no such store or person as we claimed at our interview, so the Army will take the logical conclusion that we really were spies. That means they'll likely be after us as well."

"Tybold too," Ilsa reminded them. "He'll know we've left the city."

"Don't forget the Magicians Council," Herin said with a rueful laugh. "They'll still want me. Let's stop talking and get moving."

They traveled throughout the rest of the night, stopping every few hours for a few minute's rest, before re-shouldering their packs and pushing on. By the time the first fingers of pink were staining the eastern horizon, they had covered more than twenty miles from the city, far enough so that they felt relatively safe, but not so far that they could relax their guard completely.

Herin had gradually taken over the lead as they approached the territory he was somewhat familiar with, having traveled through it on his way to Kress. It seemed like centuries ago now, and it was with some surprise that he realized it had only been a bit more than seven months since he left his sleepy little village to try to make his mark on the empire. *Some mark*, he thought to himself as he walked. *I'm now considered a spy by the Army, with the Council and the Tybold family both looking for me. I got kicked out of school and found two people that are going to be awfully hard to explain to my family if we should be lucky enough to get there in one piece.*

They detoured around a large mound that rose fifty feet above the grassland and was several hundred yards long. "This will work for now," Herin said, dropping his pack to the ground. "No one will see us from the road."

"Right now, all I want is to get some food in me and then get some rest," Ilsa said. "Can we risk a fire?"

"We can scoop out the hill a little to shield it," Herin suggested. "We'll have to burn sod though. Not much wood out this way."

"I don't care if we burn the packs," Ilsa said. "I'm frozen all the way through, and I'd like to thaw out before we sleep. Getting something hot inside me wouldn't hurt either."

"Herin, you're the expert out here. Why don't you show us how your people cut and burn sod?"

An hour later they had a small fire hidden in a shallow pit. "Ilsa, do you think you could try a reading?" Shadow asked.

"I don't think I'm completely recovered," she protested. "I don't know if I could get anything or not."

"Hold her hand, Herin," Shadow directed. "You might get something when you two are linked. It's worth a try. What have we got to lose?"

"Nothing, I suppose. Okay, Herin, let's see what happens."

Herin took her hand, listening while she went through the phrases and chants that were supposed to unlock her ability to get readings. He suddenly felt as if his hand had been plunged into the flames as heat shot along his arm, a burning sensation so painful and severe that he glanced down to make sure his sleeve had not actually caught on fire. He knew that this was a by-product of whatever he and Ilsa were doing, but the pain was still nearly unbearable. Ilsa unexpectedly dropped his hand, falling to all fours, her eyes wild and unfocused. Herin reached out to steady her before she could fall into the embers, easing her back to a sitting position.

"What the hell just happened?" he asked. "I felt like my whole arm was on fire."

"What did you see?" Shadow said, ignoring Herin, more concerned by the shocked expression on Ilsa's face. Whatever she had seen in the fire, he knew it was dangerous for them.

"Loki," she told him. "With a squad of soldiers. Maybe a dozen or so in all. They are following us."

"Already? How is that possible?" Herin asked.

"I don't know, but he's back there."

"Well, they must be pretty far behind us," Herin said. "We knew they'd be coming at some point."

"You remember that river we crossed about three hours ago? That's where they're camped right now. They are just taking a meal. They're on horseback and they're moving fast."

"Three hours behind us? We'd better keep moving then," Herin said grimly. "They must have come straight from the battlefield."

"If they traveled this far this fast they'll have to rest their horses for a few hours before moving on," Shadow said. "They probably won't be breaking camp before early afternoon."

"Let's take advantage of the time we have to put some more distance between them and us," Herin said.

"We have to rest too," Shadow reminded him. "They're still a good fifteen miles or so away from here, and we left the main road an hour back. They're going to have to track us through this grassland and that will slow them down quite a bit."

"He's right, Herin. Besides, I can't go another step unless I get some sleep."

"Two hours then, no more," Herin said. "Then we have to move again. At least we know they're coming. That was a quick vision, Ilsa."

"It just shot out of the flames. I barely had to do anything. It was stronger than anything I've done before."

Shadow kicked dirt onto the fire to extinguish it. "Two hours. Let's use it wisely."

After a few hours of sleep, they awoke and quickly gathered up their belongings, setting off across the grasslands. They halted briefly after a few hours to take another meager meal of dried rations. There had been no signs of pursuit, giving Herin some hope that they had lost Loki and his escort. The Grasslands was a large territory to have to search for just three fugitives.

"Herin? This is your country. Do you know where we are?" Shadow asked.

Herin nodded. "There is a fairly large stream off to the southwest, maybe two or three miles ahead of us. We could hit it in the next hour or so if we move quickly."

"Let's try to do that," Shadow said. "I won't feel safe until we find your village. You might as well take the lead from here on out, and I'll watch our rear."

They set off with Ilsa twenty yards behind Herin and Shadow fifty yards to her rear. Herin didn't think they were in any real danger but it didn't make sense to take chances. Part of him felt like he would be able to sense anything before it happened, but he shook off that feeling to concentrate on taking them by the shortest possible route to his village. When he had accompanied his father to Khartul all those years before, they used the trade roads. Now they were headed cross country, so he was leading them partly by guessing a bit as to the best route to take. If the map in his head was accurate, they were northeast of where his village was located.

They crossed the stream a little over an hour later, just as he had anticipated. *At least I'm still leading them in the right direction.*

"Maybe we can risk another fire," Shadow thought aloud. "Ilsa could try another Viewing. It would be nice to know where Tybold is right now."

"Let's just keep pushing," Herin said. "A fire can be seen a long way off out here in the Grasslands."

Shadow didn't argue, so they set off once more. They had traveled far enough from Khartul and the mountainous regions around it for the terrain to have flattened out. They had an unbroken view from horizon to horizon, farther than Shadow could even estimate. Ten miles? Twenty? Fifty? It was impossible to tell. The grasslands were nothing but a carpet of brownish, waist high stalks that stretched as far as they could see.

Herin seemed surer of his direction now, although Shadow didn't see how anyone could find their way in this unbroken monotony. As far as he could tell, one place looked very much like another. The first explorers here must have found it maddening. Maybe they took their bearings from the stars, like sailors on the open ocean. He couldn't imagine how else anyone could travel here if they got off one of the roads.

They crossed several more streams, some wide enough to be waded, and others so narrow a good leap carried them easily across. With each crossing, Herin grew more certain of their location. He stopped just after their fourth stream.

"It's going to be dark soon. Do you want to keep on pushing or stop for the night?"

"You know where we are?" Shadow said.

Herin nodded. "Three days travel and we'll hit the small trade route that goes through my village. That way, straight to the southwest."

"I can walk a little farther," Ilsa said. "I say we take advantage of every hour we can and keep moving."

"You're up to it?" Herin asked. It had been mostly for Ilsa's benefit that he had stopped.

"I told you before that I would tell you when I felt like I needed to rest," Ilsa answered with a bit of heat. "Stop trying to baby me, Herin."

"Fine. Let's move then," he shot back, stung by her tone. *Why can't she understand that I am trying to help her? Hell, I haven't so much as touched her other than holding her hand for that vision. What the hell does she want from me?*

His anger now drove him to set a faster pace than he had at any time during the day. When he stopped an hour later, they had covered an additional five miles, a killing pace under any circumstances. Shadow gave him a long appraising look as he dropped his pack to the ground, but held his tongue, refraining from comment.

"Was that supposed to prove something?" Ilsa said, breathing hard as she sat propped against a small boulder.

"What do you mean?" Herin asked.

"You know exactly what I mean," Ilsa shot back. "If you were pissed off at me then say so. Don't try to take it out on me by acting like we're in some sort of race or something. What do you think you're proving by walking me into the ground, that you are a big, strong man or something?"

Herin was on the verge of answering when Shadow interrupted. "Save it," he ordered. "Let's get away first and then you two can have your quarrel. Let's set out some wards tonight. We completely forgot to do that last night."

Ilsa nodded and pushed herself to her feet. "I'll take this end. How far out do you want them?"

"Let's put them at fifty yards or so. Enough to give us a good warning if anything triggers them.

Herin's estimate proved correct, and by the evening of the second day he had found the trade road he was searching for.

"We can be at my farm by midday at the latest," he told the others as they prepared to bed down for the evening.

"I'm looking forward to meeting your family," Ilsa said. "I want to see who you came from."

"Don't expect much," Herin told her. "My family isn't very interesting, and the village is going to be a lot smaller than the places you're used to."

"At least we can sleep inside for a change, even if it's in a barn," Ilsa said with a yawn. "I just want a roof over my head for a few days." She wrapped herself in her cloak and was quickly asleep.

Herin awoke in the peculiar stillness that always seemed to be a characteristic of the hours midway between midnight and dawn. He saw Shadow's still form wrapped in his cloak, breathing the rhythmic breathing of a deep sleeper. Ilsa was rolled on her side away from him. He quietly slipped from his own cloak so that he could move closer to her.

With his village so close, he wondered if they might be able to resume their relationship. It had been difficult to be so near Ilsa and yet feel so hesitant about touching her. Perhaps the safety of his home and village would allow her to allow that.

He eased down slowly, careful not to disturb her. Gently, he placed his arm across her shoulders, wanting nothing more than to hold her against him so he could feel her breathing.

Ilsa reacted as if someone had dropped a live coal in her clothing, screaming and striking blindly at him, her fingers curled into claws that left long scratches down his cheek. "Get away from me!" she hissed, her eyes as wild as a feral animal. Ilsa stared sightlessly at him for a moment, then her eyes suddenly cleared and her face took on an expression that was equal parts fear and shock. "Did I do that?" she asked in a small voice.

Herin nodded. "It was my fault," he stammered. "I startled you. I was just..."

"You have to stay away from me, Herin," Ilsa said in a cold, distant voice. "You can't touch me. Not like that."

"Like what?" Herin asked. "I wasn't going to do anything but hold you, I swear."

Ilsa shook her head. "I can't, Herin. Not yet."

Herin glanced at Shadow, unable to look at the expression on Ilsa's face. "I'm going to wash my face in the stream. Then we should go."

Shadow squeezed his shoulder in silent understanding as he passed. "Since we're all up, we might as well get an early start," he said to Ilsa in a normal tone of voice, counting on her being able to respond to their routine. She watched him roll up his pack and secure it to his back, blinking in the moonlight but standing frozen where she stood. "Come on Ilsa, we're not carrying your stuff for you," Shadow said, watching her closely.

She moved slowly, as if she were in a trance. It was apparent that she had been caught as much by surprise at her body's reaction as Herin had been. She put her pack together without a word, swinging it to her back, all the while looking off into the darkness in the direction Herin had taken to deal with the injuries to his face. Shadow picked up Herin's pack, jerking his head in the direction of the stream.

"Let's get moving," he said. "I've got this."

Ilsa stumbled towards the stream, waiting while Shadow passed Herin his burden. The cuts on Herin's face looked almost black in the moonlight. Ilsa bit her lower lip, but said nothing, merely looking away, her eyes troubled. Herin shrugged his pack into place, hopping the stream in one long leap. He set off without looking behind him. Shadow waved Ilsa across before following himself. As they always did when traveling during the darkness, they closed up the formation so that they were walking closer together. They would not lengthen it until daylight.

"Herin…" Ilsa said.

"You don't have to say anything," Herin told her without meeting her glance. "It was my fault. I should have left you alone."

"No, listen to me," Ilsa said, pulling on his sleeve so that he was forced to look at her. "I just reacted the way I did because you caught me by surprise. Give it some time and maybe we can try again when I'm ready."

"I pushed too fast," Herin replied.

"Who knows what too fast is?" Ilsa answered. "I feel like there is a slimy thing coiled up inside me, like a serpent eating away at my guts. I want to heal this, I really do. But we'll have to go slow."

"Whatever you need," Herin promised, but they walked apart from each other all the same, neither willing to risk another violent reaction.

Chapter Sixteen

Herin's first thought when he rounded the bend and saw his old village was that something happened to make it shrink since he had left. He had become so used to the heavily populated urban areas of Kress and Khartul that the village center, an area he had once thought of as spacious, now appeared little more than a small open space between shabby buildings, barely large enough for a hundred people to gather comfortably. Even the buildings themselves, as familiar in his mind's eye as old friends, now seemed drab and a bit worn. The whole settlement had the sleepy air so common to places well off the beaten track, concerned with its own affairs, and not much bothered by the fact that the outside world knew nothing about it.

The sun had been above the horizon for hours already, so there was activity in the settlement as people went about their daily chores. Herin watched them, shaking his head in wonderment. *God's balls, did everyone always move this slowly? It's like watching people sleepwalking.* The village was certainly nothing like The Pit back in Kress, or even the places they had frequented in Khartul. He knew immediately that he could never be happy in a place like this again. His horizons had expanded so much that he knew this sort of life could not hold him.

Ilsa whispered to Shadow, "My God, this place is nothing more than a collection of shacks. Herin wants us to stay here?"

"Don't worry, he won't want to stay here for long," Shadow assured her. "Look at him. He's just realizing it himself. Unless I misread him, he won't want to stay any longer than it takes for the weather to turn."

"I knew he came from a small town, but I never imagined anything like this. I never knew places like this even existed."

"There are lots of places like this," Shadow told her. "In fact, more people in the empire live in these small settlements than in the big cities like Kress and Khartul. There are hundreds and hundreds of villages like this scattered throughout the grasslands, and dozens more on each coast."

"God, growing up here must be awful," Ilsa said with a small shudder. "What kind of life is this?"

"Peaceful, if nothing else," Shadow answered. "That's worth something. The problems that plague the cities don't really touch places like this too much. They pay their taxes, and that's the only real contact they ever have with the empire. Unless there is a war."

Ilsa shook her head. "Give me the wars then. I'd go crazy out here in the middle of nowhere living in a rundown shack like these."

"Quietly, Ilsa," Shadow cautioned. "These are Herin's people and this is where he grew up. Don't put it down in front of him. You'll only make him defend it, and then you two will be at each other's throats. Again."

Ilsa said, "I'll be counting the days until we leave."

"So will Herin," Shadow guessed. "Wait until we meet his family. I doubt it will be a smooth reunion."

Herin led them along the main road, little more than a packed down dirt path wide enough for two carts to pass side by side. Some of the people stopped what they were doing to stare at them. Ilsa was certain that it was because they were strangers. She didn't know that although Chesterfield was a quiet hamlet, visitors from nearby towns were not that uncommon. What was drawing attention was the fact that all three of them were armed with bows and were in travel-worn clothing much the worse for wear. Most of the villagers assumed they were outlaws and gave them a wide berth.

Shadow didn't wonder that no one was greeting Herin. The boy who had left this place months before was gone forever. Even his appearance had changed. Herin now sported a beard and long hair, an oddity in a place where the men were routinely clean-shaven and wore their hair cut above the shoulders. Shadow thought it likely that one of the villagers would have to look Herin right in the face to see who he was, and might not know him even then.

Herin noticed the indifference and turned to Shadow with a self-deprecating grin. "I must look like an outlaw now. Guess it's the company I'm keeping."

"You left here a boy and you're coming back as a trained magician," Shadow told him. "They'll be sensing the power around you now, even though they don't know that's what it is."

"Where's your farm?" Ilsa asked. She felt uneasy in the sleepy hamlet and wanted nothing more than to leave it in the dust behind them. There was something alien to her in the slow pace of the villagers. *I guess maybe Herin was right, maybe I am a city girl after all. I'd go crazy in this place.*

"It's along that road there," Herin said, pointing to a smaller path branching off from the main road. "But I want to see what is happening around here before we leave."

He crossed the open space quickly, leading them to a blacksmith shop that opened out onto the green. Inside it looked like every smithy did, with a large anvil dominating the space in front of a bellows-fed fire, various implements hanging from hooks on the wall, a tub of water handy, and a dark smoky atmosphere that made their eyes water as they entered. The smith was bent over the anvil, carefully pounding a flat piece of iron into what looked like the end of a shovel. He made a few small taps, and then shoved it back into the fire before noticing them.

"What can I do for you?" he asked, wiping his huge hands on an apron already so dirty that it looked like it might be able to stand on its own.

"For one thing, you might try being a bit friendlier, Ram," Herin said, leaning on his bow.

The smith frowned and squinted his eyes against the glare of sunlight as he bent forward to look more closely at Herin. "Do I know you?"

"God's teeth, have you lost your eyesight as well as your wits?" Herin asked. "You must have taken one too many blows to the head. Step into the light, you big oaf."

Ram moved ponderously out from behind his anvil, and Ilsa saw that he was truly a giant of a man, though he was no older than Herin. His shoulders were so broad they looked like they might get stuck in the doorway, and his arms were as thick as her thighs. Herin turned so that his face was fully in the sunlight, grinning as recognition dawned on the smith.

"Herin? Is it you? Herin Freeholder?" He reached forward to grab Herin's outstretched hand, pulling him in to administer a rib-cracking hug of affection. "Where in the hell did you come from? I thought you were back in Kress learning how to be some big powerful magician. What did they do, kick you out for incompetence?"

Herin pointed his fingers at the fire, whispering a quick spell. The flames shot up to lick briefly at the beams overhead. "Not exactly," he said drily. His friend stared in goggle-eyed wonder at his smithy before turning slowly back to Herin.

"How did you do that?" he asked in an awed voice. His face looked less friendly than it had just moments before.

"How do you think, you dumb ass?" Herin laughed. "I went to learn magic and I learned magic. Stop looking so frightened. It's still me."

"As you say," Ram replied in a voice that suggested he was still not totally convinced. "And who might these two be? Friends of yours?"

"This is Shadow and this is Ilsa," Herin said, introducing them. "This mule of a man is Ram the Smith if you haven't already figured that out. A wizard in his own right with metal, but as dumb as an ox otherwise."

"Now there's something I've missed," Ram snorted, relaxing as he fell into a more familiar pattern with his old friend. "The stupid things you always said. Still haven't learned when to keep your mouth shut. If you two are hanging about with this one, I question your ability to choose a companion wisely. Found yourselves some trouble, I suspect. Or more likely it found you."

"What do you mean?" Ilsa asked, startled at the accuracy of the guess.

"I've known Herin since we were both babes. He drew trouble the way a pile of manure draws flies. It just seemed to follow him around. No matter where we went or what we did, sooner or later there'd be hell to pay, and Herin was always in the middle of it."

"That hasn't changed," Ilsa assured him. "It's probably worse now than it was when he left."

"I don't doubt it," Ram laughed, a great booming sound. "I'd love to hear all about it over a nice mug of ale, but I've orders to see to. Maybe later? Are you here to stay?"

Herin nodded. "Staying until the weather turns, so we'll be here for a few weeks at least. Ram, have there been any people here looking for me? Strangers I mean?"

His friend gave him a long calculating look from under his bushy brows. "Like that, is it?" he said at last. He nodded, his eyes thoughtful. "You do have a look about you, Herin. I see it now that I've had a chance to really look at you. Might be why I didn't recognize you right off."

"What are you talking about?" Herin asked. "What look?"

"The look of a man who's had to watch his back more than he should. Someone's after you, is that it? That's why you came here?"

"I needed to be somewhere quiet for a bit, that's all," Herin said, evading the question as best he could.

"I see. Well, if I'm any judge, I'd say you three look like you could handle anything that might come your way. You've changed a bit, Herin, you really have. You look harder now. I'm guessing there's a story back of that somewhere."

"We can talk later," Herin promised. "But you haven't answered my question. Is there anyone looking for me?"

"Not that I know of and I'd know of it if someone had," Ram answered. "But tell me this, Herin Freeholder, who might be looking for you?"

Herin smiled at his old friend. "Might be the Army, might be the Council of Magicians, might be one of the First Families from Kress."

"I don't know what a First Family is, but it sounds like you've been a pain in somebody's ass," Ram said with a shake of his head. "Again. We'll talk when I'm through for the day if you've a mind to, but I'll keep my ears open. Anyone sniffing around anywhere in the county, I'll hear about it and let you know. You heading out to your place now?"

"Yes. We'll stay there."

"Does your family know you're coming?" Ram asked, his eyes holding an expression of amusement. Herin shook his head and the smith laughed. "There, you see what I mean? Trouble and Herin go hand in hand like he was born to it. I wish I didn't have these jobs to see to. I'd hike all the way out to your place just to watch." He went back into his smithy, chuckling to himself.

"Do you think it was a good idea to tell him we were being chased?" Ilsa asked as they walked out of town.

"He'll hear every bit of gossip from miles around," Herin told her. "It always ends up in his shop. Now he'll be able to pass that on to us. Besides, there are no secrets in a place like this. Not enough people to allow you to hide anything like me coming back home. Plenty of people saw us come in, so we would be the center of gossip no matter what we said to Ram. He'll talk to his customers today, and they'll all know I'm back and maybe in trouble."

"That's what I mean," Ilsa replied. "Won't that lead Tybold right to you if he passes through? They'll all know that you're back home. What if somebody tells him where you are?"

"You don't understand," Herin explained. "If any outsider, much less one as arrogant and blustering as Tybold, was to ask questions about somebody from around here, they'd get nothing to help them. People here don't look kindly on outsiders, and they'd never give up any information that might get us in trouble. Don't worry. What I have done is to activate a network that will be more efficient than if we set wards everywhere. If Tybold shows up anywhere in the district poking around, we'll hear about it before the day is out."

"What's it like coming back here?" Ilsa asked, switching subjects. "Do you miss it?"

Herin looked off into the distance before answering. "You know, I thought I really would as we were getting closer. But now that I'm here, all I can think about is how small it all looks. I don't ever remember thinking that when I lived here."

"It was all you knew then," Shadow put in. "You had nothing to compare it to. This was your whole world."

"I suppose you're right," Herin admitted. "But it's a little unsettling all the same."

"Think of it as a warm-up for what is going to happen when you see your farm," Shadow warned, a smile tugging at the corners of his mouth.

Herin had been thinking the very same thing ever since they had entered the village. *God, what is that going to be like? Ram might take me coming back in stride, but it's a sure bet Da won't be pleased at all. Not after all the shit he gave me when I told him I was leaving in the first place. He'd better not say too much...I'm not taking that from him anymore, not after all I've been through.*

"You haven't said much about your family," Ilsa said, as she walked beside him.

"With good reason," he agreed. "First of all, there isn't all that much to tell. Besides my parents, I have a younger brother and a younger sister. Everyone works the farm and that's all they are: farmers. Not a very interesting story."

"Come on, there's more to your life than that," Ilsa said teasingly. "What about what Ram said? That you were always in trouble."

"Not the sort of trouble like we're in now," Herin answered. "He means minor stuff. Getting caught eating fruit from someone's orchard, letting the pigs loose, things like that."

Ilsa started laughing, and Herin looked crossly at her. "Setting pigs loose?" she cackled. "That was your idea of a dangerous prank? Setting pigs loose?" She went off on another gale of laughter, while Herin pretended to ignore it.

"Will your family be glad to see you?" Ilsa asked, finally getting herself under control. "Or will they just lock up the pigs?"

"We're about to find out," Herin said with a touch of hardness in his voice.

They were standing at a gate set into a neat rail fence, but it was obvious Herin was hesitant about opening it and passing through. Ilsa saw that Herin's house was much like the others in the village, a roughly constructed dwelling that was made of clay and thatch. Tiny windows were set in the wall to allow some light inside. A garden carpeted the entire front of the house save for a stone walkway that wound its way to the front door. Beyond it she could see open fields, snow covered now but soon to be dark with plowed soil. A large barn stood just behind the house, with a penned in area to both sides. A lone horse stood in one of the pens, with two cows in the other. Chickens clucked at them from a henhouse as Herin led them around the side of the house towards the barn.

"We're not going inside?" Shadow asked with surprise.

"I know we'll be welcome inside the house," Herin answered grimly. "It's outside I'm worried about. My father will be in the barn."

As they approached the door to the barn, the sound of metal on metal drifted out to them, muffled a bit by the wooden walls of the structure. Pushing the heavy door open revealed a middle-aged man sitting on a crate, a scythe resting in his lap as he slowly and methodically ran a sharpening stone over the surface. A wooden box of tools lay at his feet, along with some rags and a small jug with a cork stopper in it.

It was obvious that the man was Herin's father. He had the same bulky build, the same set of the shoulders. Herin lacked some of the lines that had been worn into his father's face, but the resemblance was remarkable. The man heard the creak of the door and looked up, his face changing as he caught sight of his eldest son.

He spat into the dirt and gave one last hard scrape of the sharpener before carefully setting the scythe up against a railing.

"I know this can't be good," he said sourly as he eyed Herin. "What brings you home at this time of year? What happened to school? Don't tell me all that money went to waste."

"It's nice to see you too, Father," Herin said angrily.

"Save the bullshit for your mother," his father growled. "She'll love having you home no matter what kind of trouble you've gotten yourself into. Spit it out, boy, don't keep me in suspense. Start by telling me who these two might be."

Herin introduced Shadow and Ilsa. His father grunted in acknowledgement but made no move of friendship, standing with his thick arms crossed in front of him. "Your woman?" he asked Shadow, who shook his head.

"Yours then," he said to Herin in a tone that clearly showed his disapproval.

"Ilsa is my friend," Herin acknowledged. "She saved my life."

"Did she now? And where did you meet her? I didn't think there were any women in the school, and I would have thought you would be too busy to go out gallivanting around in the city. So where did you meet her?"

"I'll tell the whole story later so I can just do it once," Herin said. "We can talk at dinner."

"We'll talk when I say we'll talk. Now answer me boy, where did you find your slut? A blind man can see what kind of woman she is."

Before he was even aware of what he was doing, Herin landed a solid punch to his father's jaw, knocking him off his feet and depositing him unceremoniously on his back in a pile of hay. He stood frozen in shock for a moment, before stepping forward to offer a hand to his parent. His father waved him off as he struggled to his feet, his dark eyes flashing with anger.

"Oh shit," Ilsa breathed under her breath, knowing what was about to happen. Shadow took her by the arm and pulled her to a bale of hay stacked off to the side.

"This must have been coming for years," Shadow whispered. "Best we just stay out of the way."

"How dare you raise your hand to me, you ungrateful puppy!" his father roared, throwing a punch of his own at his son.

Herin was prepared and easily dodged, back-peddling to keep away from his father's attacks. He caught the next punch in his hand and threw his father's fist violently away from his body.

"Stop it!" he commanded. "Are you going to let me talk or are you going to make me hit you again?"

"Fuck off," his father snarled. "You always thought you were better than everyone else in the family. Always talking about being a big shot magician. Now here you are with these two outlaws and you want me to listen to you? Go to hell and get off my farm!"

Herin and his father circled each other warily, like two wolves fighting for pack leadership. His father was bleeding from Herin's first punch, his nose swelling to twice its normal size. Herin's face was as rage-filled as his father's as years of frustration finally boiled over into open warfare.

"Stop it," Herin shouted. "Listen to me!"

"I listened to you enough over the years," his father shouted back. "Always going on about things you knew nothing about. Power and magic and the empire and getting out of Chesterfield. Thought you were too good for us, didn't you? Always thought that. Like we were beneath you just because we liked living here."

"Is that what you think this is about, you stupid, old goat?" Herin screamed. "You think I give a rat's ass whether or not you live here? I could care less. If you like it here, stay here. But I wasn't cut out to be a farmer and that's the long and the short of it. You damned, stubborn, ignorant bastard, what makes you think I care what you do with your life? I just want you to let me live mine. That's all; just let me live my life the way I want! Why is that so much to ask?"

"I'll not have you looking down your nose at me or the way I live!" his father yelled back, his face flushed with anger

"Clean the shit out of your ears!" Herin cried. "I'm telling you as plain as I know how; I don't care about how you live! Just stop making judgments about me!"

"Judgements! I'll judge you right enough when I see what a muck-up of your life you're making," his father hollered, matching Herin's roars with roars of his own.

"It's my life," Herin bellowed. "I'll do with it what I wish, and if it turns out to be fucked up, then at least it was my doing and not someone else's."

Ilsa heard the door creak and turned to see a boy in his late teens enter the barn. He was tall and lanky, with a pleasant, friendly face. He saw Shadow and Ilsa and crossed to where they sat. "Heard the yelling all the way out in the field," he said with a grin. "There's only one person that can make Da that mad. I thought I'd come and say hello to Herin." He stuck out his hand. "I'm Hanthor, Herin's brother. You friends of his?"

Shadow made quick introductions. Hanthor smiled at Ilsa and shook his head. "You're from Kress? Are you two together, or are you with Herin?"

"Shadow and I aren't together," Ilsa told him, declining to define what her relationship might be with Herin. Hanthor laughed.

"No wonder they're squaring off. Before Herin left, Dad gave him specific instructions to stay away from the 'stinking whores and cutpurses' I think was the way he put it. Convinced everyone in Kress is going straight to hell. No offense, but seeing you two coming in with Herin would set Da off right away. Come on, we might as well go up to the house. They'll be at this for another hour or two yet. Herin used to be pretty stubborn even before he left. I doubt the time away has improved his patience any. Are you hungry?"

Ilsa warmed to Herin's sibling immediately, liking his easy-going manner. She nodded and hopped from her seat. Shadow was already moving towards the door, convinced that Hanthor had judged it correctly. Neither Herin nor his father showed any signs of being willing to listen to the other.

"Did this happen often?" he asked as Hanthor led them to the back door of the simple dwelling.

"Damned near every day there towards the end," Hanthor said. "You know, before Herin left for the city. It's been kind of peaceful around here since he went away. I guess things will liven up a bit now." The prospect didn't seem to faze him a bit. In fact, Ilsa would have guessed that he found the whole thing amusing.

"Is it a good idea to just leave them alone?" she asked. "What if they hurt each other?"

"They'll yell themselves out after a bit and then come up to the house for something to eat," Hanthor assured her. "After they've fortified themselves, one of them will say something to set the other off and they'll be at it all over again. Da just doesn't realize Herin has no intention of being a farmer, and Herin can't see that Da is just scared."

"Scared?" Ilsa asked. "Scared of what?"

"Scared that Herin is going to go away and never come back again," Hanthor told her.

She looked at him in wonder. "Does everyone in your family have some kind of magical gift?"

"Magical gift?" Hanthor said with a lift of his eyebrows. "That? Hell, if you spent your whole life listening to those two, it would be pretty easy to come up with that. Come on, my mother will be glad to meet you. She'll want to know all about what Herin's been up to." He led them inside.

Hanthor proved to be right. The argument went on for more than an hour before they stomped into the house. Even then, it crackled like a brush fire, sometimes almost sputtering out, only to be whipped into flames again by a stray comment. Finally, they both sprang to their feet in the common room, ready for another round of fighting. No longer willing to endure such childishness, Ilsa took matters into her own hands. She stepped between them, pushing on their chests until she had created a space large enough to hold her.

"That's enough," she said emphatically.

"Who are you to tell me what to do in my own house?" Herin's father roared, beginning to move towards her.

"Leave her alone," Herin cried, moving forward himself.

Ilsa pushed outward with both palms and shouted, "*Letta! Aptr eda sitja! Hljoor roeda ein til annar!*"

Herin flew backwards in one direction while his father shot backwards in the other. They both crashed heavily against the wall while Hanthor looked on in wide-eyed amazement. Herin tried to get to his feet but found he was helpless to move. The curses emanating from his father proved that he had discovered himself in the same predicament.

"What have you done, Ilsa?" Herin protested, struggling to get upright but unable to do so. "Let me loose."

"Save your breath, both of you," Ilsa said disdainfully, standing between them with her arms folded and a look of disgust on her face. "I don't know which one of you makes me angrier. You are an arrogant bully," she said to the older man. "You made your son's life miserable just because he didn't want to be like you and live the life you live. There is nothing more selfish than a parent denying their child the freedom to be who they want to be, just because it isn't something the parent approves of."

She turned her ire on Herin. "And you should know better. You're arguing for no reason. You know damn well you'll be leaving here with the first thaw, but you still argue with your father about staying here. Why? You're not going to convince him that you should leave, and he's not going to convince you that you should stay. Both of you need to just shut up so the rest of the household has some peace."

Hanthor shook his head slowly in admiration. "I can't believe it and I saw it with my own eyes. All this time I thought Herin was making things up. I didn't think magicians really existed, but I can see now that they do."

"Lucky for you," Ilsa said, pushing past him into the kitchen. "I just wanted a little peace and quiet."

"They can still yell at each other," Shadow pointed out.

Ilsa turned and smiled. "No, they can't, they really can't. Watch."

Herin was trying to say something to his father but no sound came from his lips. He stopped after a moment, puzzled. "Ilsa, what did you do?" he asked.

His father's face was mottled with rage as he tried to shout at Herin, but nothing but spittle came from his mouth. There were no words. He turned to Ilsa and spat, "Witch!"

"Nicely done," Shadow said, grudging approval in his voice. "Nicely done indeed."

"They can't talk to each other?" Hanthor asked with a curious expression on his face.

Ilsa shook her head. "No. Any words addressed to the other will result in nothing but silence. They can talk to others, but not to each other. Maybe that will cool them down."

"I doubt it, but it's worth a try," Hanthor agreed. "At least it will be quiet for dinner."

Ilsa helped set out plates, taking her time about it. When she re-entered the living area, it was to find two chastised, though still angry, individuals. "I'm fine now, Ilsa," Herin said pleadingly. "Can you please remove the spell?"

"I might," Ilsa answered. "But only if you can convince me it's a good idea. How do I know you won't be right back at it again?"

"I don't suppose my word is good enough?" Herin asked peevishly.

"It will be if you really mean it," Ilsa answered. "What about you?" She looked at Herin's father closely to gauge his reaction. He nodded.

"Fine, just remember I'm keeping a close eye on both of you." She whispered a counterspell, flicked her fingers, and the enchantment disappeared like smoke in a strong breeze. Herin moved his arms experimentally, stood slowly, then gingerly moved his legs to try to get some circulation back. His father stormed off into the kitchen to fill his plate. His eyes avoided Ilsa's as he silently took his place at the head of the table, glaring off into space at nothing in particular.

Herin shook his head as he slowly walked to Ilsa, a slightly embarrassed look on his face. "You must think I'm a fool," he said, "Home less than half a day and already at his throat."

"I'm not saying you don't have reason to be provoked," Ilsa replied evenly. "But you should be able to rise above all of that now. You don't have to prove anything to your father. And your background here is just that, background. It doesn't define who you are."

"You're right," Herin admitted. "But it's like somebody else takes over whenever I am around him."

"Was it always like this?" Shadow asked, coming over to join them.

"No," Herin answered, staring bleakly into the kitchen, and into the past. "This was unusual. Most of the time it was much worse. Dinner isn't going to be all that pleasant, but I promise to behave myself."

"You won't have to worry about that anymore unless I read your father wrong," Shadow told him. "He won't dare make any sort of move with Ilsa here. Didn't you see the look when she released him? He's afraid of her. Not only is it obvious that she is a powerful magician, but she is also a woman who dared to stand up to him. I'm not so sure the second thing isn't more important than the first."

"He'd better get used to it," Ilsa warned. "I'm not going anywhere. At least not until the snows go away for good. I think I'm still frozen right down to my bones."

The meal was more congenial than Herin had believed it would be, made possible in large part because his father kept a sulky silence at his end of the table. Freed from her husband's normal monopoly of the conversation, Herin's mother proved to be a lively and interesting conversationalist. She kept up a steady stream of questions about life in Kress, keeping Ilsa and Shadow involved in what could have easily been a conversation between Herin and her alone. Herin's sister, Willow, a girl of eight or nine, sat quietly and listened to the stories with wide-eyed interest.

As soon as the meal was over, Herin's father pushed his way back from the table, picked up his coat, and stomped off in the direction of town. "Don't mind Malcon," Herin's mother said as he left. "He will come around, just you wait and see. It's just that with him and Herin…"

"I don't think you have to explain it to them," Hanthor said with a laugh. "They had a front row seat earlier this afternoon. It's pretty obvious how Herin and Da feel about each other."

"I'm sorry, Mother," Herin said. "I don't mean to provoke him, I really don't. But he just won't listen to me. Everything I say just seems to set him off."

"Give it time, Herin. Now, how long are you staying before you leave again?"

Herin looked at her in surprise. "What makes you think I'm leaving?" he asked.

She smiled indulgently at her eldest child. "You've been in Kress for months. You're never coming back here to stay. I know that and so does your father. It's a big part of why he's so upset. He feared when you left the first time that you wouldn't be coming back here ever again."

"I would have thought he'd be happy about that," Herin said with a frown.

"Herin, you were our first child," his mother reminded him. "No matter how gruff he might look on the outside, he's never going to get over you not being here. There's a part of him that will always remember you as that little toddler who used to follow him everywhere he went."

"Herin? He followed Da around?" his brother asked in surprise. "All they've ever done is fight, for as long as I can remember."

"When Herin first learned to walk, you couldn't pry him away from his father with a crowbar," his mother said fondly.

"Tagged along with him so much that your father used to bring him inside and order me to keep him busy so he could get some work done. I think he took for granted that Herin would always be here. Whether he realizes it or not, there is a part of your father that regrets not spending enough time with him."

"I didn't know," Herin said softly.

She smiled again. "You weren't meant to. But I know that he thinks part of the reason you went away in the first place is because he didn't spend more time with you. He gets so angry with you because he's angry at himself."

"Will that ever change?" Ilsa asked.

"Give him some time. He's as stubborn as Herin, so he won't change easily. But I'm sure I don't have to tell you that." She looked into Ilsa's eyes and a silent message of understanding passed between them. Ilsa realized that no matter what treatment she could expect from Herin's father, his mother was on her side.

"Let's see to your sleeping arrangements. It will be a bit cramped but I think we can re-arrange the beds in here."

"That won't be necessary," Herin told her. "We can sleep in the barn."

"In this weather?" his brother objected. "It's freezing out there."

"We've been sleeping out in the open for the past week," Herin told him. "The barn is cozy enough. We've got plenty of hay to keep us warm."

"Are you sure?" his mother said uncertainly.

"We'll be fine, Mother," Herin assured her. "Believe me, I've slept in far worse places these past months. Just give us some blankets and we'll be as snug as if we were in here. Besides, I think I need to give Da some space for a few days."

"So how long will you be here?" Hanthor asked.

Herin shrugged. "Depends on the weather. I am hoping it won't be more than two or three weeks, but we don't want to hit the road again until well past the first thaw."

"Good," his brother replied. "Maybe you can teach me some magic."

The two weeks first stretched into three, and then into a fourth as the weather stubbornly refused to change, with a cold snap moving in shortly after their arrival and dumping several additional feet of snow on what had already fallen. As each day passed, Herin grew more and more concerned that his whereabouts would be discovered by Loki or by other detachments sent out by the Army. It took a reading from Ilsa to reassure him that all pursuit had turned back for the winter, so they had a breathing space for a little while.

As it became apparent that they wouldn't be able to go anywhere and they weren't being chased, Herin found himself relaxing for the first time in what seemed like ages. No longer having to look over his shoulder, he spent each day working on his spells and hoping for an opportunity to resume his relationship with Ilsa. The spellwork went well, but there was no change in Ilsa.

At first glance she appeared to be handling the aftermath of her attack successfully. But at night, she still refused to allow Herin to touch her, insisting that she needed more time. He tried to be patient, but there were still moments when he had to fight not to say what he wanted to say, knowing it would serve no purpose and would only cause Ilsa to push back at him. She seemed paler than she should have been and often retreated to a solitary corner of the barn, complaining of headaches.

The fourth week turned into a fifth, and then a sixth, before the weather finally began to change. Herin awoke one day to find that tiny green buds had appeared on the trees, and for the first time there was a warmth to the breeze, a promise that spring was finally stirring in the land. He and Shadow began making plans to leave as soon as the roads were passable.

"Next week for sure," Herin said one morning as he and Shadow took an experimental stroll along one of the country lanes near the farm. "We could probably even leave the day after tomorrow if we were willing to travel through a little mud."

"There's no point in doing that," Shadow said. "If we wait a few extra days everything will dry out and we'll find it easier going. Are you still coming with me to Nelfheim?"

"I don't know for certain," Herin told him. "I haven't been able to get Ilsa to talk about what we're going to do when we leave here. I am worried about her."

"There isn't much you can do about it."

"You've seen her and I know you've heard us at night," Herin answered quietly. "I've tried and tried to be as patient as I can. I'm afraid that she'll never be the same as she was."

"She won't be," Shadow said bluntly. "And the sooner you realize that, the sooner you'll be able to move on. What she went through would have killed most women. Given the circumstances, she has adjusted better than anyone could have reasonably hoped for. But she will never be like she was. She can't be after something like that."

"Where does that leave us?"

Shadow shook his head. "I can't answer that. Can you two still carve out something for yourselves? Only the gods know. All you can do is to try to meet her halfway to wherever she is. Your magic together is stronger than ever. That should give you some hope."

It was true. Herin and Ilsa had taken advantage of the time to practice spells together every day, and the magic had grown to the point where he almost felt like he could experience it through Ilsa rather than with her. In some ways that was cause for optimism, but in other ways it made it doubly frustrating that he couldn't make the same progress in their personal relationship.

"Yes, the magic is powerful," he acknowledged. "It's the rest of it I'm worried about. I don't even know how to talk to her anymore."

"There's no magic to cure this, Herin," Shadow counseled. "You'll just have to do the best you can and see what happens."

The weather continued to warm, hardening the roads enough that they could begin to make their plans in earnest. To pass the time, Herin and Shadow spent a few hours each day helping to prepare the ground for planting. Herin had offered to do the work magically, an offer Hanthor had enthusiastically seconded, but his father had angrily refused, so they had settled for putting in the physical labor as a way to repay his family.

Finally, the time had come to go. Herin announced at dinner that they would be leaving the next morning. His announcement was met with less surprise than he had anticipated. His mother saw his expression. "We all knew you would be going as soon as the weather cooperated, Herin. I will have some food ready in the morning."

"Thank you for your hospitality," Shadow said. "We appreciate it very much."

"Obligations to guests are always met," Malcon said, with a glance at his oldest son.

"Do you have to leave?" Hanthor asked, clearly disappointed. He had spent many hours with Herin and Shadow, and they had been able to teach him a half dozen minor spells. It was clear that he didn't have the same talent for magic that his older sibling possessed, but he had managed to learn a few things, enough to make him eager to learn even more.

"It's time," Herin answered absently, watching Ilsa across the table. She had been even more distant and withdrawn than usual, and he wished he could break through the stony reserve she had adopted over the past few days. "We'll wait until the sun is up so it can dry out the roads a bit."

Ilsa had said nothing during the meal, and the food on her plate was untouched. She raised her head and looked at Herin. "I'm not going with you," she announced. There was a stunned silence at the table.

"What do you mean?" Herin demanded. "You don't want to go to Nelfheim? We don't have to go there. We could go somewhere else if you like."

"No, I mean I'm not going anywhere with *you*," Ilsa told him, now glaring defiantly at him. Shadow watched both of them with a worried expression on his face. He could see, even if Herin could not, that there was something more to come.

Herin's father was looking at her curiously. Shadow pushed his chair back a bit, watching closely, but not saying anything. Herin was clearly caught by surprise. "I don't understand," he stuttered in confusion. "Are you saying you want to stay here in Chesterfield? I thought you hated the idea of small towns."

"I do," Ilsa replied. "You don't understand. I'm not saying I'm settling in Chesterfield. I'm leaving, just not with you."

Herin's face went slack and he stared at her, hurt and confused. "Not going with me? Why? Where are you going to go?"

"I don't know for sure. Back to Kress, I suppose," Ilsa told him. "I can do that easily enough. With luck, I can be there in a few weeks."

"But why?" Herin asked, beginning to get angry. "I don't understand. Why?"

Ilsa said firmly, "It's something I need to do Herin. It has nothing to do with you."

"Nothing to do with me? What is that supposed to mean?" he sputtered, almost too angry to speak. The rest of his family had the uneasy looks of people who were hearing things they wished they weren't. His mother made a slight motion of her head, and they all quickly pushed back their chairs and moved silently out of the room.

"Explain," Herin demanded, barely able to control his temper. "I don't understand. Haven't I given you your space? Haven't I been patient? Why are you suddenly leaving after all of this time?"

"Herin, this isn't easy for me," Ilsa told him. Her eyes held a haunted look and her face was as hard and set as if it had been carved from marble. "It isn't something that I just decided five minutes ago. I've been thinking about it for weeks now and I know it's what I have to do."

"That doesn't explain anything," Herin shot back. "What do you mean it's something you have to do? Why go back to Kress of all places? If you don't want to go to Nelfheim, we'll go somewhere else. But at least talk to me about it."

"*We* aren't going anywhere," Ilsa said quietly. "There is no 'we'. This is where we go our separate ways."

Herin looked like someone had suddenly punched him in the gut. "Why? At least tell me why." His anger was gone now, replaced by shock.

"Can't you just let it go?" Ilsa begged. "Can't you just let me go?"

"After all we've been through together, no I'm not letting it go without an explanation," Herin insisted. "I deserve that much. What did I do to drive you away?"

Ilsa wrung her hands together as she searched for the right words. "You didn't do anything wrong, Herin. I'm grateful for everything you've given me. If you hadn't found me in that tavern I'd still be nothing more than a serving girl with no future. I'm a different person now. Stronger. Part of that is because of you. But I can't change the thing that happened to me, and it is making me go in a new direction. You can't help me and it will only be harder if you try. I have to go on alone."

"What kind of things?" Herin asked. "You're not making any sense. We can work past that, I know we can. You've come a long way since that day and you can go farther still. Why won't you let me help you?"

"That night changed everything," Ilsa answered. "I'll never be the same, no matter how long you wait. Sooner or later you're going to resent me for not being what you want, and when that day comes it will tear us both apart."

"No," Herin argued. "No, it won't. I've stuck with you this long; I can certainly stay for as long as it takes."

Ilsa sighed. She tried to make her voice strong, but it wavered still. "I don't want you Herin. It's just that. I want to be alone."

"I still don't understand. Why?"

Ilsa looked at him and her face was sad. "I have to go to Kress by myself." She paused. "I'm pregnant."

Both Shadow and Herin were stunned by her announcement. "Are you certain?" Herin asked.

Ilsa's face showed no joy and her eyes were as cold as ice. "Oh, yes, I'm certain."

"That changes everything. You're right about that. But now of all times, I'm not letting you go back to Kress."

"You're not letting me?" Ilsa said scornfully. "I don't recall asking for your permission."

"I didn't mean it that way," Herin said hastily. "I just meant you'll need me now more than ever."

"No, I won't," Ilsa replied. She looked at Herin with something like pity in her eyes. "The baby isn't yours Herin."

"What...?" Herin could only whisper.

"It isn't yours," Ilsa repeated. "The fact is, I don't know who the father is. That's why I'm leaving and why you aren't coming with me. You could never be happy raising another man's child. Sooner or later you'd hate the child, and then me, and we'd be in a place we could never get out of."

"How do you know it isn't mine?" Herin demanded. "You don't think you got pregnant from that night?"

"Actually, I do," Ilsa said. "God knows there was enough opportunity for it. Shadow will tell you I am right, Herin. Magicians don't breed with each other."

"I've never heard of it happening," Shadow admitted. "But I don't know any other female magicians either. Just because I haven't heard of it doesn't mean it hasn't happened. I never heard of two magicians being able to do the spells you two do together either."

"I know I'm right," Ilsa insisted. "If magicians could reproduce there would be a race of magicians running everything. No, whoever the father is, it's not you, Herin. You have to accept that and let me go."

"I have to do no such thing," Herin protested. "I'm not letting you go back to Kress by yourself, and I don't accept that I'm not the father. What if Loki sees you? What if he kills you?"

"I've made up my mind," Ilsa argued. "Loki's in Khartul, and even if he comes back to Kress, I know enough magic now to take care of myself. The baby isn't yours, Herin. Think about it. We had sex and nothing ever happened. But right after that night I've missed my normal cycle and that isn't a coincidence. I've never missed one before, never."

"We were close enough to that time, too. You don't know for sure it isn't mine." Herin's face was as hard as stone.

"But I am sure," Ilsa told him. She spoke so softly they could barely hear her. "This is goodbye Herin. I'm not staying here tonight. I'll go into the village and get a room at the inn. It's better that way."

"Better for whom?" Herin almost shouted. "Whatever you say, I'm not leaving you."

"You don't have a choice," Ilsa told him. "I'm leaving you. Go and find another destiny out there somewhere. But it won't be with me." She pushed herself away from the table and went to where Herin sat frozen, as if she had cast a spell on him. She kissed him softly on the cheek, tears finally beginning to flow slowly. "I'm sorry it has to end like this Herin. This is how it has to be."

"Watch him, Shadow," Ilsa said through her tears. "Please don't let him follow me." She stood in the doorway for a moment before slipping out of the house. Herin got up to follow, but Shadow stopped him by grabbing him by the arms.

"Let her go, Herin."

"I can't," Herin said.

Shadow looked at him with sympathy. "You have to. She doesn't want you. What are you going to do, force yourself on her? After what she's been through how do you think that will help anything? You are going to have to move on."

"Fuck that," Herin snarled. "I don't have to do anything but what I think is right, and the right thing to do is to go after her. That child is mine, Shadow. I know it."

"You two were lovers for months and nothing happened," Shadow reminded him. "Then right after Loki's scum raped her she winds up pregnant. What makes you think it's yours?"

"I just feel it," Herin said stubbornly. "Ilsa is just scared because of what she went through, but that baby isn't from one of those thugs."

"She's scared all right, and with good reason. She is going to have to look at that child for the rest of her life and be reminded of what happened to her. Let her go. It's going to be easier for both of you in the long run."

Herin refused to be convinced. "Easier? You think this is going to go away somehow? How can I go with you knowing my child is growing up without me somewhere in Kress?"

"Dammit, Herin, it isn't yours!" Shadow snapped, finally losing his patience. "Ilsa doesn't think so, and I've never heard of any magicians having children before."

"I'm not letting her go," Herin insisted. He pushed Shadow aside and lunged for the door. Shadow quickly whispered a spell to keep the door closed. Herin stopped before he even touched the handle, the scent of it warning him. "Why are you doing this?" he asked, as he started a counterspell. He snapped his fingers and pulled on the handle. Nothing happened.

"I'm not an apprentice," Shadow reminded him. "You won't get through there unless I remove it myself."

"This isn't any of your business," Herin raged. "This is between me and Ilsa."

"I'm just trying to give you time to think this through." Herin rattled the door, but it refused to open. His shoulders sagged suddenly in defeat. Shadow kept silent but alert. Herin slumped to the floor with his back against the door, his eyes unseeing, all of his attention turned inward. Shadow had seen that same look before on soldiers coming from battle, wondering why they had escaped death while their comrades had not. He knew that Herin would need time and space to heal from this. He sat in a chair by the fireplace, watching and waiting for Herin to make the next move.

The morning sun found them in the same position. Shadow awoke from a light doze with a start, but quickly relaxed when he saw that Herin was still sitting against the door, eyes closed in sleep. A quick glance out the window told him that it was close to dawn. He slowly stood and stretched. He walked to Herin and kicked him lightly on the sole of his boots.

"We should get ready to go," he said as Herin sleepily looked up at him. "It will be light soon and we can get an early start. Get in a couple of hours before breakfast just to work up an appetite." The weak attempt at good cheer fell on deaf ears.

Herin pushed himself upright, pausing for a moment at the door until Shadow removed the spell, and then moving silently into the other room. Shadow followed cautiously but Herin headed directly for the barn, where he began pulling things together in preparation for travel. Shadow made no further attempt to engage him in conversation, knowing that Herin would talk when he was ready. It took very little time to get their packs prepared and ready for the trip.

Behind them the house showed signs of activity, with a light in the kitchen giving evidence that Herin's mother was awake and beginning her day. Shadow was prepared for an argument if Herin tried to leave without saying goodbye, but to his relief he headed inside. Shadow left his pack outside the house before following.

"Goodbye, Mother," Herin said woodenly. "I don't know when I'll be back this way again, but I will try to send word when I have the chance."

"Just take care of yourself," she said, kissing him with a worried look on her face.

"Thank you again for all of your hospitality," Shadow said. Herin went back outside and hefted his pack to his shoulders.

"What happened, Shadow?" she asked.

"Ilsa left him, as you heard. She's pregnant and she told him the child isn't his. She doesn't want him to follow her. He's taking it hard."

"Not his?" The look on her face showed her confusion. "But how…?"

They had not told the family the story of what had happened in Khartul other than to say they had fled the city. But Shadow didn't think Herin's family should think ill of Ilsa. It was unlikely that she would ever come here again, and he saw no harm in sharing the information with her.

"Ilsa was raped before we left Khartul," he said quietly. "She doesn't believe the child is Herin's, she thinks it's from one of the men who raped her."

"Oh, God…the poor child. What is Herin going to do? What is Ilsa going to do?"

"She said she's going back to Kress and she doesn't want him following her. We were originally going to head to Nelfheim. I'm hoping I can convince your son to keep to that plan. But knowing Herin, I doubt very much if that is going to be easy."

Herin's mother shook her head slowly. "He won't listen to her. You know that as well as I do. Those two need each other, Shadow. Anyone can see that. He'll follow her no matter where she goes. Please don't leave him alone. You've seen how he is with his father."

Shadow's expression clearly showed that he did not know where the conversation was headed. "I don't understand," he told her. "What does his father have to do with this?"

"You are more to him than a friend, Shadow. And much more than a teacher." She smiled sadly. "He has never had an older man he could trust. He'll need that now more than ever. Neither one of those two will ever be completely whole without the other. It takes no magic to see that much."

"Ilsa seemed very sure that they needed to be apart," Shadow answered.

"Of course she did. She is confused and hurt and thinks the way to help herself is to forget anything that reminds her of her old life. But Herin isn't ever going to accept that. I know it. You won't be able to stop this. He's going to go after her."

"How can you be so sure?" Shadow thought she was probably being swayed by a motherly instinct of some sort to protect her child if she possibly could.

"I see things sometimes," she told him with a knowing look. "In the fire, usually. Just quick peeks you might say."

"You are a Viewer?"

"I can see things," she repeated without going into further detail. "I'm only telling you because I think you might understand, being a magician yourself and all. Herin's father doesn't know. Nobody knows, including Herin, and I'm going to ask that it stays that way. But you have to trust me that there is something connecting those two that isn't finished yet."

"I promised Ilsa I wouldn't let him follow her," Shadow insisted. "I don't see how he can help her if she is determined he stay away."

"Sooner or later he is going to go after her, and on that day you'll have a choice. Either you help him or you let him go."

"I have my own task," Shadow argued. "There are things that I must do."

"I know. But you are connected to all of this as well. I felt it as soon as I saw the three of you together. There are larger forces at work here. Every man has to choose his own path. I pray you choose wisely. Watch over him as much as you can, Shadow. He needs a friend, especially now."

They said their goodbyes to the rest of the family. Shadow was a little surprised to see Herin's father embrace him in a rough hug. Herin was plainly taken aback as well. "Godspeed boy," he said gruffly, before shaking Shadow's hand and turning away to go about his chores.

They walked silently to the end of the road connecting the farm to the trade road through town, each lost in his own thoughts.

Shadow was mulling over the revelation that Herin's mother could do some magic, at least had the ability to conjure up visions. *His brother had some ability as well. Maybe what I was always taught isn't right, maybe magic is hereditary in some families. Herin is different from every magician I ever met, and then there is Ilsa...God's teeth, could there be a mistake here? Could the child be Herin's? Damn! I wish I could get at the old library back home and see if there is anything to explain this.*

They reached the end of the road and Shadow forced himself back to the task at hand. They should turn left to head west to Nelfheim. A right turn would take them back into town. He wanted to say something, but some instinct warned him that silence was his best option. Herin needed to do this on his own.

"I'm going to town," he said firmly. "Don't get in my way, Shadow."

"It's your decision but I don't think it's the right one."

"You don't have to come," Herin reminded him. "You have your own task out in Nelfheim."

"A small detour won't hurt. I've waited this long. Another day or two won't make a difference. I think I'd better see this through."

"See what through?"

Shadow shrugged. "Whatever you've got planned right now. Your judgment isn't clear, no matter what you say."

They walked in silence but Shadow could feel Herin's anxiety. Several times he was on the verge of saying something, but anything he said at that moment would almost certainly do nothing but make things worse. One way or the other, this had to play itself out.

Herin went directly to the small inn just off the center of the settlement. The main room was deserted except for the proprietor, a middle-aged man who was wiping off tables. Herin wasted no time in pleasantries. "I'm looking for the girl who spent the night here."

The man stopped and looked up in disapproval. "Herin Freeholder, I know your family raised you with better manners than that. What about a 'Good morning' or 'Greetings'? You just barge in here demanding information? What has gotten into you?"

"I'm sorry, Mr. Johansson," Herin apologized. "I'm just in a little bit of a hurry, and it's important I talk to her as soon as possible."

"Talk to who? I haven't had a guest here in weeks. Not much business until the roads get better."

"Nobody stayed here last night?"

"No. Sorry." The man went back to wiping tables.

Shadow listened to the byplay and realized Ilsa had used that story to give herself a ten hour head start. It was likely she had taken the road during the night, but in which direction? Once the sun was up, she would have certainly struck out cross country to make it more difficult to track her. She might be twenty or thirty miles away from them by now.

Herin went back to the road and stood staring down its length for some time, lost in thought. Finally, he turned to Shadow. "She could be anywhere, couldn't she?"

"She planned this pretty well," Shadow agreed.

"I'm still going to look for her."

Shadow nodded. "I know."

"What are you going to do?"

Shadow rubbed his beard thoughtfully. "I need to know what the empire is planning to do. It was my mission."

"So this is where we say goodbye." Herin said, sticking out his hand.

Shadow hesitated, the words of Herin's mother echoing in his head. Maybe there was something bigger at work here than his mission to find out about a fleet of ships. "If you want some company, I'll come with you."

Relief fought with puzzlement on Herin's features, with relief finally winning out. "I'll be glad for the company. Any suggestions about which way to go?"

Shadow shook his head. "None at all. It's up to you."

Herin stared in both directions. Making up his mind, he set off eastwards, Shadow falling into step beside him. They walked in silence for a few miles, Shadow allowing his friend the time and space to come to grips with this new development.

"Why this direction?" he finally asked.

Herin answered quietly, "I don't know what else to do. We'll go back to the beginning, back to Kress and see if we can pick up her trail. I can't let her go, Shadow. I know she's making a mistake, and I have to find her before the baby comes."

Shadow knew the chances of locating Ilsa in the teeming crowds of Kress were thin, but he also knew that it would be a waste of time trying to convince Herin of that. For better or worse, they were committed. "Let's go then," he said, picking up the pace. "Let's go back to Kress."

End of Book One

The story continues in Book Two, *A Time of Chaos*

Made in the USA
San Bernardino, CA
28 April 2017